The Gatekeeper

Tomorrow's Assassin

Samuel T Fuller

Raider Publishing International

New York   London   Swansea

ISBN: 1-934360-42-2

Published By Raider Publishing International

www.RaiderPublishing.com

New York   London   Swansea

Printed in the United States of America and the United Kingdom
By Lightning Source Ltd.

The Gatekeeper

Tomorrow's Assassin

Samuel T Fuller

Dedication

"To my wife, Myris Jane"

Acknowledgements

I especially wish to thank Liz Kent, a wonderful professional, who inspired, advised and encouraged me to write this book.

Also to Adam Salviani who, with great patience and kindness, guided me along the road toward publication

To the owners and staff at Torbay bookshop, Paignton, who were always most helpful and encouraging.

Finally, to those many kind friends who I used as sounding boards – so often…..many thanks.

Time is widely accepted as being split into three distinct zones. The past, measured by personal and factual accounts, or hearsay. The immediate, defined as the present moment, and the future, which for most, thankfully remains unknown.

STF March 2007

Chapter One

Late Summer - 1951

Fitful moonlight began breaking through gaps in the low, dark cloud that set course toward the West. What had been a soft on-shore night breeze now ratcheted up, threatening a full storm force blow. Long stemmed grasses that marked out the boundaries of Cley Marsh began to bend in a series of pulsating waves, imitating the involuntary action of taller reed stems rooted in deeper water.

The coastal water margins of Cley-Next-the-Sea, Salthouse and Morston formed natural buffers between steeply rising shingle and cobble beaches and low-lying Norfolk villages, flanking the narrow A149 coast road. These were lonely, unforgiving places, where on a stormy night, imagination and the roar of scouring surf urged people to stay in the safety of their homes. Business on the marsh was best done in daylight.

A sudden spatter of cold rain tormented the surface of open water. This erratic beating quickly turned into a rapid tattoo, as remnants of water-laden cloud fled to join the black mass heading inland.

Police Constable Frederick Fisher pulled hard on the front door of his cottage, making sure he heard the familiar click as the catch locked home. He turned the mortice key in the lock then put his weight against the door, just to make certain it held fast.

It was only after these actions that Fred turned to face whatever the night was going to throw at him. He was not a nervous man. Twenty-nine years as a police officer, had moulded both his portly frame, confidence in his ability to apply the law and his quiet acceptance of life as a village copper.

Fred settled his heavy cape around his shoulders, fastened its collar chain, adjusted his helmet strap and pulling his bike from the porch, set out for the coast road. Once or twice, the gusting wind threatened to send him into a ditch, but after twenty minutes of determined peddling, Fred arrived safely at a point on the A149 where a track led off across the marsh.

George Wright, who had the village beat at Kelling, loomed out of the darkness.

"Evening, Fred," George said in a quiet voice, "looks like the weather can't make up its mind. Let's hope this rain clears otherwise it's going to be a wet night for us."

Fred offered George a rain-speckled grin, "Personally George, my boy, I prefer it. Honest people like to keep to their beds on nights like this."

The two constables peddled onto the track in silence, heading for the distant high wall of shingle that divided the marshland from the beach. There was little point in using cycle lamps to light their route. These lights would only serve to advertise their presence.

Their duty orders were plain enough. At midnight, they relieve the manned check point on Cley marsh, at the shingle bank end of the track. They maintain a silent watch until relieved by officers from Cromer, set to arrive in the morning, sometime around eight.

Verbal orders were they were to stop and detain anyone they find in the area. So far, the only results from these vigils had been the grim discovery of four bodies. Four separate incidents, four very dead, relatively young, fit looking men. Each corpse, either anchored to reeds beneath the surface or floating in clear water, all within yards of the shingle bank.

Each on-site medical examination appeared to show death had occurred no more than a few hours before discovery, with rigor-mortis already starting in secondary muscle groups. There was some variation in tissue discolouration but apart from that, there were no obvious signs indicating how any victim had met their end.

Following each post-mortem, opinion as to actual cause of death went unannounced. This action led to wild speculation in the press, but this clamour soon faded following the news that all the bodies had been members of the crew of a Norwegian cargo vessel, recently lost off the Norfolk coast. This plausible explanation seemed acceptable to most people, who nodded knowingly and then went about their own business. However, most people did not include those curious types who lived close to the marsh area, or those having half an eye on prevailing sea states or storm conditions or perhaps those who had a relative working at Lloyds Shipping. If you had been amongst the curious, you might have registered half an ounce of doubt about the whole, 'bodies on the marsh,' affair.

The darkness and gusting on-shore wind made progress painfully slow. Finally, just on midnight, Fred and George reached their watch-point at the shingle bank, where they gratefully dismounted from their bikes. Two colleagues, normally stationed at Blakeney, loomed out of the darkness with the news that there was nothing to report. Then they were off like cloaked bats out of hell, peddling like mad for Blakeney and a warm bed. Envious eyes soon lost them in the dark.

Parking their bikes against a convenient stand of reeds, Fred and George made their way as quietly as possible up the shingle bank. Luck was now with them. Breaks in the cloud allowed sufficient moonlight to see along the bank in both directions. They also had a view of the beach to the seas edge, plus views of the marsh.

Pulling their capes around them, they squatted back-to-back on the loose, smooth shingle. Spiteful showers of rain came and went, but in between, the heavens cleared allowing the relief of a silvery three-quarter moon and thousands of bright stars.

Time slipped by without a single sound, other than the uninterrupted movement of the sea, claiming then replacing small pebbles on the beach.

Finally, George's muted voice broke into Fred's thoughts, "This is the last place you'd connect with murders. Do you make sense of this business Fred?"

Fred let his mind drift for a few more seconds, then half-turned toward George, "Well, according to the meeting at the incident room, the Superintendent said we shouldn't do anything to fuel speculation, but the truth is, in all my years in the job I've never seen anything like this. Bodies appearing out of thin air, it was enough to scare the pants off you. It didn't look too good on us either, that last one turning up right next to where we'd been all bloody night. The relief stumbled over it as soon as there was enough daylight to spot it."

George swung fully round so that he could look straight into Fred's face, "That's the whole point, Fred. There's more to these deaths than the bosses are letting on. Personally, I reckon it's connected with the military and they're keeping quiet. Look at those three deaths over near Thetford, a few months back. Turned out to be military, some sort of chemical weapon that backfired."

Fred drew up the collar of his cape as the moonlight disappeared and horizontal rain like penny-pieces battered both men. The squall was over as quickly as it started with a bright moon appearing to paint out all but the most persistent shadows.

"It's no good us fretting, George. I'm as worked up about this business as every copper within two hundred miles, but death on this scale is not just your everyday slaughter. There's got to be more to this than you can shake your stick at. Whatever or whoever's behind this little lot is going to take some finding, you see if I'm not right."

"It's plain murder alright," growled George, "according to the CID chat in the incident room, every single one of these lads were selected and topped with some sort of poison."

"And I suppose the Chief Superintendent popped into Kelling Police house and told you, the village bobby, personally how the hell they were silently dumped on our patch, without so much as a whisper or by-your-leave?"

"Okay," replied George, "but whatever we say, this business has got everyone jacked up, chasing their tails. Spot checks every day and night, road blocks, everyone in the force on the knocker, express messages flying in from everywhere in the country, but still no result. Not even a single clue as to who they were. Photographs, fingerprints, you name it."

Fred didn't react to George's comment. He knew enough about George to know he didn't get easily rattled. He'd been decorated for gallantry in the army and you didn't get that for sharpening pencils or entertaining the troops.

Fred also felt mystified by what had happened. It was as though these young men had dropped out of the sky. It didn't make sense. He was fed up with fending off questions from villagers, from women who were worried sick about their children's safety, from irate squires demanding to know what the police were doing. Roping in all the known villains, questions, meetings, briefings followed by further briefings. Fred could well understand the frustration in George's quiet voice. Professional patience was not a piece of kit buckled on with a pointy-helmet.

George shifted his aching muscles, removed his helmet and rubbed his handkerchief around the lining. He knew Fred often found his military rawness slightly jarring. He also knew he had an awful lot to learn, but sitting on a beach waiting for something to turn up might be okay for the Micawbers of this world but wasn't, in his opinion, the right way to crack this particular walnut.

"What I find so frustrating," said George, folding his handkerchief and sticking it back into his pocket, "here we have someone acting like a modern-day Jack the Ripper, dumping bodies in our marsh and we haven't a clue as to who or why? Not so much as a reserved medical opinion on how they died. Not a peep on the wireless, unless they covered it while we've been sat here, and another thing that really bugs me, don't you find it strange how the newspapers have suddenly gone cold on the whole business? One day, banner headlines, and the next, it's back to good old stripper Jane and Fritz," George paused for a moment and settled his helmet back on his head, "not like the local press to give up on a horror story happening right on their doorstep. It just doesn't make sense, unless of course it's..."

Fred gave an interrupting, labouring sigh, "Have you ever considered, for one tiny moment, someone's already in the frame?"

"How do you mean?"

"Well, who's to know? Maybe some society sort, perhaps a Dad with clout and, hey-presto, it's all nicely covered up," Fred let the thought germinate, "after all, it's all happened before. Take those serial killings. The nasty one's up in Whitechapel."

"Whitechapel?" Echoed a mystified George.

"You remember. The ones you were just on about, Jack the Ripper and all that."

George stared into Fred's moonlit face, "You can't be serious?"

"Of course I'm bloody not!" Fred choked as he tried to keep his voice to a whisper, "All I'm saying is maybe there's a touch more to this affair than the usual run of deaths."

The wind had suddenly dropped to a whisper. Somewhere out on the marsh, a startled bird rose into the air with a screech. Seconds later, a vixen called. Its high-pitched snittering call signalling its presence in the shadowy reed beds.

Fred tapped George's shoulder, "Now there's one lady who may get some help bagging her supper tonight. Look what's making an unwelcome entrance."

George's eyes followed the direction indicated by Fred's outstretched arm. Neither of them had noticed the silent approach of a thick, low blanket of white mist. It hugged the surface of the sea like a close friend, then unrolled, advancing up the beach rapidly, filling the gap between the sea and the shingle bank. For just a moment the mass seemed to gather itself before tumbling down onto the track. In moments, the tall reed beds and open expanses of water began to slip beneath its veil.

"That's all we need," murmured George, standing up and pulling his cape around his shoulders.

"We've certainly drawn the short straw when it comes to observation jobs. If this lot gets any thicker, we'll be lucky to find our way off the marsh."

Fred stood before whispering his reply, "Well George, it may be difficult for us, but that skinny vixen may find it helps fill her stomach. And, a further consolation may be that a stranger is going to be worse off than we are, so let's be like her and use our ears."

George nodded. They both stood on the bank, capes pulled tightly about them. The surf told them that the tide had turned. It was now pummelling the shore line, setting up a pale phosphorescent glow. Moments passed into minutes. The narrow column of mist continued its snake-like journey, sometimes pausing, reluctant to let go of the tallest reeds.

George uncovered his wrist and looked at the luminous dial of his watch. Twenty long minutes had passed. As he lowered his arm, there was a sharp sound of a splash.

George looked at Fred and pointed away to his left. Fred nodded in agreement. It had been a clear single noise, as though something heavy dived or had fallen into the water. The direction could not be in doubt. As George saw Fred's acknowledgement, he set off running down the bank, into the thick mist, Fred following hard on his heels. They sent shingle cascading, stones flying everywhere.

On reaching the track where it bordered the marsh, they both pulled up sharp. They stood, hardly daring to breath, each eager to solve the cause of the splash. The mist appeared thicker around the margins where it was sheltered from the wind by the shingle bank.

"What the hell was that?" Whispered George.

"No point in whispering, George. Whatever or whoever caused that splash must have heard us galloping off the bank. It couldn't have been anything lightweight, not displacing that amount of water."

"We could split up and search the edge in either direction?" George suggested.

Fred held up a hand, "Now just you hold on, George. There's no point splitting up in this mist. If it is our mystery man, he'll try to move away as quietly as possible. We'll hear rather than see him."

"If it had been a person, surely there would have been more than just the single splash."

"Not if that person was already beyond the struggling stage. Our villain could have slid away while we were busy skiing down that shingle bank," Fred knew how angry George was, he felt no better, "One thing you learn in these marshes George, sound carries miles across water. Ask any seaman, or better still, any poacher worth his salt. Anyway, if someone or something had blundered into that water we'd have heard them splashing about. Step off this track in the wrong place and you'll be up to your unkers in four foot of water and bottomless slime, so just think on, my lad."

The two stood motionless listening. The last of the pebbles they had dislodged slithered and rattled to a grateful stop.

Desperately hoping for another sound, they both tried to control their breathing.

Natural sounds of the marsh went on about them, frogs croaked, small fish plopped and bad tempered birds snapped at each other.

"Maybe it was just one of our lads out of his area," George whispered.

The answer from Fred was a long time in coming. When it did, his 29 years of service came through, "Relax George, we're the only two live human life forms selected to haunt this marsh west of the Weybourne track. Whatever made the noise that brought us down that shingle bank, I'd

14

say was well and truly within our patch. The Cromer lads have got the main road and all points east of the Weybourne track."

Fred eased his shoulders and hooked his thumbs into the breast pockets of his tunic. He hoped the hushed tone of his voice sounded more convincing than he felt.

"The Blakeney lads have a perch on top of Cley Mill, so that's the west side covered. That being so, I think we can safely say we have this marsh bottled up. Let's stay put. When this mist lifts, if there's anyone here with us on our boggy bit, I'll let you have first go at him. And that's a solemn promise to you my eager young friend."

George stifled a laugh with his gloved hands. He liked Fred's dry wit, although he chose not to dismiss from his mind the feeling they had human company. He was itching to have a swan around, get the circulation going and hopefully flush out what had caused that....

"I've a flask of tea in my saddlebag, George," Fred's forced whisper cut across George's thoughts, "we'll get ourselves on the outside of that. Nothing can move in this lot, without making a racket."

George nodded, still only half-listening to Fred. He might have guessed that Fred would come prepared with tea. He had to admit, there was no point in blundering noisily around.

Being close to where they had propped the bikes, it took less than a second or so to find them. George pulled the bikes carefully upright, as Fred began to undo the straps on his saddlebag.

"Another five minutes and you'll see this mist disappearing toward the main road. It's amazing how quick this lot moves once the breeze picks up."

As if to reinforce Fred's words, both men watched as tentacles of mist, like long white fingers, began drawing the blanket away from the seaward side of the marsh.

The moon played its part by shedding brilliant white light across small lagoons of open water. Only the fuzzy heads of tall, willowy reeds bent to point the way the mist was travelling. Everything else seemed frozen in time.

Fred had almost retrieved the flask when he became conscious of George's hand gripping his arm. He slowly looked up into George's face. George was staring steadily over Fred's shoulder at something in the marsh, his eyes locked fast on whatever lay behind Fred.

"I think we may have to delay that tea," George's voice was quiet, but had a firmness that left no doubt in Fred's mind, "I'm sure I'm looking at the cause of our splash."

Fred slowly turned, allowing the flask to slide back into the saddlebag. It took some moments before Fred saw what was holding George's attention. At first, he thought he was staring at the moon's reflection in the water, but a second later he was not so sure. Some twenty yards away, floating in the black water was what seemed to be an oval shaped white disc.

As if to help Fred decide what the object was, it seemed to tilt towards them, its features unmistakeable. Then it seemed to be drawn down below the surface. The moonlight was playing tricks, distorting what was obviously a piece of paper, cloth or the upturned belly of a dead fish.

The cycles fell sideways onto the reeds as both men started to run along the track between the bank and marsh, each dreading that every step took them closer to what could be another marsh victim.

The moon's glow brightened, bathing the whole shimmering expanse of water with pin-points of silvery light.

George found a spot that looked solid enough to take his weight and stepped gingerly out onto a narrow clump of reeds.

"Now slowly does it old son. If it is a body, he'll be in no hurry," Fred's voice was meant to be encouraging but somehow George felt distracted. He'd thrown off his cape so as to leave his arms free, just in case he went swimming.

A few more hesitant steps on the spongy raft took him out to a point where he felt he was within grabbing distance of the object.

Fred's voice floated across, "The area you're heading for is notorious for the depth of its mud, don't slip whatever you do."

George deliberately straightened up, looking very hard at Fred. He held up the extended palm of his right hand, which in police parlance clearly meant 'Stop!' Or, in this case, an unmistakable 'shut-up!' George just about caught the hissed apology from Fred.

Slowly, and with some misgiving, George edged further along the reed clump, which by now was slightly under the water. He really didn't need reminding about what lay below his feet. Two more hesitant steps and George was staring directly down at the white disc, which now floated a few inches below the surface.

Moving even more cautiously, George slowly crouched down. It was a man's face alright. The remainder of the body was trailing, out of sight, deep in the water. He knelt down on his knees, feeling the freezing water fraternizing with his knees, then thighs.

Telling himself that one lifeless body was very much like another, George reached deep down into the water, brushing aside strands of weed that floated amongst the man's hair. George avoided looking directly into the face. He grasped a good handful of hair and strained back, to raise the head. This took all George's strength and drove his thighs deeper into the water. It felt just as though whatever had hold of its lower body was reluctant to let go.

Finally, the face came to within an inch of the surface. Minute silvery bubbles of air seemed trapped between the partly opened lips. With a final heave, the face came level with the surface.

Black water sluiced in and out of the open mouth. In the isolated silence that surrounded George, he imagined he could hear the water gurgling in the man's throat or hear words struggling to come out of the mouth. Finally, George met the glacial, half-closed eyes. He was staring straight into death. The look that once seen could never be forgotten. He knew the message so well. He told himself to get on with the job.

George reached down into the dark water and took a good grasp on clothing. With this grip he raised the head, bringing the head and shoulders free of the water, onto his small swamped island.

The heaving, rolling movement must have released one of the man's arms from beneath his body. White crooked fingers sprang straight up into George's face. Thick twisted weed, like ropes, curled through and around the fingers. This weed was defying George's attempt to raise the corpse from the water. For a heart shuddering moment, the body seemed to fight to remain submerged.

From the path, Fred saw George rest for a few moments then remove his handcuffs from his tunic pocket. In seconds, one of the bracelets was around the base of a broad stem of reeds while the other enclosed the exposed thin white wrist.

Satisfied the body was now securely anchored, George took his time straightening up. He eventually stood, water pouring from his drenched trousers.

Taking his handkerchief from his pocket, he tied this around the top stem of the tallest reed, where it hung like a limp victory pennant. The task done, George picked his way exhausted back to the path.

Fred slapped George on the back, "Had me going there for a minute lad. I thought he was going to get away from you. I'm not so certain I would have come after you if he'd won the tussle."

George's strained face relaxed, he smiled, "If you'd like to get to a phone Fred, I'll wait with our anchored friend. He's not much on conversation but I think he won't be going too far. Oh, and by the way, do me a favour and leave that flask of tea. You could be gone a while."

Fred knew that George was handing him the better of the two options. He preferred to have the chance to get to a phone, rather than squat on the track and wait for a relief. They retraced their steps to the bikes.

George swung his cape, allowing the thick serge to drop over his shoulders. At least the extra layer of uniform would help him gain some warmth, against the beginnings of a pale dawn.

George accepted the offered flask from Fred, "Try not to be too long. I think the mist has a mind of its own. It's on the way back. The breeze must have swung round. You'll be peddling against it getting back to the road."

Fred checked his watch. Almost six hours had passed since he had met George on the road.

"You take care of yourself, George. If the reluctant corpse decides to disappear, don't go swimming after it or you'll be the one tied to the undertaker's reed."

"The what?" asked George.

"Undertaker's reed, that's what it's called round here. You'll know it when you meet it again. Best place for you is the top of the bank. Dry those trousers off in the wind. Just relax and watch what's going on."

George smiled. With a hesitant wave Fred headed for the coast road. This time he made certain his front lamp was working. The dim grey light of dawn was going to have to compete with the mist. As George had said, the mist seemed to be hitching a ride on a changing wind.

Patchets hotel, a converted 18th century manor, was set on a small rise just to the landward side of the main coast road, almost opposite the marsh track. Fred had known the place before its conversion, when the original owners, Mr and Mrs Woodhall lived there. Tragically, both died during the war, killed in a raid while visiting London.

Grace, their daughter and only surviving Woodhall, now retained just one wing, plus the stables and grounds, as a family home. She had a grown family of her own. In fact, she had been Mrs Brandon, wife to Detective Chief Superintendent Alan Brandon since the nineteen-twenties. They had one daughter, Clare.

Leasing off half the house as a hotel and becoming equal partner in the hotel business proved a great success, with very few inconveniences. Part of the lease agreement had resulted in the hotel having its own approach road leading off the main house drive, so there was little or no disturbance from arriving and departing guests. The

19

grounds, through which the drive came up from the road, were landscaped and beautifully kept by the hotel company.

There were other compensations. Like having full and unrestricted rights to all the facilities provided by the hotel, including catering if required. A further advantage was being able to accommodate and entertain family guests in an environment other than their own home. All told, the arrangement certainly suited the Brandons'.

Being the local beat officer, Fred had known the Woodhalls and later, the Brandons for years. The Brandons also had a small home in Norwich and in London, but spent most of their time at Patchets. This had certainly been the case since the marsh incidents had begun.

All these thoughts passed through Fred's mind as he battled from the track onto the deserted coast road. The recessed walled entrance to Patchets came into sight. It was an ideal site for the local public call-box. Sheltered from the worst of weather, its illuminated interior had offered a welcome break on many a stormy night.

Fred Fisher arrived, separated himself from his bike and entered the kiosk. For two seconds, he had considered peddling straight up to see if Mr Brandon was at the house, but he quickly saw no point in that. If he stuck by the book and notified the Information Room at Police Headquarters, they would know who gets tipped out and when. He would get no thanks for short-circuiting the call-out system.

Lifting the receiver, Fred rattled the cradle in a series of swift morse -type depressions. To the man in the street, these rapid stuttering movements meant nothing. But to those initiated into the world of telegraphic communication, these energy releasing manipulations saved time, wear and money. Fred had been taught this trick by a GPO engineer. It was handy when Fred's pockets were short of change.

Bang on six, the reserved Alice Braithwaite was in her seat at her PBX Mk11 switchboard, adjacent to the post office counter at Cley-Next-the-Sea, ready to start her shift. Suddenly an irritating clattering signal caused her to drop both her needles and wool.

She quickly looked at the indicator, then at the large clock above the board. Alice then released a long, meaningful sigh. She deftly pushed forward the communication lever, not needing to enquire who was making the call.

"Mr Fisher," she said, with steely authority, "when using post office telephonic communication equipment, even at this ungodly hour of the morning, please do so in the prescribed manner, by placing two pennies in the appropriate slot. Now, what is it this time?"

Fred made a quick but flattering apology and within two clicks he found himself connected to Police Headquarters, Norwich. Being a public line, and not wishing everyone in the women's circle to know what had taken place, Fred used a prearranged code, then gave the location. This was sufficient to report the incident.

Five minutes later, obeying instructions, he was cycling back along a mist-free track. There was no sign of their relief. Typical, Fred thought, though he knew it wouldn't be long before the cavalry arrived.

When Fred had left for the phone, George had taken the flask and climbed the shingle bank. He sat and watched the grey morning light chasing away the night. He also watched the wide rear of Fred's figure retreating heavily towards the road. He asked himself how on earth Fred's bike had managed to survive so many years without crumbling under the weight. He smiled and poured himself some tea. The mist now deepened. George reckoned the probable cause was the breeze stalling the vapour's movement against the wall of the shingle bank. The majority of the mist lay like a great bedspread, over the western-end of the marsh, toward Weybourne.

George had just finished his second cup of tea when he heard wings beating furiously and the squawk of ducks. As he watched, three grumbling mallards appeared out of the mist like aircraft rising clear of cloud. They beat a tight turn, still yelling their displeasure at something. Then they turned to fly away in formation toward Kelling.

George's mind settled. For the tenth time, he looked down into the marsh and saw the handkerchief hanging limply from the reed and the white hand still held fast by the handcuff. He stared at the dull metal, trying to recall ever having to use them before? He hadn't. This was the first time, and they appeared perfect for the job.

Thankfully, the face had submerged, no doubt drawn down by some unseen force. George gave an involuntary shudder. At least he no longer felt watched by those half-closed accusing eyes. But, for some reason, he couldn't detach himself from the face beneath the water. Perhaps it was because here was an innocent victim of a will-o'-the-wisp serial killer, a deadly spirit, who left bodies like others leave offerings. Why this spot on the marsh and how did they arrive? All the roads, tracks and beaches were watched. Just how do you walk your victim considerable distances, then under the noses of the law, take life without a sound?

Perhaps they were religious sacrificial victims, willing to face what came. Even so, they still had to pass the manned police checkpoints. He reached for the flask. No point in keeping the last of the warm tea for Fred. If George knew him, he'd slide up to Patchets to see if he could beg a drink from the hotel kitchen, before heading back. He'd have to be careful not to be seen by the Brandons. Every bobby in Norfolk knew the head of Norfolk CID, had a home there.

The flask had barely started to tilt, when the clear sound of wings beating water signalled another group of mallards were fighting their way into the sky. Like a squadron of scrambled fighters, they broke through the top of the mist, rapidly gaining height, pouring scorn like bullets on whatever had crept up on them. Their leader confidently steered them south.

George noticed that this second scurry had taken place no more than two hundred yards or so further east than the first eruption. Whatever had put them to flight was keeping to the margins of the marsh and sticking to the mist. Whatever was moving, it seemed to be drawing a straight line for Weybourne.

Shortly after this, a third flight of birds rattled out of the mist, some distance further away. George, puzzled now, kept his eyes firmly fixed on the area of this last disturbance. He had little chance of seeing whatever it was at that distance, but guessed he was looking at a point a good mile away. If that was true, it was beyond the Weybourne track and therefore well beyond where the westerly checkpoint was set. Whatever the disturbance was, it had followed the ground immediately between the seaward edge of the marsh and the bank. All neatly shrouded by mist.

As there had been no repeated police whistles, he could only assume it must have been the hungry vixen, trying for a fat duck breakfast. George rubbed his eyes and stared again. He had excellent eyesight but, at that distance, people were just specks.

As he watched, he saw a speck appear, just for an instant, out of the mist then disappear again. He told himself he could have been mistaken.

Changing his position, George spotted Fred's figure steaming along the track, taking full advantage of the off-shore breeze. Fred's smile faded when he found there was no tea left. Outwardly he greeted this news with heroic resignation. In his mind, George deserved the tea for playing nursemaid to the floater.

"Well, at least our body is still with us," he observed, turning and grinning at George, "We're to sit tight while the Information Room sets the rest of the county alight with news of your find. Mr Brandon is at Patchets, so he'll be tipped out with the rest of the cavalry. The fat's well and truly in the fire and our beloved beat sergeant from Cromer, is at this very minute legging it to our aid."

George sat grinning at Fred. Both men looked bleary eyed, in need of shaves and a good breakfast.

"You should have been here an hour ago," George yawned. "I think I spotted someone making off over the other side of Weybourne. Whoever or perhaps I should say whatever it was, put up a few ducks but faded into the mist. Thought it may have been a poacher at first, but it couldn't have been two-legged because the lads on the Weybourne track didn't give us the whistle."

Fred's face changed, "How long ago did this happen?"

"I'd guess it started just under an hour ago," replied George.

Fred's serious expression became deeper, "Sorry mate. If you're right on the timing, the Weybourne lot were pulled off the marsh about five, to an incident on the coast road. It seems two of your Kellingites were setting about each other."

George's eyes widened, "Blimey! There was I thinking everything at the Weybourne end was covered. Meanwhile, it's possible our villain has bolted through the hole."

"Well, we don't know that for certain. But, I must admit, it's possible."

Silence cloaked both men. They were having the same terrible thoughts.

"Look, I'll leg it back to the phone and get what you've said to the bosses. They'll get some bodies down onto the Sherringham side of the heath. Whoever it is will be in the bag, if we work quickly. Don't fret. They'll turn up your prowler."

As Fred said this, the sound of a car's engine broke through his words. Detective Chief Superintendent Alan Brandon's car came into sight. In two minutes, he was stepping out of his car.

Fred saluted. "You were pretty sharp sir, if I might say."

Alan smiled, "That's alright. I had just got back from Cromer when I got the call that you had another body?"

"Afraid so," said Fred, "P.C. Wright spotted the body. He's managed to secure it but there's little chance of getting it out without the net."

"That's on its way from Cromer. Did either of you hear or see anything other than this reported splash?"

Fred stepped back, allowing George to explain what he'd seen during Fred's absence. Alan listened intently. Then he asked George to go through it again, making certain he had every detail.

"Excellent, very well done, you've handed us the best lead we've had in this business. It's the most damnable luck the Weybourne track team were withdrawn at about that time!"

Alan spun round, walking quickly back to his car. "Looks as though you've done well to get the body tethered. Must have been a struggle clearing it from the reeds. Well done."

George always felt slightly at a loss talking to top brass, "Did the only thing I could do sir. He didn't want to come out and I wasn't for going in."

Alan smiled at him, recognising tired embarrassment. "Well, at least you found a decent use for handcuffs. Look, hang on until the Crime Scene unit arrives. I'll get some lads stopping and searching everyone moving towards Sherringham. Looks as though whoever it was, is heading that way," he smiled, "Well done again Wright."

With that, he raised his hat to them both, leapt into his car and was away along the track.

Fred laughed, "Did you see that, George? He's still got his pyjamas on under that mackintosh of his. The Information Room sergeant must have rung just as he was climbing into bed, poor beggar."

Grace Brandon rolled over and flung an arm across the bed to where she expected to find a snoozing Alan. Before opening her eyes she searched the empty space beside her. She quickly assumed Alan had left the bed to visit the bathroom, but when he failed to appear, she grudgingly opened her eyes. He was gone. So were his clothes. She left the bed and almost tripped over the telephone cable that now trailed from Alan's bedside table, across the carpet and disappeared under the bathroom door.

So that was it, she thought, Alan had either received a call or wanted to make one without disturbing her, so had taken the telephone into the bathroom, leaving her to sleep.

Although she found herself slightly upset at the thought of Alan having to dash off, she knew there must be good reason. Especially as he had managed so little time for rest, since the wretched marsh business had begun.

She smiled with relief as she looked through the bedroom window and saw his car sweep up the drive. At least she could make sure he had a good breakfast.

As she returned the phone to the bedside table, it rang. Grace lifted the receiver.

"Hello," she heard a male voice say, "is that Superintendent Brandon?"

"No," Grace said, "this is Mrs Brandon."

"Sorry to disturb you ma'am, this is the control room, at Norwich. We need to speak to Mr Brandon very urgently. Is he at home with you ma'am?"

Grace gave a kind laugh, "No, I'm sorry, but I think he's just driven up to the house. If you like to hold on, I will see what's happening."

Grace left the phone and pulling on a housecoat, she went out onto the landing, just as Alan came through into the hall.

"Darling, it's the men in blue. You know who I mean, those people who see more of you than I do. But, please don't go off again until I have given you a proper breakfast." She blew him a kiss and went back into the bedroom.

Alan spent some time speaking on the hall telephone, then made two further calls, after which he appeared in the bedroom, muttering something about 'the luck of the devil'. He then proceeded to remove a heavy sweater and his suit trousers, under which he still wore a full set of pyjamas. He looked up and caught Grace grinning.

"Oh, it's alright Grace I haven't quite lost my marbles. I just threw on the first things that came to hand over my pyjamas and dashed out to arrange something."

At that point, Grace knew better than to ask what needed arranging. Thirty minutes later saw them both showered changed and ready to face the world. Breakfast was the only meal that Grace tried to ensure she had Alan to herself, whatever the coming day might hold. She knew this day would be busy for Alan. Each of the hours filled to bursting with crime and criminals, whereas for Grace, it could be long hours rehearsing for a concert, meetings with agents, or committee work. What she enjoyed best of all, was being mother to their daughter Clare, a hard working, always busy medical student, based at Cambridge.

While Alan munched toast and swallowed tea, he began wading through a raft of reports from his briefcase. Grace picked up the Eastern Daily Press that Alan had brought in. All their daily papers came via the hotel reception. An excellent arrangement, providing a multiple-choice of reading.

She glanced at the headline. 'Norfolk woman foresaw train smash!' She did not have to read further. After all, she was the woman referred to. Since the incident and the subsequent interview on the wireless, she and Alan had not had much peace. Although Alan was the most patient of men, Grace's 'gift', if such ability can be called a gift, was about as far from a benefaction as you could get. Grace preferred to call it a curse.

She had first noticed her ability to foresee events when she was just eight years old. Her father had taken her to a local fun fair. It was his intention they should enjoy a very fast ride on a roundabout, called the 'Whip'. As they were walking towards the pay-desk, she suddenly saw one of the carriages rise up away from the guide rails. Almost in slow motion, she saw horror etched on the faces of some of the riders who were thrown out. Others, trapped within the carriage as it turned over seemed frozen to their seats. Grace heard horrible screams and then all went black.

Grace gradually became aware that she was sitting on the grass, her father's arm around her shoulders. He asked if she was all right. Her father's concerned voice had registered on her mind at the same time as she clearly saw there had been no accident and the carriages of the Whip were slowing to disgorge its load of chattering, happy smiling passengers.

Grace told her father that she had become faint and would rather not go on that particular ride. Her father was comfortable with that and bought her a drink. Grace then decided to tell her father what she had seen.

She had just finished and was waiting for her father to say it was all imagination, caused by excitement, when they both heard a muffled explosion. People were running through clouds of dust from the direction of the Whip. Screaming blotted out the noise of fairground music. Grace's father had led her gently from the fairground, without enquiring as to the cause of the noise and panic.

Over the years, Grace was to experience many such premonitions, often leaving her deeply shocked and distressed. It was only later, when she achieved her ambition to become a professional pianist and fell in love with and married Alan that life, at last, seemed to turn around.

All went well for a number of years until they went to Scotland for a concert engagement and short holiday. They arrived at the Hydro Hotel. As Grace excitedly left the car, she seemed to lose her balance. Supporting herself against the car, she looked up and was horrified to see thick smoke pouring from a room on the second floor. As she stared, bright red flames shot through the smoke. She clearly saw a woman appear amongst the flames screaming for help. At this point, Grace collapsed.

Just two days after their arrival back in Norfolk, the daily papers carried a front-page account of a fatal hotel fire. A picture, taken at the height of the blaze by a guest, clearly showed a woman trying to escape from a window on the second floor, just as Grace had described it to Alan. Also in the picture was the name of the hotel. It was the Hydro.

Alan was frustrated and saddened, but no longer disbelieving. Often, Grace had recounted what she had seen, describing her intuition, her sudden flashes of a sixth sense sometimes involving serious crime. The unbidden, uninvited side of Grace's character could appear without warning, causing great physical and mental sorrow. He knew it to be like having the worst of all nightmares.

A visiting senior officer once rashly commented on how devilishly lucky Alan was to have a secret aide for solving the unsolvable, thereby opening the door to higher promotion. Alan's chief, who was present, had responded, 'better an open third-eye than a blinded green-eye, eh?'

Alan slowly put down the report he had been reading. He stood and crossed over to the window, where he looked out across the familiar marsh. Grace glanced at the heading on the form. It was a post-mortem report. Grace didn't say anything for a while, but she knew that sad look.

Finally she said, "What is it darling?"

Alan remained facing the window. "It's another damned body I'm afraid. It was discovered a short time ago by young George Wright. You know, the P.C. that looks after Kelling. I'm sorry my sweet but it looks as though you will have to be on your own today." As he spoke, he avoided looking directly at Grace. He wanted to avoid what he knew she would see.

Grace joined him at the window. They both stared at the marsh.

"Is it the same? No marks indicating the cause of death?"

She waited for the answer as Alan moved behind her. He wound his arms protectively around her. "Yes. I'm afraid it seems that way."

Her eyes closed for a few seconds. She twisted round to face him. "You must let me try to help you, please Alan let me try. It might not work, I know that, but at least give me a chance."

Her eyes searched his. He knew she was right. The only way to ease the tension he knew Grace felt was to allow her to unlock what was deep inside her. Alan knew she might not be able to help him. After all, it wasn't as simple as opening a door. Grace was no séance medium. She had always been the reluctant traveller.

Alan placed his finger under her chin and gently raised her head so he could kiss away the small tears that suddenly appeared. "Fine, dearest girl, you are now one of my team. There's one rule, as always. You don't keep anything bottled up inside, and the first inkling or premonition, you tell me straight away. This matter has already cost the lives of four or five people, so no keeping secrets or locking me out. Is that a deal?"

Grace smiled, "Of course darling. No secrets, ever."

Grace couldn't help the relief she felt. If she had powers at all, she certainly had no control over them. They controlled her. If there was anything out there on the marsh to feel, it may just seek her out.

The early sun bore through the blue serge worn by Fred and George. It seemed an age since the Superintendent had left them. The CID team had arrived as promised. Fred and George were ushered to one side, while the boffins photographed, measured, sketched and nodded. The cast-net did its job recovering the body in seconds.

Once clear of the water, on the narrow strip of reeds previously occupied by George, the examining, measuring and sampling of the scene began again.

The Inspector in charge of the boffins handed George the now redundant handcuffs and again invited them to leave.

When the Inspector had moved a few yards away George covered his mouth and said quietly, "It's our body. Why should we have to depart?"

Fred had trouble controlling his tired grin. "You sound just like a boy who's just had his ball taken from him."

They both turned their backs on the scene and walked the short distance to their bikes.

"Seriously now George, he's right to want us away, preservation of the scene and all that."

They watched as an undulating flight of Sandwich Terns, like a squadron of Mustangs, flew in from the direction of the road. Their stooping landing approach intersected the path of some Herring Gulls, causing a flash of grey, white and black. There was no love lost, and the clash resulted in a little aerial agitation. Wings flared as flight paths were rapidly changed. Fred loved watching birds, all except perhaps the gulls. They always seem to be angry over something. Their constant shrill keening reminded him of mewing cats or whining children. For him, the Tern was neater, except for his unfortunate Mohican haircut he always seemed too busy to scrap. Though, on second thoughts, he had to admit, they did seem to gain some benefit from being around aggressive birds.

Fred tore his mind away from his thoughts of wildlife. George followed him as he crossed to where the body had been laid out. Fred bent down and covered the face with his handkerchief. He knew he was losing a handkerchief, but the half-closed eyes had a deep sadness that disturbed him. Being sheltered by the reeds, what breeze there was, passed over the body without causing a ripple, so he reasoned the handkerchief would stay put.

He didn't particularly like dead bodies, but everything about this one seemed particularly strange. He'd have felt more comfortable if there were wounds or signs they had drowned, but this business was weird. He couldn't shake off the feeling that the moment he turned his back, the eyes would open or a finger would twitch. It was as if the body was a flesh-dropping zombie of the type he'd seen at the cinema in Cromer.

Fred shuddered at the thoughts he was having. Where wounds were present, the cause of death could be seen and was, well, more normal. With this lot, it was unnatural.

George nudged Fred, "What's got into you? Let's get going. The 'plain-clothes' gruesome-twosome can get on with their business. Don't need us cluttering up the place. Anyway, the marsh is now swarming. There's nothing to keep us here."

George looked up. He saw the Superintendent's car coming. "Now we're for it. He thinks we're well out of here."

The car cruised to a halt, the passenger door opened and Grace Brandon said softly, "Good morning Mr Fisher and you too, Mr Wright." The greeting was accompanied by a small thermos. "I thought you might need some strong, hot tea."

Alan indicated to the CID Inspector to draw his team away from the body for a few moments. This was quickly done. Alan then took Grace by the arm and led her carefully to where the body lay. He felt Grace shiver as she saw the still form. Grace never faltered. She stepped forward onto the reeds and knelt down beside the still figure. Everyone watched as she slowly removed the handkerchief.

Stretching out a hand, she touched the face with the back of her fingers. She quickly withdrew her hand, as though she had received an electric shock. Alan gently raised her to her feet.

Grace walked a short way along the very edge of the marsh. She stood for some seconds. Then, taking hold of Alan's hand she whispered, "This is where he stood."

Grace crouched and ran her fingers lightly across the shingle that fringed the marsh. She looked around her and then repeated the movement with her fingers.

She paused as if something was puzzling her. Alan laid a gentle hand on her shoulder. It was as if he was trying to comfort her.

Almost absent-mindedly, Grace reached up and patted the hand as if saying, it's alright. Then Grace ran her hand over the ground again, this time much slower.

"Of course," she spoke very slowly, as if suddenly understanding something very important. The words were also spoken very quietly, so that only Alan could hear her, "Of course it's here, right here." Her voice trembled.

"Alan, this place is the threshold, this is a portal! All around us now there are thousands of voices. The movement of time rushing by like a great wind. Can't you feel it? Listen."

Alan didn't answer the question. He knew he wasn't supposed to answer, just be there, close to her and listen.

There was another pause. Grace rose up and slowly returned to the body where she gently replaced the handkerchief.

Returning to the path, she said to Alan, "I need to walk up there, on the shingle bank," Alan knew that Grace was seeing far more than he or the others could. He followed up the bank, allowing a short distance to develop between them. He knew being too close could break her connection with whatever was there.

They climbed the steep bank, stopping only when she crested the ridge and had full sight of the sea. The sea state was short, often referred to locally as lumpy. It was a muddy brown colour. The suspended silt from the seabed had not had time to settle.

In the half-distance, impatient white horses raced each other along wave-tops before disappearing into watery valleys. Despite the warmth of the sun, the water looked heavy, cold and uninviting. But Grace dearly loved the solitude of this place.

The marsh held for her a wonderful sadness. It always reminded her of the opening movement of the opera, Peter Grimes. She stood recalling the movement with the evocative title, Dawn. The scene brilliantly reflected the soft, haunting notes, echoing through the shingle and out over the stands of tall reeds, where birds hung on the breeze, wings and tails flaring, compensating for the currents of air that mischievously try to unbalance each flight.

Grace looked along the beach in either direction. To the left, the slash of brown shingle curved out of sight, through the point she knew was destined to be a bird sanctuary and on to Blakeney Point. Undisturbed, the shingle ran like the horn of a great buffalo, towards the blue, washed-out sky. To the right, it likewise followed the hint of a curve for a little over a quarter of a mile, where the remains of the old coastguard station scarred the beauty of nature.

The derelict station looked naked. Its gaunt window spaces staring back at her like giant black eyes.

Alan watched Grace. Her raincoat, now exposed to the blustery wind that haunts this coastline, danced and tugged at her slim frame. She was forced to take a step back to gain her balance. At the same time, she raised a hand to Alan as if to warn him not to join her. Alan remained where he was.

A fleeting shadow, cast by a lone black-backed gull, etched its way in from the sea and up the stony bank, making her look up. It donated its squawking cry to the scene and then, as if in a hurry to be elsewhere, wheeled away over the marsh.

Alan found this distracting but didn't take his eyes off Grace. He had good cause to believe in her ability to feel things that were beyond his imagination.

Once, just for a split second, she turned to look at him. Her eyes full of sorrow, her expression one of total sadness. He was tempted to speak to her but resisted as she again turned away. He knew she might never tell him what she was feeling. He would wait.

A few moments later, she turned towards him again, tears welling up in her eyes, "I can't put this any other way, Alan. These deaths are journeys. They end or begin here, right here where that poor man died. There is a second man, I can't see him clearly, but he is the spawn of evil."

Grace looked down at the shingle and frowned, as though trying to understand what she was seeing, "He hides his face from me but he can't hide the evil he brings. He has death in his black heart." Grace looked for some seconds across the marsh towards the coast road, "There is also his nemesis, the means of his defeat. He is also a traveller. He is close by, very close. He hunts the second man, but also invites danger," she reached out and squeezed Alan's hand, "be very careful, Alan."

Her face looked pale and drawn. She held her head in her hands. Then her hands fell to her sides as though they were great weights. Grace looked exhausted. Alan carefully brought Grace down the shingle bank.

On returning to their car, Alan had a short conversation with the CID Inspector, then he and Grace headed back toward the coast road. At the track's junction with the coast road, the Super's car stopped level with a convoy of cars.

It was too far away to make out what passed between the drivers, but a moment later, the Super's car continued on it's way. The convoy turned towards the shingle bank. Obviously, the coroner and the CID team were descending in force.

Two minutes later, Fred and George had mounted their steeds and were peddling for their respective villages. When they reached the point on the track where it joined the coast road, they saw two uniformed constables. No doubt placed there to stop the public gaining access.

George looked at Fred, "Seems all the road blocks, night watches, cordons, meetings, incident rooms and going round the whole damned county on the knocker, hasn't brought us a single result, has it?"

Fred corrected a slight front-wheel wobble, no doubt caused by tiredness. "You surprise me, George. Life's nothing like a Cagney film where the goody shoots the baddy and rides off into the sunset, all within two reels. What you've just witnessed is something you'll be able to tell your children about, one day. It's called factual police work. Now go and tuck yourself up with a copy of Moriarty's Police Law and have a good day's sleep."

They nodded in agreement, smiled and parted.

Chapter Two

On reaching the house, Grace had wanted to rest. Alan could tell she needed to get over their excursion.

"Why not try to sleep, Grace. I'm expecting some calls so I'll catch up on some paper-work."

He followed her to their bedroom and made certain she was comfortable. Alan then opened the windows a fraction and closed the heavy curtains, so as to shut out the bright sunlight. Finally, he quietly changed his jacket for a more comfortable lightweight type then crossed to Grace and kissed her forehead. She was already half-asleep. Smiling, he closed the bedroom door without a sound.

Alan descended the stairs, switched off the phone extension to the bedroom and sat down at his desk. In front of him was a canvas pouch containing paperwork. He knew without looking that every file would relate, in some way, to the marsh affair. Every day, these papers were ferried to wherever he was working, by area car. Copies were similarly distributed to all Alan's team, in their endless trawl for leads.

A number of times the phone rang, but none of the calls gave him the news he was waiting for. Despite the intensity of the police sweep from Sherringham golf course to Weybourne, nothing had turned up.

After no more than an hour, he began feeling restless. He stuck to his task and pulled the next sheet in front of him. It was a quickly scrawled pencil note. A shed had been broken into at the rear of allotments. The owner of the shed had not yet been located. Alan cursed himself for not noticing the single flimsy sheet before.

He read it again and then grabbed a map of the area. He studied this quickly and reaching for the phone, dialled Sherringham police station. The ringing tone repeated itself a number of times before a very tired voice answered. Alan identified himself, "What the hell's going on? Why wasn't the phone answered immediately?"

Sherringham's Sergeant Bell, shot to attention, "Sorry sir. There's just the two of us on duty and we've only just got in from following up the report from P.C. Wright."

Alan's voice became more understanding, "Look Sergeant Bell, I'm looking at a scrap of paper with your name on the bottom of it."

"Oh yes sir, the shed's a stone's throw from Hoggs Bottom, just where the coast road ducks under the railway bridge. We met the area car driver while we were by the bridge. He told us he was on his way to you with reports, so I took a chance and wrote that note. I also used his radio to tell control about the shed. I couldn't leave the sweep at that moment. Hope you understand, sir?"

Alan smiled to himself. He knew exactly how hard police officers were working and if anyone was at fault, it was himself for barking.

"I do understand, but it's vital we quickly find the owner of that shed. It's quite possible the figure seen by P.C. Wright may be responsible. We need the owner to give us a full description of anything missing. I want that list circulated by express message to every copper in Norfolk ASAP." Before finishing the call, Alan remembered to add his thanks for all the good work.

Alan sighed and drew the papers together again, with the note referring to the shed on top. Instead of placing them back into the cardboard file, he carefully placed them into the side wallet of his briefcase. He cursed himself again for not seeing the possible significance of this note earlier.

Alan then rang the Information Room and told the duty officer he was to be informed of developments. The D.O. told him that two other members of the team and

Sergeant Friar had just telephoned querying ownership of the allotment shed. This news pleased Alan. It seemed he wasn't the only one reading circulated messages. Picking up his briefcase, he made his way back to the bedroom to check on Grace. She was still sleeping. Quietly placing his closed briefcase alongside the chair on which he had previously placed his coat, he retreated. He needed to think through what Grace had said, before meeting with David Long, his Chief.

Alan entered the hotel and collected a newspaper from a selection kept for guests. He acknowledged the smiles from the receptionists, and told them where to find him if Mrs Brandon or anyone else telephoned.

As usual, he avoided the gaggle of guests in the lounge and passed directly into the Smoking Room, a room avoided by most guests. It had been the library during pre-war years, deliberately decorated to resemble the atmosphere normally found in a London Gentlemen's club. With discreet lighting, scattered large leather armchairs, plus the occasional rustle of a newspaper, it would allow his mind to work through problems without distraction.

As far as Alan could see, there was only one other occupant. Apart from the bottoms of smart fawn cavalry trousers and heavy brown brogue shoes, the type preferred by Alan, the remainder of his companion lay hidden behind an opened copy of the Times. From the drift of pale blue smoke, rising above the paper, he was a man, like Alan, who obviously enjoyed a pipe of tobacco that was pleasantly familiar.

Choosing not to disturb the reader or become involved in conversation, he crossed to an alcove where he sat in one of the deep armchairs. He took a great deal of pleasure in slowly filling his reliable briar pipe, lit it gratefully and settled down to look at his copy of the Eastern Daily Press. It was not very often that he had the opportunity to actually smoke his pipe. Grace thought the smell repugnant, so he had reduced its use to the outdoors and the odd occasion when he could sneak into the hotel smoking room.

He glanced at the main headlines, "UN Troops fight to close triangle." Alan knew one or two young policemen who had fought in the Second World War and now found themselves recalled on Z reserve to fight in Korea. He silently thanked God that he had a daughter and not a son.

At the bottom of the front page there was a short 'stop-press' report of another body being discovered in Cley Marsh. It rated three lines. Alan's eyelids drooped. He became mildly aware of the other occupant of the room folding his paper and leaving the room. Alan sank lower in his chair. He removed his pipe with a well-executed, sub-conscious action and knew very little else.

"If it please you sir, would you like tea?"

The enquirer was Elsie, one of the hotel staff, who sometimes helped Grace out in the house. The words, when spoken for a second time, roused Alan. Tea, he thought, what tea?

"I was just enquiring Mr Brandon sir, if you would want tea?" repeated Elsie. She was smiling down at his obvious confusion. She knelt and retrieved his newspaper from the carpet where it had fallen from his lap.

Rather embarrassed, he thanked her and asked for a tray to take through to the house. It wasn't his habit to fall fast asleep in public rooms or transport tea trays from the hotel into the house.

He rose rather stiffly from the chair. Elsie smiled again and went off to arrange the tea. Alan stretched and looked around. He recalled that his companion had left. The Times now lay on the arm of the chair he had used.

Alan crossed over and glanced down at the paper. It struck Alan that the paper had been extremely neatly folded, and if Alan didn't know better, he would assume the late reader had purposely left it so positioned to catch Alan's eye.

The selected front page quarter, carried an article headed, 'Home Secretary to make statement on the Norfolk body case.' This was followed by the news that the Home Secretary, after meetings with senior police officers, would shortly be making a statement in the House of Commons on the affair.

Alan was not shaken by this coincidence. He knew that his Chief was to go to London to attend a meeting at the Home Office. Also that the public were entitled to more information than they were, up to this point, getting.

Elsie's return with the tea interrupted Alan's thoughts. He followed her out to a recess set to one side of reception. Here, he waited for a second while the small green baize door, marked 'strictly private', was unlocked by the duty manager.

Then he and Elsie passed through into the quiet of the house. This secluded access to and from the hotel was another of the contracted benefits negotiated by Grace.

Alan took the tray, thanking Elsie for her usual kindness. He slowly mounted the stairs, wondering how on earth, tiny young maids managed to carry such cumbersome loads, without spilling half the contents.

With a display of dexterity that surprised him, he somehow managed to open doors and side step around furniture, all without spilling a drop of the tea or hot water. Negotiating his way across the bedroom, he finally placed the tray thankfully on a small table. Alan exhaled deeply. Actually, it was more like a vast sigh of relief. He realised he must have been holding his breath the whole way up the staircase.

The dim, cool interior of the room was still as he had left it. The heavy curtains remained drawn, although occasional movement caused by the breeze from the open window, allowed shafts of bright sunlight to flicker through. Only two sounds broke the stillness, the distant sound of waves breaking on the beach and the equally soft regular sigh of Grace's breathing.

He tip-toed across the carpet, his intention was to close the window. As he carefully drew the curtains aside, he noticed what appeared to be small specks of green moss lying on the inside of the sill. He was absolutely certain they hadn't been there when he had drawn them. He immediately thought they had been carried in, by the soft breeze, but just as quickly, dismissed the thought. He saw they formed a very faint regular shape, as if deposited by the heel of a man's shoe. He looked again. Now he was certain. The moss was identical to a small growth of moss he had noticed earlier on the balcony.

Quietly, Alan raised the partly opened lower half of the window. Yes, he was right. Clearly imprinted on the surface of the balcony was an imprint, which also appeared to have been made by the heel of a shoe. It was obvious that access to the balcony could have been gained from an adjoining fire escape.

Alan began to move back from the window when he saw a man who was in the process of walking fairly quickly, towards the side of the building. In spite of the weather being sunny and warm, the man was wearing a light tan, belted mackintosh, something like the officer's type, worn by Alan. The brim of a hat was pulled down over his face but it didn't prevent Alan getting a glimpse of how pale he was. He was of medium build and quite tall. This impression was gathered in the seconds it took for the man to pass out of sight.

Alan crossed to the phone but realised he had switched that line off. As quietly as possible, Alan returned to the hall. While doing this, another thought struck him. He was sure the man had been his companion in the hotel smoking room. The trousers and shoes were identical. Using the hall phone, he spoke to the hotel receptionist.

In two minutes, Alan learned that the man could be a guest who had booked in early that morning. He had completed the usual register entry and had produced his identity card.

Alan asked if he had been seen lately. He was told that the gentleman had left the hotel some time ago, evidently to go for a short walk. Alan finally enquired whether the man had luggage with him when he arrived. There was a short break while enquiries were made from the porter. Evidently, he had arrived with just small hand luggage.

Careful not to wake Grace, Alan returned to the bedroom and worked through the room, noting every item, searching for change. Grace's heavy gold necklace lay where she had left it on the bedside table. Beside it lay her purse. Nothing appeared to have been taken. Not a damn thing, but someone, probably the man he'd seen, had been in the room and obviously hadn't entered for the fun of it.

Alan spotted the suit jacket that he had changed out of. He had left it draped on the arm of a chair. It was now on the floor. As he picked it up, he noticed one of the pockets had been turned inside out.

Alan's eyes went to his briefcase. It was open. Withdrawing the papers from the side wallet he quickly scanned them. The top sheet no longer referred to the shed that had been broken into. A puzzled Alan found himself reading a brief report from Fred Fisher, describing a small white metal object, similar to a badge. It had been discovered that morning by a County Roadman. The only reason for the note's inclusion in the area car mail was that the object was found on the grass verge at the entrance to Patchets. Fisher had closed his report stating that the object was now held at Salthouse police house along with an appropriate entry in the property register.

That's it, he thought, whoever entered the room was after information, not jewellery, but why the interest in a small item of lost and found property?

It was only then that Alan looked towards the bed. Grace had quietly sat up and was smiling at him.

"Let me guess, you've lost something?"

"No, darling," he said, "I tried to get in without waking you," he crossed over to her, kissing her on the cheek, "you needed that rest."

In spite of Grace having smiled at him, her eyes betrayed the fact that she was still affected by what she had seen on the marsh. Alan went to the tray and poured some tea. It was still hot. He handed the cup to Grace.

"Sorry to be such a burden, Alan my darling. I can't help what I see. I know it's not easy for you." There was a long pause.

Alan sat down on the edge of the bed, took her hands and kissed them, "You really mustn't worry, darling. That dead man out on the marsh, he is beyond pain or fear now. He's at peace. You let me do the worrying. You just rest and drink your tea."

Alan rose to straighten the half-drawn curtains, but before he was halfway across the room, she stopped him, "Please Alan, I wish you would stop treating me like a small child," Grace said these words kindly, not wishing to hurt him, "I really do need to talk this through. If you have any trust in what I tell you, now is the time to have faith in me."

Alan smiled at Grace and sat on the edge of the bed again. It was Grace's turn to hold hands, "This terrible business on the marsh is so very strange. I find it hard to believe myself, but I know what I saw. One thing is for certain. I won't blame you if you choose not to act on what I say."

Alan now placed an arm around Grace's shoulders, "Come on darling. It's me, remember. I've been with you so many times when you've seen the unexplainable. Whatever you saw out there on the marsh or on the shingle bank needs to be talked out, sorted through, just like sorting coloured beads from a bag."

She looked up into his eyes, she felt warm and safe when she had his arms around her.

"Come on Grace, we've been through this before. It is not your imagination working overtime. If you say something strange is out there, then it is. We've worked through so many problems together."

"That's the whole trouble Alan, this time I'm not sure I can explain. For the very first time, I'm really puzzled by what I saw, what I felt," she paused, "I don't understand what I was seeing or what I was hearing. Those buildings I saw, well it's not our marsh, the marsh we know and love. The noises were strange, unknown to me." She squeezed Alan's hands in hers, as though imploring him to believe her.

"I felt so remote, so alone, even though my mind was calling me, telling me it was bright sunlight and that you were with me, I felt so isolated. The whole thing seems so unreal and yet, I know what I saw. The terrible things I have seen since we have been together were not the same as this. This is very different, so very unbelievable. I'm worried you will think it's imagination."

Alan poured Grace some more tea. Clasping the cup with both hands, Grace slowly drank the strong liquid. She knew that, once again, because of her, Alan may be risking everything he had worked so hard for. No matter how grotesque, how bizarre the picture she painted, he would listen and accept it as the truth, as she had seen it. What worried Grace was Alan's colleagues, how they might react. Was this a fantasy too far?

She patted the bed, "Please sit with me." Alan smiled and sat close to her. "Alan, what occasionally happens to me is very hard for most people to understand. They classify it as an over-active imagination, an illusion, even delusion, imagination, mumbo-jumbo. It is all the same to them. The strange thing is if you ask around you'll find a high percentage of people, who at some time in their lives, sense they have done or seen something or been somewhere, that cannot be explained from their memory."

"You mean Déjà vu?"

"Something like that," said Grace, "the problem is getting them to admit it, especially in public, where their standing or future could be in the balance. Now, what happens to me is an uncontrollable, advanced Technicolor form of the same condition."

Alan looked at her, "I believe you have a very special gift for occasionally seeing, but I'm not sure where this is going?"

"Have you ever walked along a street in a strange town. You are positive you've never been there before. You suddenly feel you can describe what lies around a corner. On turning the corner you are proved right enough for it to be unsettling or rather strange?"

Alan got up, crossed to the small table and poured some tea for himself, "I can truthfully say I don't think I have. And, in any case, I leave such things to you." He smiled and offered Grace a biscuit from the tray.

"Alan, all I am trying to do is to give you an example of those 'things,' I sometimes feel or see. It is like being two people, living outside your body. You feel different, very much alone. Especially when something happens you can't understand or explain."

Alan gave her the knowing look of a sympathetic parent, "Darling Grace, I do understand and I will, I promise do anything to make you feel better. So, why not tell me what really happened out there on the bank?"

. Alan's reaction worried Grace. She felt he was being crushingly patronizing. They had been through several of her supernatural experiences in the time they had been together, but try as she might, Alan just didn't have the right kind of soul to grasp the nettle. She often felt isolated by her visions, even from him. To Grace, it was like being the only person with eyesight, watching something evil approaching. Everyone else will help but are still blind to the danger. Certainly, what had just happened on the shingle bank had made her think she was perhaps, just a little insane.

She leant over and kissed him fondly. "Let me sort out my thoughts and then, we'll talk."

Alan knew better than to press her further. Leaving Grace to relax, Alan went back into the hotel. Ten minutes later, he returned to the house.

The mystery man had evidently returned early from his walk saying he had to leave straight away on business. Having paid for the one day, he had collected his few things and gone.

The entry in the hotel register gave his name as Smith with an address in London. This, according to the clerk was verified by the details on his identity card. The man was last seen walking down the drive toward the coastal road.

As Alan had turned to leave the desk, the clerk had told him that on first meeting the man, he and the other receptionist, had assumed he was Alan's brother. The likeness was evidently quite staggering.

Chapter Three

As Alan turned his car into the entrance to Cromer hospital, his eyes took in the 1920 brown stone pile, with its forbidding high arched windows and depressing paintwork. The sight of this sombre, rambling assembly must have been more than a little off-putting to anyone hoping for a miracle cure. New white paint marked a space in the car park reserved for 'Board Members Only'. Alan parked. For some reason, this simple act of defiance, made him feel good.

He was not surprised there were very few people around. It felt that kind of echoing place. Walking quickly through the main entrance, he turned right along the dimly lit, drab-olive-green painted corridor, faithfully following the tired red on cream signs, which read Mortuary & Chapel. Feeling less than encouraged by the prospect of what lay ahead, he began to whistle softly. Once or twice, he met nurses who gave him a stony glare. This worried him until he realised what tune he was quietly whistling. It was hardly the place or time for 'The Sun has got his Hat on'.

Gathered in a group outside the Mortuary entrance were four men. One was Detective Sergeant Charlie Friar, who introduced the three others as Vincent Lawrence the County Senior Pathologist, Guy Watson; Senior House Surgeon and the District Coroner; Mr Clifford Balls.

The moment they entered the Mortuary, Alan's mind flooded back to his time he had spent six months as Coroners Officer, which meant attending and witnessing every post-mortem in his district. The smell of formalin had often made him feel very sick. It was the only time in his life when he wished he smoked cigarettes. He even envied the elderly Mortuary Assistant, who constantly had a lighted cigarette stub between his lips, as he dissected body parts.

Alan was not surprised to find that the passing years had not relieved him of his aversion to this particular chemical. Everything within the room reeked with the pungent aroma, including the slabbed and sheeted bodies. The smell was enough to make anyone immediately sick.

Alan advised Charlie Friar to breathe in and out through his mouth. He explained that by doing this, he could avoid most of the smell. Charlie, wondered why his boss thought mortuary visits were new to him, so he simply raised his eyebrows and nodded.

All five now donned surgical gowns, masks and gloves. While dressing, Alan apologised for the need to call such a meeting. He explained it was vital the body be examined quickly. While saying this, an attendant, who seemed not to want to look anyone directly in the eye, appeared from an inner room, and in a lisping soft Welsh accent, not directed at anyone in particular, announced the deceased was now in the dissecting room. He made it sound as though the deceased had walked there of his own accord and was now waiting nervously to have a tooth extracted.

The next hour and a half passed unpleasantly slowly. The pathologist, assisted by Guy Watson, worked methodically from the brain through the throat, chest, stomach and bowel without uttering more than an occasional, "Hhhmmm," or soft drawn out, "ahhh, yes."

An ancient clock, high up above the door, noisily ticked away every second, apparently as methodical in its approach to time, as the medical team were trying to be, in their pathological deliberations.

The remaining observers looked on, maintaining a respectfully sufficient distance to avoid complaint, but close enough to view every cut and thrust.

With organs neatly arranged on a stainless steel side-table, the two medical men set about slicing into them as though they were carving a splendid Sunday lunch. The

48

slicing and re-slicing, followed by separating and re-examination was accompanied by a new series of high 'ah's and low oh's. This audible language of an ancient secret society then led to a rather lengthy animated whispered conversation, resulting in a somewhat taciturn sign of agreement.

Alan correctly gathered they were ready to disclose their preliminary findings, or lack of them.

Outside in the fresh air of the car park, all five gratefully accepted the strong, damp morning breeze that helped drive the stench of formalin from their clothes. Alan listened courteously to the two doctors and coroner for some considerable time before agreeing that, as a result of what they had witnessed and discussed, absolutely nothing was to be uttered outside the group. They were to remain strictly silent on the subject, particularly to any press enquiry, until the matter had been properly notified to the Chief Constable and higher authority.

Alan and Charlie Friar then left for Police Headquarters at Norwich. In the car, Alan noticed that despite exposing their clothes to an enforced gale, blowing through fully open car windows, the formalin still tenaciously clung to life. This odious smell obviously intended to stay with them like a phantom lodger.

"Well, Charlie what do you think?"

Charlie was busy lighting a cigarette. After a number of puffs, mainly directed at his clothes, he coughed, "Well, I must be honest, I don't quite understand how the blazes anyone can drop dead without cause? According to them, every organ was in perfect shape. The heart showed no obvious sign of distress, clotting, blocking, or muscular spasm outside its natural function. You name the test. They did it, and still no declared cause. All five apparently just ceased to live. Cause of death, as yet unknown!" Charlie inhaled tobacco smoke deeply, "Personally, I don't think the Chief is going to be too happy about it. Four stiffs was way over the top and now we're here with number five. The newspapers will have a field day. I can just imagine the Eastern Daily Press headline. Mysterious plague strikes

Norfolk or, Mystery killer stalks Cley marsh, or something like it. Can't strangle press speculation, although at times I'd like to."

Alan had to bring his racing thoughts back from elsewhere, "Charlie, unlike the ink-jockeys, we have to be patient and let the medical people do their stuff. However, what I found strange was that the mortuary crew chose to play such an open game. Medical men like lawyers tend to drop back into the old professional vernacular when uncertainty reigns. They close ranks and give us non-medicals a holding titbit. I would have felt happier with a stab at a possible cause. There must be something, somewhere that has been overlooked, and I'm not just talking about accepted medical matters. There's nothing normal about these deaths."

Charlie looked across at his boss, hoping the look implied his total support for his view, while lighting another cigarette.

The Chief Constable, David Long, had been waiting impatiently for Alan's arrival. He wasn't best pleased at being told there was another body. He had been pacing his office floor for thirty minutes before the door finally opened and in walked Alan followed by the familiarly, rumpled figure of Charlie Friar.

"Well, what the hell's going on Alan?" He went to walk towards them but for some reason changed his mind. He pulled out his handkerchief and held it to his nose, "Hell, you smell like a pair of damned mortuary assistants."

He pushed two chairs over to the wall furthest from his desk, opened the only two available windows wide and waved them to sit.

"This," he said from behind his handkerchief, "I hope is going to be good news!"

Alan smiled. He knew David Long. He, Alan and Charlie had all joined the police on the same day. They had all been through initial training together and pounded their first beats from the same section house. They had in fact been friends. Although their journey through the job had taken each of them along a different path, to their present ranks, there was still a great deal of personal respect between the three men.

"You'll recall sir, that the body found in the Cley marshes during the early hours of this morning was the fifth in that area. From the medical examination of the previous four, and the one undertaken this morning, it would seem cause of death remains uncertain. There were no signs of violence or trauma on any of them and that includes unexplained bruising."

David tapped the top of his desk with a pencil, a sure sign of growing impatience.

Alan continued, "Both Vincent Lawrence and Guy Watson have conferred and agreed that, on preliminary findings, the latest victim, like the other four, died from what seems to have been simple failure of the heart to work."

"Heart attack," David said sharply.

"No," replied Alan just as forcibly, "Guy Watson said quite clearly that with a heart attack, the cause can be readily identified. In these particular cases, the visual signs were absent. The heart simply stopped. In other words, there were no classic signs of failure or attendant trauma. If you must know, he said it was similar to a light being switched off!"

David frowned, "I know who Vincent Lawrence is. Remind me who the hell Guy Watson is." David was now showing the classic frustration brought on by a lack of expected results. This was a habit he constantly criticised, in junior officers.

Charlie interrupted, "He's the senior house surgeon at Cromer hospital. He's attended all the PM's so far. Sort of long-stop for Vincent Lawrence, may I smoke sir?" Charlie tried the neat trick of rolling the request to smoke within the information requested by the Chief.

David stared at Charlie. Then half smiling, he said slowly, "No Charlie, you may not smoke in my office, and stop trying to get permission by going under the wire.

Anyway, it's about time you gave up that damn filthy habit. You'll end up with lung disease. Get on with it, Alan."

"Well sir, the bodies were all found, as I said, in the marsh within a quarter of a mile from the old coastguard station. Before you ask, it's no longer in use. In fact, it was abandoned just after the war and has never been occupied, officially, since."

"What does 'officially' mean?"

Alan regretted using the word 'officially', "Evidently, there have been occasions when it was thought, by Customs and Excise that contraband may have been run in on that beach. Personally, I don't think this case is connected with C and E problems."

"Alan, give me something positive that I can carry forward to tomorrows briefing. The Inspectorate will expect some meat on the bone they hand to the Home Secretary. What we have so far won't go down very well, will it?"

Alan sighed, "The Inspectorate will have to accept the truth. Despite every effort made by all agencies, none of the deceased have been identified except as blood types. All bodies were fully clothed. None of which carried labels or other identifying marks. The shoes in each case were new but without maker's identity. There were no marks of wear on any of the shoes suggesting the men had travelled any distance."

"What do you mean by distance?"

"The shoes were lightweight, each bore slight scratches indicative of walking a few yards on shingle. No more than that."

David smiled with relief, "Well that's it then! The conclusion is obvious. They're foreigners, dropped off by boat onto the beach. That would account for the slight wear in the shoes."

Alan shrugged. Allowing his Chief one positive thought? "That's not the opinion of forensics. They hold the view that each of the deceased died a short time after putting on the shoes and clothing. In fact, they say the shoes indicate no stretch wear, plus there is a suspicious lack of associated staining within the shoes."

"Which means what?" Asked a resigned sounding David Long.

"No good honest sweat. Just the walk up from that beach, over the shingle bank and down the other side would have provided some human evidence of wear."

David sat back rubbing his chin, "Okay Alan, it may be simpler if you tell me what we do have."

Alan started to count off on his fingers, "One, apart from this last one, they were all aged between thirty and forty, the last one, around fifty. Two, all found within the same tight area. That is to say, on the margin between the shingle bank and marsh or in adjacent water. Three, all fully clothed but no identification marks or labels. Not one of them had documents but all had British bank notes in their pockets. Strangely in mint condition, none of which were sequentially numbered. Four, the boffins are not convinced the currency is genuine, although, at this moment, they are not able to prove forgery. Five, none have been identified by appearance, body marks or prints, notwithstanding exhaustive searches by our service, Interpol or FBI."

"What about scars?" Queried David, "They sometimes score high when it comes to turning up a name."

"Not one has a scar of any type. Hard to believe, but true. Not one small scar between them."

David's face looked bleak, "What a bagful to go to glorious Whitehall with."

"There is," Alan offered, "additional evidence, which may provide the break we are looking for. We believe a man was seen moving away from the scene just after the fifth body was found."

David sat up in his chair, "You're referring to this sighting by P.C. Wright?"

"Yes, I think he was right. I'm almost certain that sighting will produce something. Also, I believe a third man is here. It seems he may have shown up seconds after the first sighting. Almost, as though he was hot on the heels of the first. It's possible he too stuck close to the marsh using the mist or lack of light for cover. We have a fair description of this man, which is being circulated."

"You continually refer to these characters as men? No women involved?"

"No evidence of women so far," replied Alan.

David rose from his chair. He crossed to a small table on which were several cups and a steaming coffee pot. He slowly poured the coffee and handed a cup to Alan and Charlie.

"Well, it doesn't sound as positive a list as I hoped for." The Chief's face was one of senior disappointment.

"But we are slightly better off than we were a few hours ago sir, and there are two other points I have to raise."

"Two other points," said David, attempting a sip at his coffee.

"I want the army engineers brought in to floodlight around a hundred square yards of the marsh from dusk to dawn until further notice."

David's jaw dropped.

Alan continued, "I want trip flares fitted by those same engineers, on all dry approaches?"

David slowly placed his cup on his desk, "You seriously want me to call in the army to light up an area, already covered by our standing watches?"

"Yes, I do sir. Eyes are no good at night and ears have almost failed us, so far. I need those lights in today and working by dusk, then our men can be positioned outside the area and arrest and detain anyone moving."

"Are you completely out of your tiny mind? Do you know what that would mean? The Home Secretary would think we've gone mad."

"I don't care much about that, sir. This whole business is to say the least, peculiar. And in any case, the precedent's already set."

"Precedent, when? Not in this country it hasn't. Don't make a fool out of me Alan! Where do you think you are, bloody Chicago!"

"No sir, 1920's, Sidney Street, London. The Commissioner of the Metropolitan Police applied for and

54

got permission from the then Home Secretary to use the Guards from Kensington Barracks. And, if memory serves, those troops didn't just supply trip flares and lights, sir."

David sat and stared. For some time he tried to grasp the breadth of Alan's request, "Alright, alright, you've made your damned point! But, Alan. Think man, blazing lights, trip flares. You'll have the Admiralty, RNLI and coastguard bobbing around like scalded cats. Coastal lighting has to be strictly controlled because of navigation, doesn't it?"

"Sir, if we had these arrangements days ago, we might not be here having this conversation. We've a real problem at night and we have no realistic option."

"How do you know there will be more activity?"

"Sir, I feel we have to accept it is reasonable to suppose there will be and we need to give my men every chance to put a stop to this business. You may recall," continued Alan quietly, "my wife has been of assistance to us on several occasions," before the Chief could react, Alan continued, "Grace was out on the marsh shortly after the fifth body was found. It is her view that this man died from a force we are not aware of. She spent some time on the margin and up on the bank, and... well, she is of the opinion that our number five is not the end. And, that all the deaths are connected to that one spot on the marsh. Evidently it has something to do with a door or something."

The Chief sat, his eyes closed.

"Well sir, Grace hasn't told me everything yet, but she is convinced these people are not of our time and more use will be made of this area."

"Not of our bloody time!" The words seemed to strangle David. He repeated the words, "What on earth do you mean, not of our time?"

"I don't mean visitors from another planet, sir. I'm sure Grace simply meant not perhaps of twentieth century."

The office became very quiet as David slowly put his cup down. Charlie half-choked on his coffee. Alan looked very uneasy.

"What I am saying is we now have five, not four suspicious deaths on our hands. All enquiries to date result in one inescapable fact and that relates to this small patch of ground. Grace has had some success, in the past, where normal police-work failed. Certain facts from, shall we call them, her experiences, have resulted in positive results. Now, she hasn't said much about this present business yet, but I would like your permission to follow up whatever lead she can give us."

David closed his mouth and cleared his throat. He spoke slowly and clearly, "Alan. You, Charlie and I have known each other for a good many years. You will appreciate what you are implying is a little difficult to accept?" He looked hard at Charlie Friar, then back at Alan, "I suggest you look again at what you are saying. The consequences of making such a statement outside the confines of this office, would be far reaching," he held up his hand as if to quickly mollify Alan, "no one appreciates the pressure and I know…"

Alan interrupted, "I'm sorry if you feel that I am out of my mind but I can assure you the information I have given you should be followed up in the manner I am advising," Alan leant forward as he spoke, as if to lend weight to his words, "at this Home Office meeting you can stall by simply saying that enquiries are continuing. I urge you to understand that I would never have come to you with such a request if I wasn't sure of my facts. What Grace has said in the past had proved absolutely correct."

"Okay, okay. Let's calm down. Alan, do you know what would happen if I went to this meeting with the HMI's and Home Secretary, requesting military equipment and assistance to prevent bodies from somewhere materialising in your marsh? You, my friend, would be retired immediately."

He stopped, his eyes narrowing. The silence returned. David slumped forward, "Oh for God's sake, Alan. Can't you see my point? It's all very well in the confines of this office talking about defensive circles, flares, floodlighting and Grace's premonitions. But in all conscience, tell me how I go to the Home Office with what you've just suggested. They would want my head removed for medical examination, as well as my resignation! In reality, we've nothing to give him except your job, and yes, yours too Charlie!"

The words, "yours too Charlie," were shouted as if to bring Charlie fully into the debate.

"Give me facts, Alan, not some dream-like scenario. Not some third world fiction from a producer's cutting room floor. At least support this claim, with some facts, real substantiated evidence. See this from their point of view. We are policemen, not airy-fairy script writers."

Alan let the air cool. David was right to falter. There had been other conversations like this in the past. Alan got up, walked across the floor and poured some more coffee. He took his time stirring sugar into his. Then he remembered he didn't take sugar in coffee. He counted to ten very slowly.

"Like it or not sir, you asked for the facts and I have given them to you. You have everything we have, plus an opinion from a source which has, whether we like it or not, been one hundred percent right in the past."

"Alan, Alan, Alan," shouted David, "just listen to what you are asking. You expect me to tell the Home Secretary's committee that somewhere on Cley marsh or on some cobblestone beach, there is a mystical spot where people appear out of the blue? The idea is so damned preposterous. I'm not wearing it Alan! It was different when Grace's gift, call it what you like, gave us a face, a gun, a knife, even a ship's name, but this? This is straight out of science fiction, blasted comic book stuff, on the counter of any penny bookstall!"

All the three men fiddled with pencils and shuffled papers. Charlie Friar eventually broke the silence. He used a tactical soft voice knowing that would achieve more than being bullish, "Forgive me sir. There are a lot of things we don't understand in this life. It's not so long ago we would have left rockets to films and comic books, but along came World War Two, and V2's landed on us by the ton.

Thousands killed. Now I think we all accept rockets exist. Half-modern man's thinking comes from stumbling into what we later choose to call proven facts," he paused, not knowing how or whether to go on, "Sir, I'm not trying to be flippant, all I am saying is, we have trusted Mrs Brandon before. When she first voiced her premonitions, fears, call them what you will. Well, I must admit we all ducked. After all, who wants to admit following a line of investigation built on a nightmare," he coughed nervously, "As you know her intuition, call it what you like, proved absolutely correct. Her information shortened the length of our enquiries and led directly to those responsible. Not one of us can deny that. She's not one to have fanciful delusions.

I know her methods are, well, a little unusual. But, as far as I'm aware, she hasn't sent us on any false trails. If she says she saw this or that, then I'm all for following it up."

Alan looked gratefully at Charlie. David Long threw up his hands. It was a gesture of surrender, "Yes, Charlie, you're quite right. But, and I mean this. What has been said in this office stays in this office. It remains between the three of us until we know more. Alan, I want you to make double sure this morning's team keep their mouths shut tight, and I do mean shut tight, on their medical findings. Or should I say lack of them. Also, I want you to bring Grace to see me when she has had a chance to review what she has said. If I am to be hung out to dry, with you lot, I want to know everything she knows. Okay?"

Alan nodded.

"You can have your lights and flares. I'll ring Thetford camp. I'm sure the R.E.s there would enjoy a romp on our marshes. Just make damn sure our men don't go blundering into any trip flares. Oh, you had better make sure P.C. Wright meets them and guides them to the exact spot you are talking about."

The phone rang. David picked it up, listened for a second then replaced the handset. "You two had better get back to the mortuary. It sounds as though your tame

Pathologist has come up with something from the latest body."

Chapter Four

"So," said Charlie, as they walked out into the fresh air, "I think that went reasonably well," he reached into his pocket in search of his filthy habit, "I must say I was surprised the boss swallowed your advice on recruiting army assistance."

"Why?" Questioned Alan, "We should have pulled them in from the start. By the way, did you manage to contact George Wright and Fred Fisher?"

"Yes and judging by their reaction you'd have thought I'd handed them a pay rise."

Alan didn't say anything more until Charlie had lit his cigarette and they had crossed to the car.

"About Grace and the help she might be," Alan delayed unlocking the car, "thanks for what you said. Do you recall the last time she helped us?"

"Shall I ever forget it?" Said Charlie, expelling lungs full of calming blue smoke, "I've never seen anyone look as smug as David when he read the morning papers," Charlie grinned, "I can see the words now. 'For his superior leadership in what had been a lengthy and dangerous investigation'. Grace's name was never mentioned, but that was her wish."

"That's very true," smiled Alan, "let's hope the Home Secretary takes a sympathetic view of our using the army."

Charlie chuckled, "You can bet your boots on one thing. If it goes belly side up, you'll be up to your armpits in slurry playing the violin and I'll be lucky if I get to resin your bow. Now if the idea wins prizes, that's different.

We'll be able to sit and listen to David tell us what a good idea he had."

Alan couldn't help smiling at Charlie's cynical wit. He unlocked his door and climbed in. Still thinking of Charlie's comment, he leant across and slipped the catch on the passenger door. Both men sat for a moment, grateful to be free from the atmosphere caused by David's understandable but grinding caution.

There was a great deal of difference in their ranks, but Alan felt that David's reluctance to unbend in the privacy of his office was a little hard to take, especially in view of the past. Grace found the needle in the last big haystack and David was always loath to admit that.

Charlie brought the silence to an end, "Do you know, this particular job is much the same as when Grace put us onto that boat business? The Chief spent all one night with me down at Tilbury docks closeted in a Lascar toilet, before he grudgingly admitted her information was right. More than once he said, if the source of our information ever came out, he'd see us both back on the beat, and he meant it! As it turned out, he made Chief Constable shortly after the case, you just sat grinning and I? Well I got married," Charlie lowered the window and flicked out the remains of his Craven A, "we ought to listen to Grace. Though I must say, I wouldn't want her gift. I couldn't sleep nights," Charlie shivered, "No bloody thanks!"

Alan smiled. It was true. Grace's ability had certainly put an end to the careers of more than one serious villain. The down side to her sudden premonitions, and some of them were horrendous, was the strain she felt until facts proved her right. Although still a brilliant concert pianist, she now accepted far fewer engagements, unless they were for what Grace called, her good causes. Then, she travelled any distance to perform. Her 'good-works' stage varied from grand concert halls to hospital wards, factory canteens and anywhere a piano could be found.

The journey to the hospital went quickly enough, though getting parked presented its usual crop of problems.

In the end, Charlie scribbled 'Police on Call – Please call at the Mortuary', on a piece of card and left it on the windscreen.

The stout double doors to the Mortuary prevented most of the sickly smell of formalin from entering the corridor. But, it would be true to say that the nearer you got to those forbidding doors, the more conscious of its cloying presence you became. Alan and Charlie took deep breaths and entered. The procedure to gown-up took just a few minutes. It always seemed strange that no matter how many times these gowns were laundered, they always reeked of that insidious, aqueous solution of formaldehyde.

"A clean pinnie reflects a tidy mind," whispered Charlie as they passed through into the dissecting room.

"Ahhhh," exclaimed Lawrence. He didn't turn round to greet his visitors, but kept his back to them, remaining hunched over a stainless steel table that served as a bench, upon which he could closely examine organs removed from bodies.

"Come on gentlemen, please don't be shy, you can come much closer. Come and take a really good look at this amazing little treasure." His enthusiasm could be likened to that of an eight-year-old who had just discovered the sweet ecstasy of Turkish Delight. He beckoned them forward.

Pushing Alan forward, Charlie whispered, "After you sir. Rank has its privileges."

Spread out on what is best described as a carving salver, was a human brain, sliced like a cut loaf. To the uninitiated, this splayed mound of tissue appeared not unlike a whitish, greyish cauliflower. It still held some of the pinkish-brown lined qualities of life. The tissue had been sliced so thinly across its axis, that it reminded Alan of paper thin parma ham. Lawrence was in the process of examining one particular section under a magnifying lens.

"Do take a look. I totally missed this little beauty during the initial rummage. Both Watson and I missed it. Then back in the office, something told me to look again. I came back and had a further look."

Alan and Charlie looked quizzically at each other.

"Do you know," Lawrence went on, "the feeling I had missed something just wouldn't go away. Guy Watson will be so cross not being here."

He handed a large lens to Alan who seemed to be having trouble, and handled the heavy instrument rather gingerly. Alan was quietly troubled when he noticed that Vincent was wearing two pairs of protective gloves, whereas he and Charlie were barehanded.

"Come, come Superintendent, surely you're not squeamish."

"Of course not," Alan replied, "we have no wish to disturb you. An explanation and report would have been sufficient."

"Oh no Superintendent, not in this case," said a buoyant Vincent, "I want you to see why I missed it, and have sight of the position in which it was found. Prevents doubt and supports continuity of professional evidence eh, Superintendent?"

Charlie leant a little closer. Alan still couldn't see whatever he was supposed to be looking at. With a smile Vincent passed him a more powerful lens. Alan adjusted his position and concentrated on the small section indicated by the tip of Vincent's finger.

Almost buried in the curious formation of tissue, he saw what at first, seemed a natural fold in the tissue. As Vincent stretched the flesh and drew his scalpel across the section, he saw what Vincent had found.

Vincent quietly said, "You see? It's so small, truly like a small whitish seed, that during initial sectioning, I failed to spot it. It is truly amazing isn't it? See how it absorbs the colour of the surrounding tissue perfectly Mr Brandon? In its position, it looks part of the crenulations of tissue. That's why it was important you see it, in-situ as it were."

Alan passed the larger lens to Charlie who peered, then let out a soft low whistle. He had great difficulty in seeing it, even with the lens. He managed a whispered, "It's so tiny. What on earth is it?"

Vincent shook his head, "You might well ask, old chap."

Re-grasping the lens, Vincent returned to staring at the object, "Trouble is, I was looking for the usual things, discoloration, staining, haemorrhage or some evidence of seizure, even some kind of malformation, but not this tiny fellow. Mistakes occur of course, and I admit, in my previous examination I missed it. I suppose I had pre-formed notions. Unforgivable, quite unforgivable."

Lawrence went on, as though speaking to himself, "After all, we had seen no evidence of an external wound, scarring etc. However, I hurried back and amazingly there it lay, whatever 'it' is." As he finished speaking, he demonstrated his skill as a surgeon by slowly removing the object from its lodging. It was, as he described, truly, minuscule.

Now that it was clear of the tissue and placed on a glass specimen slide, the object was easier to see. It appeared as though it was made from a stainless whitish hard material. Perhaps no more than two millimetres long and perhaps, less than one millimetre at it's widest point. Lawrence then examined the implant area.

"Is it possible," asked Alan, "to give us any idea how long the object has been in the brain?"

Lawrence looked at Alan, as a patient father would look at an innocent child. "You are joking, aren't you? Given that you are looking at a medical impossibility, plus the fact that we have absolutely no idea what the object is, I think your question is somewhat premature, don't you?" Lawrence turned back to the sectioned brain, "There appears to be no evidence of rejection. We have no idea what the material is." Lawrence rubbed his chin. "I have nothing on which to form..." His words faded, as he peered and probed deeper into the surrounding tissue.

"If my life depended on an answer, Superintendent," he began slowly, "I would still be as lost for the truth, but I will hazard a guess that it could not have been there long. This peculiar presence, does not meet with anything I have ever known." He threw up his hands in quiet frustration and breathed a long drawn-out sigh. "How can I provide you with an opinion?"

Charlie repeated his low whistle. He asked, "Could it be the very tip of a fine hypodermic needle?"

Vincent brought an even larger lens from an instrument cabinet. After a few minutes examination he gave up. "Well Sergeant Friar, I would say that is a very good guess. Though the object seems uniform at both ends and appears to be closed."

"Could it be a minute capsule?" Asked Alan.

Vincent stood back and scratched his head, "You might well ask. I haven't the faintest idea. Your use of the word capsule suggests an enclosure of some kind. I suppose we could X-ray it, if we had a machine that could magnify a thousand times. But then that produces it own problems. If you are right, by doing so we may destroy what, if anything is inside it."

Alan moved his attention back to the brain tissue, "How do you think it arrived in the brain?"

Vincent looked long and hard at Alan. "Before you arrived, I had a search for an entry route or path. Evidence of disruption, truth is I can't find one. Whatever delivered that into the occipital left no trace, and I mean that."

Vincent moved over to a medical waste-bin and dropped his outer layer of gloves into its open mouth, "You can, of course, have the body examined and gain a second opinion?"

This question hung in the air for some seconds, each one heavier than the last. Alan had heard Vincent make the offer, but deliberately held back, hoping Vincent would think his option was being seriously considered. Alan slowly raised the knuckle of his right forefinger to his lips as though pondering on the possibility, "Could he have been born with that inside his brain?"

As he asked this question Alan remembered where he was and what he had been handling. Feeling suddenly repulsed, he quickly wiped his mouth with his handkerchief, while watching Vincent slowly shake his head.

"I can only say that, in my experience and in my opinion, the chance of that happening is a million to one. Common sense dictates that the object must have been inserted. When, why, how? I don't know. It's a complete mystery."

Vincent watched as Charlie slowly circled to the far side of the examination table, as if by doing so, the mystery would resolve itself.

"Mr Lawrence, the object was undeniably there. We must assume our friend was carrying this around in his brain when he was alive. Bearing that in mind, would he have been affected by its presence?"

Vincent Lawrence tilted his head to one side. He took his time, "Well, your point is well taken. By affected, I take it you mean medically, physically?" He paused, "The area of the brain, as I said, is the occipital. Affects may have included loss of some vision, difficulty in certain limb movements, memory loss, confusion to say the least, but where does this lead us?"

Alan interrupted, "Just supposing the man did suffer one or more of these effects. It is reasonable to suppose he could not have travelled far without some medical or other assistance?"

Lawrence remained deep in thought.

"We must assume," Alan continued, "our man arrived at the scene of his death, having travelled some distance. Given what you have said regarding the possible affects. Would you say he was capable of surviving a journey on foot?"

Vincent looked uneasy, "Superintendent, our chosen professions are worlds apart. I do not like speculation. I've shown you what there is. Please don't ask me to theorize into your world."

Alan bit on the word 'theorize', "Mr Lawrence, at some time we all have to speculate, whether we like it or not. Please bear with me and answer my question."

Vincent's face stiffened; a verbal frost had materialised. He turned away from Alan and appeared to weigh the question, "He may well have had the object in his brain for some time. It's possible the affects may have been slight or more pronounced. I cannot say with any surety. He may well have felt nauseous, had difficulty with his balance, even vomiting. All I can do is list some of the possible affects he may have experienced. We could of course assume he may not have been affected at all."

"You mean speculate?"

Vincent grudgingly replied, "Yes... if you must."

Alan nodded, "Leaving this matter aside for the moment, can I ask you to confirm that, it seems, very little time passed between the time of death, in each of our cases, and the recorded time each body was found?"

It was Lawrence's time to smile, "Surely you haven't lost your notes, Mr Brandon. As with the previous findings, in each case there was less than an hour or two between death and discovery. Now, I have supplied you with some of the pieces to your puzzle. It is for you, Superintendent, to solve it." The frosty moment had passed.

"I expect," said Alan, "that the brain from each of the other bodies will now be re-examined to see if they all carry a similar mysterious object?"

Lawrence smiled, "Oh, I think you can rest assured we shall be doing that."

They each used the glass again to look at the object and the point in the brain from which it had been extracted. Each agreed it was hardly surprising that the object had been missed in the original sectioning.

Vincent Lawrence left them saying that he was off to get Guy Watson. Hoping he may have some opinion that may be useful. Alan and Charlie both felt Lawrence had gone to cool down. They didn't like questioning professional people, especially doctors. Any question arising from their findings was immediately seen as a direct attack on the medical profession as a whole, or the individual's professional competence.

Charlie suggested a turn round the car park might do them both the world of good. They were quite pleased to leave the slide, the capsule and sliced brain, in exchange for a few minutes in fresh air.

Twenty minutes later, they were back grouped around the table. Guy Watson was examining the brain.

"Now, where is the little marvel?" He said.

Charlie looked at Alan, who looked at Vincent. They all began a frantic visual search of the table, over, under and around it. The slide with the precious object was missing.

At first, it was assumed that when Vincent Lawrence left the examination room, he had set it aside. Vincent remembered that it had been left next to the large lens. The usual comments were made, about it not being able to walk away on its own. The fact was, it was missing and someone must have removed it in the twenty minutes they were absent.

Alan immediately flayed himself for failing to ensure the security of the sample. He bit back on recrimination, knowing that it was his responsibility for allowing the loss to occur. He and Charlie left the mortuary at a run. They already knew that accusations of unprofessional conduct would inevitably follow and rightly so!

Visually checking for anyone acting suspiciously, they finally stopped when they reached the hospital reception.

"This is ridiculous," shouted Alan, "who the hell are we looking for? Whoever did it must have known what he was looking for and where he was likely to find it. He's had the best part of half an hour to walk away."

With a great deal of embarrassment he and Charlie made their way back to the mortuary. On reaching the lobby, they checked all the rooms adjoining the examination room. In one, they found what they were looking for. Sitting at a table with the Racing Times propped up in front of him, a pencil in one hand and a cheese sandwich in the other was an elderly porter. As they entered, he leapt to his feet.

"Have you been in the examination room?" Charlie shot the question at him.

"I might have been. What's it to you?"

He then saw Dr. Watson, who had caught up with them. "Sorry Dr. Watson. I was just about to take my break when these two burst in."

"Answer their question, Mr Benson. Have you been in the examination room in the last twenty minutes?"

"Well," he scratched his head with the pencil, leaving a fine lead tracery etched onto the bald pate, "now let me see," the words came out extremely slowly, "I went to there, yes. Had to, it's part of my duties, as you know, as the unofficial mortuary attendant. I don't get paid for ..."

Alan spoke quietly, "Did you see anyone in there?"

"Not alive I didn't. As a matter of fact, I was on my way when I saw these two," Benson pointed at Alan and Charlie, "come busting out of there like a pair of greyhounds. They flew off down the corridor followed by you and Dr Lawrence. In a right state they were too."

Alan, tried to calm the situation, "Please, Mr Benson, did you see anyone else enter or exit from that room?"

Benson looked thoughtful, took a bite of his cheese sandwich and placed the remains back on the table. "No, just you lot galloping off. Well, hang on a minute. Now you come to mention it," he rubbed his unshaven chin, "there was this other chap who watched you lot charging off. Looked across and gave me a look as if to say, bloody barmy. Anyway, he nips in, only gone a second. I thought he was one of you lot. As I say, he's out again, smiles and walks off. Had a white coat on like yours. Pleasant sort of chap."

Charlie, who was quietly fuming, said, "Look Mr Benson, did you know this man, perhaps seen him around the hospital before?"

Benson, who had taken an instant dislike to Charlie, spun on him, "No, why should I? I'm not security as well as everything else round here. If you want someone to do that, get yourself a copper."

"They are the police, Mr Benson," said Dr Watson.

"Let's start again, Mr Benson," said Alan, "I'm sure you want to help us as much as possible. This man, what was he like, how was he dressed, apart from the white coat?"

Benson warmed to Alan. He guessed he was junior to Charlie, who he saw as a blustering senior officer type. "Well now," said Benson, beginning to feel he was of some importance, "he was quite a slim chap, very tall, about the same height as you. Dark penetrating eyes he had, like yours? Cold like, looked right through you. Had on what could have been brown trousers under the white coat."

"Anything else you can think of?" Alan encouraged.

"Not as I can recall. Oh yes, there was one thing. He was carrying a mackintosh. I thought that strange, it being rather warm outside. He went off casual like, towards reception."

Alan shook hands with Benson, managing to palm two half crowns to him without the others noticing.

"Sorry to have interrupted your lunch-break Mr Benson. Thanks so much for everything, very helpful."

Alan and Charlie walked the corridors to reception but the trail was cold. Now on his own, Benson opened his hand and grinned at the sight of the two half-crowns. Not bad, he thought, for two minutes conversation. He searched in his pockets and brought out his purse. Carefully opening it, he took out a brand new five pound note and smiled again, "A crisp fiver from a pathology student. Plus five bob from a copper. Not a bad day, not a bad day at all."

After an embarrassing few moments thanking Guy Watson and Vincent Lawrence, who surprisingly took full responsibility for leaving the slide unprotected, Alan and Charlie slowly walked back to the car.

"Of course," Alan said, "you know full well none of that was Lawrence's fault. It was entirely down to me, sort of crass idiocy I would expect from a probationary constable. I must have been out of my tiny mind, leaving the damn slide exposed like that."

Once in the car, Charlie raised his hands, "I'm just as guilty. Never in a million years would you imagine someone trawling through a mortuary dissecting room, on the off chance of picking up something worth nicking. Whoever did this trawl knew what was going on in that room. They took a big risk making that quick visit and that proves they know what that object is and what it does. It was shopping to order alright, and I'll bet you he was under orders to get that tidbit back."

Alan smiled, "Well, all's not lost then. Messrs Lawrence and Watson are now busy examining the other deceased to see if they have similar objects, and I'll wager they all have them. As a certain long-nosed fiddle playing detective would have said, 'the game's afoot'."

Charlie smiled, opened a window and lit a cigarette, "Now, all we have to do is find him."

"Look Charlie, you nip off and telephone a description to I.O. Remind them it's a match with our previous message. And get someone up from the station to take a statement from Benson. There's just a slim chance friend Benson may well have seen more of our tall suspect than he's letting on. It's even possible he may have a side-line in turning a blind-eye. Get whoever takes the statement to walk him round the hospital on the off chance he may pick out the runner or find that damned white coat in a bush. It's also possible one of the other porters may give us a character reference and, while you are at it, see if Benson has any form with Records. If he has a sheet, they can squeeze him and find out exactly what happened. Meanwhile, I'm off to make some notes."

Charlie smiled at Alan, "Anything else I can do while you're busy?"

Alan was tempted to tell Charlie, but smiled instead.

Alan was still writing his notes when Vincent Lawrence appeared, "Saw your car. Glad I caught you. Can you pop back and have one more look at our number five? Hope you don't mind."

As Alan exited the car, he heard Vincent saying, "This is all theory, of course, but it may help."

71

Alan caught Charlie as he was about to leave Reception. On reaching the examination room, Vincent unlocked the door and uncovered the body. He seemed quite pleased with himself. Alan and Charlie were baffled by the sudden change in mood. Vincent pointed to what appeared to be a small, very faint mark just above the right shin. Once again, he handed them the lens, and indicated they should examine the mark.

"OK," said Alan, "we give up. It could be a birth mark, or something like it. What are we looking at?"

Vincent smiled. It was obvious he loved scoring points, "Well, gentlemen, if I didn't know better, I would say that is a scar, resulting from a surgical procedure... but one that has been closed without stitching. My guess is, and I warn you again, this is theorizing, Mr Brandon. This closure could only have been achieved with some type of 'flowing' process," his hand rippled across the body demonstrating the motion.

"The skin and sub-tissue being fused, perhaps an extremely advanced form of remedial surgery, totally unknown to us."

Alan smiled broadly at Lawrence, who returned the grin, "Thinking back to our previous conversation, theorizing can be a little difficult for you, Mr Lawrence?"

"I don't mind you saying that at all, Superintendent. As I said, this is my professional opinion. Anyway, to continue, beneath the skin there appears to have been no cause for a procedure in either the tissue or bone. However, I'm fairly sure there has been a procedure carried out. The method is very difficult for me to understand and I..." here Vincent paused for theatrical effect, "have been practising surgery, at a top level, for many years. If I had to sum up what you are looking at, I would say healing has been achieved by causing the affected tissue and bone to reform, without an apparent structural change. Shall we say, much the same as ice?"

"As ice?" Muttered Alan.

"Yes, ice simply melts and then reforms, fully functioning within its original form, exhibiting little or no evidence of change. Broadly speaking, a surgical procedure based on the same principle of dynamics and physics, may one day result in regeneration, with no body parts missing or evidence of disturbance."

The length of silence that followed reflected the level of disbelief registered by both Alan and Charlie.

"How do you know this?" Alan asked finally.

"I don't," Vincent replied, "and there you have me, Superintendent. Perhaps it's just wishful thinking or even speculation and therefore I would be unwilling to repeat what I have said in front of the press," he smiled, "Oh, one last point. If what I have said is near the truth, then we may have the answer as to how our magic object was inserted into the occipital."

They smiled and shook hands. Outside once again, Charlie lit another cigarette, "It's a bit much to take in, all this business, men performing surgical magic, isn't it?"

"Perhaps we are not thinking wide enough, Charlie. We may have to change our minds about a lot of things before this business is over."

Alan dropped Charlie at his house. Then, he turned his car towards Patchets, his mind filling with what he'd seen and what Grace had said. As he drove through the limited suburbs of Cromer, he didn't notice the large dark car that joined the traffic behind him. It negotiated itself snugly in, following Alan's every move. It stayed far enough back to be just another car.

As Alan turned into the drive to the house, he was still searching for a credible solution to recent events. Remembering to leave his jacket, with its lingering smell of formalin in the car, he removed his old golfing jacket from the boot and wore that to enter the house.

Grace was in the dining room when Alan let himself in. She went out into the hall and helped him off with his jacket. She tried desperately to accept the whiff of preservation fluid.

"Really darling, no wonder neighbours are beginning to talk about you being a poor policeman. Just take a sniff at that jacket. It's disgusting, and damp. Where on earth have you been?"

She gave him a peck on the cheek to show he was loved and brightly told him there was a cold meat salad for supper. Alan gave her a tired smile and headed for the bathroom.

It wasn't until he was doubly sure that the hot shower and brisk scrubbing had removed all the smells of the mortuary from his body that he towelled himself dry, climbed into a change of clothes, put on his favourite slippers and went down to join Grace.

Passing through the hall, he grabbed a newspaper from the table and decided against mentioning he had seen enough cold meat for one day, thank you.

Alan plodded through the meal, trying very hard to put aside the comparison between cold roast lamb and sliced brain tissue when Grace suddenly announced the news that their daughter Clare had decided she would stay with them for a few days.

Grace was obviously thrilled they were going to be together, "Perhaps Clare and I could go into Norwich, have lunch then go to the cinema or something?"

She couldn't help noticing the suggestion failed to grab Alan's full attention. Grace knew that look all too well. Alan could never hide the more horrendous side of his job from her. He tried hard, but they were like peas from the same pod. She looked at him across the table and smiled. Grace reached out and touched his hand. Alan looked up and returned her smile.

He had allowed his mind to wander, letting Grace's comforting words flow over him. He was half listening to the soft music from the wireless when he suddenly latched on to the word 'visitor'.

Alan raised his head, "What was that, dear?"

Grace repeated, "We had a caller today. When he first arrived I thought you had decided to come home early and forgotten your key."

Alan grew attentive. "What do you mean, caller?"

"Someone who calls at the door and usually rings the bell, darling," Grace said, now grinning broadly.

"Grace, please tell me what you mean?"

"This chap came to the door. I thought how like you he looked when he was standing in the porch. It was you to a tee. Raincoat, just like yours, even had the same type of hat. Slightly younger I would say. Turned out he was from a London building company, following leads."

"What did he want?"

"As I just said, he was calling to see if we required any building repairs. I assumed he had been into the hotel and they had directed him here."

"Did he look like a builder?"

"No, as a matter of fact, he was far too well spoken and had good clean hands with well kept nails. I assumed he was recently out of the forces, trying to make his way into civilian life. I felt quite sorry for him really. He seemed totally unsuited to building work, even if they do have large offices in London."

"Grace, be an angel. Please don't give me his history. Just tell me what happened?"

"Oh, I showed him that small damp patch on the wall in the boot- room and he made some notes. He said to tell you he would be in touch with you shortly."

"Is that all? Did he say anything else?"

"Well, that's when I gave him coffee. That seemed to please him, funny really," Grace allowed herself a wistful smile, "He had so many of your mannerisms. Strange don't you think?"

Alan tried to reject the thought of Grace flirting with a salesman.

"He seemed really interested in you and your police work. I showed him your photograph. You know, the one of you when you were interviewed by the papers over that terrible Tilbury business."

Alan half smiled, "Did you ask him and his family to dinner?"

"Now," said Grace, realising Alan was teasing her, "you're being silly, Alan. As I said, he could have been your younger brother. He was extremely charming. He even said he had followed your recent career with interest. And he understood the terrible pressure you must be under."

"Did he say what particular pressure?"

"No. I think he was interested in what the papers had printed about the bodies on the marsh. I did ask if he knew the area and he said it certainly interested him."

"Did he tell you where he lived?"

"He didn't say directly, just that it took ages to visit us. The strange thing is, the more I think about it the more I'm certain I've met him before. I'm not saying that because he looks so much like you. It's as though I have this deep feeling he's been in our company at some time recently."

"Tell me Grace, what exactly did he look like?"

"Well darling, excuse the repetition, but he really could be your brother, even down to his choice of clothes."

Grace crossed to the mantelpiece and took down a silver framed photograph of Alan and placed it in front of him, "There, you couldn't have a better description than that."

"One last question and then I promise I'll let you relax. Did he arrive by car?"

"Now that is strange," Grace smiled, "he walked away. He must have left his car in the hotel car park."

Alan excused himself and went to the telephone. He wanted to make sure the description of the mysterious thief at the hospital had been circulated. The call brought news that the description had been widely circulated to beat and vehicle patrols. Also, that items missing from the break-in at the shed had been confirmed as a railway maintenance crew donkey-jacket, pair of old overalls and a plate layer's hammer, of the long handled variety."

"What on earth is a plate layer's hammer?" Alan enquired.

"You might know it sir, as the hammer a lineman uses to knock home the securing cleats or chocks on the line. Oh, and to occasionally tap wheels of railway wagons, when he's acting as a wheel-tapper."

Alan felt as though he didn't want to go along that route. He thanked the Information Room sergeant and rang Charlie.

"Our second man may be at least as far as Cromer, Charlie. Get your lads onto this railway angle. He probably looks like a scruffy wheel-tapper, whatever that is."

Charlie laughed, "Cromer's full of them, doing that spur line."

"Also, Grace had a visit from what could have been our hospital runner. It seems earlier today he turned up at Patchets, posing as a building rep. He's obviously very active and has knowledge. Get his description round the garages, you never know, and check the only two car-hire firms, at Cromer and Blakeney."

"I'll get them both checked. Did Grace say he had a car?" asked Charlie.

"No, she never saw one, but he's either mobile or he's the original Flash-Gordon. One more thing, he's a spitting ringer for me."

Later, Alan joined Grace listening to the news. He then decided it was his moment to tell Grace that the Chief Constable had asked if she could brief him on her visit to the marsh. He passed on David Long's request in as few words as possible. He noticed a shadow cross her eyes, although she continued to smile. They agreed the following Monday would be soon enough.

Grace looked tired and he guessed she was still upset by what she had seen out on the marsh. She had told him some of the details, but he felt there was more, much more to come. As always, she would take her time. The first explanation of what she had seen on the marsh was like a single-line pencil sketch. It was this outline, short on colour and detail that he had used to brief his Chief. Now everyone had to wait for the colour and detail to be added.

Previous incidents had taught Alan not to rush Grace. Not to question what or how she put words or paint scenes, until she was completely ready. Pain often filled her eyes as she set each word free. Coaxing her to return to what she had seen was always distressing, and could be disturbing for Grace.

This process was worrying because he knew what could happen. Letting everything out in one desperate rush had, in the past, resulted in her breakdown. The recovery had taken a long time. Patience was the key.

Alan looked across at Grace. She asked, "What have you been up to?"

Alan smiled, "What do you mean? I haven't been up to anything."

"Well," she said, "whatever it is you are totally forgiven, providing you throw away that disgusting old jacket."

Alan gave her his best pleading look, "Couldn't I keep it just for gardening?"

Grace laughed, "No, we would have all the neighbours complaining about their prize blooms failing." He laughed with her.

Clare arrived in the late evening. Suddenly, the house was full of girlish laughter. Grace ushered Alan into his study, while a certain amount of serious women's talk took place in the kitchen. Alan was pleased to hear the laughter that Clare always brought to the house.

Chapter Five

The man, Victor Grech, who was dressed in long dark clothing, lay as though exhausted. The coming night painted the culvert, in which he crouched, even darker. He shared the drain with constant running water and other things that scurried quickly away, voicing challenges to his presence in their world.

Some way off, Grech heard an unnerving sound. It was naturally strange to him, yet it thrilled him. The noise was high-pressure steam being forced through valves, depressing pistons and transmitting power through linkages to steel wheels on steel rails.

He edged himself a little closer to the top of the culvert and waited. Finally, a single bright white light appeared in the cutting. Grech watched it advance for a second then he ducked back into the culvert. Although there was still some time to go before the full darkness of night, the shadows gave him confidence he wouldn't have been seen by any watcher. He had selected this culvert most carefully. It lay in a straight stretch of track running through a steep cutting and was about midway between a bend in either direction.

Although Grech had spent most of the day playing hide and seek with a small army of policemen, he hadn't heard or seen one for at least an hour. He hoped this meant he was free to make yet another of his many moves.

He bobbed up, checking the position of the engine. Judging by its progress, it seemed to be moving a little above walking pace. Grech eased himself over the edge of the culvert, crouched to make sure he didn't have unexpected company, then stood up.

Grech looked exactly as he intended. On his head was a battered cap. His stained overalls had seen at least three lifetimes and his railway jacket had more holes than a fishing net. He held a large bag in one hand and a long handled hammer in the other. Satisfied with his appearance, he stepped out onto the track, between the lines.

Keeping his back to the advancing engine, Grech walked steadily on, the long handled hammer perched over his shoulder and an adopted limp, for increased effect. He was desperately trying to ignore the slow rumble of the advancing engine.

Grech judged it was still some short distance away when he heard a short warning bleep from the train whistle. The driver proved he was alert and had seen him.

He staggered, as if suddenly shaken awake by the warning. He looked round and made what appeared to be a painful but rapid exit from between the rails. He heard the screeched release of steam, as valves operated to apply brakes. The steady roll reduced to a long-drawn panting crawl.

Grech's alarmed eyes turned up appealingly toward the driver, who was now leaning far out of the cab, wondering what deaf idiot would walk in front of his engine.

As if rehearsed, the engine drew level with Grech, spitting steam everywhere. With a shrill scream the protesting brakes brought the thirty tons of locomotive to a gasping halt. It now stood, its asthmatic blackness streaming in water vapour.

Grech gazed up in disbelief. He'd read all about such antiquated monstrous machines, but to be standing alongside one, staring up at the fire-lit cavern of the footplate, drew the right expression of surprised shock expected by the driver and his mate, who now gazed down in some puzzlement.

"What the bloody hell were you doing?" The driver called, "Walking along the bloody track in the half-dark as though you were deaf. The rest of your lot finished at the last section."

Grech called up, "I've been cleaning culvert twenty-seven and was left behind."

It was a risk, but the chances of the driver knowing the culvert number or caring about anything except signals, was remote.

The driver, his face glistening with sweat, wiped his hands on some cotton waste and took a second look at Grech, "Whatever got into you, completely ignoring my warning signal? Walking along between the rails like Old Nick himself. Would have served you right, if I'd run you down."

Grech put on a more piteous look and shook his head, "I'm sorry driver, my leg's so sore I just couldn't jump out from between the rails any quicker."

The driver shook his head, "Well mate, you've a long, dark walk ahead of you if you're making for the sheds," he used the cotton waste to wipe his face, then turned to his fireman and said something. Grech waited while the steam warmed his legs and sewed pearls of moisture over his ragged clothes. The driver leant down, taking a good look at the infantry of the railway. He seemed to make up his mind.

"Look, you'd best nip up and tuck yourself in here. We're not allowed passengers in the cab, you know that, so keep under cover. No showing yourself. Your bloody line foreman is at the bridge with the police for some reason so keep your head down."

While he was saying this, Grech painfully climbed the four high steps onto the footplate. The second he was on, the driver released the brakes with a gush and nudged the regulator. The engine moved forward and slowly increased speed to a fast amble.

Grech ducked behind a cowling, tucking himself as far into the shadows as possible. The young fireman crouched down beside him and smiled, "What happened to your leg then, pal?"

Grech realised his fake limp had worked, though he couldn't remember which leg was supposed to hurt. He thought it might be easier to stick with the truth where he could.

"I tried to help one of the crew last night. He was sort of, unwell, just passed clean out. He was bigger and much heavier than I thought. I twisted my knee handling him. He was alright though, I left him sleeping it off like a baby. Dead to the world he was."

The fireman laughed, "He ought to take more water with it."

"Yes," said a puzzled Grech, "he ended up doing just that."

The fireman patted Grech's shoulder and went back to raking his firebox.

A few minutes later, the driver shouted a warning then sounded a warning blast on the steam whistle. On the bridge, four policemen and a civilian watched keenly as the engine bowled out of the darkness and passed under their vibrating feet.

The driver allowed plenty of steam to blow off, enveloping the bridge and masking out the receding faces. He also worked the whistle again as if thanking them for their waves. They were back into darkness in seconds.

The driver beckoned Grech to stay low, but come forward, "Look pal, we've got a clear road through to Cromer. I can't carry you into the station or the sheds because of the brass, so I suggest I drop you off at the water tower just short of the Cromer signal. Is that alright with you?"

Grech waved a reply and retired into his cover.

Twenty juddering minutes later, the engine reduced speed until it was travelling at a slow walking speed. Grech climbed down the steps and dropped off, making sure he held tight to his bag.

With steam billowing around him, he waved to the crew then quickly stepped into the darkness, beneath the water tower. He allowed a few minutes to pass as the noise of the receding engine faded away then added a further two more to gain his night vision.

Once the night sounds seemed to contain little else except the ratchet of crickets, he moved silently along a beaten path. A small, low square building loomed up in front of him. He sank to his knees and listened. Grech wasn't about to blunder into any more helpful friends. He strained to hear if anyone was about. Not a man-made sound came to his ears. Grech moved in closer. Then he cautiously circled the small brick hut. There wasn't much to it. One chimney, two small windows, each heavily shuttered and a wooden door that appeared padlocked. Whatever was in there obviously deserved some security and shelter from the weather.

Grech peered closer at the padlock. He suddenly realised he was looking at a metal back-plate, hasp and a padlocked bolt, but not one screw or bolt appeared to penetrate the door or frame. In other words, the locking system was fake! It looked genuine enough from a distance but it was obviously for decorative purposes only.

Grech pulled at the door. It resisted for a second then gave grudgingly, complaining like mad, as he pulled it further open. He passed into the inner darkness, quickly pulling the door closed after him. A wonderful door, he thought. Anyone trying to creep up on him would create enough noise to wake the dead.

Scrabbling through his pockets, he found what he was looking for. A second later, the inside surrendered its secrets to a minuscule hand torch.

It was immediately obvious that Grech had stumbled upon a maintenance crew hut. There was a long central table, complete with oil lamp, an open hearth complete with the still-glowing embers of a coke fire, coat pegs on walls, from which countless caps, coats and overalls hung, waiting for absent owners and chairs enough to seat a dozen men. The windows were fitted with what appeared to be old black-out shutters, which Grech closed. Standing against the walls either side of the fireplace were deep wooden chests. Each of these held every type of line working tool imaginable.

Grech's thin lips almost made it to a smile. Working quickly, he placed the hammer he had taken from the shed into one of the tool chests. He buried it deep, so it would not be taken as anything but a regular tool. Then he stripped off all the railway clothes and hung them amongst and beneath the pegged clothes.

Three quarters of an hour later, Grech had used the facilities he found in the hut to clean himself of all the grime he had acquired since leaving the marsh. It was only when he felt presentable that he laid down on one of the tool chests and rested. Sleep came immediately and cloaked the hours that passed until with a start, he was wide awake.

Grech crept through the darkness and nudged open the door. The first streaks of a grey dawn had etched themselves across the sky. It was time he was gone.

Using the light from the torch Grech gave his face and hands another good rub with a damp cloth. Then he took some time examining and brushing clothes he took from his bag. He worked equally hard on his shoes. Satisfied with the result he dressed, took a last look around the hut opened the door and left carefully.

Grech followed the same path that brought him to the hut from the railway line. This path now led him to a narrow lane. By following this for about half a mile he realised that he was close to a road. From the shelter of a hedge, he watched as men appeared from a housing estate opposite. Each one of them hurrying along, heads down lost in their own thoughts. Grech reckoned they were on their way to work.

He waited for his opportunity. As soon as there was a break in the pedestrian traffic, he broke through the hedge and stepped out onto the pavement. He turned in the direction most of the men had taken and walked briskly along, setting his pace to that of others. Twenty minutes of hard walking brought him to a small parade of shops.

A queue of men had formed on the pavement. Grech stepped into a shop doorway, trying to judge what was going on. A bus appeared, all the men, like sheep filed on. Grech stepped out and continued his walk in the direction the bus had taken.

The last shop in the parade was a workman's café. All the lights were on but there were no customers. Grech watched from some distance away. Then suddenly he heard the sound of another bus. It was still some way off. Grech ran back to where he had seen the men standing. The sign on the front of the bus simply read 'Cromer Bus Station.'

Within a moment he was on the bus and seated, along with about six other passengers. The conductor approached him. Grech dug into his pocket, offered a pound note and apologetically pointed to his mouth, making guttural sounds.

The conductor took the pound, mouthed something about people with money to burn and counted out a vast number of silver and copper coins. He gave Grech a ticket and disappeared to the platform at the back of the bus.

At the first compulsory bus stop in Cromer, Grech took his chance and left the bus. He tried to walk at a regular pace, as though he was local and knew where he was going. He avoided the eyes of fellow pedestrians and did his best not to obstruct or be obstructed by groups of people waiting to cross the road at busy intersections. It was still quite early, but preparations for the working day in Cromer had obviously started. He frequently passed patrolling police officers who seem to accept they were looking at the usual flock of early morning movement.

Grech continued to walk quickly and during the time it took him to walk from one end of the town to the other and back again, Cromer passed from preparation to full business mode. Reaching an older area of town where Victorian red-bricked terraced houses huddled directly onto pavements, Grech slowed his pace.

There were now breaks between the houses, which had been in-filled with industrial units. His eyes rested on one large warehouse-type building, the site of which sent a thrill through him. This feeling never registered on his thin pale face.

Bending down as if to tie his shoe lace, he realised he was by a bus stop. He rose and stood alongside it, as though waiting for a bus. Immediately opposite was a grim looking run-down public house. The Bird in Hand exhibited a badly hand-scrawled sign, half-heartedly advertising rooms for rent.

The dirty windows, faded paintwork and dilapidated state of the slated roof told him all he wanted to know. As far as Grech was concerned, the pub couldn't have been in a better position. It stood immediately opposite an imposing walled site, bearing the gold and blue crested arms of H.M. Crown Property Services.

Grech allowed the feeling of satisfaction to linger. He was one small step closer to assuaging the anger that filled his days. As he watched, a woman who looked positively ancient, appeared from the side door of the pub carrying a bucket. She walked over to the kerb and threw the filthy contents into the gutter. The black water, if that's what it was, took its time finding its way into a nearby drain. The woman straightened up and rubbing the small of her back looked up and down the road. After a second, she spat into the same gutter, wiped her nose on her sleeve and waddled back through the same door.

Grech didn't cross to the pub and try the accommodation door. Instead, he turned and walked back into the town. He browsed around the many shops until he came to what he was looking for. A hairdresser's. There were no customers. It was still early, though the barber was standing at the entrance to his shop with a hopeful, expectant look on his face.

For twenty minutes, Grech fended off the chitchat and questions wonderfully well, while the barber crooned, shaved and trimmed his customer. Satisfied with the result, Grech paid the man, replaced his hat and walked out, having heard all the news about police activity and bodies on local marshes.

Grech once again felt a little glow of satisfaction at helping to provide the barber with news to tell others. He was, after all, the author and producer of the tale. Leaving the barber's, he walked into a second hand clothing shop and purchased a large canvas holdall. Into this he placed his own bag and several items from his vast pockets. He also purchased various items of clothing which he also folded into the holdall. He then visited a number of shops, where he made several other purchases.

Now carrying the luggage expected of a bone-fide traveller and satisfied he looked respectable enough for the part, he returned to the Bird in Hand pub. Grech tried the small side door displaying the words   'Rooms for rent.' On entering he was satisfied to see the inside of the pub looked worse than the outside. He felt these conditions assured him the privacy he needed.

Avoiding the questioning gaze of the tattered woman he'd spotted earlier, he negotiated a room from a swarthy man who claimed to be the owner. Refusing to enter into any conversation other than terms for a room, Grech was shown upstairs to a front bedroom overlooking the CPS site.

He took his time examining the room. Everything was sad and carried the ingrained dust associated with consummate neglect. Even the weighted leaves of a potted aspidistra hung in need. Grech drew strength from this apparent lack of interest in hygiene. Later, he investigated the intricacies of the plumbing and managed to enjoy a lukewarm bath. He then dressed and after securing his bag in a stout cupboard, he pocketed the key to his room and left the pub.

Strolling around the town, he stopped off at a café for a meal, walked on the pier and enjoyed every amenity it offered. He also visited one or two of the seafront hotels where he sat in the public rooms reading papers. It was while he was in the saloon of the Palladio Hotel that he made a slight error of judgement. He had chosen a secluded armchair set to one side of the main windows overlooking the pier. He ordered a glass of water from a waiter and settled back to scan yet another daily paper. He allowed his eyes to close and was soon fast asleep. He woke suddenly to find a uniformed police officer accompanying another man in civilian dress at the far end of the bar. They were busy speaking to a barman.

Grech rose slowly, folded his paper and as if he had all the time in the world, looked through the window waved to an imagined person outside the hotel and left the room. Setting a very steady pace, he casually strolled up the side of the hotel looking into shop windows.

At the top of the street, he saw two more police officers stop and check the identity documents of a small man. Grech crossed the street and entered the grounds of a large church. Finding the main doors open, he passed through into the dim quietness of the interior. He sat, picked up a leaflet and studied it carefully, silently cursing himself for being too confident. He watched others and what they did. Grech imitated some of their actions which included a period kneeling. Cramp suddenly shot through his knees. He stood and passed slowly around the church looking at memorial and other tablets.

Judging that sufficient time had passed, Grech left the church by another door letting into a narrow side lane. Emerging into the main street he was relieved to see no sign of the police. Finding himself at a cinema, he paid for a seat and snoozed several hours away.

Much later, he returned to the Bird in Hand. Entering via the side-door, he went directly to his room, anxious to avoid futile conversation. The first thing he did was examine the lock on the cupboard. It was still as he'd left it.

Before going to bed he spent some hours sitting in his darkened room, watching the comings and goings at the site opposite. Like a ragged bird of prey, he singled out one particular security man and noted his duty periods at the gate.

Very early next morning, before the security shift changed, Grech casually crossed the road and struck up a conversation with the man. As a result, they met at lunchtime in the public bar of the Bird in Hand. The security man was obviously well known in the bar. Clearly no stranger to drink, he enjoyed every beer bought for him. It transpired the man was recently married with a child on the way. He was broke, owed back-rent and was in need of cash. He was also under the threat of dismissal for bad time keeping, supposedly due to his supervisor's ex-military attitude.

Within the hour, there was a bond between the two and by the late evening of the second day, a sum of money, equivalent to the security man's three months wages had changed hands. Once this transaction had taken place, Grech relaxed. He continued his occasional meetings with his new CPS contact, who supplied several small bundles, including papers.

The papers turned out to be copies of load consignment notes. These defined files for destruction at a London address. Under the heading 'Strict Security', each note listed destination, date of load and routes to be followed. A footnote at the bottom of page stated that loads from the CPS were highly classified documents, and that unauthorised routes and stops would result in instant dismissal.

This particular requirement caused Grech some concern until his next meeting with his CPS contact.

"Don't go fretting yourself. That bloke ignores every rule in the book. Stuff the rules, he says."

Grech passed him another drink, "You mean he just stops anywhere he wants?"

"Not on your life. Always the same stop. He says he's been route-checked and booked four or five times, but it don't make no difference. He's still humping that load down to London."

Grech was keen to know more, "He's certainly taking a risk, where's this café then?"

The CPS man scribbled some notes on a scrap of paper and pushed it across to Grech, "There you are friend, chapter and verse. It's all there. One day, he'll get what's coming to him!" This last sentence carried its weight in venom.

Grech took a quick look at the note. It named the café and according to the scrawled words, the driver was known everywhere as 'Walrus', due to the blubber he carried.

By arrangement, a final meeting took place in the bar of the Palladio Hotel. The CPS man, sober now, seemed a little scared and looked around the bar before seating himself next to Grech.

"Look, I've got what you want, ammo too," An oily paper parcel changed hands under the table. "Listen mister, apart from a few friendly drinks I know nothing right? I've a family and don't want no trouble, so this is my end done. The stuff you're interested in leaves the depot as per schedule."

Grech pushed the parcel into a bag and handed the man a further three months wages. As the man took the cash, Grech grabbed his wrist in a vice-like grip, "It would be best for you, and that family of yours, if you forget we ever met. You do understand that, my friend?"

"Look, that bundle I've just given you can't be traced back to anyone, especially to me, so I've never seen you or it before. As for that swaggering bastard Walrus, the depot could do with a permanent change of night driver, so I don't give a toss."

"Just make sure he's the only one who needs replacing," said Grech, "it would be a pity if I had to call on you and your little family."

The CPS man looked across the table at the small figure with burning coal black eyes and knew he had every reason to keep his mouth shut tight.

Shortly following this meeting, Grech returned to the Bird in Hand, packed his bag, looked carefully at the night load schedule, paid his bill and told the landlord he was off on business up north.

In fact, Grech didn't go far that day. He walked as though intent on going to the railway station, but just before reaching it, he turned into a filthy little side-street of forgotten run down terraced labourer's cottages. At number three, he knocked and was let in.

The inside of the house made the street outside look spotless. The owner looked at the small man in long dark clothes and saw no threat.

"A note in the window says you have a room for rent?"

The owner looked Grech up and down, "This lot's coming down in ten days so you're welcome to the room till the wrecking crew arrives. Rent's five bob a day, paid every morning to me! Pay for your own electricity in the slot and get all your own food and drink. No questions either side, right!"

The 'no questions asked', especially appealed to Grech. He had plenty of time. Grech had time to be almost agreeable, "I won't be here that long." He handed the owner a pound.

Just after dawn the day before the load was due to leave the depot, Grech caught a train to Chelmsford. Here he changed to a local train, finally alighting at Ingatestone. He walked to the Brentwood side of Mountnessing and obtained a room at The Crown Inn, within sight of a scruffy transport café. The landlord of the Crown had shown some concern about noise from heavy vehicles manoeuvring at the Café. Grech hurriedly assured him it was of no consequence, as he was partly deaf.

Once alone in the room, he went to the window where he had an excellent view of what came and went at the Café. Grech was well satisfied with his accommodation and timing. In fact, things seemed to be going very well.

Chapter Six

Fred Fisher left the rear kitchen door of the Duck Pub. This was his usual exit point when he was about to commence his duties. He felt unusually pleased with himself. He had managed a fine plate of pickles and ham from the bone, eased along with a few slices of freshly baked bread. This splendid meal was helped down with two halves of best bitter.

Sucking hard on a Fielding's 'Special' peppermint, he wheeled his cycle down the Drift, and out onto the tarmac strip that led toward the coast road. All seemed right with the world. On reaching the first of the cottages that bordered Bucklers Lane, he touched his helmet, in a form of polite salute as he passed Miss Hopkins. She was busy sorting her window boxes. She usually did this, at about this time. Good weather and bad, she made it her business to mind what was going on in those boxes, and in areas beyond the foliage.

He felt quite right to give her a look of pure innocence as he passed. Sharp-eyed she may be, he thought, but she could never have actually seen him emerge from behind the pub. At one time, she had been quite sweet on him, but that was when he was in short trousers and she had freckles the size of pennies, and pigtails.

He took his time mounting his cycle. This was a manoeuvre not without its attendant risks. He chose a smooth section of tarmac and then, giving two or three powerful scoots, to work up a respectable gliding speed, he placed the body of the law, firmly on the well-polished Brookes saddle. He was off.

Libby Hopkins gazed longingly after his retreating figure. He certainly looked a fine figure of the law to the smiling admirer. She was sure there was a certain set to his shoulders, even extra power to his peddling, when she was around.

You don't fool me Fred Fisher, she thought, I know you only come down the Drift to pass by my door, hoping to see me. You're just as shy as you were when you were sweet on me at school. One day my lad, you'll get a puncture, and then you'll need my bucket of water to mend it, see if you don't. She closed the window, still smiling, knowing Fred would be calling again.

There was no traffic on the coast road and Fred made good time to the marsh track. Apart from the immediate area in which the body had been found, the marsh had been re-opened to the public.

The thinking was that with the army now based squarely over the site, and with all their coming and going, there was little point restricting public movement. The night watch outside the floodlit area continued, although this duty now fell to the lads from Cromer, much to their annoyance.

Fred loved everything about the marsh. It was a wonderful area in which to wander and think. Fred always did prefer the country. He hated it when they were short-handed in Cromer. He didn't care much for doing beat work amongst traffic and families on holiday. Screaming children were not his cup of tea. People wearing excuses for shorts they wouldn't be seen dead in at home, especially when seen from the rear. If only people could see themselves, he thought.

He glanced up as a string of terns flew over. This is what he wanted. Retirement was not far off and he could see himself in a cottage close to the marsh. Not for the first time his thoughts turned to Libby Hopkins. Well, I could do a lot worse, he thought.

He could then spend every day, summer and winter, out in the marsh, interspersed with visits to the Duck Pub. Fred was lost in his favourite daydream, when he heard his name called. He applied his brakes and looked into the marsh. His name came again. A second later he spotted the caller. It was Harold, or as he was officially known, the Reverend Harold Crumb. Vicar of St Margaret's at Cley.

"Hello Harold," Fred waved a greeting. He left his cycle beside the path and crossed between some clumps of reeds towards what he knew to be open water.

"Over here, Fred," called Harold, "take your helmet off and keep low."

Fred did as he was asked, making his way to where Harold had adopted a crouch. Fred too, crouched down.

"Take a look."

As Harold said this, he parted the reeds, as if he was opening a velvet curtain at a village hall concert. There, not more than thirty yards away, and swimming in a tight little bunch, were five white birds with reddish beaks.

"They're just terns," whispered Fred.

"Ahhh," whispered Harold, tapping the side of his nose, "not just terns, my dear Frederick. I will bet you a pint they are Caspian terns!" He said this, with the confidence of one who knew such things, "Hydroprogne-tschegrava. Usually up in the Baltic this time of year."

Fred didn't feel like losing a pint, "Okay," he said, "I believe you, but there's many a Christian who wouldn't."

"Then, my dear respected constable of this parish, they'd lose their hard earned money in pints."

It was smiles all round as they regained the path.

"I didn't see your car as I left the coast road, or at the weir," said a puzzled Fred.

Harold looked somewhat crestfallen, "Truth to tell Fred, I fear she's on her last legs. Had to leave the precious old girl parked at the lay-by. Engine was complaining a little. Unfortunately, not the pretty young thing she was. Do you know," he continued, "I bought that old Morris Eight in 1927, when I first came to St Margaret's. She's been a powerful friend to the distressed...and a few hitch hikers. Plus," he paused as if in some great sadness, "a lot of good war service on poor quality oil. I feel she needs a good bit doing to her, and between that, the repairs to the battlemented South porch, the transept window and work on the brasses, especially to the Symonds family, I am torn as to know what to do."

"Get a bicycle, reverend sir," said Fred, "get a bike and a healthier way of life." Fred was still slightly puffed after his cycling.

"What like you, my athletic or is it arthritic friend?"

The two men strolled along the path making their way toward the distant shingle bank. A gaggle of avocets, using their long blue legs to wade through the shallow marsh water, were spooning their bills searching for shrimps, insects or their larvae.

Harold grinned and pointed, "Obviously enjoying freedom from their nesting duties, do you think?" Then Harold quickly pointed away to their right, "What a glorious sight, Fred, so very, very graceful."

He had spotted a small group of Oyster Catchers, rising over the reeds. These were totally missed by Fred, who had his attention held by the small encampment of military.

"Oh dear," said Harold, "not quite what you expect on the marsh."

Fred nodded, "Just a small cordoned area. I don't suppose they'll be here too long."

"I won't enquire too closely. I'll just take your word for it."

Taking a well-earned breather at the end of their walk, they were surprised to find a line of trampled reeds leading off in the direction of Cley Mill.

"Looks very much as though someone has blundered their way across that lot," said Fred.

"Or, chosen to carve there own way through the marsh, to the road," suggested Harold.

Fred knelt down looking hard at the trodden grasses, "It obviously runs parallel to the marsh track. So, why do that?"

Harold shook his head.

"Unless," Fred offered, "in a panic, they couldn't find the track in the dark or wanted to stay clear of whoever might be on it?"

"Could be poachers saw you or George Wright out here and wanted to sneak off?"

Fred's mind was working overtime. It was possible it wasn't poachers, but someone keen not to be seen moving on the marsh? Fred turned to Harold, "One thing's for certain, no one in their right mind chooses to tread a new path into an area like that when there's a perfectly good track already there."

Harold edged further out onto the grasses, "Not very sound under-foot and you can't see exactly where it goes. It seems to bear to the right fifty yards further on. Water's pretty deep too."

Fred pulled Harold back, "No further, can't have you wandering off into that wilderness. You may be doing the Lord's work, but unlike him, you can't walk on water."

Harold pursed his lips in a rueful smile, "I'd say whoever made that track was in a hurry and up to no good," he placed a steadying hand on Fred's shoulder, "Tell you what I'll do," said Harold, "I'll get a message over to Roger Markham at Blakeney Point. Let him have a look at that path. If he says that route is possible and can safely bear the weight of a man, then it may well be local poachers. And, if it should turn out there's a bit of poacher-watching to be done, I'll let you know straight away by phone, and I'll be the first to volunteer."

The two men parted at the lay-by, where Harold's arm, barely visible through the cloud of blue smoke, waved an eager farewell.

Fred reached Patchets, and entering the hotel, asked at the desk if he might have one of the free marsh maps provided for guests. It clearly showed all aspects of the marsh and safe approaches to the shingle bank and beaches.

Sitting at one of the side tables, Fred traced a rough pencil line through the area where they had seen the beginning of a newly trodden path. He looked hard at the pencil line and scratched his head. It just didn't add up. Carving a new path through a dangerous area of marsh, in the dark, was suicidal. Unless being spotted posed a greater threat than finding himself up to his neck in deep water and slime. Over the years and certainly during the war years, that particular part of the marsh, running toward Cley Mill, had claimed more than one foolhardy poacher. In spite of large notices and fencing, one or two people a year, usually visitors, sadly ended up in trouble.

Fred was ferociously nibbling the end of the pencil when he finally concluded that whoever had chosen that route must have seen the main track leading from the shingle bank and deliberately ignored it. Whatever threat compelled the runner into those reeds could only have been to avoid discovery at all costs. What or who would do that? The police or perhaps someone else, like the figure spotted by George?

Fred folded the map and placed it into his tunic pocket. He left the hotel and rode his bike along the margins of the marsh where it met the coast road. He hadn't peddled more than two minutes before he saw a trodden area exiting the marsh. He told himself it was possible someone could have just waded around at that point. Fred dismounted and crouched down, allowing his eyes to track back into the thick, tall impenetrable reeds. Someone had exited the marsh at that point. Fred took the map from his pocket and marked the new position. He turned around looking for a reference point. The entrance to Patchets was no more than a hundred or so yards away.

Fred decided he'd wait for Harold's call then, if it proved worthwhile, he'd get on to the CID at Cromer. There were enough mysteries in Cley marsh, without the added red herrings left by the poaching fraternity. Putting the map back in his pocket, he cycled off to the Salthouse police house. There was a phone to be nursed and if things worked out, calls to be made. It wasn't until early evening that Harold phoned. Roger Markham had confirmed he would look at the path with them in the morning.

The slow creak of the bedroom door slowly opening and the softest whispers of cautious movements disturbed Fred Fisher. He had been awake for some time but lay, trying to push away the jumble of thoughts that prevented him getting back into his usual deep sleep.

He lay perfectly still. The darkness of the room coming and going as a bright moon played hide and seek with banks of thick cloud. The tick of the alarm clock was the only sound. Fred's mind was now fully alert, although he cunningly kept his eyelids closed. The soft movement came again. The feathery lightness of each change of position seemed to indicate that whatever was making the noise, was making its way very, very slowly towards the bed.

Fred waited, knowing that to make his move too early would give away the only advantage he might have. A distant roll of thunder thumped its way in from the North Sea. Fred cursed under his breath as he lost the soft sound. After a second, it was back, and closer. The distance between the bedroom door and his bed was no more than eight feet, so whoever was coming for him was intent on his not being aware of their presence, until they struck. He sensed what seemed to be the lightest touch at the bottom of the bed. It moved very slowly up the covers. Then, the cat mewed. Its purring breath met Fred's ear. With some relief, Fred realised that his night prowler was his cat, Spike.

After some seconds the rising concern felt by Fred subsided. He managed a sleepy smile, remembering that his furry companion disliked thunder and the rain that usually followed.

After pulling himself together, he thought he might just as well get up and make a cup of tea. A crash of thunder, this time closely followed by a flicker of lightning announced the storm was approaching the coast.

"We're in for another downpour, Spike. Not a good night for the boys on the marsh," Fred said quietly, looking toward the now prostrate feline.

He eased himself out of bed, allowing Spike to spread himself out on the top cover. You'll be down in a flash when you hear the milk bottle moving, Fred thought, as his feet search for his slippers.

Fred didn't allow Spike in the bedroom at night. Cats had their place and it wasn't upstairs in bedrooms. He shrugged into his dressing gown, realising he must have left the living room door ajar. It was the only way Spike could have got to the stairs. But Fred could have sworn that he'd closed that door. It was part of his regular routine.

He didn't put the landing light on, he didn't need to. He'd been in that police house long enough to know every inch blindfold. Fred counted each of the stairs that creaked as he descended to the lobby. In front of him was the front door, to his right was his office and to the left was his living room and kitchen. Lightning struck again, producing an immediate rapping of thunder. The flash lit up the passage. He had almost reached the living room when he realised the door was open. In the same moment, he sensed the office door was also wide open. Now that, he thought, was queer. A flash and a further clap of thunder barracked across the nearby fields, its echoes making the stacked china on the dresser, dance a jig.

He paused trying to take in what he was looking at. Had he been so tired that he had completely missed out his nightly routine?

A voice was beginning to shout warnings in his head. White lightning streaked in again. It lit up the inside of the police house like a searchlight, probing all the corners, sending horse brasses jingling. The light that immediately exploded in Fred's head matched this flaring brilliance. The pain, that was its identical twin, shredded its way down to the base of his neck where it joined the dark pool of oblivion. A fleeting shadow fell over him, as he collapsed onto the stone-flagged passage floor.

Spike, now seated at the head of the staircase, looked at the movement. His luminous green eyes glowed in the blackness that followed the lightning.

The figure of a tall man stepped across the prone figure and crouched down. A glove was removed and ice-cold fingers felt for signs of continued life from a carotid artery. Seconds passed. More lightning illuminated the scene as the crouching man rose up. The glove was placed back on the hand. The figure now moved back into the office.

Using a shaded torch, the man crossed to a small cabinet marked 'Lost Property'. He opened this and removed what seemed to be a small white metal object. This he placed into a pocket. Then he went to the desk and examined two large books. After carefully examining them, the man tore a page from one of them. This he crammed into the same pocket. Returning to the passage with several papers in his hand, he quickly examined them by the light of a torch. He discarded most and let them drop silently to the floor. Two were examined more carefully. He let one of these fall from his fingers to join the others. Then, most carefully, he studied the final paper and placed it into his pocket.

He knelt down and shone the torch in Fred's face. He felt for the pulse again then switched off his torch. The man crossed to the front door and opened it carefully. He seemed to listen for some time before turning up the collar of his mackintosh against the heavy rain. He pulled down his black felt hat and left without a backward glance.

Outside, spattering rain bounced off the front door step, drummed on windows and ran gurgling into drains. The occasional lazy roll of departing thunder beat a path into the heart of Norfolk. Lightning was searching elsewhere for things to see. The hall clock ticked away several minutes before an enquiring Spike slowly descended the stairs. He sniffed at and around Fred for some signs of movement, but failed to raise even a twitch of a finger.

Cats have no personal attachment to their providers, so the inspection was soon over. Owners may feel they have unswerving loyalty from cats, but this allegiance soon changes if the provision of food and shelter is not forthcoming.

Spike sat by the still form and cleaned himself. Boredom soon set in. He wandered into the living room and from there out into the kitchen. Having decided that little was likely to change, until his provider woke from his sleep, he settled down, doing his best to ignore the tail of the passing storm.

Out in the dark passage, blood seeped from a head wound, trickled its way beyond the hairline and fell into a small pool.

It was the continuous double ringing of the telephone that finally prized itself into the skull of Fred Fisher. Its persistent shrill jangling drove him to attempt getting to his feet, but this was not so easy. His feet were several miles away and would not obey the commands he was passing. Through increasing waves of nausea he tried to raise himself from the floor, but it was no good. He decided it would be easier to drag his useless body across the floor into the office. After what seemed an age and a thousand miles, he managed to reach up and knock the telephone receiver from its cradle to the floor.

He lay beside it for a full minute, tuning his mind to the stream of abuse from an irate Alice Braithwaite, "For the Lord's sake, Fred Fisher, you're really trying my patience. Stop wasting my time and answer me! Are you going to take this call or am I going to..." she got no further.

Her ears detected distant slurred groans as Fred tried get his mouth around words. He gave up and tried repeating the one word, "Help!" two or three times, before slumping again into unconsciousness.

Alice tried again, "P.C. Fisher, what on earth's wrong. Will you answer me?"

She received only a long silence. Being an operator of many years experience, she knew full well that the line was open, and that someone had answered her summons. The number she was calling was an official police telephone, not a public line. She was conscious of her duty to resolve the matter, officially.

Somewhat torn between the beginnings of alarm, curiosity and downright annoyance, Alice kept the line open, but by several deft movements, changed the direction of her call to George Wright, the constable at Kelling.

The phone rang only once before being answered. A female voice told her that Constable Wright was out viewing storm damage, but she would get a message to him, as soon as he arrived back at the Police house.

Alice was a little puzzled. She was sure Constable Wright was unmarried. She also knew there was no clerk employed to answer that telephone and she thought she knew the voice, but couldn't quite place it. Alice prided herself on identifying just about every voice she had ever spoken to, on or off the telephone. Having concluded it must be a visiting cleaner, she said for him to get over to Fred Fisher's as soon as he could. Knowing how friendly Fred Fisher and the Reverend Harold Crumb were Alice also telephoned the vicarage.

The effect of this last call resulted in a double arrival at the Salthouse Police house. Harold met George Wright peddling like mad, half way along Bucklers Lane. George gratefully abandoned his cycle in favour of a lift with Harold. On reaching the front door, they found it standing ajar.

George, being in front, opened the door fully. Fred's feet came into view, the rest of him was spread out alongside the office desk. A trail of dried blood marked his efforts to get to the phone.

Fred was dreadfully pale and the collar and front of his dressing gown were soaked in blood. His eyes were only half-open and he was obviously sliding in and out of consciousness.

It didn't take too long to have Fred removed to Cromer Hospital and notify police headquarters of the apparent attack on Fred Fisher. Harold, being Fred's close friend went with him in the ambulance, promising to let George know immediately of any change.

The police house at Salthouse became a sudden hive of activity, with senior CID officers and FPO's coming and going. Being the only uniformed officer present, George felt slightly uncomfortable, almost out of place. He obtained permission to remain at Salthouse to assist in enquiries. It was some hours later, when everything that had to be done, had been done that George sat at Fred's desk and wrote his own statement.

Having done this, George found himself trying to figure out why someone would want to break in, search the office, attack Fred and then leave without apparently taking anything. Apart from a few scattered carbon copies of reports, fowl pest notices, some hand-written notes on wild bird trapping, nothing appeared to have been touched. He crossed over to the desk where all Fred's paperwork lay. He sifted though it but nothing sprang out at him.

He looked at Fred's Daily Occurrence Book. George could see several entries relating to Fred's visits to Cley marsh. The more he looked at an entry Fred had made about his last visit, the more George became attracted to it.

'*Signs of someone forcing a path through the marsh, beginning close to where the body had been found and possibly exiting onto the coast road, adjacent to the entrance to Patchets. The route possibly runs close to and parallel with the existing marsh track. This matter may be connected with sighting(s) made by PC Wright (vide DOB418). This may also by linked to the finding of a metal object (badge-type?) found on verge adjacent to Patchets. (See – Property - 134).*'

George tilted the book, studying it more closely. By chance, sunlight caught the page at an angle. Very faintly, he could see the final line of writing had been slightly smudged. Like a damp cloth or glove had been lightly drawn across the words, after the ink had dried.

There wasn't much of a mark and it was only when he held it to the sunlight that the smearing became more obvious. Looking back at rough notes Fred had earlier made on pieces of paper, he compared the entries in the D.O.B.

George could see how fussy Fred was to get everything right in that book. First, he worked his thoughts out roughly. Then, in his best hand writing he transferred the notes into the DOB. No scratching out, no blots. The smudges were not his work.

As far as George could see, the only rough note that was missing, appeared to be the one relating to the last entry. It wasn't screwed up in the fireplace or waste basket. Quickly scanning other pages, George was convinced that whoever had smudged the entry, it wasn't Fred Fisher! It had to be someone examining that particular entry, having been out in the storm perhaps?

George picked up the Lost Property Register and turned to entry 134. No sign of smudging. But there were marks on the tips of pages, as though the corners had been thumbed over with the same damp glove. A search though the buff envelopes stored in the property cupboard, failed to find the one marked '134'.

George reached for the telephone. One lost property item and maybe, a rough note on Fred's D.O.B. entries? He dialled the CID office in Cromer. They could shoot him down as a plodding beat man, saying they already had the details, but he had to make sure.

In reality, George's theories went down well. George closed the D.O.B. and carefully placed it into the desk drawer. He smiled as he realised that the only eyewitness to the incident was Spike, and he was too busy tucking into food supplied by Fred's friend, Libby Hopkins, to be interested in anything else.

Later the same day, George Wright was in the office at the police house when Mrs Brandon and her daughter Clare arrived. They explained they had visited the hospital and Fred was quite comfortable, even wondering what all the fuss was about. Mrs Brandon told George that although Mr Fisher had received a nasty cut to the head, which had to be stitched, X-rays had thankfully shown no fractures or worse. Their visit to Salthouse was simply to ensure Spike was being looked after. They offered to take Spike, but George explained the cat was quite happy, providing food was put down regularly.

After making sure all was well with George and that he was now happily settled in the house at Kelling, the two ladies left, but not before Clare had found a private moment to press a tightly folded note into George's hand.

George was stunned. For a second, the veiled movement worried him. He was certain Mrs Brandon must have noticed and be wondering why Clare was passing clandestine notes to George? Clare, for her part, was not sure if her mother had seen the long look and smile she had given George, as the note changed hands.

George deliberately delayed opening the note. He spent some time trying to imagine what the contents might be. He had always thought of Clare as someone out of his league, beyond his dreams. Not being able to contain his curiosity, he slowly opened the note. His smile gradually faded. Then he laughed outright. The writing was more of an untidy scrawl and quite difficult to read. He was more than a little disappointed, to say the least. It read, *'Look after Spike - and make sure he doesn't get upstairs!'* It was signed, *'Fred.'* PS. *His fish is in the larder, he likes it cooked and boned! Get him to Libby H, if in doubt.'*

Grace Brandon had always enjoyed her link with her husband's police work. The visit to Fred Fisher had gone extremely well. Also the meeting with George Wright at Salthouse had brought back certain memories. She had seen both the note and the smile. Grace remembered how she too had smiled, that first moment she realised that a very young Police Constable had come into her life. She knew her daughter and idly wondered if George Wright knew his fate was sealed?

Alan helped Grace from the car and led her into the police headquarters building. He wondered how Grace was going to react if David Long appeared a little patronizing towards her. It had been some time since they had last met and regardless of her information being spot on, there was always that little niggle in Alan's mind as to the way David treated Grace. She had been the only informant pointing the way to the truth in the Tilbury Docks case, but David was always visibly uncomfortable with Grace's premonitions. When the information was tested, found correct and the villains tried and sentenced, it was a different story. All smiles and private congratulations, but here they were again at the start of another mystery.

Grace appeared unfazed by David's wide smile and warm handshake. She was very pleased to see Charlie

Friar was present. She knew him as a friend and ally. However, she also knew that once passed the coffee and biscuits stage, it was going to be questions and two spoonfuls of doubt with each, please. She wasn't wrong about the coffee and biscuits. The welcome she received was as warm as the coffee and as sweet as the biscuits. What was surprising was the fact that as soon as this interlude was over, David settled her into a comfortable armchair and simply said, "Grace, I understand you may be able to help us with our enquiries into what happened on Cley marshes?"

Grace was pleasantly surprised, because she knew that David Long, continued to see her form of interpreting what she saw, as highly suspect, mumbo jumbo. But, contrary to her innermost feelings, here he was being encouraging rather than discouraging. She smiled at David. The small butterflies that usually invaded her stomach at this point, decided to remain small and she told herself that whatever she said, there was bound to be the usual scepticism.

Grace decided it was best to just describe the pictures she saw, not to interpret, but paint the canvas with a broad brush. Let the doubting Thomas's do the rest.

Grace relaxed, "I must begin by explaining that the area I saw is known to all of us as the old coastguard station, the one that lies on the shingle bank some two miles east of the Cley Channel and Mill. It's the only one on that section of beach, agreed?" They all nodded, "Fine, to help me, could I ask that you leave any questions you have until after I have explained what I saw."

David Long asked her to continue. Grace took a handkerchief from her handbag and with this in clasped hands, closed her eyes, relaxed and began, "What I saw was the area I have just referred to, but, I believe it is some time in the future. The sea had been pushed back a considerable distance. Perhaps by some type of new sea wall or something like that. At first it was difficult for me to believe it was the same area, but it was. There were a large number of buildings. They looked somehow, futuristic. Smooth domed structures and inverted dishes. This is how I saw it. There was a guarded perimeter, but no obvious wall or fence. I didn't understand what was happening but things were very different. I had the distinct feeling of oppression, secrecy and extreme danger. There were some towers, masts and lots of flood-lights."

David made as if he was going to interrupt but Alan stopped him. She seemed to become increasingly restless. Her eyes were closed tightly and her hands worked on the handkerchief. David looked at Alan and mouthed the word, 'Sorry'.

Grace paused, as if finding her way forward, "There are shafts, leading from what appears to be the perimeter, down and out into the sea," her hands worked again, her eyes moving swiftly beneath the closed lids, "then, a man suddenly appeared a few yards outside the area formed by the towers and lights. I think he was very close to the point where Alan and I stood. At first, he seemed to appear in a very fragmented form, like looking at someone reflected in a cracked mirror. This man faded and was gone. Then, at the same spot, another figure appeared. He also seemed to fragment, but then appeared again, this time like a shadow. A number of figures appeared. When they first emerged, they seemed incomplete, but within a split second, each became whole. They materialise, yes that's the word. They materialise a bit like a person coming through a net curtain. The first figures were unsure, they seemed confused. I saw each of them, in turn, try to walk back. But as they reached a certain point they seemed to falter and collapse. Then another one appeared who, for some reason, seemed different. He was much shorter, dressed in long dark clothing. He seemed surer of himself. He set out, away from the shingle bank, heading along the margins of the marsh, toward Sheringham. He gave every impression he knew where he was going. I know this man will cause many deaths unless he is stopped. Be very careful of him."

Grace paused. Her eyes remained closed. David looked across at Alan as if to raise a question, but Alan held up his hand. Grace should be allowed to continue while she could.

"There will be an explosion, more like a searing flash. This will happen where there is a small gathering of people and they will all die. I saw this man turn away laughing."

Here, Grace paused. She seemed to slowly calm down. Her eyes opened and she dabbed at them with the handkerchief. She looked directly at David and continued, "We have the other man. This one appeared seconds later. He has already been very close to us. Not you David, but he has been close to Alan and I. I somehow know he has a different purpose, just as dangerous, but this man hunts the first. In looks he is so very like you, Alan. This similarity shook me because I thought it was you. It wasn't until I clearly saw his face that I knew it wasn't. These two men oppose each other's plans. The second man will stop at nothing to find him."

Grace asked for a drink of water. Her hands shook as she took the glass. No one said anything while she drank. She put the glass down on a small table by the side of her chair, dabbed her eyes again with the handkerchief.

"Well, Chief Constable, you were anxious to know what I have seen and now you know."

David sat staring at the pencil he was holding. He wasn't quite ready when Grace had finished speaking. He had wanted to interrupt on a number of occasions, but held his impatience in check. Now, he felt more than a little embarrassed. This was mainly because of the nature of his first question. It was never easy, especially with Grace.

"Thank you so much, Grace. I know this can't be easy for you. Now, please don't think I doubt anything you've said, but... is there the remotest chance that some of what you've just told us, could be part of something you've read or perhaps a film or...?" He raised his eyebrows, allowing the question to peter out.

Grace looked strained but amazingly calm. She just smiled softly at David, "Do you remember the last time I helped you? It was much along the same lines. Something

I had seen," here, she pecked at the air with the first two fingers of both hands, as if highlighting the word 'seen'. "and do you know what you said, after I told you what I had seen?"

David smiled broadly, "Sorry my dear Grace, but I just had to ask, didn't I?" Grace relaxed as David went on, "Your description of the shingle bank, and in particular the old coast guard station site, implies it had been replaced by some sort of ultra-modern military, I think you said, 'futuristic' installation." Grace nodded at David. "What do you mean by 'futuristic?"

"Well," Grace paused and thought hard, "Something of the type you might see in a child's comic book."

David ventured, "Like one of Dan Dare's adventures in the Eagle comic perhaps?"

Grace failed to smile, "Yes David, something like that. I'd no idea you were an Eagle fan, or were so well read."

David noted the look of concern, "Is it possible that you can tell us where these people come from?"

For a second Grace relaxed, "It's alright David I am not saying they are little green men from Mars. As far as I can tell," she paused, her eyes clouding again, "these people, shall we call them travellers, are simply out of step with time itself. They are certainly not of our time and they certainly bring death with them," she shrugged her shoulders, "right now, I feel as lost as they must be."

As David heard this, he pressed a button on his desk. Almost immediately, a smart young woman came in, armed with a notepad and pencil. She sat close to Grace and made detailed notes of her replies, as David, Alan and Charlie quietly gleaned as much information as they could.

It was just after six when Grace, Alan and Charlie left the building. Charlie excused himself saying he wanted to get to Cromer as soon as possible, to check on Fred Fisher's progress.

Alan took Grace's arm and told her how very, very proud of her he was. She felt the tension drain away. She

109

had once again, bearded David in his den. She also felt that this time, he actually believed what she had said. It would be so easy for someone like David to dismiss what she was saying, as delusional. After all, seaside piers were full of Madam this or that, all predicting the future. With Grace, it was different. They were not guesses. Her premonitions had been proved stunningly right. Hers had always been based on some fearful event. For her it was never easy to calmly announce someone was going to die. There was no sense of victory, only a mind-numbing sadness, each time her prediction resulted in one or more bodies.

Grace decided a long time ago that if she was to lead a normal life, she had to fight to subdue the depression brought on by what she chose to call, 'the other side'. On this occasion, the first step would be to allow Alan to buy her a first class meal, plus a glass or two of fine wine.

She enjoyed having David believe her, this was something of a relief. Besides, over dinner she may be able to put the future out of her mind. She may even have the opportunity to tell Alan her good news. Grace had received an invitation to play at a charity concert at the Royal Albert Hall. To receive such a high-level invitation, after so long away from that particular platform, was a thrilling compliment, and one she found difficult to keep to herself.

Grace pondered on the fact that such an invitation meant having to go to London for a whole plethora of meetings, rehearsal discussions and pre-concert practices, to say nothing of the stresses of the actual performance. Would it all be too much?

Grace felt she should decline the invitation. She told herself it was selfish to be so self-centred, at a time when Alan had his hands full. At the same time, she did feel thrilled by the prospect of returning to the platform, helping to raise funds for such a good cause.

Grace chose her moment like a General committing his cavalry. She struck just as they were enjoying their first glass of wine. It was immediately plain Alan was truly thrilled for her. He brushed aside Grace's concerns and insisted she play, and that he be there to support her.

Grace felt so relieved and relaxed that she almost mentioned her suspicions of Clare's feeling for a certain Police Constable, but she thought perhaps that little morsel of news could wait. If what she suspected turned out to be true, it wouldn't be long before Clare would make her true feelings known to her father.

Chapter Seven

The articulated lorry stopped with a lurch. Escaping air from the hydraulic brake system hissed sharply, then subsided as the driver removed his size twelve boot from the brake pedal. Oily mud-stained water poured from every point on the heavy rig, cascading onto the thick mud-rutted battlefield that posed as a lorry park. There were no other vehicles around. This was unusual though not terribly surprising since the completion of the bypass.

Scores of illuminated red light bulbs announced to the world that this was Mary's Transport Café. Each of the bulbs reflecting harshly in the rippling puddles, as each raindrop did its best to shatter an oily mirror. Large yellow lit misted windows promised hot food and steaming mugs of tea, plus the bonus of a break from the black tarmac that superimposes itself on the mind of every lorry driver. Especially on the lonely night run.

The recent arrival was an unusually large drawing unit, with dark blue paint work, tethered to a faded all white trailer of the container type. No name graced its tall sides, but on the doors of the towing unit and above each of the displayed index plates were the letters CPS, surmounted by a large crown. To most people, this meant nothing, but to the police and certain others interested parties, it meant 'Crown Property Services'.

An overweight, rumpled figure of a man dropped from the driver's cab door. The mud that rose into the air as feet met ground, neatly turned in, liberally coating the sagging dark blue overall slacks that clung, defying gravity from somewhere below his belt-line.

The man reached up and swung the heavy door closed and, although he was now the specific target of penetrating rain, he took his time satisfying himself that the cab door was properly secure.

He made a great play of putting the keys in a cavernous pocket then jogged like an overweight whale, to the shelter offered by the café porch. His scuffed high-reach, red-laced boots and oiled crew cut hair, reflecting the fact that he saw himself as an athlete, a mauling boxer, capable of taking on anyone. An impression he loved to give but visibly denied by his heavy, over-ripe pear shaped frame.

Before entering this parlour of fried delights, known amongst the trucking fraternity as 'Mucky Mary's', he shook four pounds of water out of his short hair, flicking oily hands through it then, sure that he was looking like his favourite boxing hero, he pushed his way through the paint faded, swinging door.

The familiar fuzzy, fluctuating sounds of Radio Luxembourg met his ears. Jazz played out over the air in a mysterious undulating motion caused by long-distance signal interference. The door squealed shut behind him and he stood for a moment enjoying the smells that met his flared nostrils. He wasn't known throughout the A12 trunk route as 'Walrus' for nothing. He was proud of this nickname. He accepted it meant he was seen as a hard-man. Someone with a reputation, you didn't upset!

In reality others saw him as a joke, as a flashy, overweight lump, looking for a heart attack. But, there was one title he did hold. He could eat his way through anything Mucky Mary could provide. Money had been won on it.

Outside, the rain continued to sheet down as though gills, not lungs, were the order of the night. The place was empty of customers except for one small man, who didn't look up as the fat man entered. By the way he ignored the grand entrance it was obvious he wasn't impressed or at home to polite conversation.

The small man slowly wiped a porthole in the steam that covered a window and peered out into the night. He appeared to look long and hard at the one solitary lorry. Then he abandoned the porthole to the persistent, creeping condensation. It seemed he wasn't in any rush to do anything.

Two male café staff went sullenly about their business. One occasionally visible through the kitchen hatch and the other wiping grease around tables. Both had cigarettes hanging unattended between their lips, apparently excusing them from conversation.

The driver reached up and took his time pulling the collar of his overalls high onto his neck. Then he crossed over to the row of metal stools in front of the counter. Demonstrating his ability to do two things at one time, he climbed onto one of the stools while reading the chalked spam menu. His ears caught the sound of the man by the window push his chair back, get to his feet and walk slowly to a point somewhere behind his stool. The Walrus didn't feel crowded, so he ignored the move.

The infamous Mary appeared from the kitchen, the obligatory cigarette gracing the corner of her mouth, hung limp as usual. Unlike her employees, a steady stream of blue smoke did nothing for her blood-shot eyes. She came through from the back, nodding a casual greeting to the driver, but instead of meeting his eyes, she stared over his right shoulder.

"Excuse my curiosity but, is that lorry yours, my friend?" The voice had a brittle quietness, like a small child shuffling on broken glass.

It made the fat man stop reading the menu. In a tired, irritated movement, Walrus turned partially round to view the speaker. The questioner was of no height, had no spare weight and a very pale face. His clothes were long, too long. They were dark and, apart from being heavily creased, from what may have been a country walk on a rainy night, there was nothing, aside from the mud stains, that stood out.

"Not that it's any of your business, slim, but no, I don't own it. Therefore, it can't be mine. I just happen to be the hero who has to cab the frigging heap! Listen shortstop, I'm not your frigging friend either. What's it to you anyway? You're not big enough to be curious about anything let alone a real wagon like that!" He liked what he said. It made him laugh and slap the counter with pleasure.

The driver's hunger overcame his need to show off, "Now go away. I want to eat something as big as you, little man!"

The small man looked down at the floor, "My name is Victor Grech and I'm sure you will want to know that."

The fat man slowly unwound himself from the stool. Balancing on the balls of his feet, he waited for the trouble he hoped might come. He'd gone a few rounds at fair ground booths when younger and liked to think he could handle himself. He liked the look of the odds and felt it might give Mary a thrill to see him in action.

The small man's shoes were the only surprise. They were black, light leather. The sort office managers minced around in.

"Mine is Bert Manning, they call me Walrus because I eat things bigger and more threatening than you for breakfast." He looked across at the table cleaner, to see if he was enjoying the show. The cleaner looked up and gave a submissive nod.

"What are you, a carrion-crow practising to be an undertaker? Now go away before you get badly hurt. I can't stand dwarfs dressed in black. They're unlucky!" He laughed again. This time, the staff grinned. It didn't pay them not to.

"I asked you a very polite question. I also told you my name," the man said in a whisper, "I thought you may be able to give me a ride towards London." Grech then made a curious move backwards, away from Walrus, as though already making up his mind his hope for a ride had gone.

Walrus saw the move and contemptuously turned his back on the excuse for a man, "Fat chance, I'm not allowed passengers mister, that's even if I wanted the company of a circus midget, which I don't!" The word don't, was spat out, "Now, if you don't mind, I want to eat." He climbed onto the stool again.

Grech backed away another step, as if physically struck by what Walrus had said. His eyes hardened and his thin mouth tightened, "I need to get to London quickly. It wouldn't do you any harm to help me get there, and by the size of you, you could do with taking a rest from eating." These words, spoken no louder than his previous whisper, carried an anger that smacked of splintered ice.

Walrus's face took on that tired, 'I'm really going to slap this one,' look. He slowly got off the stool and turned to face the man again, "Look skinny, I've just told you. No lift! One more remark earns you a visit to the mud. Now stop bothering me. I won't be so polite next time, Okay!"

The two male night staff quietly joined Mary. If trouble was coming they wanted to be close to the pick-handles that were neatly placed under the counter. It would not be the first time that the night shift had been called 'to-arms'.

"That's so very inconvenient," the thin man spoke even more softly, almost to himself, "but, I suppose it was kind of you to be on time." Grech's right hand went between the folds of the newspaper he was carrying, "It just proves you can rely on Government transport to run on time? Oh," he actually seemed to chuckle, "and you can bet your precious life on that!" Those last few words came, almost as a comic afterthought.

Walrus clearly felt the draught that came with the quietly spoken words. He noticed the man's penetrating black eyes were everywhere, on Mary, her staff and on him. One of the men behind the counter suddenly came to life, "Now come on you two, we don't want any trouble here."

He started to move, as if to back up his words. He stopped dead. They all saw what seemed to be a type of handgun in the man's right hand.

"The keys, if you please. And if I were you, I wouldn't try to do anything stupid, like proving just how very brave you are."

The gun thrust forward as if underlining the acidity in the words. Walrus looked helplessly toward the others. His hand was already groping in his sagging trouser pockets. He was not about to argue with a maniac holding a gun. After all, his load was just old papers, no value to anyone. The keys, thrown in a perfect arc, landed neatly in an outstretched left hand.

"That is extremely kind of you, and now, ask yourself, is there anything I can do for you? Can I offer you something to ease your hunger perhaps?"

In the fraction of a second that passed, the fat man nick-named Walrus, knew what was coming. He had time to open his mouth and half raise a hand, when he saw the gun kick up.

The retina in his eyes registered what appeared to be flame. The last thing he heard was his scream. The last thing he saw was his own death. All four people left in the locked café, didn't hear lights switched off, signs turned to closed, hysterical laughter, a lorry start up or the long drawn-out grating of gears, as it suddenly jerked forward. Neither were they aware that the rain continued to wash across the now darkened lorry-park. It was a truly, filthy night to be out.

Wind driven rain continued to work hard through the dawn. It filled every rut in the lorry-park to the brim, despite gravity doing its best to sluice gallons of the yellow muddy mixture out into the road. Normally, the constant coming and going of heavy transport helped to displace most of the water, but this had been no ordinary night.

The first clue that things weren't quite right at Mucky Mary's was when the morning shift arrived, just before six. The two cyclists, having battled their way the half-mile from Mountnessing village, to this isolated shoulder of the B1002, saw no other traffic. In fact they saw nothing unusual until they reached the miserable excuse for their place of work. Not one red light bulb blinked a welcome in the yellow lake that served as a lorry park.

Thinking they had totally mistaken the day for a Sunday, they peered through the windows, seeking a ready answer. What they saw through the grimy glass was a grotesque scene. A fat man was lying straddled amongst a certain amount of collapsed furniture. He seemed to be covered in blood. That was enough to send the day shift peddling like fury for the nearest telephone.

The first Essex police car arrived just after six forty-three, after which the water in the lorry-park took on permanent waves caused by the rapid movement of police vehicles. Commercial traffic was beginning to pick up and a few lorry drivers tried to gain their usual access for breakfast, but one look at the number of pointy helmets kept their wheels turning.

Teleprinters throughout that county started their insistent chatter just after seven-thirty, carrying 'Express' messages describing the carnage at Mucky-Mary's. The first circulation briefly outlined the incident. Others that followed were more specific.

Soon, on-duty policemen everywhere in the country were made aware that Essex police were looking for, as they put it, 'the person or persons responsible,...anything suspicious,...do not approach etc., etc., etc.'

Inside the palace of fried delights, the pungent aroma of violent death fought to take over the breathable atmosphere from the resident reek of truckers fare. Detective Constable Bob Fuller was the first member of the local CID to arrive. His eyes took in tell-tale signs that lay like unread pages of a book. He noticed all the tables appeared to have been cleared and then wiped down with a very greasy cloth. That is, all except one. This unspoiled surface was immediately adjacent to a front window. On this table, a lonely cup remained uncollected and still contained most of its brown, cold contents, as though whoever had sat there, decided not to drink it. Or else chose not to because something far more important was about to happen.

D.C. Fuller also noticed the chair closest to the cup, had been pushed back. As though the user had risen from it and walked away, leaving it parked clear of the table. Next, he looked hard at the window. Years of fry-ups and neglect had done a good job on all the café windows. It had left a misty film on which the tired, curious or, just bored traveller, could simply doodle away time. He looked more closely. The window surface had a perfectly round smear drawn through the film. The type of mark someone might leave who had sat at the table and wanted to look into the lorry-park, maybe showing an interest in something or someone arriving?

Carefully, he drew the chair back to the table and sat down. He then tried to look through the smudged circle. To get the view he wanted, he had to adjust his seat twice, to get his head low enough. After a minute or two he straightened up. He was sure that whoever had sat at that table and cleared that patch had either been a child or a very short adult.

He removed the cup and saucer from the table, taking great care not to smudge any prints. Cautiously he tipped the contents of the cup into a glass then placed the items into a cardboard box.

Another point crossed his mind as he looked at the body of the fat man. It seemed he must have collapsed backwards, between the stools causing them to topple sideways. The pattern suggested the dead man might have been standing slightly away from the line of stools when shot.

He bent down and picked up what looked like a piece of blood stained newspaper. It seemed to be the corner of a page. The name Eastern Daily Press was quite clear. He also noticed traces of what could be oil. He sniffed at the paper, He had smelt that oil often enough in the navy. It was gun oil! Bob Fuller placed the paper carefully in the box with the crockery.

The foot-ring on one of the stools clearly showed traces of yellow mud of the type found in the lorry-park. He reckoned the fat man came in, sat on one of the stools at the counter then dismounted for some reason. Perhaps speak to someone standing behind him.

A quick glance told him there was no crockery, cutlery, food or whatever on the counter. This, he assumed, meant whoever had chosen the stool, had only recently arrived at the café. It seemed they hadn't been there long enough to be served. Whoever had sat at the window may have been waiting for the dead heavyweight, now glued to the floor.

By the time senior police officers arrived at the scene, Bob Fuller was well on the way to guessing how, but was now faced with who, why, when and what for? He had learned to 'observe' and note the unusual on the recent course he'd attended, and from a number of books he purchased on forensic science. He didn't intend to investigate the larceny of cycles, for much longer.

As soon as he had passed on his thoughts to the arriving group of senior officers, he was reminded, in no uncertain terms, that his duty was to attend the scene, and to ensure nothing was touched before the arrival of the senior investigating officer. He was then invited to return to his station and continue his routine investigative duties.

Feeling it was their loss not to use his professional abilities more effectively, he dutifully handed over the cardboard box containing the cup, saucer and oily paper, and left for Brentwood.

His observations, however, had not fallen on stony ground. The cup and saucer were checked. It was found there were two sets of prints on the cup. The first were identified as having been made by one of the café staff. The second had not been made by anyone present. It was therefore assumed they belonged to the person responsible for the multiple killings.

One of the prints also matched a mark on a new ten-shilling note, found in the cash register. This note was the only one in the till. It was rightly assumed that business in the café, prior to this customer's arrival, had apparently been non-existent.

So, there were a few things they knew about the suspect killer. It was assumed by the size and form of the print, it was a man. That he had enough money to change a ten-shilling note for a cup of tea and he had probably driven away in the vehicle brought in by the dead customer. The other bodies were quickly identified as café staff. There was no weapon left at the scene, therefore the killer was armed and extremely dangerous.

The personal belongings found on the dead heavyweight led very quickly to his CPS employers, at their document stores in Cromer, who provided a complete description of the vehicle. They also supplied a schedule of its regular time of departure, strictly enforced A12 route and were stunned to learn that the driver must have left the A12 at Ingatestone, joined the B1002 and stopped at the café. It was off his assigned route to Silvertown in East London where he had been due to arrive between three and four in the morning. His supervisor emphasized such deviations from prescribed routes, to visit unapproved cafés, were not permitted. He seemed completely oblivious of the fact that their driver was now dead, along with three other persons.

The driver was a local Cromer man, his name was Albert Manning, single, lived in lodgings and had been employed by the CPS for a number of years. He'd always done the regular night run, five nights a week. He was totally disliked by his colleagues. There was a history of his being particularly disruptive and abrasive towards them. During the war years he had been considered medically unfit for service due to flat feet. He also claimed to be a conscientious objector, based on religious grounds. As a result, he had been drafted to work in the coal mines.

The trailer had been loaded with 5 tons of Government or Court papers, defined as being outside the realm of public interest or simply time-expired. They were to be destroyed by fire at the H.M.G. furnaces, sited in Dock Road, Silvertown. London, E16.

Given the time the crime was discovered and the distances involved, it was obvious that the killer had hours to get wherever he was going. He could now be somewhere in East Anglia, in London, or anywhere. By four in the afternoon, every policeman in the country was looking for the CPS lorry.

The crew of a car from the Metropolitan Police garage at East Ham was carrying out checks on likely parking spots on their patch, when the driver pulled onto the forecourt of the Manor Way Transport Café, just north of Learoyd Gardens. Heavies were stacked in several rows, at the sides and back of the café. It was the usual place to take a break before joining the queue of wagons waiting to deliver to the Royal Albert Victoria or King George V docks, or to stop after making a drop.

The observer, a young probationary constable, climbed out, leaving the driver to rest his eyes and keep an ear to the radio. The observer took his time, wandering through the ranks of parked trucks. He had almost reached the chain link fence that separated the café from Manor Way School, when he spotted the rear of a trailer that looked as if one of the back doors was slightly open. A broken seal was lying on the ground.

He didn't wait to inspect the index plate. If it was the lorry they were after, and if the person responsible was still with it, he was known to have been involved in a shooting in Essex. Their orders were absolute. 'Report and wait for assistance to arrive'.

In just over ten minutes, the sight of policemen, blossoming in and around the forecourt, brought out all the customers, resulting in some confined but good natured confusion.

One at a time, drivers were seen, questioned and allowed to leave. It had become obvious the man they sought was not present. The café owner was all too ready to cooperate but still miffed about losing trade. When told a lorry on his property had been involved in a multiple murder, he lost a bit of colour and quietened down. It transpired that he had actually seen the wagon arrive early that morning. He was very busy at the time and didn't actually spot the driver. He assumed he had come into the café and had a meal. Lorries kept arriving and leaving, so he couldn't tell whether that particular wagon was still parked or if it had been driven away.

The police made a count and found there had been twenty-seven vehicles present when their target vehicle had been spotted. This being so, it was not surprising that at least one lorry could have been parked, so as to be fully masked from the café, by others.

A detailed search of the trailer revealed that the CPS door seals had been cut, the trailer lock broken and unbolted. Two seconds work with the right tool, readily carried in the cab.

Inside the trailer, lying on the floor was a complete load manifest containing brief details of every file carried. The interior of the trailer was sectioned off and marked alphabetically. There was very little disturbance of the load, until they arrived at the compartment marked, G.H.I. This compartment, like the others, was in fact a sectioned trolley, something like a very large laundry basket on wheels. This, in turn, was split into three sub-compartments. The 'G' section had been completely pulled out. Most of the contents were still lying within their sealed cardboard pouches, but one marked 'Galleon Affair' had the seal broken and was empty. So, it looked as though the killer had not just hijacked the lorry, satisfying a fetish for unusual means of transport. This was a planned interception of the vehicle to lift specific documents due for destruction.

This news was quick arriving in both the Essex and Norfolk Police Headquarters. No time was lost in towing the lorry to the MP Garage, where CID officers took it apart in their quest to find anything that could assist the enquiry.

George Wright's telephone rang. He climbed out of the bath, tucked a towel around himself and padded down the stairs, into the front room that served as his office. He had been enjoying the freedom of having his own house, even if it was also the Kelling Police house. Just for a moment he hoped it might be Clare, but it wasn't.

"Come and get me, George, I'll be waiting for you outside the main reception. Don't be long mate. I look a bit conspicuous."

George was both disappointed and stunned. His caller had rung off before he could utter a word. He dived into his clothes, donned his crash helmet and was gone, all in ten minutes.

The sound of his motorcycle, as it roared up to the front entrance of Cromer hospital, had quite a disturbing effect on staff and patients. But no where near as alarming as the sight of the pillion passenger, as it left the hospital grounds two minutes later.

Fred Fisher was clinging to George as though his life depended on it. His bright white helmet was in fact a large head bandage with the ends flying in the breeze behind him.

There was no conversation until they stopped outside the police house at Salthouse. Fred dismounted clutching a small holdall, which evidently held everything Fred had scooped from his locker. He was shaking like a leaf. George assumed it was shock, but Fred had other ideas.

"What the bloody hell were you doing? I've just escaped from hospital and I've no wish to be sent back. You're mad, George. Stark, raving bonkers. If I'd known I was being collected by a speed-merchant, I would have rung Harold Crumb at the bloody vicarage."

George felt genuinely sorry for Fred. He was obviously in shock and totally undone by his first motorcycle experience.

Fred certainly looked strange with his head in a white turban and bruising that had spread down beyond both cheeks. He resembled a cross between a masked Indian bandit and Dick Turpin.

George opened the door of the police house and out rushed Spike. He was obviously thrilled to see the main provider of his food, although even he took a second look at the face. Fred picked him up and returned the show of affection.

They were standing just inside the door when Charlie Friar drove up, closely followed by Harold Crumb. Within an hour, with Fred properly dressed and sorted, they were comfortably seated at the Duck pub.

Charlie filled Fred in on all the happenings, including the incident at Mucky Mary's. Although it was some way from their patch, it did involve a local who had been the driver. He had been employed by CPS Cromer and had been driving one of their wagons.

Fred sipped at his pint. It was good to be back amongst people he knew and trusted. He took a longer draught from the glass, just to make certain the nutty quality was still there. With deeper satisfaction, he wiped his mouth and muttered, "Strange."

Harold, who was about to imbibe, lowered his glass, "What is?"

Fred smiled, "Well, I was just thinking, life goes on quietly for years, and mark you I'm including the war years. Then, all of a sudden, things start popping."

Fred took another long swallow, while the others waited, admiring the weight of bandages and blossoming bruising. "You take the break in at my place. Whoever paid me a visit ignored those valuable silver-bowling cups on the hall table and the money I left lying on the desk. He gives me such a wallop then takes a rough sketch I made of a path on the marsh and a metal badge thing from the property cupboard. Now that's what I call strange."

"Was there anything special about the drawing?" Charlie asked.

Fred looked from Charlie to Harold for agreement saying, "No, just a single line drawing, roughly done on a free map of the marsh."

Harold nodded, "Strange thing to take. Do you think it was possibly taken to wrap up something?"

125

Fred put his glass down, "Sometimes I despair of you Harold. It was one of those very small maps Patchets give their guests, not a four-by-two sheet of wallpaper. Don't know why I scribbled that path on it. It just seemed peculiar, seeing as how it ran so close to the main track."

Harold brightened, "Fred, one bit of positive news. You recall I said I would speak to Roger Markham and ask him to look at it?"

Charlie broke in, "Isn't he the chap that manages the bird sanctuary on the marsh. Lives in a cottage out near Blakeney Point?"

"Yes," confirmed Harold, "sorry I should have said. Well, he has had a look at what we took to be a track left by someone out by the shingle bank. He also had a quick look at what we took to be the exit point, close to Patchets. In his opinion it was probably a one man effort. Judging by marks he found, whoever did it, crouched for some time in two or three places, one of them close to where your metal object was found."

"Is tracking one of his specialities then?" Asked George.

Fred drained his glass, "You could say that. Nearest thing to a blood-hound we've got in Norfolk, ex-Kenya big game man."

"And another thing he told me," said Harold, "you know that description you chaps have been putting round, the tall chap?" They all nodded, "Well, it seems The Linnet has been hired out to a new tenant. Our harbour master says it fits him to a tee."

"What's The Linnet, when it's at home?" Asked Charlie.

"In this case," said George, "she's a ketch, tied up not too far from Roger Markham's cottage. She's on a buoy at the top end of the Cley channel, just in sight of Blakeney quay. Water deep enough to keep her floating." He knew where Charlie was going with his question.

"Has this tall chap been seen on the boat?"

Harold nodded.

Charlie left the table and went to the phone. He rang the only yacht chandler in Blakeney. Two minutes later he had confirmed the sighting.

Charlie made it plain it was time he and George were leaving. When Fred rose from the table, he was told to remain and relax. He wouldn't be involved in police matters until he was declared fit to return to duty. Charlie crossed to the bar and paid for another round of drinks for Fred and Harold then, with smiles all round, he and George headed for Blakeney.

Charlie reversed the car into the large covered yard kept clear for the lifeboat crew. Taking binoculars from the glove compartment, George quickly spotted The Linnet. There was no sign of movement on the boat. A further sweep of the binoculars told him there was no sign of the tender either.

Charlie left the car, and walked the length of the quay amongst a throng of visitors. Taking his time, he searched each landing point until he spotted the dingy. It lay, partly hidden, alongside the steps opposite the hotel.

Charlie went into the hotel and used the telephone. He then rejoined George in the car. Taking it in shifts, they watched and waited for the tall double of their boss, to appear. The crowds gradually thinned, the tide changed and boating activity settled toward thoughts of dinner. It was almost seven when Alan drove up.

"Sorry chaps. Our venerable harbour master has just returned from a trip to Norwich. He called in at Patchets to tell me about this man Stolland. Evidently, he claims Stolland has business ashore and won't be back on The Linnet until around midday tomorrow. I think we'll arrange to join him for lunch."

Chapter Eight

By nine the next morning, Alan had waded through sheaves of telexes, countless copies of typed statements, and had coped with a lengthy and bruising conversation with David Long.

Evidently, the Home Secretary's private secretary, or some such Whitehall clerk, had been jerking strings. It had all been very stiff over the telephone and David was left in no doubt. The H.S. wanted to know, as soon as possible and certainly before the PM's question time slot in the House, what connection there was, if any, between the murders in Essex and theft of restricted files from a Government store in Norfolk.

Alan half-heartedly drafted a suggested reply for David's approval. It was a task he hated doing because whatever he wrote, David would comb through the language, adding a politically tuned word here, an oiled phrase there. Only then would the required reply clack its way onto the telex machine at the Home Office.

Joined by Charlie, they commenced trawling through clippings from various daily newspapers, reporting what journalists took to be facts arising from the café murders. For a journalist, the word 'fact' could be any comment thrown away by an untried witness, then written with a very broad technicolor brush, whereas Alan and Charlie were somewhat confined by the narrowness of legal definition.

The discovery of the lorry abandoned in London carried half-page pictures, mostly of the Manor Way Transport Café. One London daily included a picture of a London Transport Bus, route 101, with a caption suggesting this was the means by which the lorry driver had made his escape. Also under a banner headline, claiming an exclusive, a broadsheet newspaper claimed that an arrest of the Essex café slayer would take place within hours. This must have been a comforting thought for readers.

Coffee brought a short respite from newsprint, allowing Charlie to brief Alan on Fred Fisher's progress and confirming the list of missing items from the Salthouse police house. That over, Alan glanced at his watch again and announced it was time to leave for Blakeney.

The main street leading down to the quayside was as obstructed and busy as usual. Alan eventually managed to tuck the car into a slot at the back of the police station. Then, he and Charlie made the short stroll towards the quay.

"I must say I'm looking forward to meeting my double."

"He may not be so keen to meet us though," promised Charlie, "he has some explaining to do. And, I don't like colleagues getting whacked!"

Alan stopped as they stood aside to allow a large fish van to negotiate the narrow street, "Just you remember, Charlie, we have enough evidence to make him a suspect only. Strong suspicion yes, but, I don't want any smart lawyer shaking him out simply because we have leapt in too early."

Charlie nodded, "Fair enough."

"Don't get me wrong, I'd give a great deal to know exactly why a person would break into a police house, turn it over, then attack one of our men, all for a slip of paper and an ounce of metal. The answer lies out there on the marsh. Young George Wright did well. He's got his wits about him and right now, we need that."

Charlie thought for a minute, "While we have George Wright in mind, he could be useful to us in CID. Won the Military Medal in the last lot you know." Charlie paused, hoping for some sign of agreement.

Eventually a thoughtful Alan stopped scratching his chin, "Yes, I did know, I agree he's smart. What was he in?"

Charlie dug into his memory, "Couldn't be a hundred percent sure, but I think he started off in the navy, then somehow ended up in the P.B.I."

Alan nodded, half-turned away, then frowned, "P.B.I? Never heard of that, what's PBI stand for exactly?"

"Poor Bloody Infantry, I think."

Alan smiled, "Well whatever it means, he's obviously got what it takes and Charlie, I promise we won't let the grass grow."

Appearing out of the crowd was a uniformed Constable. He crossed over to Alan, and saluted, "Sir, The man Stolland has been involved in an incident in Cromer. He's been taken to Cromer hospital and admitted for treatment."

"What sort of incident?"

"As far as we know, he was seen on the knocker by a resident in Eccles Row."

"Making enquiries at the houses?"

"Yes sir, door-to-door in Eccles Row. That's close to the railway station."

"What were his questions about?"

"He was trying to find a man he called Grech or something like that? It seems this car mounted the footpath, hit Stolland and drove off. The constable that attended thought it was you when he first saw Stolland, but quickly realised it was the man you wanted to question."

"Where is Stolland now and is anyone with him?"

"CID officer is with him at the hospital."

"Has the car been traced?"

Found at the Railway Station car park, parked round the back of an old shelter, empty I'm afraid."

Alan gained all this information as he and Charlie headed back to the police station, where Alan phoned the hospital.

Alan looked pleased as he finished the call, "Well Charlie, luck's going our way at last. It seems Mr Stolland has been very fortunate. According to the doctor, he's extremely agitated and has already tried to discharge himself, claims the accident was his own fault. Says he stepped into the road in front of the car. Evidently, his injuries are not serious, though he does have a broken arm. That's been set and plastered, quite a bit of bad bruising too.

The medics are all for releasing him as soon as they are sure he has no head injury. The x-rays will give them that information. Evidently he could be released into someone's care, so to help out our friends at the hospital, I've arranged for the Cromer area car to go and collect him. He'll be told they are taking him to the station so that he can make a formal statement regarding the accident. Once there, purely by chance, he'll meet our police surgeon who will persuade him, one way or another, to be our guest overnight. It's my opinion, after the shaking up Stolland's had, he'll settle for a safe night's rest, even if that is in a police cell. In the morning he'll be offered a lift back here. I'm banking everything on him returning to the Linnet. Oh, just one more thing. He's confirmed as tall, medium build, with penetrating eyes. Also, it seems, he's rather aggressive when he can't get his own way."

Charlie's eyebrows shot up, "It really is your brother then?"

"Thanks Charlie," Alan rubbed his hands together, "well, our man is as safe as money in the bank, so who's for a tour of The Linnet? It's too perfect a chance to let the opportunity slip. We can run the rule over Stolland's little nest before he gets back."

They made their way down to the quay. A seasonable mist was beginning to form, but you could still make out the channel. Charlie opted to row while Alan sat at the blunt end and steered. They both looked totally out of place and a number of times Charlie managed to scoop several gallons of water into the boat and over Alan. Fortunately, the channel was wide and their line of advance unobstructed by other boats. Even so, other boat people watching the dinghy's erratic progress were left wondering why so many changes in direction were necessary in water as calm as a mill pond.

A little further along the channel, the mist chose to drift like so many linen shrouds, sneaking amongst the moored craft and muddy shingle banks. Alan eventually got the knack of tiller-work and soon had them nudged up to the clinker built hull.

The Linnet was an absolute delight to the eye. They both climbed, rather inexpertly over the aft counter and were astonished at the tidiness of the deck. Nothing was out of place. It reflected the care lavished on it by the owner, and obviously by its new tenant.

Securing the tender snugly on the seaward side, they both made their way to the hatch leading below. This was fastened with a stout-looking brass lock and draw bolt.

Charlie slipped the bolt, turned his back on Alan, fumbled in his pocket and within seconds the hatch seemed to slide open.

He whispered, "Okay sir, the lock hasn't suffered and will re-lock when we leave."

Alan smiled at this assurance. He knew Charlie and was sure it would. The saloon was as snug as the deck. Fortunately a small waterproof hand-torch was found clipped onto the bulkhead at the head of the companionway, alongside a pair of fire axes.

Alan said, almost to himself, "Thought of everything when they fitted her out, didn't they?"

It took several minutes of careful examination before they found what they were looking for. The locker door opened at a touch. Inside, lying on top of several charts and other papers was Fred's tourist map. It clearly showed a faint pencilled arrow, beginning close to the shingle bank and almost adjacent to the main track. Where the marsh met the coast road was a pencilled cross and question mark. These two points were joined by a dotted line. At the bottom of the map was a pencilled note that read; *'Path appears to enter reeds and turn sharp left towards the coast road. Seems to run within feet of and parallel to marsh track - WHY?'*

"Gotcha!" Mouthed Alan, "Mr Stolland you're ours now. We have attempted murder, breaking into the police house, plus theft of evidence. But I think we'll let Mr Stolland have just a few more feet of rope. Just to see where it leads."

Charlie had been rummaging, "Well, we have Fred's paper, but that metal item doesn't seem to be here? You would have thought they'd be together?"

"Unless of course, Stolland had good reason to take that with him?" Suggested Alan.

Placing the paper back exactly as it was found, Alan indicated it was time to leave. Charlie followed, making sure things were Bristol fashion, especially the lock and bolt.

On their return to the quay, the tender was made secure using the type of amateur knots Stolland had employed.

It was after 11pm when they arrived at Cromer police station. Stolland had been made comfortable and was very satisfied with the meal that had been provided. Alan was immediately struck how very much alike they were. It seemed that Grace and everyone else that had commented on the similarity had been right.

Alan explained in some detail, that extensive enquiries and efforts to find the car and driver responsible for the accident were in progress. Stolland appeared guarded but was obviously relieved at the lack of positive results. He also seemed reluctant to talk in detail about the incident, saying it had all happened too quickly to take in. This attitude was far from convincing and certainly not the usual demeanour of the innocent pedestrian, injured in what appeared to be a deliberate hit and run incident.

Alan's trump card was played when he drew Charlie aside and, making certain Stolland could just hear, suggested Stolland's version of events could be true and that it probably was a simple accident, with the driver losing control of the steering, mounting the footpath and not realising injury had been caused, drove off. On their return, Stolland was positively relaxed. He claimed to be a

Southern Irish writer, renting The Linnet to finish a novel. He claimed he was in Eccles Row collecting local colour.

Finally it was suggested, as it was rather late and as he appeared comfortable, he should spend the remainder of the night at the station and go home after a decent breakfast. Stolland, seemed to accept the invitation.

Before leaving the station, Alan went to the duty room to see the desk sergeant, "Has any of Stolland's property been taken into our possession?"

Sergeant Bell looked confused, "No sir. As he was not under arrest, he was transferred from hospital to here with everything still in his pockets. Do you want me to turn him over?"

"No. That's the last thing I want. But when the car crew get back, get them to check every inch of the inside of the car to see if they can find a small silver metal object. Mr Stolland might be tempted to use a temporary police safe deposit box. Oh, and make sure nothing of this conversation gets back to Mr Stolland."

Safely out in the car park, Charlie lit up as usual, "I take it we're still banking on Stolland having that, whatever it is, on him?"

"Charlie, I'm willing to bet you he had a right shock when that item went missing. You mark my words he'll stick to that little item as though his life or someone else's depends on it."

"You don't think it's just alloy scrap then?"

"I have a strange feeling that particular piece of metal was the magnet that drew Stolland to Fred Fisher. The map is a blind. He's hoping we swallow his bait and forget all about what you call, alloy scrap."

Charlie stubbed out his cigarette, "Well, wherever his secret lies, he's certainly happy to bunk down in the cell tonight. Mr Stolland certainly seems to have enemies of the planning and killing variety."

They separated, agreeing to meet at the Harding's Hotel at eight the following morning.

The new day began in bright sunshine. Alan was first to arrive. He thanked the manager for use of a service room on the second floor. It wasn't the first time the hotel management had provided the loop-hole through which comings and goings had been observed. It was perfect for the job, with a small bay window overlooking the whole quay.

Charlie joined him, having already telephoned the station at Cromer. It seemed that Stolland had voted to leave their kind hospitality at ten.

Making themselves comfortable, they settled in. Alan knew he was putting a lot of eggs in one basket. If Stolland decided to do a runner and disappear, David Long would make the Russian pogroms look like Sunday school outings.

Just after ten, a knock on the door of the room heralded coffee and a message to ring Police HQ. Alan was in no rush because he knew who wanted to talk to him. He wasn't disappointed.

"Alan, what the bloody hell's going on. I have just spoken to the Duty Inspector at Cromer who informs me that the man suspected of being involved in the attack of Constable Fisher has just walked free from the station, under direct instructions issued by you. Now, is this true?"

Alan waited a few seconds, swallowed hard and quietly replied, "The Duty Inspector is correct sir. I decided not to move on Stolland at this time."

"Not to move on him at this time? Man, you had him locked up. What better time do you want? Tell me that!"

"I feel we would achieve more by having the man outside. He'd be no use to us decorating a cell in Cromer."

"I take it he is being followed? Tell me he is!" The Chief Constable was grasping for the straw marked survival.

"Well sir," Alan began, "at this very moment, he's in an area car being given a lift back to Blakeney. It's my belief," said Alan crossing his fingers, "he will want to board the boat he's leased."

"And if he damn well doesn't," barked David, "answer me that." The Chief was definitely feeling the draft. His dreams of a retirement knighthood were turning to ashes.

"Sir, I've every reason to believe the man is on his way here now. I don't want to tip my hand until I am good and ready to lock him up. By letting him have a free run, he will assume we are not in possession of evidence, just suspicions. It's my guess he'll either try to move that evidence or destroy it. He's no stranger to the law and he most certainly isn't a fool."

"If he's, as you say, no fool, then all the more reason to secure the evidence that came to your hand. Listen to me Alan, the first thing he'll do will be to destroy what evidence you had. If you've been fool enough to leave that slip of paper on the Linnet, he will destroy it the first chance he gets. You can say goodbye to that for sure."

"We don't intend," Alan continued quietly, "to give him the opportunity to destroy anything. Besides, if he intended to destroy that particular piece of paper, he would have already done so. For some reason, he wanted that scrap of paper intact, and us sniffing for it. As I'm in charge of this investigation...."

"For the moment!" Interrupted David.

Alan chose to ignore the threat, "As I am in charge of this case, and I accept I am, I'm willing to take that particular risk."

David Long took a deep breath, "Now listen carefully to me Alan, we've been friends for many years, but I have a number of influential people who are starting to look at me sideways. Whatever you are up to, make damned sure it's watertight. I don't want a smart suited barrister getting promotion and a fat fee out of the Norfolk Constabulary. Do I make myself crystal clear?"

"As usual, you have left me in no doubt, sir." Alan replaced the receiver, uncrossed his fingers, loosened his collar and returned to the service room.

Charlie looked up as he entered, "Everything okay, as usual?"

"Oh, yes," said Alan, "Just as you would expect it to be." He had no sooner said this when he was again summoned to the telephone. Alan's return to the service room the second time was a quieter affair.

Charlie watched him come through the door, draw up a chair and sit, slowly shaking his head in disbelief.

"Now what's happened?"

"It seems that, as calm as you like, our plausible friend told the car crew to drop him in Sherringham. Said he wanted to organise some bits from the shops and that he would probably have a pint, then continue on to Blakeney by bus. The crew's reason, excuse call it what you will, was they were simply detailed to transport a male passenger home to Blakeney. So thinking it was okay, they dropped him. They even made sure he had the fare for the onward trip! That was about half an hour ago."

Charlie sat stunned for a moment, "Let's get onto control and have that car directed back to Sherringham to grab him."

"Too late," said Alan, "I've already done that, but Stolland has disappeared. A train left Sherringham shortly after they dropped him. He may be on it, he may not. In any case, everything that moves will be searched. The bus station's getting a visit, etc., etc. Right now, all we can do is let everyone else run around. At least we have a good description and that plaster-cast sticks out like a sore thumb."

"What are we going to do, sit on our thumbs?"

"Have patience, Charlie. He may be up to something right now, but I have a strong feeling he will want to arrive without being driven down to the quay in a marked police vehicle. So we sit tight and hope David's telephone is defective. One thing I'm not about to do is lose sight of that boat. He'll be back."

Lunch was delivered on two trays and just after, at 4pm, tea arrived. They were just thinking about ordering dinner when Charlie called Alan to the window. A taxi had appeared on the quay. Stolland took his time getting out. By the time both of his feet were on the pavement, Charlie was out the door and making for the stairs. He called over his shoulder, "We'll want to know where he picked up our friend."

Alan continued to watch Stolland, who gave every impression of being in no hurry. His general demeanour gave nothing away, but his eyes were everywhere. He made sure no one was particularly interested in him before paying the driver. He then very slowly made his way across the quay to where The Linnet's tender was secured. He was obviously suffering some acute discomfort because it took him an age to untie the line and get aboard. A number of people offered to help, but their repeated offers were met with a polite smile and shake of the head.

He watched Stolland struggle to paddle the dinghy away from the steps, using a one armed sculling motion. Somehow he drove the tender forward, occasionally turning his head as if looking for someone or something on the quay.

Having made it to The Linnet, Stolland took an age to secure the dinghy and clamber aboard. After another good look back towards the quay, he went below.

Alan found himself grudgingly admiring the persistence, doggedness and pure tenacity displayed by Stolland. Whatever was driving him on, it certainly took courage.

Charlie was back in the room well before Stolland had made it a quarter of the way along the channel. Alan ignored him until he saw Stolland go below, it was only then he turned to Charlie.

"That cab was flagged down not far from Cromer railway station just under an hour ago. There were no stops, other than traffic, between there and here."

"Was there any conversation?"

"No," replied Charlie, "He was as quiet as the grave. The driver said he looked badly beaten up, worn out."

"Did the driver mention anything about being alerted to people of Stolland's description by the police?"

"Yes, he received the usual visit, but a fare is a fare. He intended dropping into the station as soon as he got back to Cromer."

"That was very public spirited of him."

The evening parade of strollers along the quay began. Hotel guests, expectantly looking forward to dinner, shared the evening air with those preferring fish and chips from newspaper. Every one of them possibly dreaming of owning one of the boats that swung at moorings.

Alan trained his binoculars on The Linnet for the hundredth time. She was now showing a light in the saloon. Alan switched the binoculars to the quay.

Pedestrians parted as another taxi defied signs limiting vehicular access, manoeuvred its way onto the very edge of the quayside. The passenger chose to remain seated. With the binoculars, Alan clearly saw the side of the man's head. He appeared to be staring out along the Channel. Not as someone might who was simply admiring the view. This was the fixed, steadfast concentration of a hunter watching his prey.

Alan sensed something was about to happen, "Charlie, get down and see what you can make of the passenger in the taxi. We may have found someone else who has an interest in Stolland. You never know, it could be his nemesis making a house call."

Alan continued to watch. The passenger got out, said something to the driver and raised a pair of binoculars. He seemed to be looking directly towards The Linnet. To steady the view through the glasses, he leant his elbows on the quay handrail. He adjusted them once or twice then lowered them slowly. He walked further along the quay, eyes firmly on The Linnet.

Training the binoculars once again, he seemed to grow twitchy. He edged further, another yard or so, as if to remove an obstruction from his line of vision. This new position seemed to be more to his liking. Quite a few people were now between him and the waiting taxi. Alan saw Charlie, appear, jacket off, sleeves rolled up and obviously enjoying his Norfolk holiday.

Charlie strolled or rather rolled up to the taxi and placed one hand on the driver's door, as if to steady himself, "Good evening driver sir, any chance of you taking me to Wells Caravan Park?"

The driver looked at him smiling, "Sorry my old pal, I can't, I'm booked and my fare's going back to Cromer."

Charlie tried again, "Won't take more than half an hour, I'll make it very worth your while." As he said this, he took out his cigarettes and offered one to the driver.

"Sorry pal, honest, if I could I would, but this guy has already paid me best part of the fare and as I said, I'm booked solid."

Charlie gave the driver a big beery grin, "It's okay old mate. I understand perfectly. Looks as though you've got yourself a travelling tourist, interested in the birds is he?"

The driver looked around as though trying to spot his fare and then grinned at Charlie, "Certainly had a grand tour of Cromer before we started for here, but it's the first time he's used those binoculars of his. Still money is money and the clock's still running."

"And quite right you are sir," burped Charlie, "would you kindly give me one of your cards so I can give you a buzz if I get stuck?"

The driver reached down to the carpet on the passenger side. "Here, you might as well have this one. My passenger took it and then dropped it on the floor, obviously doesn't want it."

Holding the card by its outside edges, high in the air, Charlie put on a slight wobble as he waved an exaggerated farewell to the driver. His imitation of a man who's the better side of a few beers was professional.

Shortly after this, the fare returned to the taxi. With a last long look across to The Linnet, the passenger climbed in and the taxi drove off.

Alan smiled as Charlie re-entered the service room.

Charlie laughed, "Well, we can now get hold of that driver and find out exactly what our little friend was up to. With any luck, we should have a few prints on this card. It's the cigarette card type, laminated, so we might get lucky."

Alan took the card carefully by its edges and placed it in an envelope, "You never know Charlie, you just never know."

George Wright was busy on the boring routine of police work. He had completed a Crime Report covering the larceny of one child's bicycle, from outside a cottage in Kelling. He clipped the papers together and placed them in a despatch envelope. The area car from Cromer would collect it on the usual mail run in the morning. He kept telling himself that such mundane tasks had to be done. His thoughts repeatedly returned to Clare Brandon. No matter how he tried, it wasn't easy to forget her smile, or that her father was unfortunately one of his police bosses. Day dreaming didn't help when there were cattle movement licenses and notifications to be served, plus gypsy camps to visit. He didn't mind them. Providing they kept their hands off other people's property, like chickens, eggs and such.

He picked up an envelope, stamped it and was about to put it on the mail shelf, when his thoughts sprang back to Clare. He shook his head and dropped the envelope onto the shelf.

The phone rang. He wasn't in a rush to answer. It wouldn't do to give the impression he was sitting waiting for a call. He slowly counted to ten then reached for the phone, "Police house, Kelling, Constable Wright speaking." He had to be careful, it could be the Duty Inspector on the other end of the line.

"Hello, Mr Wright, it's Clare Brandon."

George almost dropped the receiver. He drew a chair rapidly from under the desk and sat down. "Miss Brandon, well what a pleasant surprise. Now, what can I do for you?" He hoped he sounded calm, in total control, but felt far from relaxed!

"Actually George, there are four reasons for my call. One, I wish you would accept I am a grown woman and a very happy medical student, hoping one day to be a qualified MD to boot. Two, I want you to stop talking to me as though I am a child and you are my father's age. Three, I want you to take me to a rather special dance in Cambridge next month," George's throat went dry, "And finally, why was it, when my mother and I visited Miss Braithwaite. You know, she's the telephone operator at Cley Post Office. Well, she told us a woman had answered your telephone, when she called you about Mr Fisher?"

There was no immediate reply.

"George, are you there, George?"

George gripped the desktop. He felt as nervous as when he had first given evidence in court. "Yes. On your first point Miss Brandon,"

Clare broke in, "Now George, please listen to me, my name is Clare understand? – it's 'Clare.' I am studying to be a doctor and I'm telling you I am the tonic you need to brighten your plodding life."

George mumbled, "But your father's a senior police officer and I'm not so sure he'd be too keen about us being out together. Second, the lady who answered the phone was my neighbour's wife, Mrs Mills, who's just turned sixty. She covers the phone when I'm out. At no expense to the county, I might add."

George swallowed hard. It was all coming out wrong. Why could he live through battles and face up to what that meant, but crumble when Clare was near him? There was silence at the other end. He immediately regretted what he'd said and how it must have sounded.

"George, I accept you are wonderfully shy and if I wait for you to make the first move I'll be grey haired. I do understand, really I do, but I want us to be more than just acquaintances. Couldn't you forget who my father is and think only of us as special friends. Okay? Oh, and thank you so much for agreeing to take me to the dance. You did, didn't you?"

George was trying so hard to do the right thing, "I'm not so sure Clare, what with covering Fred's patch and other duties etc."

Clare laughed and said, "Dear George, I'll drive over to Kelling this weekend and we can go for a walk, or just talk. If you like, I'll bring my mother as escort."

"Look Clare, I'm sure your mother is very nice, but would you mind if we talk alone first, certainly before your father gets to know about us."

The phone clicked and the dialling tone returned. George suddenly felt sick. He placed the receiver back on its cradle, got up and walked into the kitchen, punching the door as he went. He had never been good with girls. Since being shipped home and his eventual release from the forces, he'd not had time to adjust to female company. He was tongue-tied around girls, out of his depth. This was especially so with Clare. He knew she was way out of his league.

He'd concentrated on his career rather than worrying about girls. George had no idea what to say, how to treat them. It was okay for Clare, she had all those chaps milling around her at medical school. George came from a different background. No education to speak of. He'd been reasonably happy until Clare had appeared and smiled at him. He knew she could never really be serious about him. In any case, she wouldn't want to arrive at the dance on the pillion of his motorbike. He had to smile at the thought. The phone rang again, without thinking he went straight at it.

"Clare, I'm sorry…." He got no further.

Although the caller's surname was Brandon, it wasn't Clare. It was Detective Chief Superintendent Brandon, "That you Wright, what on earth's going on?"

The trap door opened and he fell through, "Yes sir, sorry sir, I was in the…." Again he got no further.

"Look Wright, get on that motorbike of yours and get down here to the Harding's Hotel. And Wright, don't come in uniform and don't hang around the Reception area. Come straight up to the Service room on the second floor, and make it sharp!" The line went dead. But this time, the silence was ominous.

While quickly changing into the only decent civilian suit he had, he mulled over his latest conversation. Could Clare have had time to ring her father about him? Complain at his off-hand manner? No way. She wouldn't do that. Would she? Hurt daughter and all that?

George pulled up some 30 yards away from the hotel. He wanted to rehearse again what he was going to say. His off duty time was his, to use as he pleased. This wasn't the army. It was not a police matter. He didn't feel it right that Clare should run to her father when previous to her call, George had never said a word to encourage her. He admitted to himself that he'd smiled, but that was polite. He had to admit to thoughts, some of them very romantic, but he had always recognised the social differences in their worlds and shown the respect he felt was right. Then, he remembered what Clare had said about them being special friends. Suddenly he felt much better about things. Clare must have feelings for him. She hadn't said so outright, but she had said 'special friends'.

George was now in a frame of mind to face the DCS. Or perhaps leave the job and re-enlist?

He braced himself as he made his way to the second floor service room. As he reached the door, it was opened and a waiter came out carrying a tray stacked with jugs and coffee cups.

"Ah, there you are, Wright." Alan was now framed in the door. He waved a hand ushering George quickly inside, "Don't stand there decorating the corridor, don't want the natives to know we've a cupboard full of crushers nesting in their building. You know Sergeant Friar."

The welcome was rushed but friendly. George relaxed a fraction. Obviously the DCS would not discuss his daughter in front of another policeman. Or would he?

Alan had decided to bring in reinforcements in the form of George Wright, just in case he had to split from

Charlie. His intuition was right. A few minutes after George's arrival, Charlie drew Alan's attention to the window, "He's on the move again, sir."

Alan crossed to the window, where Charlie handed him the binoculars. He trained them on The Linnet. The saloon light was out and a shadowy figure was in the dinghy, making an erratic course for the quay. It wasn't until the tender was tied to the quay that Alan was absolutely sure it was Stolland. Still struggling, he hauled himself up the vertical ladder, demonstrating some strength and a great deal of determination. He crossed toward the hotel.

"Wright," Alan said, "Get your body down to the Reception area. Find out what he's up to and for Pete's sake don't let him cotton on to you. Let me know the second he makes a move."

George was back in the Service Room in no more than three minutes, "He's asked for a taxi sir. It's due to pick him up in five minutes, by the main doors. He's no luggage so it seems he can't be going far."

Alan thought for a second, "Charlie, take my car. Follow that cab and don't let him lose you. Find out what he's up to."

He turned to George, "You and I are going to pay a visit to The Linnet to find that map of Fred Fisher's. Let's hope it's still there. If it's gone, I'll have some explaining to do. Charlie, try your best to let me know, via the Information Room, where you are and what's going on. We should be back from The Linnet in two hours. If the worst happens, we'll get ashore to Markham's cottage, on the point. We'll let the dinghy drift from the point. You never know, Stolland may believe it slipped its mooring," he added, "With luck!"

Charlie stood for a moment, "That's mud out there sir, people can get caught in it, up to their necks and beyond."

Alan looked at Charlie, then to George, "Don't worry about us. Wright's military record says he's no stranger to a little night manoeuvres on foreign shores. I'm sure we'll survive the odd ducking. Just you hang on to Stolland. Now get on your way."

Charlie lit a cigarette and smiling at George, went out the door.

Alan turned to George, "Now, Wright, I believe you and I have some pressing business to sort out." George's self-assurance plummeted. "Let's stroll down to the quay, borrow that dinghy as though we own it, and pay that visit to the good ship, Linnet."

George relaxed as they walked onto the quay, "It's not a ship sir."

"What is not a ship, sir?"

"The Linnet, sir, it's a boat. You see, you can put a boat on a ship but not a ship on a boat. That's how you can tell the difference...sir."

Alan slipped the mooring as George settled at the oars, "For God's sake Wright, relax a little. I'm sure what you've said is correct and I shall benefit from your nautical advice, but right now, let's just enjoy the water sports. You're not committing a felony or going to your execution. We're doing a little night snooping, like the excise men did in these parts years ago. Now let's paddle."

For the second time, a fine mist made the night passage along the channel somewhat forbidding. Its presence seemed to amplify every little sound.

Alan whispered, "Just the night for a spot of piracy, eh, Wright?" "It's wrecking I'm more worried about sir," whispered George, heavily engaged at the oars.

He let the thought of what they were doing run through his mind. It was not what he imagined honest police work to be. At Police College, they never taught boarding and taking over boats in the still of the night, but neither had he ever envisaged carrying out piracy with a DCS acting as Blackbeard.

Not another word was said as they approached The Linnet. She had swung round, bows on to the tidal flow that hadn't quite reached slack water. She now pointed directly toward the distant quay. This allowed them to pass alongside and under her stern, to board directly into the

146

cockpit, without anyone on the shore side, seeing them. Not that discovery was likely, in view of the mist that increased and hung like damp washing on a line.

A fitful moon peeped occasionally through high cloud and layers of mist, spinning threads of bright light along the surface of the channel. For some reason, George shivered. He was not a natural sailor. In fact, that's why he had volunteered for special operations, becoming a brown job. However, the more he thought of getting seaborne, the more he liked it.

With the dinghy secured under the stern, the two men moved through the cockpit to the hatch. Although Alan had borrowed the magic tool from Charlie, it was found to be surplus to requirements. The lock was unfastened.

This fact disturbed Alan slightly, but he assumed Stolland must have had other things on his mind when he went ashore. They descended into the gloom of the saloon.

Alan told George to keep a watch toward the quay, while he made straight for the locker, which held the charts and papers. They were all there, including the one that Fred Fisher had drawn. Relieved, Alan slipped the paper into his pocket, returning the others to the locker. He had just moved to continue a more thorough rummage, when he felt a hand on his arm.

George leant very close and whispered, "Sir, listen."

It was difficult at first for Alan to hear the sound that had alerted George. At first all he could hear was slapping water and the creak of shifting timbers. After a few seconds, he did pick up a different sound. It was soft and regular, something like regular breathing. Whatever it was drew slowly nearer. He began to recognise the sound of muffled oars, carefully used and approaching from the direction of the quay.

"Could be Stolland," Alan whispered, "We'll stay below, not to frighten him off. If it's not Stolland, then it's my guess, whoever it is, they're counting on him being asleep."

They felt, more than heard a small boat rub alongside The Linnet. It worked its way gradually aft. Then, decking creaked as weight was transferred along the line of the deck. Their visitor was making his way, as quietly as possible, along the deck toward the bows. This would place him above the forward sleeping accommodation.

Alan watched as George, careful not to make a sound, edged his way onto the starboard locker that doubled as a single bunk. Occasional moonlight suddenly gave him a restricted view of that side of the deck. Fortunately, the glass of a cabin light had heavy protective wooden slats over it, preventing whoever it was from seeing straight down into the saloon. George remained perfectly still, his face set. Alan went to whisper. George raised a finger to his lips. The look he gave Alan was a simple, 'quiet!'

It was impossible to say what the visitor was doing, but he wasn't at it long. The first hint of movement was when George saw the faint hint of a shadow reach along the deck towards him. Under his breath he thanked the fitful moon for choosing that moment to provide some light. He ducked to one side, pressing himself against the bulkhead.

He picked up the soft sounds of the visitor retreating towards the cockpit. Some faint scratching around the hatch cover followed this movement. George took a chance and had another look. He now had a clearer view and was in time to see their visitor sliding over the counter into what, he assumed, was his transport. Seconds later, the distinct sound of straining oars in rowlocks filtered through.

This time there seemed a sense of urgency in their use. Certainly the user had increased his stroke rate. In the dimness of the saloon, Alan looked across at George. When he first saw him moving, he was going to stop him, but quickly realised this young lad seemed to be in his element. It hadn't been the first time he'd waited to give someone a nasty surprise. Alan didn't raise an eyebrow when George all-but told him to keep quiet.

George climbed off the locker, "It couldn't have been Stolland sir. Too short and he really was a lightweight. As he passed by, the only part I clearly saw was his shoes. Not the type I would have worn for a raiding party, more the expensive office type."

Alan relaxed, "At least he didn't try to get below. So why did he come aboard? What was he up to on deck?" He signalled for George to follow and made his way aft, to the hatch.

He tried to slide it back. It wouldn't budge. He tried again. It wouldn't give an inch.

"I think our visitor has bolted us in."

George made his way quickly forward, into the sleeping space. The forward hatch also seemed bolted from above.

"Looks as though our little caller had no intention of being pursued?"

Alan agreed and tried the aft hatch again, "It's no use, Wright. Have a quick look for an alternative."

Their combined efforts only showed that whoever built the Linnet, made an excellent job. Apart from the two accommodation hatches, and narrow upper casements over the saloon, the rest was solid timber. George tried the casements. Normally these were ratcheted up in fine weather, to allow air to the lower deck. When closed, they were pitched at an angle and designed to allow water to run off. It was obvious Stolland had securely dogged these down. They both sat to consider what action they could take.

"Well," said Alan, "here's a fine thing. What do you think Nelson would have done in a situation like this?"

George smiled, "Possibly put his telescope to the other eye?"

Alan laughed, "Quite possibly."

George went back into the sleeping compartment. Going right forward to the bulkhead, he tried to find whether there was access into the bow sail-storage locker. There didn't appear to be. He was about to return to the saloon when he heard a noise. He looked around the bulkheads. Then shook his head and listened again. Moving onto a side-locker, he pressed his ear to the frame of the casement. There was distinct ticking, something like a clock? A clock sited on deck?

He listened again, putting his hand up to stop the D.C.S., who was moving slowly towards him. George moved away from the locker, "Don't quote me on this sir, it's only an opinion, but I think we may have a device on the main deck that's ticking."

"You mean a bomb?" Alan said calmly.

George looked toward the forward space, "That's just my opinion sir, I can't see it, but, under these circumstances, I wouldn't like to bet it isn't."

They both moved back into the saloon. Stumbling around in the half-light, they searched for something to help open the hatch. They found the two sets of brass mounts, obviously designed to hold the axes for just such an event. But strangely, the axes had been neatly removed. George climbed to the head of the companionway, just beneath the cockpit hatch. Grasping hold of the brass handrail, either side of the ladder, he swung his legs up with all his strength and smashed at the cover with his feet. George was no lightweight and he was very fit. It took all of ten attempts before the hatch suddenly gave. With a splintering crack their exit was assured.

"Sorry about the damage, but I think it's important we get at whatever is ticking."

Alan followed George up the now cleared companionway.

Snugly placed alongside the forward casement was a small canvas bag. George knelt, undid the tie fastening and looked inside. One look was enough for George. He knew a bomb when he saw it, even if it was of the home made variety. This one was very much alive and ticking.

Alan cleared his throat and whispered over George's shoulder, "Explosives are more in your line. What exactly have we got?"

150

George carefully got to his feet, "Well, not to mince words, we have enough eight-oh-eight to blow us and this boat to the other side of Wells."

"For Christ's sake," Alan said, "what's this eight something?"

"Plastic explosive, connected to a detonator which, in turn is attached to a neatly wired battery and adapted alarm clock. Amateurish but classically effective."

Alan was amazed how calm George was. He thought for a second, "Can you disarm it, or perhaps make it safe enough for us to move it?"

George knelt and began to look closely at the device, "I'd say our donor left about enough time to get himself safely ashore. Pound to a penny, he's watching the boat right now," George said this without raising his eyes from the device, "these types like to watch the results of their handiwork."

Very gently, he turned the device so he could clearly see the wiring. More to himself than to Alan, he whispered, "Ordinary clipped motor wiring connections available from any garage. Crude but neat little job."

The hour hand was missing. Then George's eyes fastened onto a terminal neatly soldered to the end of the minute hand. This hand was about to reach the vertical, where another terminal sat waiting to complete the circuit.

Without warning and all in one rising movement, George grabbed the bag, throwing his weight backwards against Alan, knocking him clean off his feet back and down into the well deck. George continued the movement, thrusting upwards. All his energy now dedicated to a round flat swing, at the top of which he launched the bag into the air, as far away from the boat as he could.

The device had just cleared the safety-rail when, for what seemed a split second, both men saw white light and felt a searing, suffocating heat.

Roger Markham was standing outside his cottage on Blakeney Point, taking a last look round, when he heard a series of sharp bangs and splintering wood. He guessed

151

someone was breaking into a boat. Unfortunately, thefts from boats were not uncommon, even in the remote estuaries and marshes of Norfolk. He lost no time in getting to his dinghy and striking out for the nearest moored boat, which was The Linnet.

He was within a yard of her port side when an explosion occurred. He saw a vivid flash, felt heat, and a great orange ball appeared to rise into the air from the starboard side of the hull.

The explosion lit up the whole channel around him. Though stunned, he quickly regained his senses, ignoring what he took to be small flaming debris striking the water all round him. Roger turned the dinghy and rowed hard for the starboard side. He rounded The Linnet, to find her hull, above the water line, partially blown away. She was listing slightly and some of the upper timbers and rigging were burning. Tiny shreds of flaming canvas floated in the air like spinning fireflies, these spiralling down, all around him hissing and spitting as they fell into the water.

Roger felt caught in a nightmare. The thought flashed through his mind that had the explosion occurred on the port side, he would not have survived to tell the tale. He rested the oars and cupping his hands to his mouth began shouting. He called out, a number of times, trying to establish if anyone was aboard.

Alan, blown by the force of the explosion, found himself lying in the cockpit, flat on his back with small pieces of burning material raining down all around him. After what seemed seconds, he heard Roger's voice and called back.

He felt stupidly helpless, like a child. He was finding it difficult to regulate his breathing or get to his feet. Rapid shallow breaths were all he could manage. He tried a number of times to rise. Though his mind was willing, his body refused to cooperate. He called out, as best he could, hoping George Wright would answer, but it was Roger's voice that came back.

Roger appeared over the stern rail. He quickly crossed to Alan and helped him sit up. At the same time he stared around him, aghast at the utter confusion. He knew the Linnet and how well she was kept. Now she seemed little more than a wreck. All he could say weakly was, "My God, Superintendent, what are you doing here. What's happened?"

Alan who was trying to control his shaking body, pointed to what had so recently been the pristine foredeck, "Roger, please check on young George Wright. I think he took the full blast. Please find him, help him. I'm okay. Just a little shaken."

Leaving Alan, Roger looked forward along what had once been the faultless starboard side. There was little left, except charred and burning timber. He turned to look back, his eyes meeting Alan's. There was little point in stating the obvious. The night that had immediately turned black after the brightness of the initial flash, now seemed filled with engine noises and beams from power lights.

They closed on The Linnet through drifting mist and smoke. Alan sat in the cockpit on a side locker, with his head in his hands trying to stop shaking and ease the pain in his ears. Eager hands reached out and strong arms lifted him from The Linnet.

He wasn't sure what was happening and before he was able to get half his mind working, the same strong hands were lifting him onto the quay.

Crowds of people pressed in around him. There was noise, a jumble of voices, none of which made any sense. Time slipped for Alan as he tried to reach out and stop it. If only he could get hold of something that wasn't spinning, allow him to grasp what had happened, what was going on. Whose were the hands that held him? His thoughts swam down into the sickening blackness again.

Charlie had been on the coast road on his way back from Cromer, when ahead of him to the North-West, he saw a massive flash. This had died to a red glow before the noise came. A low rumble, that reminded him of the blitz in London. That, he thought, was no firework. He pushed the throttle to the floor. He knew before he reached the outskirts of Blakeney that whatever had exploded, had been close. Charlie had to slow the car to a crawl as he drove into the town. There were so many people heading down toward the quay, he was forced to thread his way through them. Some were running, while others simply stood at cottage doors, talking quietly. Everyone, without exception, was looking towards the quay and the pulsating glow in the sky.

As he crept along, the people in front of him suddenly parted. A car emerged driving up from the quay. At first Charlie assumed it was an ambulance, then he realised it was a taxi. It passed slowly by, equally hampered by the surging crowd. He recognised the driver. It was the same chap he'd spoken to and accepted the card from earlier in the day. The driver looked almost frightened, certainly less happy than he had been at their previous meeting. He looked directly at Charlie with a glance of half recognition. Charlie's eyes buttoned on the passenger, who was speaking sharply to the driver and half covering his face. The driver, reacting to what his passenger said, looked straight ahead and drove on.

Charlie turned to watch, but the passenger kept his head facing the way they were going. Charlie had no chance of seeing his full face. However, there was no doubt in Charlie's mind. He was sure it was the same man he'd seen paying a lot of attention to The Linnet earlier.

He recalled the conversation with the taxi driver. He'd said the passenger was booked to return to Cromer. Charlie had seen them start on that journey about an hour or so before he went off to follow Stolland. This rattled Charlie. He was in two minds whether to turn the car round and stop the taxi, but thought better of it. That driver wasn't likely to forget a fare that yanked him backwards and forwards from Cromer twice, then placed him close to an explosion.

It was impossible to get near the hotel car park, so Charlie abandoned the car, pressing forward on foot through the crowds. A group of men were carrying someone on a makeshift stretcher, up the steps of the hotel.

Charlie had a nasty feeling in the pit of his stomach. He started to run.

Alan still couldn't focus his eyes properly but reacted when he heard Charlie's voice. He grabbed for his hand and pulled him close, "Charlie, someone blew up The Linnet while we were on it. Young George Wright saved my life. He's still out there somewhere. Find that boy Charlie. He's probably still in the water." Alan's voice weakened. His hand dropping from Charlie's grasp as he descended once again into the familiar dark pool.

Charlie's head was crammed full of doubts and questions. He desperately needed to get answers but knew he must locate George. Before leaving the hotel, he grabbed a telephone. It took barely five minutes to brief the Duty Inspector at Cromer. The sketchy briefing included setting up an incident room, briefing senior officers, describing the taxi to be located and occupants arrested for being involved in the incident at Blakeney. Also adding the fact that George Wright was missing and DCS Brandon was injured and en-route to Cromer hospital. Charlie sweated blood as he hoped he'd covered all the bases, but knew he was a long way short on detail and time. He still had no idea what had actually taken place out there on The Linnet. Certain facts were immediately obvious, but fine-detail was as hard to come by as hen's teeth. The hotel manager was his brilliant self, already setting a small lounge aside for Police and Emergency Service use.

Charlie made for the quay where he found a boatman waiting to take him out to The Linnet. The trip out was every bit as bad as driving down through the street to the hotel. The channel seemed packed with small craft of every description, searching like mad for George. Crews seemed to be using every sort of lamp to create white pools of light on the surface. Each light probing shadows or penetrating what remained of the shreds of mist, obviously in an effort to get George out of the water. Fortunately, Charlie's skipper spotted the Wells lifeboat and immediately made for her. The RNLI Coxswain was able to brief Charlie on the search of The Linnet.

Just one injured person had been found aboard, who had been removed to the shore. Charlie didn't stop him but knew he was talking about Alan. Roger Markham and some other lads had been on The Linnet dealing with the fire.

The lifeboat crew intended to run the Linnet up the Channel to the quay and tie her alongside as soon as it was light. Charlie could see shadows of men working aboard the Linnet, making the last efforts to contain the few remaining hot spots.

She was still afloat, though listing to starboard. The hull was blackened and torn. He found himself wondering how anyone could have survived such a blast.

Charlie shuddered as he looked down into the dark swirling water. He was no sailor. In fact the slight roll of the boat as it kept station alongside the Wells lifeboat was enough to remind Charlie that he was more at home on shore than on water.

Faint radio static from the bridge of the lifeboat was interrupted and the Coxswain of the Cromer lifeboat reported that he was making slow progress, searching along the seaward side of the bank toward Blakeney Point.

Charlie immediately thought this search a total waste of time. It was unlikely that George would be carried out of the Blakeney Channel and round the Point.

The Wells Coxswain read his mind, "Best let the Cromer boat do that check on his way to us. Save a crew searching out there later. There's plenty of boats bobbing around here to find him if he's to be found."

Charlie waved his thanks as they separated from the lifeboat.

Searchlights continued to knit a pattern across the water, striking and lingering on the Morston Salt Marsh that formed part of the south western boundary of the harbour.

Charlie knew what a job they had on their hands, searching every inch, let alone the entrance to the Cley Channel. Deep inside, he knew it was an impossible job in darkness, even with the occasional help of the moon and searchlights. His mind lingered on George, the man. Never one to push himself forward, quiet, almost reserved and yet a first class copper. He knew he had come through some terrible times in the forces only to end up somewhere out there.

Charlie found himself saying, "Don't fret Georgie boy, we'll find you, take care of you and then we'll find the filth that did it!"

The skipper of his boat thrust a lantern into Charlie's hand. "Don't you worry yourself friend, these lads know what they're doing and they won't give up until your man's found."

Charlie seemed to have trouble finding words to reply. He smiled and switched on the lantern as the boat swung down the Channel. They too were now joining the search.

Chapter Nine

The telephone rang. Grace hadn't been in a restful sleep. She never slept well when Alan was out of the house and a call was always half expected. "Mrs Brandon?" Before the caller had chance to say another word, Grace knew the meaning of the thoughts that had been crowding in, defying her efforts to sleep.

"Please don't be alarmed, your husband is fine," the female voice said, "but he has been taken to Cromer hospital for a routine check. He was involved in an incident at Blakeney," she paused, getting no response, she continued, "perhaps you would like to visit him? We have a car on the way to you now. Please, Mrs Brandon, believe me, your husband really is fine and in fact, forbade us to notify you. I'm sure he will forgive us for not doing what we thought was right."

Calming her mounting fears, Grace found her voice and thanked the caller. She was aware of the awful task undertaken by those who had to deliver what the police service call 'agony' messages.

She quickly washed, put a comb through her hair, added a spot of make-up, dressed and was ready just as the car arrived. The drive to the hospital was an opportunity to go over and over the message she had received. It was typical of Alan to say she wasn't to be told. He had so often arrived home with bruises etc., and wouldn't offer a single word of explanation. Well, this time, she was going to have her say. He had no right to continue in a service where she was constantly at her wit's end. Countless nights, wondering what danger he was in, or where he was.

It really was all too much. He was to retire and she was in the right frame of mind to tell him so.

It was high time to put an end to his playing this childish game of cops and robbers. She wiped her eyes with a handkerchief and braced herself.

When she was shown into the room where Alan was, she crossed over to the bed where he lay smiling at her, "My darling Grace, I expressly told them you weren't to be worried. They've finished their checks and I'm one hundred percent fit."

"You have no right to decide what I shall or shall not know. One thing for sure, you are on your very last case. It's not as though you haven't other police officers capable of doing whatever it is you were up to. But no, delegation is something you know little about. You must do everything yourself. No one else can be trusted. You always have to lead from the front."

Alan took Grace in his arms, looked over her shoulder, at the doctor and winked, "Of course my dear, now if you will help me get ready, we can be off home."

Grace jerked away, "Don't you dare patronise me, Alan Brandon. If you knew just how many times I have sat up, waiting for you to come home, only to see you limp in saying nothing had happened, everything was fine. Well, I won't take any more of your damned agony messages." The anger in her words reflecting the agony and relief she felt.

Alan took hold of her hands, "Darling Grace, I promise I will do whatever it is to please you. Can we now please go home? I think I could do with a couple of hours sleep before I speak to David Long."

Grace remained resolute, "Promise me right now you will consider retirement, or at the very least, get David to give you a nice desk job?"

"Now come on old girl, would you like me under your feet all day every day? You are a professional concert pianist. Have I ever asked you not to rehearse or go off and play at a particular concert?"

When they arrived home, Alan spent some time on the telephone in his study. When he finished, he joined Grace in the kitchen, where she had tea waiting. He told her some of what had occurred at Blakeney, leaving the business of George Wright to last.

He didn't provide details of the explosion but told Grace that George Wright deliberately shielded him from the worst and, as a result, had taken the brunt of it, probably ending up in the water. He quickly assured her that a thorough search was taking place and he was sure that everything would be all right. Not for the first time, his words sounded hollow and although her eyes continually searched for his, he avoided the contact.

Grace held her cup very tightly, "Alan, you do realise that our daughter has special feelings for George Wright?"

Alan reached for the sugar. By doing this Grace knew he was rattled. He didn't take sugar with coffee and was doing his best to stop taking it with his tea. She watched as he slowly put three heaped spoonfuls into his cup.

"Oh come on Grace, you know what young women are like. She's young, still a medical student, infatuated by a handsome young man that's caught her eye. I don't think it's serious.

"You don't think she's serious?"

"Bless you no. Besides Grace, it wouldn't be practical. He's fresh out of the army, no immediate prospects to speak of, she's at medical school. I'd say you are reading far too much into this."

Grace stood for a minute just staring at him, "Oh, I see," she said slowly, "and I suppose I was not serious, just besotted, smitten or fixated when you were just a very young constable, with no immediate prospects and I married you? Is that what you truly think?"

Alan rose from the table, crossed the room and leant against the sink, with his back to her, "What I'm trying hard to say is…that boy may be already dead. He's still missing and the last I saw of him was just a blurred shadow in the centre of a flash," he turned to her, agony showing in his face, "Grace, please, he may not have survived. Should we at least wait before we... ?"

Grace rose from the table and reached out for his hands. "No my dear," she spoke softly, "I'm putting myself in Clare's place when she hears on the radio, that the person she cares about is missing," she slid her arms around him and hugged him close, "I want to give her the choice as to what action she wants to take."

"Look Grace, I think we should wait until, well, at least until we know one way or the other. I promise it will be easier on everyone."

"And who will it be easier on, Alan, you, me, David Long, Charlie, Fred Fisher? It's Clare we have to think of. It may look to you as if I'm an anxious mother clucking around my chick, but I know what she will feel when she finds out. I've seen the looks she gives him. Clare loves that boy," Alan tried to interrupt, "no, trust me Alan, I'm her mother and I say she loves him. He may not realise it yet, but she does and she is going to be very hurt if we don't give her the right to know as soon as possible."

"Okay Grace. Tell her, but please don't assume she's head over heels in love with him. She may just feel dreadfully sorry for the chap and want to help."

Grace hugged him, "You mean the way I felt sorry for you and just wanted to help you?" She smiled at Alan. She then went to the telephone.

The first hint of day on the North Norfolk coast is a special time. A grey line drawn with an artist's brush washes up from the east, cradling the dawn that creeps its way progressively in, snaking itself around shingle banks and shelving beaches, disowning the suspicious blindness of night. Sleeping seals that have rested through the darkness open their dark soulful eyes and scent the day's approach. They stretch to ease out the hardness of their lodging, seeking the energy to move. They yawn and start the shingle cascading with their lumbering slide, down the steep beach, toward the soft embrace, promised by the dark water.

Gulls, ever ready to take advantage of the promise of food, take off crying to each other, encouraging others to lift their heads from under wings and blink at the threat of weather to come.

With this dawn came a gathering of wind. It lifted itself from the grey heaving sea, collecting moisture as it travelled then, in temper threw it earthward in hard spattering blasts, as if challenging the birds to rise.

Heading into the estuary the wind grew in strength, driving before it small ripples that quickly turned to confused short waves, each one sporting its new white hat. Within the space of time it took to announce itself as a new day, waves had become steep, the sea doing its best to discourage anyone thinking of venturing outside the protection of the shingle bank.

Pulsating waves thumped home, each like a giant's footstep then withdrawing with a soft rush like sighing breath. Clawing at the shingle, the dark foaming water ran back like Neptune's children, gathering winnings from the beach. Anything loose was snatched and taken back into the deep.

Two small seals had been reluctant to join others that had ventured down and into the waves. These two snuggled closer to the larger shape that now lay between them.

A pair of black-backed gulls, uncertain of their courage, ventured close to the group. Then, as if startled, jumped into the blustery air and just as quickly returned flapping to the shingle.

They drew near the larger of the shapes and, anxious to explore their find, tentatively pecked at it. The two small seals edged away as if to make for the safety of the sea. The gulls rose up again and waited for the movement to end. Three more black backs joined their fellows, looking to share the spoils. One, larger and more adventurous than the rest, marched through the quarrelling group and fluttered onto the back of the lifeless bundle. It pecked at it, meaning to get on with the task of feeding rather than debating a pecking order.

A loud report echoed over the shingle bank. The noise of rushing feet disturbed the gulls. Another blast joined the noise of angry squawking gulls rising away from what they considered their prize.

Stones flew everywhere as a man swamped in oilskins, lumbered slowly down the shingle bank. He placed the shot gun he carried at a safe distance then knelt beside the still bundle, recently vacated by the black backed gull. Carefully he turned the bundle over. George Wright had been found.

The Coxswain of the Cromer lifeboat heard the two shots. They were faint but distinct. It sounded like the maroon distress rocket signal, always given by the RNLI, indicating a need to launch the lifeboat. Putting two and two together, he called down to the deck. He was told that the sounds appeared to come from the direction of the shingle bank forming the far Western end of Blakeney Point. No one had seen flashes so it was assumed it wasn't distress rockets. He pushed the two throttle controls forward and headed for the Point.

Through the binoculars, a man was spotted standing over what appeared to be a body. He was waving and obviously needed their help. No more than thirty minutes later, bathed in the glow of a dozen searchlights and the bleak beginning of a wet day, a yellow oil skin covered bundle was transferred from the lifeboat onto Blakeney quay.

A silent crowd watched an ambulance begin its journey to Cromer hospital. People lingered, breathed in the smell of charred timbers rising from the moored remains of The Linnet, which was safely made fast, against the quay. Guests with sleepy eyes made their way slowly back into the Harding's Hotel, tired but with heads full of the events of the night. Very few of them knew what had taken place. Others expanded on their theories over breakfast.

Grace made some more tea. Alan had tried to sleep but hadn't made the land of nod for a second. When Grace came into the bedroom, daylight had barely made its presence felt. Alan put down the phone for the tenth time.

"Any news?" She said, putting down the tray.

Alan yawned, apologised and said, "Sorry old girl. Not a word I'm afraid. Apparently the Wells and Cromer lifeboats are out searching, as well as everyone else who has a plank to float on. Charlie's still out there somewhere. Harold Crumb has organised locals to walk both banks of the Blakeney and Cley channels, and the seaward side of what you call the shingle bank. The uniformed branch has agreed that authorised people can carry a shot gun while searching."

Grace sounded alarmed, "What! Shot guns?"

Alan smiled affectionately, "Sorry, I meant to say, two shots are to be fired if anyone finds anything. It's the only way to signal from an isolated spot if you haven't flares, and most haven't."

"Why not flash torches?" Asked Grace, absent mindedly trying to put sugar in Alan's tea.

Alan spotted this and stopped her, "Because there will be so many flashing torches searching that area that no one could tell a signal light from the glow given off by some poor chap tipping end over end in the marsh. That, my girl, is why bangs make sense. If the shooter gets no response after two minutes, he fires another two, and so on until he does get help."

Grace crossed the room to look out of the window. She said, almost to herself, "Let's just hope there are no duck poachers on the marsh then."

The phone rang. It's loud insistent ringing startled them both. Alan beat Grace to the phone. It was Charlie.

"He's been found," Alan could hear more than relief in Charlie's voice, "I don't know chapter and verse but evidently he was brought ashore and transferred to hospital. Lifeboat crews dealt with it. I didn't get ashore until he was on his way to Cromer. Evidently, it's touch-and-go, but he is alive. I've let HQ and the Chief know."

Alan felt a tremendous weight lift from his shoulders.

"The chief says you are to have bed rest. You know what he's like. He means it, Alan. You relax. I'll get up there and ring you the moment I have anything definite."

The line went dead, being replaced by the constant purring signal.

For what seemed an age Alan stood holding the phone close to his ear. Painfully slowly, he tried to place the receiver onto its cradle. It took three attempts before he managed it. He couldn't say a word. His eyes had misted over. Alan tried to push emotion aside, but the young man had saved his life. He had deliberately acted to place himself between Alan and the bomb. Grace came up behind him and put her arms around his shoulders.

The phone rang immediately. Grace picked it up. It was Clare. All she said was that a woman from the Police information room had just telephoned. George was in Cromer hospital. She was crying, "What's happened to him, Mum? I can't think straight. Is he terribly hurt? No one would tell me because I'm not family. All they would say was his condition is giving grave cause for concern. I'm almost beside myself with worry."

Grace turned away from Alan hugging the phone, "Darling please, please don't worry. I'm sure everything is being done for him. Did they ask you to go to the hospital?"

"Yes, they asked me to get there as soon as I can, so I'm leaving as soon as I put the phone down. Mum, I can't lose him, can I?"

Grace was confused, "Darling, just go to him. He needs you now." Grace wanted to urge her to wait until they could collect her, but the line had gone dead.

"Well," said Alan, "it seems you were right, as always. Our little girl has grown wings. Best give Clare chance to see my saviour before we put in an appearance. Let's pray he's going to get through this. I owe that boy my life."

Grace wiped her eyes, "Oh Alan, You don't think?"

165

Alan calmed her, "If I know George Wright, he wouldn't have asked for Clare if he felt he was going to die. We don't know what condition he is in but he's young and fit, he'll come through this. I just hope he's strong enough to survive the arrival of our daughter."

Grace smiled through her tears.

Clare was ushered very quietly into an easy chair drawn close to the head of the bed. Deeply sedated, George lay flat, with no pillow. The only sound was his soft breathing. Everything looked sterile and silent. George was covered, from the waist down by a single sheet, drawn over a frame so that it didn't rest on his body.

As far as Clare could see, special yellowish burn dressings covered his upper body, including his head. There seemed to be tubes cables and monitors everywhere. There was a small space between the dressings where his lips were just visible. Clare could hear his soft regular breathing.

A woman doctor, who had been standing alongside Clare, smiled encouragingly and spoke in a hospital whisper, "You can speak to him my dear, but please don't expect much reaction. Your young man has been through rather a lot," as she said this, the doctor placed her hand lightly on Clare's shoulder, "it is possible he may not react to your voice. Don't let that stop you. He may prefer to listen, rather than rouse himself to talk."

Clare thanked her and watched the doctor leave the room. She didn't try to touch his bandaged hands, although she so much wanted to. To bring him back to her so she could explain how much she needed him.

"It's Clare, George," she said softly, "I'll be just here if you need me," her eyes filled with tears. She fought to keep the sobs out of her words. She pulled another handkerchief from the pocket of her coat and wiped her eyes, "just you sleep George. I'm just so happy to be with you without you making excuses to get away from me."

Clare was conscious of a young nurse sitting at a desk at the foot of George's bed. She was keeping herself quietly busy, occasionally looking at monitoring equipment and noting results on patient forms. She also gave Clare an encouraging smile. The same caring nurse organised tea, making Clare feel less of an intruder.

Clare sat back in the chair, listening to the hospital at work. The steady movement of people along green and white tiled corridors, hushed conversations, trolleys clattering along and now and again the steady hollow ringing of a telephone. Clare wished she had remembered to bring a magazine or newspaper. She heard the telephone on the desk purr softly. The nurse picked up the instrument, spoke softly, then quietly got up and left the room.

Clare's eyes travelled along George's still form to the frame at the head of his bed. She noticed a large white card. It carried the words, 'George Wright Liquids Only'. Beneath that was a name, Dr Irene Webster, a contact number and the date.

Her eyes travelled on. Lying on the top of the bedside cabinet was a thin file. Clare knew she was wrong but couldn't resist picking it up. She opened the stiff blue cover. Most of the details written on the first page related to George's admission. Some notes briefly referred to the initial specialist examination. Clare's, very limited experience as a medical student, helped interpret some of the early findings but did not take beyond the fact that George was seriously injured.

The second page carried treatment instructions and a list of drugs. Clare flicked over the page. She felt her face flush with guilt. Clare had no right or professional qualifications to pry, but the notes were about George, the man she loved. Suddenly her eyes landed on one phrase that had been written in red. It simply said, 'No known next of kin - Parents deceased.' Clare was stunned.

She was still staring at the words when the nurse, who had re-entered the room, slowly removed the file from her hands. Clare looked up but was too shocked to react or say anything. The nurse just smiled, settled her back into the armchair and placed a magazine in her hands. A clock, sited above the door of the room, ticked away each minute. The door opened and a white-coated elderly man signalled that he wanted to speak to her outside the room. Clare went into the corridor where the man waited. He introduced himself and then asked Clare to sit on a nearby bench. She did this dreading what her imagination was telling her.

"Miss Brandon, I understand you are not yet related to Mr Wright?"

Clare nodded and screwed her handkerchief between her fingers.

"I also understand you have begun studies as a medical student at the medical school in Cambridge?"

Clare nodded, mopping more tears and wondering where this was leading.

"You understand that being a doctor involves us in appreciating and sometimes bearing the pain of others. You will also understand what I mean when I say, I am sorry to have to tell you that, if he survives, it is likely Mr Wright may never recover his eyesight."

Words fell on Clare's ears like a slap in the face. The handkerchief stretched taught between fingers felt the dampness of falling tears, as the shocking news came. She managed, "But you believe he will live?" She looked desperately into the doctor's face.

"If he can get through the next twenty-four hours, I think he has a good chance. It's obvious you care for him a great deal and with you to help him, he will have everything to live for," the doctor patted her hand and led her back to George's room.

Clare sat looking at the sleeping figure. She wanted to hug him, gather him up and tell him no matter what, she was there for him. They would manage.

The nurse gave her some more tea, and a magazine. She flicked through the pages but words ran into each other, becoming an indistinct, meaningless blur. Faces looked back at her, their smiles out of place in her misery. The words, 'No known next of kin', kept swimming in front of her eyes. What had happened to his parents? She continually thought how wrong she had been to read the file. If George had wanted her to know he was an orphan, he would have surely told her.

In reality, George had said very little. Their relationship was all one sided, but he had asked for her and that was everything. Clare loved him, there was no doubt in her mind, but he had never so much as hinted at affection beyond friendliness. Although he had returned all her glances, her smiles, there was never a word. She often looked around and found his eyes on her, but that is where it ended.

The file told her his date of birth. He was older, but only by six or so years, and that was nothing, she told herself. If only he had just once let her know his true feelings. She was certain he loved her, or else why in all his pain, had he asked for her. Was it purely because there was no one else? Clare watched George's bandaged fingers. There was not a flicker of movement.

The door to the room opened quietly. It was Grace. The nurse rose, whispered a greeting and offered her a chair. Grace thanked her and sat alongside Clare.

"Darling," she said, "it may be some time before George comes round from the sedation. To wake him early may cause him a great deal of pain. Wouldn't it be best to leave him to rest? There are others here too and we all thought it would be a good idea to get something to drink and eat."

Clare wiped her eyes and shook her head, "I'd rather be here. He may wake and I want him to know I'm here."

Grace hugged her, "Darling, I know you're hurting terribly inside, but I feel George would want you to be strong and rested when he opens his eyes."

Clare stared at her, "You don't know do you?" She said, choking back the tears. Grace looked at her daughter. Slowly the possibility of George not seeing filled her mind. How could she have been so naïve?

"Clare, please let's leave the room and come back a little later. I'm sure the nurse will tell you immediately if George wakes."

Clare sobbed the words, "If only he knew how much I love him and want him to be well."

Grace placed an arm around Clare's waist and guided her to the door, "Oh, my dearest Clare, I'm sure he knows."

When Grace and Clare entered the visitors lounge, they saw Alan, Charlie, Fred Fisher and Harold Crumb sitting in silence. They had just been joined by Dr Irene Webster, who had explained she was temporarily in charge of George's case. Dr Webster waited until Clare was seated and then explained that George, once stabilised, would be transferred to the Royal Norfolk and Norwich hospital where specialist treatment would be provided.

"Specialist treatment?" Said Fred, his voice just above a whisper.

"For burns," said Dr Webster, "actually, the flesh wounds caused by the blast and flying debris can be dealt with immediately, but the burns to his face, body and hands, well that's a specialist field and may take some time."

Clare tried hard to control her voice, "You mean, he'll be disfigured?"

Dr Webster turned to her, "It's too early to say if there will be disfigurement although there is bound to be scarring. He is strong, but it may take some time for him to recover from such injuries. With the right treatment and patience, I'm sure he will make a good recovery."

Clare stared at the floor, "But I have been told that George may not recover his eyesight?"

Dr Webster waited for Grace to move then sat beside Clare. She took her hands in hers.

"Clare, the last thing George needs right now is to lose hope. The specialist that spoke to you is the best in the business. If George's sight can be saved, he is the one to do it."

Absolute silence in the room made the next few minutes unbearable. Dr Webster quietly left them to consider what she had said.

Alan sat between Grace and Clare and hugged them to him, "I swear we will do everything we can to get George well. Please believe that Clare. He can live with us at Patchets, or do whatever you or he wants."

"Excuse me," the nurse from George's room was standing at Clare's elbow, "I think you ought to come back. He is being prepared for the move to Norwich and he's awake. He knows what is going to happen and that you are here. Whatever you do, please don't attempt to touch him." Clare and Grace both quickly followed the nurse.

George heard them enter the room, "Who's there?" His voice sounded muffled by dressings and extremely weak.

Clare, eyes streaming in tears said, "I'm here darling George."

Grace stood back and quietly watched her daughter with a breaking heart and a certain pride.

The lips parted, "Hello Clare. Have I been asleep long? I feel very drowsy and I'm as thirsty as hell."

The nurse shook her head and pointed to the tubes.

Clare didn't know what to do with her hands. She leant close to George, "Soon George, the nurse will give you a drink soon."

"How long have you been here, Clare?"

"Hours," she said, "I came as soon as I heard. I've been sitting quietly reading a book waiting for you to surface. My mother's here in the room and my father and his marsh gang are waiting in the lounge. I'm told there are queues of people just waiting to wish you well." Clare had to stop talking as tears again ran down her cheeks.

George sensed her tears, "Please Clare, chin-up now. Can I sit up?"

Clare again looked at the nurse. She looked sad and shook her head. Clare whispered, "Sorry George. Evidently you are in a laying down bed. Sitting up is not part of this bed's design."

She heard a noise coming from George's lips and guessed he was trying his best to laugh. Clare lightly moistened his lips with some wet cotton wool the nurse gave her.

"George Wright, you'll do anything to get out of taking me to that dance," she wished she hadn't said it, but it just came out.

There was a moment of silence. George struggled, "Please try and understand Clare. I wouldn't be right in that company. You deserve younger, brighter people around you. A man who can take you around the world, enjoy life."

Clare was shocked. She knew in her heart that George was trying to protect her. That he may have already guessed what the future may have in store.

"That's tosh, you're just making excuses because you are safe in this hospital bed, and you know it," she paused for a long time then added, "my mother thinks it would be nice."

She caught the soft rasping sound and knew George was doing his best to laugh, "I see. And how does your father feel about it?"

Grace stepped forward and taking Clare's hand said, "Hello George. Bless you for what you did. It was very, very brave. Clare's father and I would be very proud and honoured for you to take our Cinder's to the ball. Just you get well, for all our sakes."

There was another short silence. George managed a soft whisper, "Thank you Mrs Brandon, but I really did nothing."

The tears appeared again in Clare's eyes. She bent close to George's head, "You see. You can't make any more excuses and please stop making me cry. I'm well over twenty-one, a free woman and anyway, I never thought I would have to bring my mother to my courting."

The two women smiled at each other, though a deeper sadness settled in Clare's eyes. She had been hoping so much that George would have responded with different words. Just some sign of fondness. It seemed it wasn't to be.

George stifled a cry of pain as he lifted a bandaged hand and laid it gently on hers, "Dearest Clare, right now, there are so many things, like the pain to go away. To get my head around this business, sort out a sea of thoughts. To see you laugh instead of just hearing the tinkling sound. Please let's wait and see what happens," his voice faded.

It was now so obvious that George was in considerable pain. The nurse came forward and lightly fitted George with an oxygen mask, which hissed into life. She went to the other side of the bed and pressed a red button. Somewhere, along the corridor a muffled bell started to ring.

The nurse touched Clare's arm. It meant she and Grace should leave. Clare leant over the bed, taking every care not to touch George.

She whispered, "I'm sorry my dearest, dearest George. It's just that I love you so much. Please, please get well for me and I'll take care of you no matter what the future brings."

They left the room, Grace's arm around the waist of her sobbing daughter. They both knew George was now fighting for his life. A medical team appeared and passed quickly into the room where George lay.

Alan looked up as Grace and Clare approached him. He stood and held out his arms. No words were necessary. All he wanted was to take the pain and sorrow away.

Chapter Ten

Alan slowly surfaced. Like a lumbering whale, he swam upwards from the dark, towards the light. It took him some time to focus on the alarm clock.

In the dim light, the green luminous hands registered five minutes to ten. It just couldn't be. Why hadn't he woken earlier? Why was it so dark at five to ten in the morning? Why hadn't his brain clicked into gear at the usual 6.30am?

One answer came when he swivelled his protesting eyes towards where the large bedroom window should be. The daylight, his fuddled brain told him should be there, was missing. Shutting out the daylight had obviously been one of Grace's cunning plans to keep him securely in the land of nod.

Also, some devious worm had removed the better part of his brain overnight, leaving his skull full of red topped matches. One or two ignited each time he tried to think. His eyes had minds of their own. Each seemed to move independently, both clinging desperately to the underside of its socket. His tongue felt like a piece of old canvas, liberally coated in stale Gorgonzola cheese. Meanwhile, his innate sense of surrender reassured him that if he could ratchet his eyelids to their fully closed position, he would descend gratefully back into the dark pit of oblivion.

The bedroom door opened slowly and Grace put her head round, "Good morning darling. Would you like some tea?"

A hand rose like a periscope from the ocean of bedclothes and waved a weak acceptance.

Try as he might, Alan couldn't get his head around the fact he appeared to have slept the sleep of the dead. His tousled head turned slowly to greet Grace.

He mumbled, "Sorry Grace, what's happening?"

George! The name struck him like a blow from a fourteen-pound hammer, "Grace, here I am laying in bed, what's happening with George. Have we heard anything from the hospital, has Clare rung? Is Clare here?"

Grace sat on the edge of the bed, "George was successfully transferred to Norwich. His condition is stable and Clare says he is still fully sedated, but his breathing has improved."

Alan visibly relaxed, "Thank you dear God for that."

"Clare is a little happier because, as George has no known next of kin, the hospital staff are treating Clare as his family. Also, because she is a medical student, they are briefing her on his condition," Grace took a deep breath, "now, that you know the latest, we can concentrate on you and this delayed shock of yours."

"Delayed what of mine?"

"Shock dear. It is what you have that's making you feel so dreadful."

"Oh I'm sorry, dear."

"No need for sorry dear and nothing is exactly what's happening. Well, that's as far as you are concerned anyway."

Alan felt this was a command.

Grace tucked in loose bedclothes, "You sir, can relax. Briefly, David has telephoned and you're not to think about putting in an appearance anywhere today, except perhaps to be seen by the doctor, who, you'll be pleased to know, has just arrived."

Alan put a shaky hand to his forehead and winced, "Please Grace, stop playing mother hen, my head just won't stand it, and tell the doctor to come up. Oh, and get hold of Charlie Friar for me and, oh yes, I'll have that cup of tea, please."

Grace smiled and guided Alan's hand to the cup, "Does my little soldier feel just a wee bit sorry for himself this bright sunny morning?" She kissed his cheek, happy at the thought he was sounding his old self.

Alan growled, swallowed the tea in one long gulp and groped for his dressing gown.

"You're to stay exactly where you are," warned Grace, "at least until the doctor has had a chance to look at you."

As she said this, Grace gently pushed Alan back onto his pillow and again, tucked in the covers. If Alan did resist, it didn't show.

At about this time, Charlie Friar was arriving at the quayside in Blakeney. As he stopped the car alongside the Harding's Hotel, Fred Fisher stepped out from the main entrance.

"Best not hang about here, Charlie," said Fred, "Stolland's in the bar talking to the bar manager."

Charlie followed Fred through the lobby, into the Reception, "He's a cool one and no mistake. What time did he get here?"

Fred ignored the question. He quickly guided Charlie into the Hall Porter's lodge. This provided a clear view of the only two ways into and out of the bar, direct from the street and from the hotel lobby. After quickly slipping the snib on the inside yale lock, just so they couldn't be disturbed, Fred provided the answer to Charlie's question.

"I'm told he's been here over an hour."

Fred helped himself to a sausage roll and cup of tea from a tray thoughtfully provided by the management.

"All the comforts of home I see," said Charlie.

Fred grinned, tapped the side of his nose, "Local knowledge Charlie, local knowledge. Anyway, as I was saying, he was followed to the Palladio Hotel. You know, by the pier. Too upmarket for me. Once inside, he made a quick phone call, then sat and had some coffee."

Charlie puffed away at his cigarette and listened. He kept his eyes on the lobby bar entrance, getting visibly agitated every time a small group of chattering guests strolled through the lobby, temporarily blocking his view.

"It's okay, Charlie, we'll see him if he leaves the bar. Now, according to our man, he seemed on edge, eyes everywhere. He was obviously waiting for someone or something to happen. Then, guess who showed up?"

Charlie shook his head, "I'm hoping that between the sausage rolls and onions Fred, you're going to tell me."

Fred ignored the sarcasm and sipped his tea, "Do you recall a chap called Victor Stigley?" Charlie didn't answer, so Fred provided the clue, "He's the night Supervisor at the CPS depot in Cromer?"

Charlie's stare unlocked from the bar door. He looked round at Fred, "You mean the chap who didn't have a good word to say about the CPS driver, topped at Mucky Mary's?"

Fred grinned, "The very same. Well, he showed up. Went straight over to Stolland and sat down. It obviously wasn't their first meeting. They knew each other alright."

Fred brushed pastry crumbs from his chin and reached for a ham sandwich. Charlie showed exceptional patience.

"Well, as I was saying, they had a few quiet words. Stigley puts out a hand and accepted something from Stolland. Our man wasn't able to see what it was, but it was easily palmed."

Charlie glanced at Fred, who shrugged, "I know I should stick to facts but if I were a betting man I'd bet you a pound to a ferret, it was cash in hand!"

Charlie swung his eyes back to the bar door. Fred continued, "Anyway, they both left in a hurry. Stigley shot off towards the CPS. Our man, stuck with Stolland and they ended up here."

"Where's our man now?" Asked Charlie.

"He's outside. Thought it best just in case Stolland spotted him and managed to put two-and-two together. Name is Frank Woodhouse, seems a nice young chap," Fred sighed, "of course, they're all so young now Charlie, aren't they?"

Charlie nodded. He watched a large bluebottle fall from the window, land on its back and start buzzing madly as it tried to regain its feet. Filthy things, he thought and swatted it with a newspaper. He recalled an old saying about coppers. You know you're getting old when policemen start looking young. Fred was right.

"Have we any more news of young George?"

The question was posed in a softer voice and betrayed a side of Fred that he didn't show that often. His words, spoken almost as a father would, when worrying about a son.

Charlie patted Fred's arm, "You'll know as soon as I do, Fred. That I promise."

He thanked Fred for turning out, and after making sure he was okay for transport home, he slipped out the lobby entrance and joined the young Frank Woodhouse.

Charlie knew of Frank, although he was not part of his section. He had been selected from uniform as an aide, then transferred permanently to Cromer CID.

They walked separately across the road to what had once been an old quayside warehouse. New owners had converted this into a gift shop with a coffee and tea facility above. A welcome bolt hole for visitors wishing to dive under cover to avoid rain and trawl through the displays of handy gifts from Norfolk.

Once inside, you couldn't help noticing the ingrained smell of tarred rope, oil and varnish, all promoting the right salty atmosphere. Strategically placed lobster pots, ships lanterns and glass floats guided the gullible towards the counter containing the many impulse buys. Good for the visitors thought Charlie. They like a bit of local colour.

A creaking wooden staircase, for some reason painted a bright royal blue, led to the first floor where, if you had a mind, you could accept the brightly chalked invitation to enjoy a toasted teacake and cup of tea, priced at nine pence. They tossed for it and while Charlie lit a cigarette and found a table, Frank handed over the one and sixpence, thinking, there goes this week's plain clothes allowance.

The table Charlie chose overlooked the quay and bar entrance. They sat down, trying not to look too conspicuous. Not easy when dressed in suits, while the other customers, obviously visitors, wore sensible cool lightweight clothes.

Trippers chewed on the small toasted teacakes and did their best to look as though they were enjoying the tea, the leaves of which had obviously been through the pot a few times.

Trying to blend in wasn't easy for other reasons. They were not in holiday mood and their lack of jolly holiday banter made them stand out as more than suspicious. That was obviously the opinion of the bottle-blond manageress, who a few years before, would have turned them in as German spies. Other customers chatted and laughed, while Charlie and Frank sat, watched and waited. Frank looked down at his feet. His brown suit trousers had ridden up over the tops of his heavy black boots. These definitely looked out of place, so he did his best to hide his feet under the table. He had meant to buy some shoes for plain clothes work, but his pocket wasn't quite that deep.

Other customers came and went, causing the bell suspended on a spring just above the door to clang alarmingly, with each opening. An annoying child found this more amusing than picking his nose, so he continued wrestling the door open and closed, until dissuaded by the back of his father's outstretched hand.

Charlie and Frank watched the bar door and waited. Harold Crumb arrived, his car coughing dark blue smoke. A sure sign it was playing up. A second later, Fred appeared from the hotel and both men left, trailing sufficient exhaust emissions to envelop and entertain coughing pedestrians.

Time slipped by and the tea grew cold. The oily film that now invaded the tea's surface drew Frank's attention. It's rainbow colours becoming more pronounced

179

as the tea cooled. Frank wondered what constituent of tea caused the oil to appear as the temperature dropped. He concluded its appearance had less to do with the overworked tea leaves and more to do with the cleanliness of the cup. His attention returned to the window.

Charlie groped for his lighter, adjusted the flint, lit his fourth cigarette and stared out at The Linnet. She lay tied to the quay, where the lifeboat crew had secured her. The explosion and fire had done little to enhance her appearance. She looked sad and battle-scarred. It struck Charlie that it was peculiar Stolland hadn't made straight for the boat. Perhaps Stolland was trying to gather what locals knew of the incident. A worthwhile exercise, even if it did cost him the price of a few pints. Especially, one or two may have helped in the rescue and recovery of The Linnet.

"That boat's in a right mess," said Frank.

Charlie was caught in the process of lighting yet another cigarette, "So is young George Wright and, while you're thinking on that, our boss isn't too healthy this morning. He's convinced he wouldn't be here today if George hadn't knocked him out of the way."

Frank let the subject die. He could feel a sudden glimmer of anger building in Charlie, "Are we going to lift him as soon as he shows?"

"No Frank, we're just going to watch. See what he does. As the boss says, give Master Stolland just a bit more rope. I want to see if he goes aboard. If he does, then that's different, we're ready for him. I must admit this is one arrest I'm really going to enjoy. That's why I was relieved to see Fred leave. It wouldn't do to have Fred around if Stolland resisted arrest. Fred would love that."

"Do you think Fred would have a go at Stolland."

Charlie removed his cigarette, "What do you think you'd do, if he'd almost fractured your skull? Wish him the time of day?"

Frank shrugged and wished he'd not asked the obvious.

"He's our man all right. Anger is a terrible human weakness Frank, and policemen have the same feelings as other people. Putting on a uniform doesn't change the character of the man who wears it. Don't you ever forget that, my son." Charlie stubbed out his cigarette, ramming it into the ashtray with some force, "I didn't want Fred around when we collar Stolland. Though I must admit, I wouldn't mind if he did resist. Then Frank, you can witness my using just sufficient force to affect the arrest," the two men grinned at each other.

At that moment, the bar door opened and Stolland appeared. He stood for a moment in the doorway shaking hands with two men who looked as though they could be local boatmen. Then, instead of leaving immediately, he spent a second or two looking along the quayside, first left and then right. Appearing satisfied, he made his way casually through the throng of visitors. Walking slowly, measuring his pace to that of the crowds around him. Casually, once or twice, he glanced back over his shoulder, as if half-expecting to see someone he knew.

Reaching the point where The Linnet lay, he examined the crowd surrounding the quayside, before climbing down a short ladder and stepping off, onto the deck.

For a man with an arm in a sling and multiple bruising, he was certainly lively enough. With one last glance around, he disappeared through the open hatch. Charlie watched him like a cat watching a mouse. As soon as Stolland descended, Charlie moved. Frank had to run to keep up with him.

The peroxide blond moved quickly aside, anxious not to have her feet crushed by Frank's boots. From the look on her face, she wasn't too pleased they had left without placing the obligatory service tip in one of the saucers.

The smell of charred wood hung heavy in the air as the two made their way carefully to the hatch leading down to the saloon. Charlie stopped, cupped a hand over Frank's ear.

"If he cuts up rough, don't be a bloody hero. Just watch him like a hawk and back me up!"

Stolland was in the saloon, concentrating on what appeared to be a thoroughly noisy search. Although it was full daylight on deck, the saloon was as dim as a TOC H lamp, with layers of soot on every surface. The pungent reek of acidic smoke did little to encourage visitors to stay. The racket from the quay and the clatter caused by Stolland's frantic search covered the limited noise of their climb down the companionway.

Thin shafts of sunlight penetrated through shattered timbers and deck lights, to etch small pools of brilliance on the littered deck. Airborne particles of ash danced in these shafts of light, as Stolland's search disturbed the fetid air.

The saloon was a complete shambles. Charlie and Frank watched as Stolland thrashed about, frantically turning out drawers and lockers. Every few seconds he paused to look at sodden papers, quickly discarding them, to pick up others. Stolland had no idea he had company until they were immediately behind him.

"Looking for this Mr Stolland?"

Charlie's voice was steady, his words softly spoken, but there was no hint of friendliness. In his outstretched left hand he held a small sheet of paper. Patchet's guide to the marsh, on which there were pencil marks.

Stolland froze then spun round. He automatically crouched as he turned. Fierce dark eyes flicking left and right as if weighing his chances of making it to the companionway. He glared at the paper. Then, in the blink of an eye, his expression changed, from a threatening look to a relaxed half-smile.

"Sergeant Friar. Welcome aboard the wreck of The Linnet!"

Charlie withdrew the paper and carefully put it in his pocket, not taking his eyes from Stolland, "We seemed to have startled you. Given you quite a turn I'd say. Expecting someone else were you sir. Perhaps someone who might wish you harm. Wish you into the next world?"

Stolland rubbed his hands together as if to gain time or perhaps remove ash, "No, no Sergeant, you just caught me totally by surprise. I was checking to see what the damage was. Terrible what an accidental fire can do to a vessel like The Linnet, isn't it."

"An accident, you say Mr Stolland," said Charlie advancing into the saloon, "Well, let me see sir. The definition of an accident, if my memory serves, includes the words, unplanned and unexpected. I doubt that this little fire was unplanned or unexpected," Charlie rubbed his chin, "oh no sir, the last thing I would call this little fiasco, is an accident? I would say it was very much planned by the person or person's responsible, and maybe even expected by the person for whom it was truly intended."

"Well then, Sergeant," said Stolland, "It was doubly fortunate for me that I was enjoying the hospitality of your police force at the time wasn't it?" Stolland displayed a forced smile.

Charlie waited, but a wary Stolland chose to do likewise.

"When you left the hotel bar a short time ago, you appeared to be looking around for someone. You repeated this behaviour on a number of occasions on your way to the boat, and again before you came below. Was there a particular reason for this caution, sir?"

"You seem to have been watching me very closely, Sergeant," Stolland paused as if to gather his thoughts, "I had a few drinks with friends, left their company and crossed to The Linnet. Surely there's nothing suspicious in that, is there? Now, as you can see I am very busy, so if you will excuse me I need to get on."

Stolland made as if to walk around Charlie. His tall figure slightly stooped in the restricted headroom. Frank moved and blocked his exit.

Charlie's voice grated, "Oh yes sir, you're busy, and have been for some time. I agree there's little point in prolonging this meeting," Charlie again took the piece of Patchets paper from his pocket. He held it close to

Stolland's eyes. Its bleached whiteness caught in a shaft of sunlight, "you can see this sir, clearly see it I mean?"

Stolland stared at it.

"The paper I have here was found amongst your possessions, on this boat. In fact, it was lying amongst other papers of yours, having previously been stolen from the police house at Salthouse and, at that time, a police officer colleague of ours was assaulted and seriously injured."

Stolland stared back at Charlie.

"You are being arrested on suspicion of being concerned in both those offences," Charlie cautioned him.

Stolland suddenly seemed to relax. Looking at them both, he said, "There'll be no resistance from me. Please believe I very much regret this business, especially the injury to your colleague. It was as unfortunate as it was unavoidable I'm afraid."

Visitors gathered four deep on the quayside, taking in the excitement of what one or two may have considered additional holiday entertainment. They witnessed three men, one wearing an arm in a sling plus a set of bright handcuffs, clamber from the bowels of The Linnet, awkwardly ascend a vertical ladder and, leaving sets of ashen footprints, trudge to a nearby car. One observer had no doubts as to what they had just witnessed. He stated to those nearest to him, that the plain-clothes copper in the brown suit and black boots had lifted the two dodgy ones. Those around him just nodded in agreement.

The journey to Cromer police station, was uneventful and without conversation. On arrival, Tiddy Goldsmith, the station sergeant, formally charged Stolland with the offences at Salthouse. Stolland indicated he didn't wish to make a statement or have a solicitor present. He did however make a request for an urgent meeting with the Chief Constable. Stolland then found himself back in the cell he had so recently quit. He was no longer a guest of the Norfolk Constabulary, but their prisoner.

Tiddy smiled as the cell door closed on Stolland, "If you don't mind my saying so Charlie, we're all pleased this matter involving Fred Fisher is cleared up. Sad business when a person can't sleep safe in his own home."

Charlie smiled for the first time for what seemed an age. He too felt a slight hint of pleasure. Tiddy noted the satisfaction.

"You'd better come up to the office. I've some bits and pieces for you to deal with. Also Mrs Brandon has been on and wants you to go over to the house to see your boss. He's been getting a bit bolshie. Evidently, the Chief said he mustn't stir from bed until he's been passed fit by the doctor. Oh, and Vincent Lawrence, the pathologist, said you are to telephone him as soon as possible. Something to do with results from testing capsules or some such."

Charlie and Frank followed Tiddy's broad back as he trudged up the steps from the cells. The soles of Tiddy's size fourteens just managing to fit onto each of the rising treads of the narrow stone staircase.

Charlie reflected on the sergeant's nickname. Tiddy had arrived at this label by being a touch under seven feet tall with his helmet on, and he was just as broad. But a softer, kinder man couldn't be found. The way he handled Saturday night fights in local pubs was pure magic. Respected by everyone, cop and criminal. He was a fair man that hated to lock anyone up, when a clip round the ear would get a better and swifter result.

Some time later, Frank followed Charlie into the yard. Charlie got into his car and lit a cigarette. He was obviously deep in thought, even somewhat dazed by information passed to him. He looked at Frank apologetically, as though he had just remembered he was with him.

"Sorry Frank, I'm miles away. Thanks for your help. I've asked your boss if you could be detached to us for the duration of this case. He's agreed, so get in. There are a couple of urgent matters for us to deal with. Get over to Norwich and see our boss, Mr Brandon. I've a shrewd feeling he's not going to be best pleased. So, let's ease our lot by preparing the ground, and that means our first stop is

185

to get you a decent pair of shoes. The boss would have a fit if he spotted those boots of yours."

Frank looked surprised and more than a little self-conscious. Charlie stopped at the first second-hand clothes shop he came to.

Alan was not the most patient of men, but found the wait for Charlie almost unbearable. Eventually he heard a car arrive and was out of bed in a flash. He pulled on his dressing gown and was four steps down the staircase when Grace opened the front door.

Alan shouted, "Charlie, where the bloody hell have you been?"

These words greeted the smiling Charlie, but didn't stop his stepping over the threshold. However, the caustic welcome did cause Frank to falter.

Grace was furious. Before Charlie could answer, or Frank wonder in which direction he should now be pointing, she left the door and was bounding up the stairs, bundling Alan backwards toward the bedroom.

It was immediately obvious that doctor's orders were not about to be breached by anyone. Standing in the hall, Charlie and the reluctant Frank tried not to smile, but how often does a lowly copper get the chance to see a senior police officer verbally beaten up in his own home.

Some few minutes and a hushed conversation behind a closed door later, Grace came out from the bedroom slightly flushed with victory. Slowly, she descended the stairs.

"Charlie, my husband is to remain in bed for two days. Please ensure he obeys the doctor. He may be a senior police officer and your superior but please hear what I say! He does not leave that bedroom until the day after tomorrow. Now, if you would be so good as to visit him, he would like to talk with you," she then looked at Frank, smiled, and said, "you must be Frank Woodhouse, I am Mrs Brandon, Grace actually. Would you be so kind as to follow me to the kitchen, where I shall provide you with some tea. Then you can take the tray up to the meeting."

Frank gave Grace a weak smile and followed her quietly into the kitchen, trying desperately to stop his new shoes squeaking as he crossed the parquet floor. Charlie had never seen Grace so angry with Alan. Obviously, she was finding Alan's enthusiasm for 'getting on with business', a bit of a trial.

He knocked on the bedroom door and marched in. He was used to this side of his boss. He kept his smile going.

To his surprise Alan was sitting up in bed grinning, "She's brilliant when she's angry, isn't she?"

Charlie laughed, "She's bloody superb," he said.

By the time Frank entered the bedroom with the tray of tea, Charlie had brought Alan up to speed. Alan looked at Frank, shook his hand and welcomed him to the team. Frank was a little surprised by the informality. After Charlie had explained, for the second time, the reaction of Stolland at the time of his arrest, Alan turned to Frank, "We've never met officially Woodhouse, so I feel we should just lay the ground out. Sergeant Friar will fill you in on everything that has happened so far. Your task will be to assist Sergeant Friar in all matters related to this case. You will report directly to him, and only to him. What you call each other is your affair but you will always address me as 'Sir' or Mr Brandon. I say this because you'll be meeting officials and may be in the company of the Chief Constable at meetings. You may also be required to meet officers from other forces. Don't give them cause to believe we policemen in Norfolk are slack. You have replaced a damn fine young police officer. I refer to P.C. Wright. If you're half as good, you'll not disappoint. Don't let Sergeant Friar or me down and, don't let yourself down. I don't expect to refer to these matters again. Have I made myself clear?"

Frank felt it best to simply, nod.

Alan grinned, "Good lad. Now let's have that tea."

Charlie had listened to what Alan had said and understood the reasons for it. Frank had arrived abruptly into the team, had backed Charlie at an arrest that could have gone badly wrong, and embarrassingly witnessed the dressing down of a senior officer by his wife. If he was unsure how he stood to begin with, he was certainly aware of the boss's thoughts now. Charlie was quietly confident Frank would fit in nicely - no reason to hide his feet anyway. Not now they were sporting nearly-new brogues.

"So Charlie," said Alan, handing a cup of tea to Frank, "what's this about Vincent Lawrence?"

Charlie relaxed, "Our friend Lawrence has re-examined the other bodies found on the marsh. Each of them contained one of those seeds or capsules, identical to the first one lifted from the mortuary. They'd all been positioned in the occipital section of the brain. Two of these he's forwarded to a friend of his who heads up the R&D at Mullards. A top boffin named," Charlie flicked at the pages of his notebook, "ah, here it is, a Professor Bob Willis. Evidently quite famous for being ....."

Alan gasped, "He did what? Send vital evidence to some damned boffin in the TV industry, without so much as by your bloody leave!"

Charlie waited for the colour to return to Alan's face, "Beg pardon sir but, in retrospect, it was not a bad move. This R&D at Hackney is not strictly TV based. It's one of the best electronic labs in the country. Lawrence knew what he was doing. He often sends bits and pieces to this guy Willis. He's noted for being quick and clean, and he hasn't failed him yet." Charlie paused to see if his explanation was accepted.

"Hold on Charlie. Bits and pieces from a pathologist who lives in a mortuary, to an engineer at a TV works?" Mumbled Alan weakly.

"By bits and pieces, I wouldn't have thought Mr Lawrence meant body parts sir," replied Charlie.

Alan sat stone-faced, trying to imagine what else Lawrence was sending through the Royal Mail.

Charlie continued, "Anyway, they were evidently subjected to powerful x-ray procedures. The results were stunning, according to Lawrence."

He waited for a reaction from Alan. Alan looked as though he was going to make a comment, then chose silence.

Charlie shrugged and continued, "Each appeared to contain some type of circuitry. In the opinion of Professor Willis, they could be minuscule receivers or something along these lines. In each case, they seemed to be in two distinct parts. At a guess, his not mine, perhaps some sort of receiver and transmitter. However, as he put it, he could be wrong. There was no identifiable means of opening them, whatever they are. It was all too delicate. Well beyond their capability and in his opinion, no facility exists to manufacture such a device. According to Lawrence, if Professor Willis says they are beyond modern technology to manufacture such microscopic equipment, then you can lay money on it. Whoever was responsible for their design and manufacture, plus the advanced surgical methods of insertion, have skills well beyond what's known to science today. And, before you ask sir, that last bit is the opinion of Mr Lawrence, not Willis."

"Anything else?" Asked Alan.

"Well sir, It was hinted it may be something you only see in comics and on cinema screens!"

Alan looked hard at Charlie, "And I suppose we have to thank our Mr Lawrence for that view?"

Charlie finished his tea and grinned, "No sir, Professor Willis. Evidently the future seems to be more in his line, I'd say."

Alan indicated to Frank to pour what was left of the tea. "Charlie, have we now secured all four capsules?"

Charlie shrugged, "Well, we have the two from Lawrence and evidently the two that were sent to Hackney are on their way back to us," he paused, "by messenger."

"Right," said Alan, "get those damn capsules locked up. They're not to be let out of police possession again, for any reason. What news of the taxi, the one that was busy leaving Blakeney when The Linnet was hit and have you spoken to the driver yet or better still, traced the passenger?"

Charlie braced himself, "The taxi was found abandoned at Aylsham. Well, just above Millgate, where the old crossing was. You know, not far from Blickling Hall."

Alan interrupted, "Yes Charlie, I do know."

"Well," continued Charlie, "the taxi had been driven onto the old railway track for some distance then stuffed down an embankment into a small copse. Two young kids out skylarking found it. No sign of the driver, or of a passenger, if there had been one when it was dumped," Charlie coughed, "however, there were some blood stains and this resulted in a widened search. I understand that just after dawn this morning, the body of a man, now identified as the driver, was found stuffed into a culvert some two hundred yards further along the track. From the initial examination of the body and clothing, it seems he may well have walked most of the way to the drain before being done in. A single shot through the back of the head. Somehow, the body was crammed into the drain. Whoever put that poor bugger's lights out was no lightweight amateur."

Alan held up a hand, "Charlie, I take it by using the word crammed you mean it took some doing?"

"Well, the first search missed him. It was only when water backed up following a storm that he was found by a railway gang trying to clear the blockage. The body was some way into the pipe. It must have taken some strength to put it there, it was only a twenty-four inch drain."

Alan quietly asked, "What about the passenger?"

Charlie shrugged again, "Missing sir, no trace."

"That does it," said Alan, throwing back the bed covers, "Grace or no Grace, its time I got to work. After I've spoken with the Chief, we're going to see Stolland. This time I'm going to ring the truth from Stolland. He's up to his neck in this business."

Charlie and Frank met Grace in the hall. "It's no good Grace," said Charlie, "He's on the phone to David

Long to set up a meeting and then we're taking him over to Cromer."

Grace smiled at Charlie, "Dear Charlie, I expected no less," she turned to Frank, "see what sort of crazy world you are entering. Take the hint and find a nice quiet well paid office job somewhere."

Frank smiled.

Chapter Eleven

The journey from Alan's home at Patchets to Cromer police station took half the time it would normally take. The car, with its three occupants had careered its way along as though the devil himself was driving. Charlie, who was sitting in the front passenger seat, chain-smoked the whole journey. This resulted in Alan insisting all windows were wide open. This did nothing for Frank's comfort, collecting fresh air at the same velocity as Charlie's expelled tobacco smoke.

On reaching the station yard, the car screeched to a halt at the feet of a station cleaner, Alf Tucker, who just happened to be hosing the yard down. Alan leapt out, "Do me a favour Mister Tucker, give Sergeant Friar's car a wash, inside and out, it smells like a damned ashtray."

The car's engine was off but it continued firing for a few seconds coughing like a dying asthmatic.

"Engine needs a jolly good de-coke," mumbled a grinning Tucker.

Alan tossed the keys to Mr Tucker and stormed into the back door of the station, calling over his shoulder, "So does Mr Friar!"

Tiddy Goldsmith looked up as Alan entered.

"Have an urgent message for you Superintendent. The Chief Constable telephoned and says, today's meeting with him is off, but expect a heavy meeting tomorrow morning. He would be obliged if you and Sergeant Friar could be at his office before ten so that he can brief you on who's expected."

Alan nodded and headed for the interview room on the first floor. Charlie took the cell keys from Tiddy and winked, "Any chance one of your guys can drum up some tea? We'll be in the interview room with Mr Stollard."

Tiddy returned the wink, "I dare say we can squeeze the pot for such distinguished company. Your prisoner won't need anything he's just had a nice fish and chip lunch, including four slices of bread, plus the regulation pint pot of tea."

Charlie passed the keys to a smiling Frank, "Take him up to the boss Frank. Oh, and don't forget to apologise to Mr Stolland for having to disturb him so soon after tiffin!

The interview room was regulation. One locked and barred window providing a view of the station yard, bricked walls tastefully coated in 1934 regulation green. A single fly-specked, hundred watt light bulb, hanging from twin flex immediately above a small bare table, strategically placed in the centre of the room, each leg securely screwed down to the planked floor. There were two chairs at this table.

Alongside the window was a smaller table, upon which sat an old Imperial typewriter and a supply of A4 paper. A small uncomfortable looking wooden stool was stored beneath the table, obviously there for use by the unfortunate typist.

Charlie looked at Frank, "Can you drive one of those?" He indicated the typewriter. Frank nodded. "Good, make sure you get everything that's said. We'll deal with the formal statement later."

Alan pointed to one of the chairs. Stolland sat down, "You are aware that you have been charged with…"

Stolland interrupted, "I think Sergeant Friar will have explained. I don't deny the charges. Neither do I intend to hide anything. In fact, I want to clear some of the fog that surrounds certain events. I include in that, the matter of The Linnet. If, after I've finished, you still have questions I'll answer them as best I can."

"As best you can," snapped Alan.

"Yes," replied Stolland equally forcibly, "as best I can!"

193

Alan stared at Stolland for some seconds, "These charges you face are extremely serious. If you wish to make a formal statement…"

Stolland interrupted, "Superintendent, forget the written statement. Police formalities, formal statements, it will all take too long. Forgive me repeating my warning. We are losing time! A lunatic is running loose and you insist we tiptoe through ancient police practices! If you would just let me explain. Then, you can decide where you go from here!"

Alan looked at Charlie. "Okay Stolland, I'll give you exactly ten minutes, but I warn you, if at any time I feel you are misleading us or prevaricating in any way you're back in the cells."

Stolland seemed to relax, "I need to make it clear that the less people hear what I am about to say, the better. It is best for all concerned, and I include in that, Mrs Brandon."

Alan rose from his chair. He looked over at Frank, "Woodhouse, get an area car to run you over to the hospital and see how George Wright is." He waited for Frank to leave the room. The silence was like stepping into a cold shower.

The moment the door clicked shut, Alan spun on Stolland, "Now listen very, very carefully Mr Stolland. Making threats, especially against my wife will get you an accidental fall down the cell steps. Do you understand! Leave my wife out of your nasty business, and that's the last and only time I'll warn you."

Stolland pushed back his chair, to avoid Alan's painfully stabbing finger, "But Mr Brandon, your wife is already in this business, as you put it. Isn't she?" The question hung in the air for what seemed a long time, "Look, Superintendent, I don't speak lightly and I'm not trying to be smart. I'm sure you'll see that you and I want the same result."

As Stolland said this, a knock on the door broke the tension. Tiddy Goldsmith looked round the door with a grin and passed a tray to Charlie. He turned to Alan,

194

"Woodhouse has left for the hospital as you instructed. You won't be disturbed again sir." With that, he left the room.

With each of them supplied with tea, Alan said, "It's your ten minutes. I suggest you use them wisely."

Stolland asked if he might stand, "I think better on my feet."

Alan waved a hand, "Stand on your head if it helps but get on with it."

"First, I am, as you rightly guessed, responsible for entering the Police House and taking the note. Regretfully I also knocked out your constable, Mr Fisher. I am deeply sorry and I mean that. I also entered your room at the Hotel to make a search and I recovered a certain item of state property from a local mortuary. I admit all these things, but they were all done for one reason."

"Get to the point," Charlie said.

"I am a serving Police Officer. Not in any of the forces you would recognise," Stolland took a deep breath, "there is no way of explaining this easily."

"Oh for Pete's sake Stolland," Alan demanded, "Get on with it. We'll be the judge of whether we think you're telling us a pack of lies."

"I have made, what you may call, a time shift. Some one hundred and fifty years in fact," Stolland read the incredulous look on the faces in front of him, "I said it wouldn't be easy. Before this interview's over, you'll be torn between fact and fantasy. I'll be supplying the facts and you'll be fantasizing. I don't envy you the task of taking what I have to say to your superiors."

Alan signalled Stolland to sit tight while he and Charlie went into the lobby.

"Well Charlie, after listening to what Grace said on the marsh and what she later said in David Long's office, it seems we have no choice but to believe him. This whole business is insane."

"And what if he's not goody-two-shoes, and is in fact the villain of the piece?" asked Charlie.

"I take your point, but Grace described two men and I think Stolland fits the hunter, not the hunted. Grace mentioned future time and like it or not we're stuck with Stolland." Charlie nodded and opened the door.

Stolland looked up, reading their faces, "If the tables were turned gentlemen, I too would view this business as pure madness," he looked at Alan, "trips into incredulity is nothing new for you surely Superintendent. Not with Mrs Brandon seeing what she's seen. What did you call them at the time? Hallucinations, visions, perhaps even flights of fancy?"

Before Alan could answer, Stolland went on, "And, according to my information, following the leads she gave had its successes for both of you! Am I right Sergeant Friar?"

Charlie chose to ignore the question.

"Forgive me, but I have the advantage of hindsight, historical information. I promise there's no magic here. Unfortunately, Jules Verne failed to mention the nasty side of time travel. You see, like all good policemen, I've done some homework."

Stolland's face grew serious, "The man I am after has made the same journey, I've made. His plan is to change history and we, and I mean people of my time, cannot allow that. I'm here to transport that man back and avert a greater tragedy."

"Wait a minute," stormed Alan, "wasn't what happened on The Linnet a bloody tragedy. There's a young lad lying in hospital because of the handiwork of someone who's known to you."

Stolland held up his arms, as if surrendering, "I am well aware of that, but I promise, if we don't stop this one character, you'll witness a far greater disaster. Remember, he's already responsible for the deaths of several people, five of whom you found on your marsh. If we, and I loosely say we, are to stop him, you have to know what you are up against. That means briefing you, but I see my ten minutes are up." He looked at Alan.

Alan leant back in his chair and folded his arms, "Carry on."

Stolland smiled, "I am from an experimental impulse fusion facility sited on the coast at what you call Cley-next-the-Sea."

"Does that account for your reference to my wife?" Alan asked.

Stolland shrugged, "Yes. Part of the work undertaken at this establishment involved early experimentation into something you may recognise as time-lining or time-shift?"

Charlie's eyes lifted to the ceiling. Stolland ignored the implied disbelief and continued, "The task recently delegated to me involves the security of that part of the facility dedicated to time shift. Because of its function and my position as Gatekeeper, it is my responsibility to ensure no criminal use of the facility. The greatest difficulty for you Superintendent is to accept, without doubt, that I am talking about the year 2102. Without that, there is little point in proceeding. In fact you both know too much already, but that can be remedied."

"Remedied?" Repeated Charlie, his furrowed eyebrows signalling his mounting suspicion.

"A quick, simple, painless process leaving you unharmed," Stolland waited for that little gem to sink fully home. The looks on the faces of Alan and Charlie were full of disbelief, "Right, you want proof, I'll give you proof! Take me back to Cley and I'll provide proof the gate exists."

Alan sucked on his teeth for seconds, "Perhaps later, if I feel it's necessary."

"Okay, if you won't allow me to satisfy your doubt instantly then I'll try explanation. I'm pursuing a man named Victor Grech. He is extremely dangerous. As I said, he has already killed on your patch and his intention is to kill again. Grech is utterly ruthless. He was a Class Three scientist, employed under the direction of the Head of Experimental Associated Projects for the Federation of European States. This man's name was Clive Welland. I say was, because he was your body number five. Clive Welland was an extraordinary scientist, specialising in advanced physics. He had developed a special project called PT&RS. Simply, a particle transfer and recall system, or time shift system. Later it became locally know as 'The Gate'. In brief, a method of transporting matter from one point in time, forward to a pre-determined time."

Alan held up a hand, "Look Stolland, Charlie and I have sat listening to explanations from people like you on hundreds of occasions. But your story takes the biscuit for invention!"

"I assure you the Forward Planetary Development Project, is real enough. The Gate part of that project is also real enough. Initially developed for its defensive capability, it gave us, that is to say, the FES, the ability to search forward in time to prevent incidents like that of 2016."

"That of 2016, and what pray does 2016 mean?" Asked Charlie.

For the fraction of a second Stolland wavered, "Forget that. What I can tell you is that the ability to defend will not always relate to global situations. Searching and dealing with threats from outside our atmosphere will become vital. Your grandchildren will see the need for and beginnings of such a project."

Charlie laughed, "This really is Jules Verne. Who is going to believe the crap we're listening to?"

There was no response from Alan, who held up a hand to quieten Charlie.

Stolland stared coldly at Charlie, "I can assure you Detective Sergeant Friar, whoever you tell, had better listen!" His eyes immediately softened and travelled back to Alan, "To continue, because of Grech's phenomenal ability as a physicist, he quickly gained senior status. Welland made him familiar with all aspects of the Gate. In fact, they worked like Siamese twins for about ten years on the initial particle and matter transference system. We now have reason to believe it was Grech, adapting work originally funded for Welland, who stumbled over the 'reverse' possibility."

"Reverse possibility?" Queried Alan.

"Just as it says," smiled Stolland, "travel into the past. Anyway, Grech secretly reworked certain of Welland's programme developments, gently leading Welland to the point where he couldn't help but stumbled on the possibility. Welland, stunned by his apparent breakthrough, enlisted Grech to mask screening devices, making it possible to continue tests they knew were in direct contravention to international law. Just over three years ago, when experimentation was complete and totally against the wishes of Grech, Welland declared the discovery to the Faculty, the overseeing body. As a result, all known trials ceased. Both scientists found themselves very much restricted.

The Federal States Authorities then examined this additional function in detail. They quickly decided it breached the specific terms governing the facility and, more seriously, carried an unacceptably high risk of misuse by governments or individuals. Its rapid and unanimous decision was that without some form of strict protocol, absolutely guaranteeing against misuse or abuse, the reverse aspect of the facility was to be totally destroyed. This decision was unanimously accepted and endorsed by the whole Federation."

"I ask this out of ignorance," said Alan, "but surely a controlling protocol was developed to cover the 'forward' aspect of your facility, prior to it's adoption? Couldn't the same controls be used?"

"There were specific security problems attached to travelling back to the past. I'm sure with a little imagination, you could think of a few. Individual ambition came into the equation. There were other reasons, mostly technical, well beyond my understanding. You must accept that it took some time to perfect the level of guarantee the FES insisted on. In fact, part of the answer lay in what we call a Siros key."

"What on earth is a Siros key?" Enquired Charlie.

"You referred to them as seeds or capsules I think? Siros simply means single insert reaction occipital system. It's a simple method of creating an artificial synapse."

"Please, no more," pleaded Alan, "look that one up later in the dictionary or something, Charlie. Stolland please get on with it."

Stolland smiled again, "These implants, once embedded in the subject cannot be removed by the subject, or by those antiquated medical methods available to you. To try would simply activate the key, which would cause the immediate termination of the subject."

Alan winced, "Sounds a bit dispassionate."

Charlie broke in, "Are you fitted with one of these keys?"

Stolland smiled, "Yes, of course."

"By what you've said, and what we've already witnessed, it's obvious that these keys were adapted to provide a guarantee against abuse?" offered Alan.

Stolland nodded, "The short answer to that is yes, but this provided yet another problem. Welland had designed the prototype used on forward missions. Both he and Grech had been at the forefront of that development. It transpired that Grech was in fact a brilliant designer, far more capable than Welland. Welland, being Grech's superior, was clever and wily enough to suppress certain aspects of Grech's talent. In fact, we have evidence to show that for some years, Welland kept Grech on a tight reign. To him, it was like having a genie in a bottle. The problem I spoke of was that Welland, finally gave Grech a free hand to develop the reverse key. Welland didn't know it, but at that point, he released the genie from the bottle. Once Grech produced the new key, Welland took over. He set up a series of live tests, demonstrated its safe use to the Faculty. This resulted in reinstating the project. Grech, unbeknown to Welland, now had a free hand to develop his own plan."

Charlie raised a hand, "Hang on. You said Welland and this guy Grech had bent rules to develop the reverse capability, right so far?"

Stolland nodded. Charlie leant forward in his chair, "How, if your security is so pukka, could they be so readily accepted back onto the project?"

"There are holes in every system. The short story is that Grech is extremely clever, exceptionally cunning, and no one, and I do mean no one, knew anything of his personal plans."

Charlie sat back into his chair, shaking his head and smiling.

"Well," whispered Stolland, "you might well smile Sergeant, but you know how resourceful he can be. He's led you a right dance hasn't he?" Charlie's smile collapsed.

Stolland smiled, "We are not here to score points, are we? Getting back to Grech, he lived on-site and spent all his off-duty time working through small, contained experiments with a light transference beam.

The only relaxation he seemed to enjoy lay in defeating site security force fields, upsetting security. When challenged over this, he always claimed this was purely to demonstrate where a change in site security was necessary."

"Hold on Stolland," said Alan, "I thought you were part of this security force?"

"No," replied Stolland, "I am State Police, brought in to dig about and find the rot, if any existed. By this time, live experiments were running. A volunteer would need to be single, have no known relatives and be fully aware of the particularization risk."

"Particularization risk?" Asked a puzzled Charlie.

"The process transfers the body in its matter form, or as a fine particulate, through the time distortion. At a pre-set point the matter reforms," Stolland struggled to explain, "I'm a policeman, not a scientist. But it's as though you look at something through a fine mesh, then as you watch, all the parts come together. You'll have to forgive my lack of knowledge."

Charlie still looked puzzled, "A little like an explosion followed by an implosion?"

It was Stolland's turn to frown then smile, "A rather brutal analogy Sergeant, but it's yours. The volunteer would be transported, then on receipt of a signal be retrieved through the Gate. His journey would be scrutinised against known facts. His condition would be reviewed by the medical team and the retrieved Siros key would be sent to Grech for assessment and changes, where necessary."

"Do you mean this chap Grech was given the vital task of instituting changes where he thought they were necessary?" Alan asked.

"Of course, after all, he had been the one who had redesigned the keys, which resulted in FES acceptance. It was naturally assumed by everyone that Welland was closely supervising every aspect of Grech's work."

Charlie muttered, "A bit like giving a convicted arsonist matches to play with." Alan nodded.

Stolland smiled, "Yes gentlemen, retrospection can be beneficial sometimes, but I must warn you, Grech is extremely clever. He had kept a clean sheet since re-introduction and showed nothing but conscientious compliance and boundless enthusiasm, as far as his grade security monitors were concerned. Even pointing out where lapses could occur. At that time, they had no reason to withdraw him from having responsibility for programming the keys. After all, the keys simply gave control of the subject to monitors once the individual had passed through the Gate."

"So, I suppose your man Grech built himself a position where he blended into the woodwork. He was clean?"

"Exactly," said Stolland, "the protocol itself seemed water-tight. The first volunteer took nothing through, except the clothes he wore. He was to be on the other side for a minute or two. Later, when they saw that the system worked, volunteers spent longer periods, allowed additional latitude with regard to equipment or support transfer."

Charlie nodded, "So, here you had a time-served poacher you thought had turned gamekeeper?"

"A fair assumption," said Stolland, "anyway, once a subject was through his training and due to pass through the Gate, Grech would simply supply a programmed key to the medical team, who inserted it. Grech was simply the quality control, solely responsible to ensure keys functioned within limits set by the agreed protocols. Remember, he had built himself a reputation as being very thorough in every aspects of security. The monitoring team would follow the subject throughout the test.

As I said, it would be Grech who would fine-tune the limits and review the keys performance on their return, often pointing out where changes were necessary."

Alan asked, "Were there ever failures?"

"Yes. Though I should say, it seemed so at first. One test took place into one of your worst winter night storms. Evidently, for some reason, the subject became confused. Monitoring technicians assumed the subject died through his own inadequacy. At no time did the monitors suspect direct termination."

"Termination?" said Alan.

"Termination means what it says. The execution occurs wherever he happens to be. The body ceases to function the moment the signal is given. There is an acceptable option and that is to suspend consciousness. This is where the subject is recovered and later interrogated. These were the safety features demanded by the FES."

"Wonderful world you live in," said Alan.

Stolland looked surprised but ignored the remark. "We now know that Grech deliberately designed the so called failure into the key. The object was to see if the protocols detected a fault, also whether the execution would be detectable. Grech must have been well pleased with the outcome."

Alan said, "A nasty individual. I am amazed that with all your advances in technology, you failed to identify a 'risk' when you saw one. After all, he'd previously bent the rules and that surely made him a continuing risk!"

Stolland smiled, "Considering what we have achieved since your time, I wouldn't say we've made too many mistakes. If I can prove one solid fact, will you help me get Grech?"

"No," said Alan, "not the way you mean. If Grech's done what you Say, he's as much our target as yours. You're in our time now and you'll abide by our rules, antiquated though they may be!"

Stolland looked down at his hands, "Well, will you at least take me out to Cley marsh so I can prove the Gate exists?"

Alan looked at his watch. "Yes," he said. He looked again at Charlie, "let's go and add some colour to Mr Stolland's tale Charlie."

Cley marsh looked beautifully calm. The late afternoon sun picked out the different colours of grasses, reeds and clear water. Very few people were about, which surprised Alan. They left the A149 coast road and drove slowly across the marsh.

"Now," said Alan, "it's all down to you, Stolland. This is your one chance. Don't blow it! One slip, just one move in the wrong direction and we will have you back in cells before you can whisper Jules Verne! Is that crystal clear?"

Stolland didn't take his eyes from one particular area of shingle bank. He just nodded. Alan and Charlie were both on edge. They had no idea what might happen once Stolland was out of the car.

Under Stolland's instructions, all three left the car and walked the landward edge of the shingle bank, where it met the marsh. They reached a point some two hundred yards from the old coast guard station when Stolland stopped.

"This is it, hold it here. You must trust me. I need to walk forward alone."

Charlie grabbed hold of his arm, "Where you go, we go."

Stolland spun round, frustrated, "I can't prove a damn thing to you if you won't allow me to walk forward on my own. In just ten paces I can prove everything to you."

He looked at Alan, so did Charlie. Alan waved Charlie away, "Okay, but one step over ten and play-time's over."

Stolland paced forward slowly. He was looking straight ahead along the margin of the marsh. He stopped and seemed to be speaking to himself. Suddenly, his outline grew indistinct.

Right in front of their eyes his body form began to break up. It was as though he was turning to dust. The form that had been Stolland stepped forward into a mist. In less than a second, he had completely disappeared.

Alan and Charlie darted forward. They ran on through the area where Stolland had vanished. Neither could believe their eyes. All they could see was shingle, marsh grass, reeds, a blue sky and the silhouette of the ruined coast guard station.

There was only the sound of the sea breaking on the shore and cries of birds.

"Blimey, this is going to take some explaining sir," said Charlie. They both turned around and faced towards the car.

Alan spun around, quickly looking in all directions, "Damn, damn, damn! It's as though a hole in the ground opened and swallowed him."

Charlie shook his head, "No sir, if you don't mind my saying. He's conned us good and proper. I've only ever seen things like that at the pictures and I don't envy your having to explain it."

Alan glanced at Charlie with a frustrated look that simply said, explain that if you can!

Time crept by as they again searched the shingle where Stolland had stood, but found nothing but earth and stones. Finally, both men walked over to the car and leant on the bonnet, staring out over the marsh, toward the coast road. "One thing for sure," said Alan, "He's given us that one hard fact. The Gate exists alright. He's proved that by becoming the invisible bloody man. Hell Charlie, what were we thinking of. I just let him walk away! I can see early retirement looming ahead....for both of us!"

"And not from choice," said Charlie.

"Oh come on, it's not that bad," said a voice behind them.

They both spun round. There was Stolland, solid flesh and bone.

"What the hell did you do? Where have you been?" Demanded Alan.

"All I did was contact my monitors, then walk back into my time. Give you two enough time to have a mild heart attack and then, walk back through the Gate to your time. I simply wanted to prove the one solid fact that you may not have believed, unless I did it right in front of you."

"And that was?" Blurted Alan, desperately trying to hide his relief.

"That I come from another time. Not another world where the ruling elite have two heads. Just a time that is ahead of yours. Everything I have told you is true. My doing what I have just done, is not what is strictly supposed to happen. It has caused a few ripples on the other side. But, then again, nothing that has happened was supposed to." Stolland opened the rear nearside door of the car and started to climb in. Then he hesitated and turned to look at Alan.

Alan nodded, "Well Stolland, you seemed to have proved one point, but you're still responsible for the attack on one of my officers, and I'm not sure how we're going to get round that, but for the moment, I am beginning to think there might be something in this Gate business."

Charlie started the car and they moved off. Alan turned to look at Stolland, "Why gatekeeper? That's a bloody awful title."

Stolland shrugged, "It's just a title. Until Grech's caught, no one my side of the Gate is going to rest easy."

"Why can't they just turn off his key, terminate him?" Asked Charlie, stating the obvious.

Stolland placed a hand on Charlie's shoulder, "You are forgetting who designed his particular key."

As they drove into the yard at Cromer Police Station, they just missed hitting Tiddy Goldsmith as he peddled from the yard. Alan wound down the car window, "Any messages?" Knowing the answer before Tiddy dismounted.

"Yes sir, if I were you I would make two calls, both of them life threatening. First, the chief constable is fuming and on top of that, your wife is equally upset. Perhaps you could sign the log indicating I have passed on the messages. Oh, there is one other thing. The blue bag containing Mr Stolland's possessions is in my desk. Perhaps you should take a look in it?" With that, Tiddy cycled off.

Before making any calls, Alan opened the blue bag. The first thing he saw was a small white piece of blank metal. His face broke into a satisfied smile, "Well, Mr Stolland. We seem to have found the item of lost property taken from the police house at Salthouse. Would you care to explain?"

Alan took the metal and placed the smooth side to his eye. After it had been there a second, he turned it to Alan. The blank smooth face now contained two lines of text, plus what seemed to be a number.

Charlie read off what he could see. 'Stolland Peter – State Police. Insp. Serial No. 2102.'

"You know, I was in dead trouble without this. It has a value far greater than I can tell you," smiled Stolland.

Alan failed to return the smile, "Oh, I'll bet it has,"

He turned to Charlie, "it's time you went home and I've a couple of calls to make. And as for you Mr Stolland, well you've gained a couple of points, but you are still on a very nasty, sharp hook."

Alan's phone call to Grace was a short affair. Grace couldn't disguise her anger with Alan, "You are supposed to be in bed recovering, not gallivanting about the coast enjoying yourself. You are so maddeningly pig-headed. Nobody can be trusted to do anything and you have never understood the word delegation!"

Alan tried to explain the importance of his being where he was, but it was no good. He decided a tactical withdrawal was in order. His final words were deliberately rushed, "This line's terrible isn't it? Lost most of what you said I'm afraid darling, something about being at the station was it? One last thing poppet, would you mind making up a spare bed? Peter Stolland will be spending the night with us."

Before she had time to reply, he replaced the receiver hurriedly. He felt he would give her enough space and time, to cool down.

Some time later, Stolland took up a strategic position behind Alan, as Grace opened the front door. She ducked around Alan and smiled at Stolland, "Good evening, Mr Stolland, at last we meet, please do come in, I hope Alan's trekking hasn't worn you out? He seems to enjoy playing on the beach. Like all small boys I suppose, he never knows when to stop his games." She totally ignored Alan until Stolland was in the cloakroom.

"Has David phoned?" Alan asked the question as he tried to dodge her anger and advance across the hall.

"Three times to be exact," Grace replied in a voice lowered to prevent Stolland hearing, "The first time to speak to you, something about tomorrow's meeting. The second time to find out where you were. The third time to register his obvious annoyance at not being able to speak with you. I jokingly said I thought you were probably trying to find your way out of the marshes. He didn't seem too amused."

"Actually," Alan offered a hushed explanation, "I did try phoning him. He was out somewhere, shopping in Norwich I think. I left a message to say I would attempt to call him later."

"He's your boss Alan, or have you totally forgotten that? And, you didn't give me time on the phone to tell you that Clare is here and she has brought a girl friend to stay overnight. These are the sleeping arrangements. Clare's friend is using Clare's room. Clare is happy to sleep the one night with me in our bed. Mr Stolland can sleep in the spare room and," there was a distinctly cold pause, "I have made up the truckle bed for you in your study. The other two bedrooms are stripped ready for decorating."

Alan desperately tried to think of another solution.

"Alan, I know that bed gives you no rest and backache. But, in view of the unusual circumstances, I didn't think you'd mind too much."

Alan found his voice, "That thing? It's a rickety antique, a wreck! It's, well, they went out with the ark. Why haven't you made up the camp bed in the loft above the garage?"

Grace stroked Alan's cheek, smiled and said, "Oh no dear, that may have been too uncomfortable for Mr Stolland. After all, he is a most welcome guest.," the smile broadened as Stolland joined them.

Alan felt a touch jaded as he tried to get comfortable. He hadn't switched on the light because there was no need. He knew where everything was. It was his study and everything was so familiar. The truckle bed normally resided in the loft. He had inherited it from his parents, their having purchased it while in Yorkshire on their honeymoon.

You could tell its origins, by its hard unforgiving feel and true Yorkshire 'owt for nowt', style. Sight of it, covered in dust and upended in the loft, had often offended Grace but it was, after all, a family heirloom. He just hadn't the heart to dispose of it. He had even used the argument that it might come in handy one day. It did hold good memories. The number of times he had spent a sleepless Christmas Eve, as a child, tucked warmly into its massive frame, waiting for his father to creep into the room, playing his part as Father Christmas. He had been much smaller then.

Alan moved for the hundredth time, trying to find a more acceptable position and elusive sleep. Every time he turned over, the bands of steel, forming the thin mattress support, played a twanging calypso, while the extended leg section of the frame, became unbalanced. Additional misery came from the one lumpy pillow, where he normally had two. He also suspected that the bed covers included at least one of his old car blankets from the garage.

A spasm of cramp curled his toes into a ball. His foot shot out from beneath the covers, sending him bolt upright. A sharp pain in his back now competed with the cramp for instant attention. His latest involuntary movement upset the delicate balance of the antique frame, causing the foot section to collapse. The bed had died.

He reached out for the reading lamp. It was not in its usual place on his desk. He realised Grace must have moved it. With some difficulty, he got out of the listing bed and moved sleepily forward. The small toe of his right foot struck one of the solid brass casters, fitted to the bed frame. The pain of this superseded the sum of all other pains. He managed to smother the fierce gasping howl, by placing both hands over his mouth.

Alan groped for the elusive desk-lamp. His fingers finally located its base. He snicked on the switch and delivered himself from the painful darkness. He looked round at the crippled bed. "You are gone in the morning!" He mouthed.

The next thing he noticed was a large dinner plate, on the desk, covered with a napkin. Misery spread slowly as he lifted the napkin to find a rather cold looking roast meal, congealed in a sea of brown gravy. Beside it was a note. It read, *'The meal I spent two and a half-hours preparing. The girls enjoyed your pudding, sleep well. G.'*

He nodded very slowly, "Now I know why she's ever so slightly miffed," he whispered. Replacing the napkin carefully over the plate, he put out the light and sat very gingerly back onto the protesting bed.

The black marble mantle clock, with Egyptian style obelisks and hieroglyphics, struck twice.

"And you're something else that's destined for the bin!" Alan mouthed. He almost smiled. At least he had lots of time to think out what he was going to say to David.

Chapter Twelve

Alan found the drive to Police Headquarters rather uncomfortable. The night had been an exceptionally long one. Sheer exhaustion had brought him some sleep although he was convinced he'd had no more than an hour, at most. He was equally convinced he now knew what prisoners felt like after being racked or strapped to a gun carriage.

Breakfast was something else. It had been a complete fiasco, with Grace, Clare and her friend constantly looking at Alan and Stolland, smiling, winking and saying they could definitely pass for brothers.

Then Grace insisted Stolland use some of Alan's clothes, because Stolland's looked as though they had been on him for days, which they obviously had. Grace gave Stolland, Alan's best lightweight suit, a choice of summer shirts, brand-new underclothes and, to top it all, she handed him Alan's cricket club tie.

The final blow was when she handed Stolland the Eastern Daily Press before Alan had a chance to get at it. He had stormed through it, obviously searching for something that was not there, then handed Alan, one badly mauled paper.

Grace and the girls were full of excitement over something they were not willing to share with him. Then, right in the middle of his dashing around at the last minute to find lost papers and briefcase Charlie arrived to collect them. It was not the best way to start what he knew could be, a long and trying day.

They had to wait for the Chief Constable to appear. Apparently, an urgent call had prevented him making his way to the meeting room. While they were waiting, a uniformed sergeant spoke to Charlie and handed him a sheaf of teleprinter messages.

Glancing at them, Charlie took Alan to one side, out of Stolland's hearing, "At last," he said, handing the messages to Alan, "it seems FP got a match on the abandoned Taxi, with dabs found at the café in Essex."

Alan looked, "Mucky Mary's?"

"Yes," said Charlie, "as luck would have it, a young D.C. out of Brentwood, got to the café first and preserved them. On top of that, the Met have done a match to prints found in the cab of the Cromer truck, plus others found inside the trailer at the Manor Way Cafe."

Alan nodded, "Seems someone's been busy. Can they put a name to the prints yet?"

Charlie shrugged, "They're searching records, but if this is the same villain, he's been getting around a bit, hasn't he? The vexing question is, why Stolland? What reason would he have for targeting Stolland?"

Alan raised his hands, "Why not? He obviously knows Stolland's come after him through that thing he calls the Gate."

It was Charlie's turn to shake his head, "Hold on a second boss. Didn't Stolland say he didn't join the facility until after Grech had gone through?" Without waiting for Alan to reply, Charlie continued, "In fact, there's a strong possibility that Grech may never have laid eyes on him."

Alan looked at Charlie, then over to where Stolland was sitting, "That's a good point. But he may well have cottoned onto Stolland in Cromer or have other means of knowing?"

Charlie scratched his chin and nodded, "It seems so. Anyway, he was the only passenger in that taxi when I saw it earlier at Blakeney, and when I saw it a second time heading away from the explosion."

Stolland seemed to tire of the staged whispering and came over, "I couldn't help overhearing. Do you mind if I join in?"

Alan looked at Stolland, "You might as well know. Whoever did the bombing on your late home, may be the same person who killed a local taxi driver, and before that, four people some distance from here."

Stolland rubbed at his chin, much the same way as Alan when he was deep in thought, "Your point about Grech knowing I'm after him is well made. It's obvious he's taken more than one good look at me. Know your enemy, Sergeant. Wasn't it the ancient Roman, Horace, who said, 'Fail not to show wise caution'?"

Alan smiled, "So, Stolland. The future still holds admiration for the classics. That's something, but we should remember the whole quotation. Which, if memory serves, includes the words, 'When danger encircles you, show yourself steadfast and undaunted'."

For the first time, Stolland actually laughed outright, "I'm sure all three of us will use a little care and determination in this matter."

He turned to Charlie, "In your case, Sergeant, you should take good care of yourself. As far as I know, you are one of the few, this side of the Gate, who's crossed Grech's path and lived to tell the tale. Just hope he hasn't worked out why you paid him and the taxi so much attention. I don't need to tell you how slippery and dangerous he is."

Charlie tried a nervous smile, "Thanks a bunch for that helpful thought. What would help right now is Grech's photograph and prints. I suppose you do still take prints?"

Stolland put a hand on Charlie's shoulder, "An ancient art Sergeant, but one that has persisted and been improved upon through the years."

"Well," said Alan, "Grech's better known to you. We only know his alleged handiwork. Until we can marry a face to our set of prints, we can't be sure we have a common enemy. Whoever's responsible, they've little regard for life, and that may include my Sergeants."

Alan showed Stolland the messages. Stolland nodded as he read them, "So, it seems Grech's been busy."

He thought for a moment and was about to say something when the door opened and in walked David Long.

"Good morning, gentlemen. Sorry to keep you waiting. Had a rushed telephone link-up with the Met and the Essex chief. Bad business, more murders than you can shake a stick at. Anyway, come on up to my office, it may be quieter up there."

David Long didn't take too kindly to Stolland being treated as anything but a dangerous prisoner. He was, as he was quick to remind him, under arrest for serious offences. As soon as they were all seated Alan briefed him on the circumstances, leading to Stolland's arrest.

David eyes swivelled upwards to the ceiling, "Oh, not more of the unreal please Alan. What ever happened to plain straight-forward police work?"

Not for the first time, David found himself lost for words and ended up dreading the task of having to convince others, far more senior than himself, that Stolland's story, wild though it was, could be true.

Deciding it was best to have some defence, David closed the meeting, knowing the best protection was an affable politician, and it had to be one that had previous experience of Alan's proclivity for unusual cases.

David looked hard at Stolland, "You might or might not be what you say you are, you may be his spitting image," he pointed at Alan, "but one thing is certain. Superintendent Brandon is responsible for you. As things stand, you have committed criminal acts for which you have yet to answer. You will either remain in close-custody or be escorted by my officers wherever you go. Is that clearly understood?"

Stolland smiled and nodded.

David then dismissed them instructing they should remain immediately available for a further meeting.

Thoughts tumbled through David's mind. He found himself torn between total belief in the professionalism of his officers, plus his incredible experience of Grace and her 'seeing' powers, versus the incredibility of the story surrounding Stolland. He sat for some time weighing everything he had heard. He would either end up labelled an incompetent fool by those in authority, or congratulated. Damned if I do and damned if I don't, he thought.

The threat of not taking appropriate action to contain what may be a nation-wide issue, weighed heavily. Having the threat of killers piling through a gap in time, tipped the balance. He would need to be cautious, select and balance his words carefully.

He unlocked a draw in his desk, withdrew a leather bound file marked 'Classified UK Defence Action.' He then ran his finger down an index and picked up the telephone. Dialling a number, he waited to be connected and then gave a code word. Just two minutes later, he was speaking to Sir Nicholas Folland, Home Secretary.

Thirty-five minutes later, he was in his car, on his way to London. One thought accompanied him. He desperately needed a high-level politician to make a quick decision. Not, he had to admit, the easiest task. To balance the responsibility of this business, he needed some form of large umbrella and Sir Nicholas was about as big as they came.

Outside police headquarters, in the fresh air, Stolland came to a halt, "You have to let me go back through the Gate. This time, I'm going to be a little longer."

Alan said, "We let go of your reins and you'll be off like a greyhound after your Mr Grech. No Stolland, we've already seen you fade into the ether. Until we have our hands on this maniac Grech, if there are journeys to be made, we go together."

Stolland stared hard at Alan, "You have no idea what you are saying. I cannot possibly take you through the Gate. It would destroy you, and not just mentally."

Alan stared just as menacingly at Stolland, "Come off it Stolland, I may be like stone-age man to you, but we are still made up of the same juicy body parts. It won't do Stolland."

For the first time since Charlie had cornered him on The Linnet, Charlie saw real anger in Stolland's eyes,

"Don't throw away the supporting evidence you're going to need by being an utter fool. There is no way I am going to appear at that next meeting without vital evidence. I am trying to help and I'm not about to ruin my mission by crossing you. You trusted me before. Let me go back and report what has happened. I'll get permission to bring through the evidence you badly need. Certainly your Chief will need it, if he is to swing his political masters."

Charlie lit a cigarette, "Personally, I'd kill for a photograph of Grech, plus a copy of his prints. If we could get those, we could nail all this business down to the one man."

Stolland said, "If we don't nail him, and in the very near future, this business, as you call it, will be over before we get near him."

Alan looked at Charlie. "Alright, alright but we both take him to Cley and hope to God we don't come back with just a handful of bloody shingle!"

"How long before this next meeting?" Asked Stolland.

"Why?" Replied Alan.

"Because, I may need all the time you can give me."

Alan half smiled, "Then we shouldn't be stood here, wasting it."

Charlie went through the motions of lighting another cigarette. "You know Sergeant, said Stolland, "I shouldn't do this, but I'll give you a piece of advice. If you have any shares in the tobacco industry, sell them."

Charlie grinned back at him, "And then what would I do for pleasure?"

"Continue breathing?" Suggested Stolland.

The car halted at the same spot on the marsh, as before. Alan walked with Stolland to the shingle bank, "I've half a mind to believe what you say Stolland, even though I feel it could just as easily turn out to be some fantasy, dreamt up by a criminal mind. Just don't keep us waiting too long."

With that, Alan held out a hand to Stolland. They shook hands and a second later, Stolland was gone.

Charlie had climbed the shingle bank and was watching children throwing stones into the sea. He smiled as his thoughts rambled on. He reckoned throwing pebbles into the sea was part of the human psyche, a compulsion; something children and adults have done since time immemorial. It had something to do with challenging the sea.

He put yet another cigarette in his mouth. He cupped his hands around the flaring match and inhaled the smoke deeply. He knew Stolland was right. His breathing was becoming laboured and it wasn't, as some people thought, advancing years. He was still comparatively young-ish, and could still chase the odd villain. Another thought entered his mind. He flicked the half-smoked cigarette away, watching it spiral into the air. He'd have to try and give it up. As he thought this, he knew how difficult it would be. It wouldn't be the first time he'd tried to kick the habit.

He looked at his watch for the hundredth time. Hours had passed since Stolland had gone back through the Gate. Charlie felt twitchy. He fell to wondering if Alan had been right to let Stolland go. Alan had driven off to Patchets to use the telephone. He obviously didn't want to upset the Chief by going absent again.

Charlie had never been one to envy senior ranks. He certainly didn't envy Alan's job, explaining how or why he'd allowed Stolland to disappear again!

He didn't hear the car arrive, but his mind registered the slogging footsteps, digging into the shingle, as someone climbed the bank behind him. He guessed it was Alan. Small chips of stone exploded and cascaded around him, as who ever it was, slumped down onto the stones.

"Where's the boss Charlie?"

Stolland's quiet voice startled Charlie, "Sorry I've been so long, but permissions had to be obtained to get bits through the Gate. Wasn't easy, I can tell you."

Charlie looked round. The shingle behind him, where Stolland was perched, also contained what looked like a large backpack. Although relieved at seeing Stolland, there was no way he was about to show it.

"I see you've been shopping?"

Stolland didn't answer at once, but looked back across the marsh as if searching, "The boss, where's your boss?"

An answer wasn't necessary. The car was visible threading its way through the marsh, from the distant coast road. "It's not good news Charlie," Stolland said, "Grech must be totally insane."

Charlie was going to ask what he meant, but the car was close.

Both men stood and waited. Soon Stolland began waving. He actually seemed pleased to see Alan.

Charlie wondered what had occurred, the other side of the Gate. There was a sense of urgency about Stolland, as if time was running out. Causing a small avalanche of stones, they jogged down the bank to the stationary car. Relief also registered on Alan's face. At least Stolland had returned.

"No point in rushing back," said Alan, as he opened the driver's door, "evidently nothing's been seen of the chief since he went to London."

"They've probably put him in a padded cell and thrown away the key!" Said Charlie.

"And we know how that feels, right Charlie? However, he did send a message. He met with our political masters then they all sloped off to the War Office. Then, believe this or not, it seems everyone adjourned to Number 10. He included in the message, we are to be at the War Office in Whitehall at two tomorrow afternoon, without fail, and that includes you Stolland."

"Now that is getting serious," said Charlie.

Alan turned on Charlie, "Can you get more serious than having a lunatic killer on the loose. One who has already seen off around ten people?"

Stolland broke in, "In that case, I suppose we'd better make the most of the time we've got."

Alan vacated the driving seat to Charlie and sat in the back with Stolland. He looked at the strange backpack, "I see you've arrived with something. I take it that it's more than a change of underwear?"

Stolland settled back and allowed Alan's curiosity to fester, "Just let's say we'll have some backup for tomorrows meeting. Until now, you've had to work blind. Well, from now on, you'll have a face to put to those prints."

"Great," said Alan, "let's get to Cromer. It should be quiet there and chances are we'll be undisturbed. If the Chief does turns up, at least we're on holy ground and contactable."

The journey passed without Stolland saying much about what had occurred on his side of the Gate. He simply explained his superiors finally agreed to release limited information, in a secure form. This verbal glimpse of what had taken place intrigued both Alan and Charlie. Why had the visit taken so long? Obviously, there were things that he was not going to tell.

It was not until they were inside the CID office at Cromer, with the door firmly closed that Stolland opened the backpack.

He withdrew a slim, smooth box-like object, not much larger than a box of Swan matches. He seemed to place pressure on the sides and they silently unfolded, increasing its size. He placed the object on the desk, indicating that Alan and Charlie should sit anywhere in the room they chose. They did this without comment. Stolland remained standing, positioning himself slightly behind and to one side of their chairs.

"For some little time," Stolland said, "you've both been at a loss to know whether or not to believe my story. No one can blame you. It's not every day you have a visitor from another time dropping in. I did my best to convince you of the truth, by passing through the Gate. But, I agree that piece of visible magic may not have helped you convince others."

"Or help identify Grech," said Alan.

Stolland paused, "Point taken."

Alan was staring at the box. The top of which had begun to glow with a faint luminous green light. Charlie also watched this and absent-mindedly began to grope for his cigarettes.

"Not now Charlie," said Stolland, "what you are about to see may make you choke on that weed. It may make you a little nervous, unsure of yourself, but I can assure you, it's all perfectly safe. Please stay in your chairs until I explain what you are looking at. Then do as I ask. You'll no doubt have questions and I shall answer, as best I can."

With that, Stolland walked across the room, drew the blinds and locked the office door, "Now," he said, "remember, don't move from your chairs, until I say."

There was a soft click and the room became bathed in a pale green glow. The light slowly grew, becoming brighter but cast no shadows. As they watched, there was a change. Figures of people began to appear, walking towards and around them. It was just as though they were standing in the middle of what looked like a laboratory, or an operating theatre.

Neither, Alan or Charlie recognised the instruments or equipment that surrounded them. Everything was smooth and scrupulously clean. To one side, banks of glowing panels showed what appeared to be some kind of display, each screen different to the other. There were voices, but individual words were scrambled.

Suddenly, a short, thin man was walking close to them. He stopped in mid stride. Just as if frozen in time. He was as real as if he had just entered the office. The light seemed to centre on him, his features becoming clear.

"Let me introduce you to our killer, Victor Grech. Now, please get up and walk around this man, just as if he was standing here. Take a good look at him. You won't affect the image or cast shadows. The emissions will not affect you."

Alan and Charlie stood up, not saying a word. As Stolland had asked, they walked up to and completely around the figure. They were obviously dumbstruck by the experience. The figure looked solid, but when they reached out to touch, their hands passed straight through the image.

"I asked you to take a really good look, because surely Charlie, you recognise this character? Not the first time you've seen Grech, is it?"

"Well now," Charlie rubbed his chin, "I'm not certain what our courts would think of this form of identity parade, but, for my money, that's the passenger from the taxi, alright. And the one who stared for ages at The Linnet. Did you get his prints?"

"I did a little better," said Stolland.

There was a faint whirring from a slightly larger box, which Stolland removed from the pack. After a few seconds, Stolland handed Alan and Charlie a perfect hologram of Grech, plus a complete copy of palm and fingerprints. The whirring ceased.

"Now," said Stolland, he operated something and Grech began to move again, walking round the room as if followed by a mobile camera, "Study this man, his walk, the way he carries himself. Listen and pay particular attention to his voice. Note how soft his speech is, also how deep set his eyes are. See how black and piercing they are. He also has abilities that are not obvious. Regardless of his lack of height and slim build, he is deceptively strong. He can also slip into and out of character by simply changing his clothes. He is, as I have already said, extremely ruthless and cunning. This, I promise you, is the closest you'll ever want to come to this dangerous individual."

Suddenly, from all points in the room, a voice could be heard speaking softly and yet there was an underlying ice-like clarity in the tone. He was obviously giving instructions to others in the room.

Stolland continued, "Remember gentlemen, this man doesn't develop friendships. He uses people as you might use a tool. I'm told if something was not absolutely correct, or to his liking, his eyes sharpened to black pinpoints. He showed no other emotion. It is possible he doesn't understand remorse, pleasure or that type of feeling. So don't look for compassion in this man. You will certainly be painfully disappointed.

This then, is Victor Grech, our target. It is fairly certain all three of us are now his! Please, if you do nothing else, watch your back from here on in. As we know, he moves around without too much of a problem, regardless of routine checks etc."

Alan sat down heavily and shook his head slowly, "I'm sure I don't have to say how confusing all this is, and not only because of what we've seen. If Grech is responsible for these killings, he's certainly the worst, cold-blooded bastard, I've ever come across," the colour in Alan's face drained to a pale shade of grey as he recalled the photographs of bodies at the transport café.

After some seconds he said, "It goes without saying, no one outside this room will know what we've seen. That is, unless you feel that a demonstration to others is necessary?"

Stolland replied, "We policemen are born sceptics. It will be necessary to repeat this show at the next meeting. Therefore, those attending must be completely and utterly trustworthy. For everyone's sake we must keep the time-shift element of this business fully cloaked. Forgive my repeating this, but I must insist, only those that absolutely must know, should be present at that meeting."

Alan looked at Charlie, "We agree totally. The less people know of this business the better. It's the stuff nightmares are made of."

Stolland seemed to relax a little, "I have no fear of you going back on your word. After all, the only protection you and yours have from this creature is that we work on an absolute need to know basis and trust each other. The more people who know we are on to Grech, the greater the risk. If one of us slips up and it gets out to the media, he will most assuredly, get to all of us before we can stop him."

Alan looked slightly embarrassed, "We may have to broaden the circle slightly. You'll just have to watch our every move. If there's something, someone you feel is a risk, don't waste time apologising, just say it. I'll try and cover any misunderstanding."

Stolland smiled, "And there was I thinking we wouldn't have to worry about stepping on toes?"

Charlie had been pouring over the prints, comparing those provided by Stolland with those taken from the crime scenes, "I'm no FPO, but I'd stake my pension on these being identical. Grech's the killer, alright. But there's one thing I don't understand?"

Stolland smiled at Charlie, "Only one thing?"

Charlie grinned back, "Yes, if he's from the future and he's so damned clever at getting things through the Gate, as you call it. Why has he used an old fashioned handgun on his victims?"

Stolland smiled, "That's easy. For some reason, he came through without a hand weapon. Possibly felt he could execute his main plan, then scoot straight back through the Gate before the dust settled, leaving no trace of his visit. What we do know is that he's purchased a gun locally, and let's face it, being shot with a pistol is just as lethal and looks less suspicious than being terminated by a weapon from my time. By the way, what type of gun has he used, so far?" The last two words from Stolland, hung in the air.

Charlie coughed, looked at Alan and drew out his notebook, "Point three-two Beretta automatic, soft-nosed, expanding bullets. Very nasty close up."

Alan said, "I wonder how he got hold of that in the five minutes he's been around?"

Stolland looked at Charlie's notes, "I'd say, take a good look at wherever he stayed in Cromer. I've a feeling the answer may lay there or with his contact at the warehouse the lorry came from. He'd have plenty of money to buy it."

Alan seemed surprised, "How on earth can he carry wads of cash through the Gate?"

"He didn't. We have no use for what you call cash. He had one of these," he pointed to the slightly larger of the two boxes.

"This can produce items such as your currency. Once it's programmed to the likely needs of the user, it simply replicates it. Truth is, you can't tell the notes from those you receive from your bank. Even selects random serial numbers. I should know, I've already used quite a few. One thing I've learnt, money speaks all languages. If you have money, you can buy as much help as you need. Money has no conscience and asks no questions."

Alan and Charlie's ears were pinned back by what Stolland had said.

"It can also be programmed to memorise any item from your media, newspapers, books, maps from any period, which the user researches, then feeds in. Even, tide or transport schedules. He has everything very nicely at his fingertips. As for recruiting help, and it's just a guess. He would look for a loner, someone who looked short of money. Perhaps someone from a pub or club, or perhaps just someone he met in the street. During conversations, he would buy a few drinks and get them relaxed. You know, let them talk. By doing this, he establishes himself as a friendly type, appears to have money, and is willing to listen to the individual's problems. He might even drop the hint that money is available."

"How?" Said Charlie.

Stolland looked disappointed, "Look, Grech had access to all sorts of general information, serious value to the right sort."

Charlie looked puzzled, "What would it take to get someone on his side, without question?"

"Greed," said Stolland, "just plain greed. It never fails Charlie. The sound of quick money, Grech would call up any sporting occasion from your time, and know the result. He then passes this on, giving his mark, sorry, his new acquaintance, the impression that he's a first class tipster, a real friendly track-type. He might even loan the poor chap his stake money. Then, when the winnings are paid out, well, one good turn deserves another?"

Just when Stolland had Charlie's full attention, Alan called, "Hold it right there! The latest dog results at

Ipswich can wait Charlie! Let's get back to the real issue. You say he's come back to cause a catastrophe, right?"

Stolland nodded, "That's what we believe. All his moves so far indicate he's sticking with his main plan."

"And all the killings, they are part of the plan?"

"Not at all, but it shows how dangerous Grech is. He has one driving force and that is 'the plan.' Anyone crosses his path or causes him grief or concern becomes his target."

"So, let's stop pussy-footing around," urged Alan, "we must stop him now!"

Stolland operated something and the visual display faded, "Alan, your Chief wants this meeting with his bosses to go well. We don't want to go over the whole thing twice so I ask you to be patient?"

Alan's body posture showed his mounting impatience, but he nodded his agreement. All police activity, both covert and overt had, so far, failed to give them a sniff of this man Grech, except of course, in the weight of bodies.

Alan excused himself and left the room. Charlie went round opening blinds and windows, discovered he badly needed a cigarette and started the blue haze drifting across the room. Stolland quietly placed the objects back in his pack.

When Alan returned, he looked more than a little uncertain, "Well, it's all on. Stolland, you'll need to be fireproof tomorrow if you want to survive the doubting Thomas's. Even with your picture show, it will be damned hard going. Most of our masters, especially the politicians, believe we are dealing with a straight forward, 20th Century serial killer. I can promise, they're not going to be too happy about you or what you have to say."

Charlie stubbed out his cigarette, "I'll get on the phone and see what's happening around the counties. You never know your luck, hopefully Grech may be on a mortuary slab somewhere."

"Now that's one post-mortem I'm looking forward to," said Alan with more than a hint of feeling.

As they descended the stairs, Alan caught Charlie's arm, "Grace told me on the phone that Clare has been with George and he's just about comfortable. I'm going to make sure Grech pays the full price for what he's done. I'll do the hanging job myself."

Trooping out into the station yard, they saw an area car waiting, obviously detailed to take Alan and Stolland to Norwich. Charlie waited for them to go before wading through and rechecking every scrap of information arriving at the information room. Anything new would be notified, direct to Alan.

The area car moved off, then immediately stopped. Alan wound down his window, "Charlie, we'll catch the nine-thirty-two from Thorpe Station. I'll pick up the tickets on the way home later. Save us time in the morning."

Charlie nodded, "Sounds fine, sir," for the benefit of the watching car crew, he had added the 'sir', "don't let Mr Stolland forget the backpack. We're going to need it."

Alan smiled, "Watch your back, Charlie." With a wave Charlie watched him go, then went to join the paper chase.

On the way to Norwich, Stolland quietly said, "There seems a real bond between you and Sergeant Friar."

Alan nodded, "Joined the service in London together. David Long, Charlie and I were in the same section house. Did beats together. David and I got our heads down and raced for promotion, while Charlie loved the people on his beat. He wasn't interested in studying for a higher rank.

We've been through some hard times. Charlie's been like an uncle to my daughter, especially when she was young. Grace was still regularly playing then. BBC broadcasts, piano recitals, proms, she loved her music. Charlie used to take Clare out and spend hours walking with her, while I studied and gained promotion. He married much later. Charlie has no children of his own. It's sometimes difficult to remember the difference in our respective ranks. Unfortunately, the police service respects badges of rank, rather than the quality of the man wearing them. Influences outside the force count a great deal, if you want to go higher, that sort of thing. Charlie and his wife June are just like family. I wouldn't like anything to happen to either of them. It would be like losing a brother or sister."

Stolland stared at the road ahead, his mind full of comparisons between family ties and life that now surrounded him compared to what he had known. His face did not betray his personal thoughts and memories.

At Thorpe Station, Stolland leapt out of the car immediately it stopped, "Please allow me to buy the tickets. Call it a boyhood ambition."

Alan watched as Stolland disappeared into the booking hall. A few minutes later, he returned to the car proudly waving them. "They're first class reservations for tomorrow morning, including a full English breakfast!"

The smile on his face said everything. Alan understood Stolland was perhaps living out a history lesson.

The evening went extremely well, with Grace and Clare on top form. Grace seemed thrilled about something, which she said she would explain if she received the telephone call she was waiting for. Alan quite naturally assumed it must be something to do with one of her many committees.

After dinner, Clare provided news on George's progress. She had visited him and said he seemed far more comfortable. Evidently, Sir Sidney Lisle who was a top burns specialist was to oversee his treatment. George was speaking a little more easily but dreaded dressing changes. He never complained but Clare knew the pain he must be enduring.

Stolland sat listening closely to Clare's report. Perhaps reflecting on what could so easily have been his fate. Clare also said she had difficulty in getting any time alone with George and had to be content with sharing him with crowds of well-wishing visitors, including Fred Fisher, who was now courting.

"Courting," spluttered Alan, trying to avoid depositing the remainder of his wine in his lap.

"Yes," laughed Grace, "isn't it a hoot. It seems he has at last grasped the nettle. Evidently, the lady concerned is Libby Hopkins. You know, she has that charming cottage not far from the marsh, in Bucklers Lane. Has beautiful window boxes."

Alan nodded, "Yes, nice person. Well, who would have thought it, crafty old Fred. Always did want to live near the marsh, but I think the closeness of the Duck public house has something to do with it."

They all laughed.

The only telephone call was for Grace. When she returned from the hall with a smile so broad Alan knew immediately what it was.

"Confirmation that you have been invited to play?" He said.

"Yes," said an excited Grace, trying hard not to preen too much, "it's so exciting and everything's in such a rush. A one-off concert to raise funds for war orphans. It will be wonderful simply because it will be the greatest concert since the end of the war. Oh Alan, I'm so excited but, it will mean time in London for rehearsals I'm afraid. I will stay at Eaton Walk for my rehearsals, which will be at the Royal School of Music and the Royal Albert Hall with the full orchestra. The BBC will be broadcasting the whole event and the Royal family have promised to be there."

Grace caught her breath, put on a painful expression meant for Alan, "Will you mind terribly managing for yourself for a short time, Alan dear?"

Alan looked at Grace, "It will be dreadful slaving away here, but as it's for King and country, I think we will all have to bow to the inevitable."

He looked across at Stolland and smiled broadly.

"Do we get to come to this great occasion?" Asked Clare.

Grace laughed, "Only if you promise to make sure your father wears white tie, and that goes for you too Mr

Stolland, if you come. The tickets are expensive, fifty pounds each."

"No problem there," smiled Stolland, "I am absolutely certain I can find the necessary funds. After all, I am on an expenses paid trip."

Alan's smile faltered. Stolland smiled at Grace, "Dear lady, your fund will benefit and our pleasure will be complete." He gave Alan a wink.

"No, no we can't have that," blustered Alan, "you are our guest. I insist. I will pay for the tickets and be pleased to wear white tie."

Alan's face was a picture of relief, as the matter of the ticket purchase seemed settled. Stolland's access to what he loosely described as 'funds,' had taken on all the trappings and worries of a certain King Midas. Right now Alan felt he didn't need Stolland's money machine or any other technical wizardry courtesy of the Gate.

"And when does all this begin?" Clare asked her mother.

"Believe it or not, for me it all begins tomorrow. I must first go into Norwich. Tomorrow evening, I'll travel up to Eaton Walk. I'll let you know on the phone the details of the performance and when to collect the tickets, etc. Oh, it's all so very exciting isn't it?"

Alan was grateful to finally crawl into cool clean sheets and thank his lucky stars for rescuing his conscience from a financial disaster. His thoughts ran on, pondering on Stolland's family situation. Stolland never referred to his personal or private life, which was a little strange, being so far from home. In fact, he seemed to avoid the subject as though there was a great sadness there. Did he have a special home, a wife and family? Alan made up his mind to find out.

His last thought was about George Wright. One day, he thought, I am going to find a way of paying that boy back for saving my life.

Chapter Thirteen

The next morning, Grace drove them to the Thorpe station, where they met Charlie. Checking the indicator board, they found the train was leaving from platform four. Having bought each of them a newspaper, Grace said her goodbyes, promising not to spend too much money and to work hard at her music for the concert. She and Clare then went shopping, after which they intended visiting George.

The three men wound their way through the crowds and found their carriage. Charlie was pleasantly surprised to find they were travelling in first class comfort. Dead on time and with the slightest of jolts, the train steamed out of the station. Charlie then received his second surprise. A smartly dressed steward appeared in their compartment, produced a bundle of sticks, the complexity of which would have defeated a deck chair attendant, and proceeded to assemble a respectable table. On this, he laid cutlery for a silver-service breakfast. All managed without a word.

Passing through Chelmsford, Charlie was finishing his third cup of tea, having done justice to a limited but fine post-war breakfast. He smiled across at Stolland, who was amazed at Charlie's ability to tackle the railway breakfast menu.

Just after midday, the train ran alongside platform twelve at London's Liverpool Street station. Alan woke Charlie, who had done his best to sleep the best part of the journey from Chelmsford.

Stolland had said very little as the train made its way through the London suburbs. He sat staring through the window at the bomb-damaged buildings and rubble strewn spaces, still very much in evidence.

Twice he shook his head in disbelief, finally saying to Alan, Reading about this destruction, isn't like actually seeing it. What are those tall metal structures sticking up on the horizon?"

"Dock cranes," said Alan, "they line the London docks. Some local children call them Noddies, because of the swinging, bobbing and swaying, as they move their loads. I take it that you don't have such cranes?"

Stolland smiled, "I remember seeing them in books, but we have nothing quite like that. It's best we don't discuss what we have. Protocol you know," he smiled again.

There was quite a queue to pass through the barriers at the end of the platform. A ticket collector, whose face seemed to carry as much sadness and wear as certain buildings they had passed, was automatically collecting tickets and managing to talk to his mate, without disturbing the ash on a smouldering cigarette. This seemed permanently glued to the corner of his mouth.

Indicating this Charlie said, "Now that is what I call a real cockney artist. Who said, you can't, do two things at once? Obviously, whoever it was, had never met that chap."

They made their way slowly through the crowds towards an exit marked, London Wall & Moorgate. A further sign simply read 'Taxis'. Emerging like water from a gushing tap, they found themselves in the street. Charlie pointed along the street, While Alan shouted to make for the taxi rank.

Alan and Stolland turned and followed Charlie's back. They saw him suddenly dive across the road and flag down a cab. In a second, all three were inside the taxi.

"Never," said Charlie, "ever go to a rank outside a main-line station. It's so much easier to grab a cab in the street," he turned to the driver, "Trafalgar Square please, driver."

Stolland was fascinated. He stared at everything, from boarded-up blitzed buildings, bombsites covered in luxurious weeds, buses, crowds of people, to City of

London coppers with their unfamiliar brass helmet badges. The taxi pulled up outside the National Gallery, on the North side of Trafalgar Square.

Stolland leapt out, backpack in hand. He handed the driver a white five-pound note and said, "Keep the change." The driver looked pole-axed. Stolland looked pleased with himself, "I've always wanted to say that."

Charlie looked just as amazed, "Do you realise, you've just given that chap four pounds seventeen and nine pence, as a tip?"

Alan laughed, "No wonder he's shot off into the traffic!"

Charlie continued, "That's a week's wages earned in a single journey. Oh well, easy come easy go."

Alan knew exactly what Charlie meant. No doubt, the fiver had been a product of the little black box. He was suddenly ashamed. Here he was, a Superintendent of Police, condoning a crime. However, it was too late now, and he was rather enjoying being in the company of a man from the future, though he controlled his smile.

Crossing the square, they managed to pull Stolland away from Nelson's column and trundled him forward, across Duncannon Street, to a small café. Finding an empty table, Alan resisted the temptation to let Stolland pay for the drinks.

He quietly said, "I think it best if we sit for a few minutes and work out what we do when we arrive at the War Department," Charlie nodded, "and I think it best if you, Mr Stolland, cease passing, what could be funny money. Every purchase doesn't start and end with five pound notes. People get suspicious when you buy something worth a few pence and insist they keep the change. After all, we're only a stone's throw from Scotland Yard, if that means anything at all, to you?"

Stolland grinned, "Sorry. I had no idea I was offending you, and yes, I do know the name Scotland Yard. I also know we are not more than two thirds of a mile from Parliament, just three quarters of a mile from the flats that once served as Buckingham Palace and less than two miles, as the crow flies from Sherlock Holmes', Baker Street apartments."

"Flats?" Said Charlie, in shocked amazement, "What do you mean, flats! The King's still very much in residence, and that's how we like it!"

Stolland held up his hands in mock surrender, "Calm down Charlie, I'm only joking."

Both Alan and Charlie were obviously relieved. Their second cup of coffee tasted worse than the first. Alan decided it was time to make their way to the meeting. The walk along Whitehall, to the unattractive pile known as the War Office, passed without comment.

They mounted the steps to an imposing front door and found themselves ushered into a large, echoing reception hall. Here, they met an equally large, uniformed Commissionaire, who stood like an impassable granite boulder. Such fixtures always appear to be ex-forces, sport waxed-moustache's and exhibit a pear-shaped frame over a fierce air of superiority.

Alan produced his warrant card. The Commissionaire glanced at the card, then at an appointment list, ticked off an entry and directed them to a wide stone staircase leading down into the basement area.

At the foot of the stairs was another desk, this time manned by two members of the Military Police. One of these again examined Alan's warrant card, cast a judgemental eye over all three and then led them through a long corridor, at the end of which was yet another door. He knocked on the door, and listened. Receiving no reply, he knocked again. This time the door opened and they went in.

The size of the room surprised Alan. It was rectangular and very well lit. Halfway down on the left side was a large black marble fireplace. In the centre of the room and running its whole length was a wide, green baize covered table with chairs placed on either side. The shock for Alan, Stolland and Charlie, was the number of people in the room.

Some stood around in small groups, talking in hushed tones, while others were sitting at the table. All appeared to be finishing coffee. Conversation gradually died and questioning eyes turned on them. The silence was now deeply uncomfortable. It was as though they had stumbled into a club, restricted to members only.

Charlie whispered, "I feel like one of the three stooges."

"Truer words were never spoken," Alan hissed these words between gritted teeth. He was seething.

A somewhat tired voice, from perhaps half way down the room, called, "Do please come in and sit down."

An arm, clad in dark blue pin stripe, supporting a pale hand, neatly intersected by the regulation one inch of white shirt cuff, gave a half-hearted beckoning movement.

The voice continued, "Please occupy those chairs placed across the far end of the table."

Alan and Charlie recognised the voice of the Home Secretary from his many radio interviews. It was of course, Sir Nicholas Folland. Alan assumed, they were to be seated in a position that gave every occupant the opportunity to examine them as they walked to their chairs. The same walk, of course, gave the three the opportunity to take in the variety of people present.

During the journey, Alan noted his own Chief Constable, who kept his head buried in files, apparently studying a paper of some sort. The Essex chief, raised a hand and smiled, as did a Commander of the Metropolitan police, who Alan knew, was responsible for K Division, part of the dockside area of the east end of London. At least, their presence made sense.

Seated either side of Sir Nicholas were the Joints Chiefs of Staff, flanked by what appeared to be their respective assistants. At side tables, placed along the full length of either wall, were seriously suited men and women, all apparently vital note-takers. The three took all this in by the time they reached their seats.

Alan breathed the words, "Somewhat crowded for a confidential briefing!"

Stolland placed the backpack carefully on the baize-covered table. Every eye in the room moved in unison, first to the pack and then back to the three.

Sir Nicholas rose to his feet and smilingly said, "Well ladies and gentlemen, we all know why we are here, having been earlier briefed by Chief Constable Long. As we all know, there has been a succession of brutal murders, which I also understand, may be connected to an undisclosed..." here, Sir Nicholas paused for effect and repeated, "an undisclosed threat."

A muffled murmur ran through the room, while Sir Nicholas, being a true politician, courted the appreciation of his words and delicate pauses. He again repeated, "As yet, an undisclosed threat. The three gentlemen, who have just arrived at our meeting, are here to clearly explain, that threat. So..." another courted pause, "I understand that Chief Superintendent Brandon will provide us with a full account, supported we hope, by some factual evidence?" Broadly smiling left and right, he sat down. His eyes, like those of everyone else around the table, now pinned on the three new members.

Alan took his time rising to his feet. The number of people, stacked into the room seriously offended him. This was as unexpected as it was unacceptable.

"Sir Nicholas, ladies and gentlemen, this is extremely difficult. Because of the very nature of our business, I am at a complete loss to understand the wisdom of such a large attendance. While I am not questioning the credibility, the loyalty, honesty and integrity of every person present, I do not feel..." he got no further.

Stolland had risen and stood beside him. He looked at Alan, as if apologising and reading his thoughts. Turning to face Sir Nicholas, he said, "Sir, you will forgive Superintendent Brandon for being unsure of the way forward, when I tell you that I am here to present the evidence referred to. It is I, and I alone, who insisted on an absolute 'Need to Know', classification, for today's attendance," A rumbling murmur began to build through the room, Stolland continued, "I have absolutely no

235

intention of being disrespectful to anyone present. But, what I have to say is for only the ears and eyes of the very few people who will provide the authority and action for what must be done."

The murmur, now like an approaching tube train, became more distinct. Feathers had obviously been, ruffled. Over this chunter of disbelief, Stolland continued, "They will be personally held to account, if a word of what I have to say, gets beyond this room."

To Charlie, who was amazed at the immediate wave of indignation that filled the room, it seemed as though he was inside a chicken coop, watching all the hens nodding, pecking and clucking at the same time. Bobbing heads turning left and right, hands waving to gain support as to why, their particular attendance should ever be questioned was intolerable.

The noise of offended individuals and support groups reached a crescendo before Sir Nicholas, banging the table with the head of someone's furled umbrella, brought a confused silence. Stolland sat down.

"Thanks Stolland," said Alan, "succinctly put, if I may say so."

Sir Nicholas rose and called to him several grey suited men. Without explanation, they left the room. Within the room, a succession of whispered conversations broke out. David Long rose from his chair and walked purposefully to where the three were sitting.

"Well done Alan, The only success you've had with your opening, is to evacuate the bloody room! There goes my chance of retiring with a knighthood. Why on earth couldn't you have given them something on the murders and waited for the Home Sec's reaction?"

Alan stood up, "Sir, we came to present facts and the murders are, if you'll excuse the expression, only part of today's presentation. A significant part I grant you, but this is no ordinary murder spree!" Alan was doing his best to control his obvious displeasure at his Chief's total failure to ensure attendance was strictly limited. Alan counted five, and then went on, "Now, I'm truly sorry if you feel I've handled this badly and I'm totally shattered if you feel your chance of a knighthood is shot, but I feel we can't have a lot of open-lipped, loose tongued civil servants running around knowing what Stolland has to say. They've obviously heard and seen too much already!"

Stolland admired Alan's spirit, but felt a little restraint was in order. Quietly reaching for Alan's sleeve, he gave it a gentle tug. David, who also seemed to accept what appeared to be a hint to calm the water, didn't miss the hint. Both men accepted that washing linen was best done in a laundry, not in front of such an audience. As if to underline the need for change, the main door opened and in walked Sir Nicholas. Silence descended and chairs hurriedly reoccupied.

"Ladies and gentlemen, after some consideration, I would like all attendees, except the military, civil police and the three special guests, to leave the meeting." Sir Nicholas allowed a second for the shock waves to strike home, "I do apologise sincerely for what you may consider has been a waste of your most valuable time. However, there are convincing reasons for this, so I ask you to kindly withdraw. You will each receive the usual buff paper, briefly explaining the purpose and outcome of today's meeting."

Chairs shunted back creating a further din, when Sir Nicholas raised an appealing hand, "Sorry, but this request also naturally applies to all Aides and support staff," due to the continued disgruntled muttering, he raised his voice an octave, "can I also remind you of the penalty for disclosing anything you have seen or heard here today."

Sir Nicholas removed his spectacles and pointedly looked immediately behind him. A half dozen grey suits, whose owners felt the request to leave could, under no circumstances, have included them, dutifully rose placed note-pads and pencils in government briefcases, and joined the sullen, stony faced exit queue. It took a full twenty minutes for the room to clear and revised seating positions allocated. This revised seating placed Alan, Charlie and

Stolland on one side of the table, with Sir Nicholas, Joint Chiefs and Police Officials, opposite them.

Once settled, Sir Nicholas, apparently unruffled by what had taken place, smiled across at Alan. Charlie admired the smile, wondering who his dentist was.

"Now, Detective Chief Superintendent, I hope the echo of slashing cutlasses was worth it. Perhaps your guest, Mr Stolland, who seemed so anxious to reduce our numbers, would like to begin."

Stolland rose, but instead of speaking, he began walking slowly all the way around the room, with what appeared to be a small box resting in the palm of his open hand. After a complete circuit of the room, he looked across at Sir Nicholas.

"It seems sir, there are three transmitting devices, perhaps microphones secreted in this room. I assure you, they are active."

Sir Nicholas rose. Signs of impatience clearly painted on his flushed cheeks, "Where, damn it man! Show us where!"

Stolland walked slowly to the fireplace, "One is hidden under the mantle-shelf. One behind that plaster crest immediately above the door and the other is behind the picture of the King."

This revelation caused a further delay of thirty minutes. Sir Nicholas left the room while a group of people entered, searched and found the secreted wiring and microphones. When these had been removed Stolland undertook a further check and was satisfied with the result. While this was going on, tea and biscuits arrived.

Charlie slipped out of the room and returned just before Sir Nicholas. He had found a toilet in which he could have a cigarette.

"I always wondered what our taxes were spent on," he said, "every sink in this place has its own bar of soap and towel. Talk about waste of soap ration. They have even stamped the words War Department on the soap. Not that anyone would steal it. It's as hard as a bullet and smells of Jack's fluid or whatever that stuff's called."

"Jeye's," corrected Alan.

After assurances, Sir Nicholas resumed the meeting. He smiled, thanking Stolland for his security assistance, "I do not think it wise to enquire where the meter, or whatever it was you used, came from. It's obviously not available to us, quite yet?"

The question went unanswered. Stolland stood, once again. He removed from the backpack one of the black boxes and, repeating his performance at Cromer, he placed it in the centre of the table.

"Sir Nicholas, Gentlemen. There is no short way around what I have to say. I think it has always been standard practice, to know as much about your enemy as possible. It is only fair then, that you should know yours. I say yours because from this moment, he is as much your enemy as mine, or the Superintendent's or Sergeant Friar's," as Stolland began this last sentence, he walked slowly behind and touched the shoulder of Alan and then Charlie, "under no circumstances will you take notes at this meeting or make them after it, and that includes simple diary entries. Superintendent Brandon will produce all written matter relating to this subject. He alone, will be responsible for the safe custody of all information relating to this investigation. Party politics, differences of opinion or personal beliefs or needs, must not sway your judgement in this particular matter. Your future and that of many others is in the balance here. Were it not so, the decision to allow me to make, what you may call, a time shift would not have been taken. Do I have total agreement thus far?"

Heads containing looks of total disbelief, nodded.

"A man, from my time, 2102, has already been responsible for a number of recent killings and other acts of violence. He has violated our security protocols, engineered a time shift, solely intent on personal vengeance."

Everyone, apart from Alan and Charlie tried to interrupt. Stolland held up his hands.

"Please gentlemen! I didn't come here expecting you to believe what I'm saying without proof, and that will be provided, before you leave this room. It is for you to judge and act, to enable we three," Stolland placed his hands on the shoulders of Alan and Charlie, "to stop this madman, before he carries out his plan."

Sir Nicholas couldn't contain himself, "Now look here, Stolland. If we accept what you are saying and this villain has come from the future," there was a politician's pause, "time slipping or whatever you call it, then surely he may have already had sight of how successful he was. Stands to reason, what? He could simply have gone to his local newspaper offices and looked up historical accounts, couldn't he?" Sir Nicholas shook his head as he said this. He turned to his left and right, "Damn it all, saying what I have just said makes me doubt my own sanity."

The room was now deathly quiet, apart from a clock that ticked away the seconds.

Stolland amazingly smiled, "The recorded history that was available to this man, prior to his time-slip, carried nothing of what has occurred recently, simply because details have been suppressed. The media has no knowledge and providing this blanket is maintained, no public record will exist."

"Sorry, Mr Stolland," said Sir Nicholas, "I'm sure I speak for all across this side of the table when I say, with the benefit of hindsight, I am sure all this makes sense to you, but regretfully, not to me."

"Fair enough sir," said Stolland, "let us say Jack the Ripper brought about the deaths of a number of women. These deaths are on public record. Stories splashed across your press. What of other deaths not recorded? These fell into what you might call unrecorded history. The future will not be aware of them. Our man has returned to your time to rewrite history. He is here to reshape certain reported historical events, available to him in his own time."

Sir Nicholas turned to others his side of the table, opened his hands and nodded, "I think I see your point. It's up to us to ensure nothing goes to the media, and I mean nothing! However, other than these recent unfortunate deaths, we are still a little short on facts."

Stolland looked at Alan and Charlie, then back across the table. Eyes stared back at him, waiting to see something, anything that would help them believe the unbelievable.

"My passing through time, by using what we call the Gate, is a fact that has already been demonstrated and witnessed first hand, by the police officers on my side of this table. If you have doubt, I ask you to put aside those doubts until I have completed my presentation."

Everyone maintained silence. Stolland gave a faint smile.

"I would also point out that once you are briefed, you might be at risk from the individual you are about to meet. As you know, he has already a number of kills to his credit."

Stolland asked Alan to turn off most of the lights. This he did. The black box began its show to the complete amazement of all, but Alan and Charlie. Again, the scene was a laboratory environment, with Grech taking centre stage. Stolland froze the display at the point where Grech was fully visible. He then split the display into three holograms, showing Grech's front, side and back view. Stolland waited for the murmurs of incredulity to soften.

"The man you are looking at is one Victor Grech. He is the man responsible for the recent killings I referred to. If you carry nothing else from this meeting, you must believe this, if he suspected you were aware of his plans, his face would be the last you ever see in this world. He would most definitely find you and make no mistake, he would most surely kill you, and anyone with you. That could mean your entire family. He does have the benefit of history so he can be several jumps ahead of you especially where the media records your moves. He most assuredly knows where to come looking if he connects you to his business. The only sure defence you have is to ensure that no action related to this business, including meetings such as this, becomes the subject of speculation, or common knowledge," Stolland thought for a moment, "remember, what Grech has planned is reshaping history. The murders he has committed would not have been committed had he not come back in time. I know that is hard to grasp, but it does mean that historical information available to me, prior to coming over, would not have carried news of these killings. Therefore, we could not have prevented them.

It is equally possible that Grech is blindly going forward to carry out his plan. He is an opportunist, cunning and an extremely intelligent scientist. He has already recruited local help and I feel he will recruit further assistance. He has the means to gain his ends, don't help him! So please remember one of your wartime slogans, 'careless talk costs lives'."

Stolland let this sink in. It was obvious from the hushed conversation that this whole event was grabbing at nerves.

Sir Nicholas raised a polite hand, "Is there any way you can go back to wherever you come from and deal with Grech from there?"

Stolland said, "Normally, anyone on a programme related to time-shift would be fitted with a device that would provide his or her monitors the opportunity to suspend or terminate the subject. The reasons for this can be many and varied, but, in Grech's case," Stolland held up his hands, "in plain language, I'm afraid when the instruction for termination was sent, and it was, it didn't work! We now know why. I cannot go into detail."

A shocked silence descended on the room. At last, Sir Nicholas said, "I speak for all present. No one will utter a single word about this business, to colleagues, to superiors, to family or friends. You have my absolute word on that. Also, I believe, for sake of total security, Detective Chief Superintendent Brandon, his sergeant and yourself should be the only three people who have absolute authority to pursue this man Grech, and either secure him or silence him. No one here will question your actions or contact you. It will be for you to contact us if you so choose to do. I would finally add that should you meet any obstruction, you must contact me immediately. In that one case, members will be recalled."

One of the joint chiefs raised a hand, "In that case Home Secretary, can I suggest we give this matter a code name. So we can react with appropriate speed. Something short, that will trigger instant action on our part?"

Charlie, as the lowest ranked member in the room, felt he should contribute something. He remembered Napoleon, the little Corporal, had often been the shortest man in the room, so he plucked up courage and raised a hand, "If I might suggest sir, what about the single word, 'Phoenix'?"

Sir Nicholas smiled, "Well said Sergeant Friar. Operation Phoenix it is. We all hope Grech sets fire to himself pretty soon."

This remark drew smiles from everyone except Stolland, "Shall we go on then, gentlemen?"

The visual display that Stolland provided now split into two separate displays. The ones of Grech, moved to the far end of the room. They remained perfectly clear, as if Grech stood waiting to speak.

"I'll leave our target in a position so that you can continue to look at him while I explain the reasons which appear to have created his lust for revenge and began this tragic affair."

A second, larger display appeared at the other end of the table. It was like looking at a curved cinema screen. Most of the display was text, supported by copies of photographs, which looked as though they were from newspapers or periodicals. Stolland now stood to the side of this display. As he spoke, the content seemed to flow, reinforcing his story. If he referred to a picture, a date or an article, it was immediately enlarged into a three dimensional display.

"In order to understand Grech, we have to go back in time. Prior to 1900, the family from which our man descends, lived in Poland. They were very wealthy, mainly from their iron and steel businesses. They had many other financial interests. In 1900, the family moved to Kiel, Germany, where they appear to have purchased a controlling share in the Germaniawerft Company. You may know this company. It became one of the most successful producers of German submarines during the 1914-18 war.

Following the First World-War, the family moved base to Berlin and then on to London. Their financial empire grew rapidly. Their interests broadened by the acquisition of two shipping lines, one German and one British. Within ten years, they controlled a huge percentage of the steel that went directly into the ships.

At that time, the family name was Galen. Due to an unexplained accident in the Atlantic, involving the Galen family yacht, only four members survived. These were the head of the family Franz Victor, his wife Elizabeth, their son Joseph Victor and his son Victor George. There were no other survivors and no other known relatives. I accept you may be aware of most of these details, from media reports at the time.

The family business, the Galleon Corporation, was based at their offices adjacent to Galleons Reach. This area is located on the North bank of the Thames, adjacent to your King George V dock at North Woolwich. Their iron, steel and shipping businesses, plus the many smaller enterprises in which they had controlling interests, were organised from Galleons Reach. The main family house also stood in the same grounds, as did the offices. It was known locally as, the little kingdom. You may also remember that title from your newspapers.

The Galen family had chosen to live in the east end of London. They were Jewish and, I suppose, felt at home in that area. You may also recall that at the end of World War Two, rather amazingly, Franz and Joseph Galen were arrested accused of collaborating with the enemy and the whole Galleon Corporation with trading and supplying the enemy.

These unsupported and highly questionable charges, most of which arose from one source, were brought by one, Richard Stickland MP. I can see by the nodding heads that you all know of this. Now gentlemen, you see why this room had to be cleared before this meeting could begin."

Stolland waited for the muttering to stop, "The public mood at the time was far from sympathetic towards anyone accused of being a traitor, no matter how suspect the so-called evidence. The result was the swift collapse of the Galen businesses and Corporation. In short, the family lost all finances and property overnight! The State took over. You are aware of these happenings. They have happened in your time. They are your recent events. Two of you are members of the same club. That's if you'll excuse me calling your Westminster, a club." More muttering broke out.

"Please bear with me and I will show where our killer, Victor Grech, fits into this picture. Franz and Joseph Galen, were sentenced to life imprisonment with hard labour. Within a year, both Galens were dead. The first to die was Franz of a heart attack. Then Joseph died in a reported rock fall, at the quarry where he was working. How very strange. The enquiry following the accident, found that other inmates probably murdered him. The Grandmother went to South America where she disappeared. Records show that in 1946, the grandson, Thomas Victor Galen, appeared in a charity trust home following the suicide of his mother. He appears registered under the surname Grech, a supposed war orphan from Europe. Gentlemen, here lies the family line, that tenuous connecting thread, that leads directly to our target, Victor Grech.

Now, as you are very aware, in 1948, Richard Stickland MP, inherited his father's title and estates. Immediately following this, he purchased all rights to the failed Galleon Corporation. He also obtained the properties at Galleons Reach, including the Galen family home. By the end of last year, the now Lord Richard Stickland had also obtained all contracts previously held by the Galen family, to supply iron and steel to help rebuild Europe, including Germany.

Gentlemen, with the benefit of hindsight, there are those of my time who say that a very questionable take-over or theft had occurred," Stolland held the silence that followed for a fraction longer, then added, "To even a casual observer, it would seem that the Galen family had been surgically removed from the business world, but this is where things get a little difficult for you. The remainder of the story lies beyond your time. Not wishing to suffer termination, by my monitors, I find myself having to weigh my words carefully.

Oh, I can see the way your minds are working. Why didn't I go back and quietly remove the supposed little war orphan? Before the seed could propagate, nip it out. Remember, what has happened is fact, history. It is not yours or mine to undo. It is the Victor Grech of my time, 2102, that has chosen to alter the natural order of things, to appear from your future and wreak his vengeance. He's back to settle accounts and it's my belief that the weapon he has in his possession is far, far beyond your imagination. We can't stop this man simply by putting everyone on alert, going back to a war footing or quietly hiding certain people away. Neither can we pacify Grech with a little political manoeuvring, or buy this man off! Remember. He knows most of the moves you would try to make, and I promise you this, make one false step and the result will be catastrophic, totally beyond the imagination of your 20th Century script writes. In Grech's mind he has nothing to lose and, in his mind, everything to gain."

The painful history lesson was over. Like all political meetings, the review and discussion of what was said by whom ran on for hours. In fact, it went on until the Home Secretary was certain there was no alternative but to leave Operation Phoenix to the three people sitting opposite him. At least, they were expendable, if it all went wrong.

Alan, Charlie and Stolland felt exhausted by the time they left the War Office. Alan broke the silence as they walked along Whitehall, "Do you think that lot will be able to keep quiet about what's been said?"

Stolland shrugged, "They're your people and they're bound by the need for secrecy. Which of them will dare to repeat what they've seen or heard. It would be military or political suicide, too outrageous without

246

producing some form of factual evidence to support their story? Would you, in their position?"

It was Alan's turn to shrug his shoulders, "Well, I just hope you're right. There was a complete mixture of private ambitions in that room. It doesn't do to mix politics and duty in the same glass."

Stolland smiled, "Oh come on, Alan, you're being a little pessimistic aren't you? If my guess is right, they'll drape us on the sacrificial altar, put out some bland instruction of compliance with Operation Phoenix, and close ranks."

Charlie was busy lighting a cigarette, "I wouldn't trust any of them, especially if it comes to Knighthoods. Pull the ladder up Jack, will be their motto. If it goes sour, we'll get buried, not them."

Stolland agreed, "The one point I'm really worried about is this business about Stickland. After all, he may now be in the House of Lords, but he's still an active member of your Home Secretary's political party. If my guess is right, he's a personal friend too. Did you see Sir Nicholas's face when I referred to the Stickland criminal take-over of Galen?"

Alan laughed, "Did you spot the political agony, talk about embarrassed?"

Not to be left out, Charlie thought he'd add another dimension, "And what about the military chiefs, what wouldn't they give to get their hands on that box of tricks of your's?" Charlie flicked his cigarette into the gutter, "But it's not just the equipment they'd give their pensions for, it's ten minutes inside your head, Mr Stolland. They'd be able to out-manoeuvre every single move the enemy would make, before they even thought of it. After all, what's future to them is just history to you."

Alan flagged down a taxi for Liverpool Street station. On arrival, the news was grim. They had just missed the last train to Norwich. They must wait two hours for the night milk train. This train, they were told, would stop fifteen times before arriving at Norwich, at a quarter past five.

The thought made Alan shudder, in fact this whole business was enough to make anyone quake. What was to stop anyone from the future just dropping in and changing history, personal or otherwise. Just the threat of having an open door like the one on Cley marsh made him sweat.

Chapter Fourteen

The phone rang. Charlie ignored its pleading. Someone down in the general office would answer it. He wasn't into phone calls at the moment. He moved his feet further along the top of his desk. Charlie had become a great believer in personal comfort. This was his first day back in the office since returning from the conference in London. The idea was that he should spend the whole day translating his rough notes into some sort of order.

A knock on the door interrupted his thoughts. Before telling the visitor, or who ever it was to come in, he removed his feet from the desk and adopted a studious crouch over his notes. He felt this attitude would provide the right impression, indicating deep concentration on his part, and a need to be gone, on the part of whoever was visiting.

His antagonist was a young probationer. Breathlessly, the newly appointed constable told Charlie there was a call for him.

"Why can't you transfer it up here?"

The constable looked rather pale, "Well Sergeant, I'm afraid I don't know quite how to do that yet and I'm worried I'll lose the call if I try."

Charlie face broke into a smile, "It's okay, I'll pop down with you and we'll sort it out."

With obvious relief, the constable preceded Charlie down the stairs. His new beat boots clattering on the bare wooden treads. Charlie went into the broom cupboard that now doubled as a telephone switchboard room and by pulling cords and connecting jacks, he directed the call to the CID office.

Having displayed his skill to an audience of one, Charlie grinned at the new arrival, "Just give me time to get back upstairs and throw that key. When you hear me start to speak, pull it back in line with the others."

He was still grinning when he was once again comfortable in his chair, feet back on the desk and telephone to his ear.

"Hello Sergeant Friar. We haven't met but my name is Bob Fuller. CID Brentwood."

Charlie recognised the name straight away, "You're the chap who was first on the scene at Mucky Mary's. What can I do for you?"

"Well, I don't know if this is the right way to go about it, crossing borders and all that, but I've heard something that could be related to the Mucky Mary business," there was a pause, "I have to be careful, if you know what I mean. My boss is keen on my keeping my nose on the simple larceny stuff, so it's difficult, if you get my drift?"

Charlie grabbed a pencil, "Look Fuller, I don't get your drift at the moment. Is your call connected to the Mucky Mary business or do you want to talk to me about cross border bike nicking?" The line went quiet. Charlie's tone softened a touch, "Look, I sympathise if you've a crappy relationship with your boss, but we all have to start our apprenticeship somewhere."

There was still silence. Charlie tried again, "Look, force loyalty counts for nothing when it comes to serious crime, and I think your call is connected to a serious crime on your patch. So, if your boss has a downer on you, that's none of my business," he waited, "however, bringing a nasty piece of work to book is every copper's business, so do you still want to take it outside your manor?" Charlie waited, hoping he hadn't put young Fuller off.

Bob Fuller coughed, "I'm making a bad job of explaining why I haven't taken this to my boss. I suppose I'm still pissed off at his not keeping me on the Mucky Mary's job."

"Look, from the Essex reports I've read, I happen to think you handled your end very well. It must have been a real eye-opener for a young D.C., walking in on that lot. Plus the fact you kept a cool head and preserved the scene. It's never easy handing over heavy stuff and going back to plod matters. I've had my share. It's all police work, and that's life old son. Now, do you want to talk, if so, where are you speaking from?"

A relaxed Bob Fuller replied, "I'm at my parents, I had to come home to get a decent meal."

Charlie laughed, "Okay Bob, give me the number and I'll ring you straight back. No sense in their shelling out for police business."

There was a brief awkwardness, "It's Albert Dock 1037."

Charlie whistled, "Now there's a coincidence. My people have an Albert Dock number, must live fairly close."

"They do," came the reply, "my parents know your people. They live in the next road to ours, Russell Road. We live in Burrards Road. Good old Custom House, eh?"

Charlie got on to Trunks and asked for Bob's number. A few loud clicks and the connection was made.

"So, what's all this about?"

Bob Fuller explained that he had been with CID a short time and felt he had to avoid treading on toes. Charlie heaved a sigh, sympathised once again, but was cautious in view of the obvious touchiness.

"Bob, we believe the nutcase responsible for Mucky Mary's has also killed on our ground. If you think you can help narrow the field down, we'd better get together. Where's best for you?"

Bob thought for a moment, "Any chance you coming down to Custom House? I may know someone who saw the guy with the Crown Property lorry."

"The same truck, the one from Cromer, you're sure of that?" Charlie tried to keep the gathering excitement out of his voice.

"As sure as I can be," replied Bob Fuller.

Charlie thought quickly, he knew Alan had his hands full. Bob Fuller's information may come to nothing. There had been other leads, which had all fizzled out, "Okay Bob. How long will you be at your parents?"

"I'm home for the next week. I've got annual leave to clear."

"Look Bob, I don't want to queer anyone's pitch. I had better ring my Governor and if it's okay with him, I'll pick up the wife and bring her over to my people. It's time we paid a visit. I can then pop round to you. I'll buzz you back as soon as I've jacked things up."

Alan Brandon seemed more than a little busy getting ready for a one-to-one with David Long. All he could say was to follow up Bob Fuller's information, "You go down, Charlie, take the wife and stay down there until you get every ounce of help young Fuller can give. We don't want his boss or any of the Met locals getting in a strop. I'll grease a few wheels by phoning George Fellows. K Division is his patch. He'll keep his troops off your neck. If you must pull weight, just use, Operation Phoenix. Shame about Fuller's situation, he may still get into hot water for contacting us without local permission. I seem to remember an awkward DI down that way, Billy somebody or other. He had a reputation that tended to put you off serving as a CID Aide. Bit of a stickler on job boundaries. I'll get David Long to have a quick word or two with his opposite number, it may lift Fuller's worries. Let me know if it goes sour or if you feel that Stolland and I should be there. On second thoughts, I think it best if I keep Stolland entertained this end until you tell me something different. Oh, and I'd better have your people's telephone number."

Charlie always appreciated his boss's free-hand approach. It bred enthusiasm and trust, "Albert Dock 1031," he said, "just leave a message if I'm out."

With duty calls made and confirmation of the time they should arrive at Burrards Road, plus having warned his own folks of the impending invasion, Charlie picked up his wife, and headed for London's East End.

The A12 was busy but the drive was pleasant enough. Soon they threaded their way past Chelmsford, stopped for a late lunch at the Horse and Groom on Galleywood Common, then it was down through Billericay, out onto the A13 and into the East End.

Charlie's parents were tickled-pink to see them, but as soon as it seemed decent, Charlie made excuses and left the house to walk round to Burrards Road. He loved this part of London. It was always busy, smelt permanently dusty, looked beaten up and had enough noise to drive a bolt through a wall, but it was a special place.

Although Charlie now lived in Norfolk, which he knew was God's own, he was a born East-ender. As he walked, he slid into the atmosphere. It was like putting on old shoes, worn but comfortable.

The area, alongside the Royal group of docks, had taken a regular pounding during the war. Luckily, some of the Victorian two-up, two-down terraced houses still remained. Though still bearing scars of bombing, they were for the most part, kept as clean as new pins on the inside. There was certainly visible evidence of real pride felt by families who were lucky enough to live in them.

He knocked on number forty-two's well-kept front door. The door opened and Bob Fuller shook Charlie's hand. He was young, athletically slim, taller than Charlie and had piercing blue eyes. His smile was as broad as the door frame, and he had a handshake like a steam piston on heat.

Bob guided Charlie into the front room where, after receiving the regulation cup of tea, Bob asked, "Should I call you Sergeant?"

Charlie smiled, "Definitely not, and I'll call you Bob, unless a senior officer's present. That way we can't tread on toes, as you would say." Bob smiled.

"So," said Charlie, "a few ground rules. I need to know all you know. Keep it simple, short and to the point. If this business comes to anything worth following up, we do it together. Share the problems as they arise. If we need help, we let the local boys know. Otherwise, they could get emotional. If it means turning over someone or a drum in the docks, we let the PLA peelers know we're on their patch. Jack Cousens, one of their Inspectors, lives next door to my folks. I'll do that before we invade. How's that for ground rules?"

Bob relaxed. He immediately felt he could work with Charlie.

"Okay, I'll keep this as short as I can. I know you grew up and started your police career in this area. Did you come across or recall a family name of Cash? Father works in the Albert dock as a Tally clerk. Mother still teaches at Ashburton School?"

Charlie was digging for his cigarettes, "Can we do this outside? I'm dying for a smoke but not in your mum's best room."

They moved outside, squatting on the low wall that just about separated the house from the pavement. Charlie gratefully lit up. Bob declined the offer of a cigarette. Closing his eyes, Charlie slowly exhaled a stream of smoke.

"Yes. Didn't they have a couple of daughters? Nice people as I remember lived in Leslie Road. They had a son. His name escapes me but last I heard, he was away in the navy?"

"Joe still is," said Bob, "well, I'm courting Sylvia, who's their youngest. She works in a shipping office in Leadenhall Street during the week, but does bar work at weekends in the Peacock."

Charlie butted in, "Hard on courting but keeps her busy, eh?"

Bob laughed, "Well, I'm stuck in lodgings at Brentwood. Makes life a bit difficult, but we hope to buy a small place in Romford. She can train it into the City and I can do the same to Brentwood."

It was Charlie's turn to smile, "It surprises me you didn't join the Met, would have made life easier for you both."

Bob stopped smiling, "I don't want my marriage to begin in one of these streets. Sylvia deserves better," Bob looked up and down the narrow street., "clean air and all that. Well, as I was saying, one of the other part-time bar staff at the Peacock is a girl called Ellen Thurston, lives in this road at number four. It turns out she works the early shift at the Manor Road Transport Café. Does the café name ring bells?"

"Of course it does," said Charlie, "that's where the Crown wagon was found after the Mucky Mary's job. You're beginning to get me very interested my son. Did this Ellen see anything?"

Bob smiled again, "Well, it seems that when she was interviewed along with the other café staff, she was too scared to admit having seen anything. However, she did mention something to Sylvia at the pub, the following evening. Evidently, she went out the back of the café to get some air. There's a sort of wooden fence between the rear café door and the lorry-park. She was just standing there when, through a small gap in this fence, she saw the CPS lorry kangaroo to a stop. At first, she thought it was going straight through a chain link. The fence separates the café from some school playing fields."

Charlie held up a hand, "What does kangaroo mean?"

Bob jerked his hand across his body, "She said it was jerking forward as though the driver was new to the job. As though he wasn't used to manoeuvring a wagon of that size in a tight space. Anyway, she watched this for several minutes. He had two or three goes at parking it. It crossed Ellen's mind that the driver wanted to get the lorry as far round the back of the café as possible, trying to get it out of sight. It eventually stopped and the driver seemed to have trouble switching off the engine. From what she said, it sounded as if he didn't know that diesel engines have to be choked off. Anyway, the cab door finally swung open and this man dropped out. According to her, he was a right weird looking character. At first, Ellen thought the lorry had been nicked or something. She said he stood, leaning back onto the cab, sweating and shaking like a leaf. She didn't know whether to laugh or cry. He seemed a dwarf compared to the regular Crown driver.

Anyway, he looked around then ran to the back of the trailer with something in his hand. Ellen saw one of the big back doors open and legs disappear into the trailer. She said it was so strange because he wasn't dressed like a CPS driver, no blue overalls, coat or cap. She also noticed he was wearing really lightweight shoes."

"What's so strange about that?"

"Blimey Charlie, no heavy trucker wears lightweight shoes. They wouldn't last a week! Neither would his feet. Another thing was, they were thickly covered in what seemed to be dried yellow mud. For someone who's dead fussy about his feet, he doesn't seem to mind where he's putting them."

Charlie nodded, "Did she get a good look at his face?"

"There's no doubt about that. That was what put the wind up her. She said there was something evil about this bloke. It wasn't his build, because he was a real lightweight. Didn't look as though he could punch his way out of a paper bag. But, what did put the wind up her were his eyes. He had a very pale face and sunken, black eyes. Ellen later said they were like black prunes floating in sour milk. At first, she was scared stiff he'd seen her. He paused for a good couple of seconds, looking straight at her. Then shot off to the back of the lorry. When she calmed down a bit, she told herself she'd imagined he'd spotted her. That he couldn't have seen her through the gap in the fence. She decided it was none of her business and went back into the café and got on with her work. Anyway, she couldn't get those eyes out of her mind. When she tried to blank the business, she found herself shaking. Her boss asked her what was wrong, said she looked upset and pale, so it obviously showed. He was all for sending her home."

Charlie broke in, "Did this chap go into the café?"

Bob shook his head, "No, Ellen was sure he didn't."

Charlie thought for a minute, "Did Ellen tell any of this to the local peelers, when they turned up?"

Again, Bob shook his head, "No, she kept it to herself. It was when she got to work at the Peacock that evening, she was chatting to Sylvia and mentioned it. Then, the evening before last, they were both serving when Ellen spotted this small bloke come into the Public bar. She said she suddenly felt him looking at her. It petrified her because she thought he'd come for her. Sylvia saw Ellen's face suddenly go pale and she started to shake. She grabbed her and took her through to the Saloon bar. When Sylvia got back into the Public, she saw him. It was obvious he was the one that Ellen had seen. He was exactly as Ellen had said, a small ferret-faced bloke, with a wicked stare. Anyway, she said she noticed him because he was so strange. He didn't bother with a drink, never approached the bar. Got into conversation with a local and seconds later, they both left the pub. In Sylvia's opinion, this lorry driver, if that's who he was, knew this local chap, or seemed to. The local appeared pleased to see him. That's if hand shakes count for anything."

Charlie was listening intently. He knew Stolland should be here, listening to this, "Bob, did Sylvia know who the local chap was?"

Bob shook his head, "I have to put my hands up to that one. I didn't ask. She started to get a bit weepy, upset, you know what girls are like. I've made arrangements to see Sylvia later. I'll get her to bring Ellen round tomorrow morning."

Charlie parted from Bob, thanking him and his folks, agreeing to meet in the morning. On his way round to his parents' place, he was tempted to call in at the Peacock. It had been his local until he transferred to Norfolk. He decided against it and walked on.

He walked into Russell Road, looking across at the iron railings surrounding his old school. Childhood memories flooded in. The times he'd fled over those railings chased by the caretaker's dog. On one occasion, he'd left the backside of his trousers flying like a banner on those same railings. He hadn't realised how athletic he must have been as a small lad.

He listened to the continuous clatter of weaving machines coming from the open windows of the mat factory. Coconut matting was the nearest he had ever been to carpets in his parents' house. It struck him that the noisy clatter, made by the looms in the factory, had never bothered him as a growing youngster. He smiled as he realised why. He was born into the clatter of this road with its tight terraced houses on one side and factories on the other.

His first job had been in Barnards, which stood alongside the mat factory. Long days spent at furnaces as a rivet boy, tending the white-hot metal. This particular part of hell's kitchen was the Grab factory, where the din of heavy metal production was appalling. The noise created by weaving looms was nothing in comparison.

His parents' house stood immediately opposite the Grab factory. He turned into the porch and automatically reached to place his fingers into the letterbox. He felt for the string that hung on the inside of the door. On this was a key. He drew it through the letterbox and used the key to open the front door. For as long as he could remember, the same key had hung behind that door. There was never a need to have a second key in their family. This method of entry was common in the East end. Breaking into someone's house was almost unheard of. The poor didn't steal from the poor.

He walked through the passage with its green distempered walls, to the sound of laughter. He found his family gathered around the kitchen table. It was good to be visiting his folks.

The next morning he walked with his wife and parents to the trolleybus stop outside the Peacock, and saw them off. They were happy enough to go up West for a day's tour round the shops, plus a lunch at Lyons Corner House, all on Charlie.

He'd already phoned Alan and brought him up to date. Alan had thought it best if Charlie questioned the girls, then let him know the result. He would then judge whether Stolland and he, should join Charlie. Although

258

Charlie accepted this, he felt the presence of Stolland could tip the odds against them, especially if spotted by Grech.

He was also concerned about Stolland's accommodation. Neither his nor Bob's parents were in a position to take in more visitors. Charlie tactfully voiced his misgivings, "Perhaps the local nick could provide B and B?"

It was now Alan's turn to be unhappy. He thought Stolland had already sampled enough cell hospitality. The conversation ended with a laugh when Alan suggested Stolland could bring the truckle bed with him. Charlie's parting shot was that Stolland could always return to his own time and write a book entitled 'Travels with a Truckle bed,' or better still, take it back to his time.

On reaching Bob's house, Charlie met Sylvia Cash, who turned out to be very good looking with lots of dark hair and Ellen, who was equally good looking. A natural blond and it seemed about the same age. It was not hard to see why the girls were friends. Apart from hair colour, they could have been sisters.

When the four were alone and settled in the front room, Charlie raised the matter of Grech. The atmosphere immediately changed. Ellen's face grew quite pale. Her bright, china blue eyes clouded and tears were quickly dabbed away with a small handkerchief, which from that point on, spent most of the time screwed into a ball.

Charlie spoke very slowly and quietly, "Ellen, have you seen this man since he walked out of the Peacock?"

She nervously, and equally quietly said, "Yes, I was walking home from the Peacock. I try not to get into conversations in the street, but a few of our neighbours were standing at their front doors talking. Obviously, something had happened. I heard one of the Scrivner boys had been over in Poplar and got into a fight with a local bookie's runner. The boy, Barry it was, had used a razor on the runner. I wasn't surprised. Barry's a right villain. Even at school he'd carried a razor. He once threatened a teacher with stitching. Anyway, no one was going to let on to the police, so Barry, as usual, just walked away. The runner was taken to Poplar hospital where he was fixed up."

Charlie placed a hand on Ellen's arm, "Where does this Barry live?"

Ellen looked at Syliva, as if in surprise, "They all live in Hoover Road. You must know that family. Old man Scrivner ran the family business for years. Rathbone street market, pawnshops scrap metal, you name it. They have it sewn up. Any bit of trade that makes money. Old Mrs Scrivner, she does the money lending down at the dock gates. Down there regular, every Thursday night collecting in from the men as they get their wages, then re-loaning out to wives on a Monday. If not loans, it's popping rings. I will say one thing for them. They're as good as gold to local people. You know, down on their luck pensioners and that sort, who are a bit short. In fact, they helped quite a few old people right through the war. But it still doesn't do to cross them."

Sylvia butted in, "Or set up in opposition!" This came out with obvious feeling.

"What does that mean?" Charlie said, looking across to Sylvia.

"Well, it's well known they have a heavy side, especially that Barry. A right squirrel, he's not called, the Scribe for nothing."

Charlie raised his eyebrows, "Scribe? Why Scribe?"

Sylvia undocked her lips from a teacup, "In plain English, Scribe means he leaves his mark on you, if you offend the Scrivner family business or are found trying a bit of fiddle on the side. Barry doesn't use a pen, he uses either an iron bar, his fists or razor. He's not particular, real black hearted and quick to lose his temper. It doesn't pay to be in his debt either."

Sylvia fiddled with teacup, quickly looked at the others, "Bob had a run in with Barry when he first applied to join the police. Although Bob had been friendly with Freddie, the older brother, even run a barrow for him as a kid. When young Barry found out he was going into the police, he left a cat with its throat cut on the doorstep. We all knew what it meant."

Charlie also knew what that meant, so he let that last bit slide. Bob was big enough to look after himself.

"Ellen, when did you last see the small man?"

Ellen again used her screwed up handkerchief, "It was as I was walking from my neighbours. There's this street light just up the road. He was standing under it, just staring at me, following me with his eyes. I know that sounds a bit melodramatic, but he really was just watching me like a cat watches a mouse. If he meant to scare me, he did a good job of it. Anyway, I didn't want to walk into my house because he'd know where I lived, so I walked around until I found myself at Sylvia's. I looked round, but I think he'd gone."

"When I opened the door, she was in a right state, I can tell you," Sylvia said, "She had some tea then my Dad and I walked her home. That little toe-rag wasn't anywhere to be seen. My Dad would have done him, he's hard enough. He's one of the few that's given Barry a clip on the ear."

Charlie's memory was reeling back to when he used to sell bundles of firewood for the Scrivners. He'd enjoyed going round the streets with a handcart, selling the bundles at a penny a go. Freddie Scrivner told him that if a pensioner was hard up, just them a bundle and don't take their penny. Unfortunately, Freddie, who always seemed to be laughing, went on to work as an auxiliary Fireman during the war. Sadly, he died in an air raid in 1941. Charlie travelled from Norfolk to attend the funeral. Old man Scrivner shook hands with Charlie outside Trinity Church, saying it was good of him to say his farewells.

Breaking out of his thoughts, Charlie said, "Who was the local man you saw in the Peacock talking to the small chap?"

"I'm surprised you've had to ask, that was dear Barry," Ellen said.

Charlie nodded, recalling they had, at first said they didn't know him.

Charlie turned to Bob, "Do you know his latest form."

Bob shrugged, "Locals are all aware of what goes on, but I think he enforces whatever his family decides has to be done. He's been lifted a few times, but somehow, no one ever comes forward with evidence. Not even those he's marked. It's the rule of the east- end. As the Italian barber in Butchers Road, Lucianno Trementini says, 'Non vedo, non sento, non dico, nulla'!"

"Can we stick to English, Bob?" Charlie said.

Bob was grinning, "Sorry Charlie, it means see, hear and say nothing! In other words, you don't stray outside your village, and you mind your own business."

"That barber in Butchers Road taught you well," said Charlie, "but, if this Barry has been playing away from home, he may have some recorded form. It's worth a check. To save time, I'll get it done from Norfolk. If he's been done anywhere, we'll know."

Ellen suddenly started to shake. Sylvia hugged her, "It's going to be okay Ellen. Nobody will lay a finger on you. You'll see to that won't you?"

The question had Charlie's name on it. Charlie thought for a moment. He knew that if Grech suspected the girl could connect him to the lorry, or even place him with Barry, she'd be as good as dead. Grech's previous form showed he'd killed for less. The answer was to shorten the odds of Grech finding the girl.

"Right, I need to use your parents' phone Bob," said Charlie, "and you young lady, are going on a holiday."

Ellen looked up, "How the hell can I do that with two jobs on the go. And, anyway what's my mum and dad going to say?"

Charlie smiled at her, "You just leave everything to me, including your parents. I'll even supply a sick note to your boss. You won't have to worry about what your boss might say. I'll fix the lot, including any cost involved. This is where we use the system, while you," he pointed a friendly finger at Ellen's tear stained face, "you enjoy the fresh air of the seaside."

Charlie left the girls in the front room drinking tea, while he got on the phone. In no time, Charlie got through to Alan and quickly explained the position, plus what he was proposing.

Alan laughed as he agreed. He suggested he get the sick notes for both Ellen and Sylvia and forward them to Charlie. Alan also explained, in this case, it would be better if Ellen remained with someone she knew and trusted. The phone calls ended with the message that the appropriate forms, completed and signed by a qualified doctor, would arrive by special delivery, the next morning.

Things had moved very quickly. By that evening, Charlie was back speaking with both girls. He explained the plan and although at first there were concerns, mainly centred round suitable clothing, etc. By ten o'clock, everything was ready and at eleven, Charlie's car pulled slowly into Burrards Road. It cruised to number forty-two and quietly parked. Not a net curtain twitched. It took just five minutes to transfer two girls and their hastily prepared luggage into the car.

Charlie looked at June, his wife, "You are an absolute angel. You've got the route okay?" June nodded, but knew Charlie would insist on going through it again.

"You join the A12 at Gallows Corner. An Essex Police car will then escort you all way to Cromer. Any problems let them deal with it. Just drive carefully, and ring me the moment you're home. I love you very much, so don't pick up strangers." With that, and a quick kiss, the car whispered away.

When June had first heard of Charlie's intention to transfer from the Met to Norfolk, she saw herself living in a thatched cottage with roses round the door. She would be a respected member of village community, doing good voluntary works. Now, after more years than she liked to recall, she was quite used to Charlie and his police work, plus acting as an unpaid member of the constabulary from time to time. She smiled to herself as she drove along the A12. She certainly did her share of voluntary works.

June checked in her rear-view mirror for the tenth time. The Essex patrol car had tucked nicely in behind them. It was a long journey, during which the girls settled down to sleep. June couldn't remember exactly how many times their home had been used as a hotel for guests of the Chief Constable. However, on this occasion, June was looking forward to the two girls staying. They seemed nice and if June played her cards right, their presence could lead to shopping sprees in Norwich.

Charlie had found it easy to fall asleep. One minute he was looking at his watch, guessing how far June and the girls had reached and the next, something was screaming in his ear. It was the telephone. As he rose to grab at the receiver, he glanced at his watch. It was a quarter to four. June's voice had a tinny sound, but it was a relief when she said, "Good morning darling. You can go to bed now. The cat and kittens are in from the cold."

Charlie laughed, "Did everything go okay?"

It was June's turn to laugh, "Yes, of course it did. The only problem we have is deciding who gets up and cooks breakfast. You look after yourself, and Sylvia says, love to Bob, and they both say, thanks for the seaside holiday. Seriously love, do take care."

Charlie laughed, "Don't worry and tell the girls their respective mothers will be ringing the girl's bosses at a respectable hour, explaining they have had to go to a doctor. Sick notes certifying their sickness are organised. They're not to worry about their jobs, just relax. Oh, you will be receiving some money delivered from Alan. Actually, it's being supplied by Mr Stolland, who says to tell you, it will help you entertain the girls."

Putting the phone handset back on the cradle, Charlie suddenly remembered what Stolland had said about banknotes. That no one could tell his from the real thing. He went weak at the knees. Charlie lit a cigarette. 'Oh well,' he thought, 'it's too bloody late now. I'll have to put that little matter right when I see Alan.'

Breakfast at Russell Road was rather late that morning. His mother woke him just after ten, with the news that a car had arrived from Norfolk and the driver was sitting downstairs tucking into toast and tea.

Charlie leapt out of bed, dreading the thought of a police sign on a black car, sitting outside their front door. He needn't have worried. A quick glance through the window told him that it was the old blue Austin fourteen from Cromer.

Opening the kitchen door, he was greeted by the sight of Frank Woodhouse, mouth full of toast, grinning like a Cheshire cat, "Hi there Charlie, your boss thought you needed some real help, so here I am loaded down with one manila envelope and orders to remain as long as it takes."

The envelope contained the sick notes for the girls. Charlie studied each of them in turn. The signature was a scrawl, "Who signed these?"

Frank took a second to drain the last drop of tea from his cup, wiped crumbs from his chin, and looked at the certificates, "Well, your boss went over to see a Dr Watson at the hospital. I think they are probably his monica. Terrible scrawl though?"

Charlie smiled, "Did my boss let you know what's happening?"

Frank eased himself from the table, smiled at Charlie's mum, who was hovering with the teapot and said, "No, he said you'd brief me."

It took Charlie an hour to wash, shave, dress and explain to Frank what had occurred so far. He had just sat down for his own breakfast when Bob Fuller arrived. Introductions followed accompanied by more tea.

When all three eventually left the house, the industrial din from the factories opposite had been clattering out for some hours. All three climbed into the car with Frank driving.

"How on earth do you stand the noise?" Asked Frank as they settled into their seats.

Charlie and Bob looked at each other, turned to Frank smiling and said, "What noise?" All three laughed.

"Where to?" Enquired Frank.

Charlie thought for a second and then said, "I didn't say much in the house because I don't want our families drawn further into this business. It's bad enough we're staying with them. I think your folks Bob, and mine are risking enough, without any more shop talk in either house. Agreed?" Bob and Frank nodded.

Charlie relaxed, "Lets go see if we can dig up old man Tate."

Bob leant forward from the rear seat, "You mean the Tates in Clever Road?"

"Got it in one," said Charlie, "my dad was talking about the Tates. Evidently, Jimmy Tate has disappeared and the old man's sprouting money, treating everyone down the pub. Let's see just how hospitable he is."

Frank didn't start the car, "Can I have a brief on these Tates before we arrive on their doorstep?"

Charlie apologised, "The Tates were as poor as church mice in my time and gossip has it nothing wonderful has happened to change their fortunes. Jimmy, the son has convictions for blowing safes. It's thought he learned his trade in the forces. If I say it, as one who shouldn't, he is reckoned to be the best safe man in London. He last went down for a job at Stratford. Caught red handed in the Co-op one night, didn't put up a fight, just laid his tools down."

"He's a bit of a hero to young villains around here, sort of Robin Hood," said Bob.

Charlie continued, "It would be handy to know where old man Tate got his wind-fall. After all, it can't be from hard work."

The drive round to Clever Road took no more than five minutes. There were five or six women standing in a bunch a few yards from the Tate's front door. They stared at the car as it approached. The car might have not had police written all over it, but these women were experts at recognising bizzies. They each adopted facial expressions designed to beat hot metal.

Bob recognised at least three women as immediate neighbours of the Tates. They all turned away and drifted further along the pavement. Mrs Tate opened the door. She looked very tired and red eyed.

Charlie smiled, "Good morning Mrs Tate. Would it be possible to speak to Mr Tate?"

The woman looked hard at Charlie and in an exhausted voice said, "Haven't you lot said enough."

Old man Tate appeared from the kitchen. He was white as a sheet and equally red eyed, "What the bloody hell do you lot want. We've just had one visit from your lot. Bugger off, leave us alone for God's sake."

Charlie held up both hands, "Mr Tate, I'm sorry, obviously you're very upset. Can we please have a moment of your time."

Charlie got no further. Mrs Tate flew into a rage, "Bloody coppers, all you ever think about is pushing decent people around. Why don't you go back up to Abbey Arms and find out why that heap came down here first thing this morning to tell us Jimmy had been murdered. Not content with that, they turned us over. Now you're here!" She struggled to contain her tears, "What more do you need to know."

Mr Tate grabbed hold of her and putting his arms round her, helped stem the tears, "He's dead Mr Friar," he said, mumbling the words as though he still didn't believe it, "Shot through the bloody head and he never once offered violence, ever. You know that?" There was a pause, "You'd best come in, don't won't every bugger in the road knowing."

They all went into the small kitchen. Mrs Tate sighed, "Best make some more tea." She detached herself and went through into the scullery,

Charlie's heart went out to her. A typical mum, he thought. The worst news ever and her first thought, is to make a cup of tea.

Old man Tate closed the door behind her. "Let her be doing something." There was another embarrassing pause, "It's not right. Something smells about this lot Mr Friar."

In the past, the old man had always spoken to Charlie in a friendly way. Charlie had done a few years as a local beat-man in these streets, before transferring from the Met to Norfolk, and was well known and respected as a fair copper.

"What's happened to Jimmy?" Charlie said this very quietly.

The old man looked into Charlie's face, "Don't you know? We thought that's why you were here?"

Charlie shook his head.

"About two this morning, mum and I were woken by banging on the door. It was the bizzies from the Abbey. They dropped the news on us and then went through the house like a dose of salts. Took away some bits they found in Jimmy's room. It seems Jimmy was doing a job. A safe, somewhere up by the Bridgehouse. Shot through the head, twice! Bang, bang!" There was a pause, "You knew Jimmy, Mr Friar. Never went tooled up for violence. He was just a peter-man, a real professional."

May Tate, came in with the tea. It went quiet while each of them drank. The strain caused by the silence was unbearable. Charlie coughed as though apologising for speaking.

"Ben," He used the old man's first name out of respect. "Do you know who's dealing with this locally?"

May said, "That tall Inspector with the Adolf moustache. The one that had young Billy collared and put down."

Charlie recalled that Jimmy's older brother Billy went down for receiving.

Old man Tate broke in, "Billy's due out. He's different Mr Friar. You can take it as gospel. When he knows, he'll kill the swine who topped our Jimmy. The law won't have to worry about catching him. Our Billy will do him. He's as good as dead."

"There's no justice in doing it that way Ben. If Billy goes after this gun, he'll end-up back in the nick. Why not let the police do the job. That way, you'll have your justice and have Billy home, safe and sound?" He changed tack, as if talking to himself, he said, "Seems like you just turn a corner and get some luck and then this happens."

"Luck, do you call this luck?" said the old man.

Charlie patted his shoulder, "What I meant was, the lads in the Peacock said your luck had just turned, had a few bob to treat yourselves for once?"

"You can't call that luck Mr Friar. It hasn't brought Jimmy luck has it? No amount of money can ever bring my son back," For a minute, the old man choked back his tears, "Things seem to be coming right. We could have all had a right old knees-up. A little while ago, Jimmy met this right decent little sort. Everyone in the pub seemed to be taking the piss out of him. Well, Jimmy straightened them out. He looked hard up, a bit rough. So Jimmy treated him to a drink or two. Got chatting, even fixed him up with a crib somewhere down in Lockhart Street, Stepney. Anyway, long story short, this cove turned out a bit creepy, looked like the Co-op undertaker, but a decent sort. Free handed, you know. Jimmy pulled his leg. Crappy dresser, but did he have a talent. Was a real cracker when it came to picking a winner. Dogs, horses, he was spot on every time. Well, Jimmy and me, we followed his tips and cleaned up.

Then we had a few beers over at the Bridgehouse. We get talking and he gives me four aways, plus four homes on the pools. They only came up didn't they, paid out nicely. I tried to give this sort a handful, but he wasn't having any. Said Jimmy was helping him out with a little bit of business."

"When was this," Charlie said.

"Not long ago, said he had a small demolition job to do. Wanted a timer system, whatever that is. Somewhere up on the coast, in Norfolk I think. Well Jimmy's dead now so it don't matter."

Charlie leant close to the old man, "Now look here Ben, it's very important we speak to this little man. Have you any idea where he is now?"

Ben Tate blew his nose and took a long time folding his handkerchief, "Don't know where he is now. Evidently done a runner from Lockhart Street, but you could go on the knocker down there. He sometimes drinks at the Bridgehouse. We called him Vic. Now, Mr Friar, with respect it's time you were gone."

Charlie thanked Mr and Mrs Tate for their courtesy and was sincere in his sorrow for their trouble. He also asked Mr Tate to think over carefully what he had said about Billy, not taking the law into his own hands. As they were going through the door into the street, May Tate placed a hand on Charlie's arm, "Mr Friar, you're one of us east-enders. You get that swine for us and mark his card good and proper."

She pointed to the old man who was going back into the kitchen, "He seems to think it was that Scrivner boy, Barry, but I don't. He's a violent streak in him a mile wide, but he's no shooter. Just do your best to keep my Billy safe, that's all I ask Mr Friar."

Chapter Fifteen

Grech left the underground at Great Portland Street station. Climbing the stairs to the Euston Road exit, he stood for some time staring about him. In front of him was Albany Street but, in order to reach it, he had to negotiate his way across busy Euston Road. The noise of heavy vehicles starting away from traffic lights and presence of heavy exhaust fume distracted him.

Grech walked across the wide pavement and placed his hands on the railings separating the safety of the footpath from the road. He felt very uneasy. There was so much traffic, so much noise and so many pedestrians. His agitation clearly showed to others around him.

"Feeling alright, Guv?" The unexpected question came from a man selling newspapers, "It's alright my old cocker, thought you looked a bit rocky on your feet like?"

Grech looked into the man's eyes. He was surprised to see real concern. The newspaper seller stepped forward, laying a kind hand on Grech's arm, "Seen too many people come unloaded crossing this road. I'll give you a hand across if you like?"

Grech shook his head and pushed the offered hand aside. He turned away, his thin face making it plain he needed no help. Unsolicited generosity was new to Grech, and not a sentiment he wished to encourage. He turned his back on the man.

Following a stream of people, he dodged his way across Euston Road. On reaching its North side, he looked over his shoulder, out of curiosity. The paper seller was still watching him. He even grinned and waved. Grech ignored the raised hand and quickly passed into the comparative calm of Albany Street.

Quickening his pace for a short distance, he looked at the house numbers. Then he slowed to a more even pace, studying more closely the four storey houses that still lined its West side. He noted with distaste their somnolent grandeur. Although terraced, each was complete in itself. Boundaries set by neat black and gold painted railings, guarded tidy but tight basement areas. Broad granite steps led up to imposing front doors, mirrored by the steepness of the servants' steps that led down from pavement to basement level. Access to these lower courts was via narrow wicket gates. Compared to the industrial clamour of Euston Road, the elegance of Albany Street quietly reflected what had once been a genteel part of London.

Removing his eyes from house numbers for a second, Grech could now clearly see the entrance to a police station. Its elevated blue lamp hanging above the stepped entrance. The sight unsettled him. He hesitated, took from his pocket a piece of paper and began to examine it very carefully. To a passer-by, he seemed to have stopped in order to refer to directions.

He folded the paper and continued his slow walk looking up at the house numbers. He paused then tried one of the wicket gates. It swung open. He quickly descended the stone steps to the basement and crossed the flagged area to a broad, half-glazed door. The brass plate affixed to the door simply said, 'Domestic entrance'.

He stood for some seconds listening then he knocked very quietly. There was no response so he tried again. There was still no response so he tried again, a little louder. Still receiving no reply, he tried the polished brass doorknob. It turned easily in his hand, the door swinging open without a sound. He entered, closing the door behind him.

Totally puzzled but pleased by the lack of security, Grech passed into what was obviously the kitchen. To his far right was a large black range on which a kettle simmered gently. A door immediately opposite was open and through this came the mellow sound of a chiming clock.

Grech knew that the police station was just a shout away, but couldn't resist the urge to pass up into the main house. This was, after all, the main London home of his enemy, Lord Stephen Stickland.

He tiptoed forward, taking care not to disturb a large tabby cat that left its basket by the range, and wound itself around his feet, purring like a rivet hammer. He discouraged the cat by lifting it away with the toe of his shoe. The cat looked at him disdainfully and returned to its basket.

Grech silently crossed the kitchen, passed through the door and slowly mounted a narrow carpeted staircase. This gave access to the family entrance hall. Grech couldn't believe he hadn't been challenged. Taking his courage in both hands, he coughed quite loudly and waited. There was absolutely no reaction. The only sound was the ticking of a hall clock. He was about to cough again when he suddenly saw a small envelope lying on the front door mat. Grech assumed the letter had recently arrived through the letterbox and lain undiscovered.

He picked up the cream envelope and saw that it was hand written and addressed, Private & Confidential, to Lord Stickland. Scrawled in the top left corner were the words, 'By hand'. On the reverse was an embossed Home Office seal. This, he thought, was his key to legitimacy. He could talk his way out if caught by simply explaining he was there to deliver the package. He called again softly, enquiring if anyone was at home.

As there was still no answer, Grech stepped into the hall. Placing the envelope into the inside pocket of his coat, he made his way to the sumptuously carpeted main staircase and climbed to the first floor. If challenged, production of the letter would add a ring of truth to his story, that he had simply tried everything to raise someone to whom he could deliver the letter.

At first floor level, he opened a number of closed doors before he found what he assumed was Lord

Stickland's library. The size of the room presented Grech with a problem. Searching the room for a diary or something of the kind would take time. He was tempted to leave while he still had his freedom, but the reason for his visit fuelled by the hate he had for the name, reinforced his determination. He began his search.

Thirty-five minutes of thorough but careful searching went by before Grech found a small document case, tucked into a drawer of a desk. He opened its main compartment. This contained many papers. Some carrying the emblem of the House of Lords, others referred to club memberships and business correspondence. He replaced them and closed the case.

He was about to put it back when his fingers rubbed against the catch of a small side pocket. Unfastening this, he withdrew two sheets of paper that made Grech's thin lips part in triumph. The first referred to the Motor Vessel Galen Empress, now owned by Stickland, clearly authorising the unrestricted provision of fuel, from H M Government reserves, for National and International industrial promotions. Grech glared at this for some time. The second was a certificate, stamped and signed by the Minister of Supply and Fuel. This certificate also carried an endorsement stating that the cost of any fuel issued, was to be set against the issuing ministry.

Grech stood with fists clenched, staring across the room. He gradually calmed down and replaced the papers, ensuring nothing looked out of place. He had no reason to remain in the house. He had all the answers he needed. Retracing his steps, he silently returned to the basement kitchen. Crossing over to the range, he stroked the cat and moved the kettle slightly to one side. He was tempted to leave the letter he had found by the front door, but changed his mind. He closed the kitchen door, climbed the basement steps and passed through the wicket gate, all without being challenged.

Grech could not believe his good fortune. He strolled to the Regents Park end of Albany Street and enjoyed the feeling of success. So far, everything had worked out. There had been several annoyances since his arrival, but these he had dealt with in a very sharp and positive way. He almost enjoyed the feeling that he could outwit anyone who tried to get in his way. As this thought slipped into his mind, he clattered straight into a rather well built woman, who was briskly walking in the opposite direction. She almost knocked him off his feet and then belaboured him for being drunk and for not looking where he was going. Grech was still staggering when the woman swung her brightly coloured heavy bag at his head and continued her journey along Albany Street. Grech was angry, but was content with the thought that at least he was not the poor man who was married to her.

He was not to know, but his assailant was none other than the Stickland's Housekeeper, Mrs Ellen Sparrow. On placing her key into the lock of the basement door, she was surprised to find it unlocked. She was immediately alarmed. But on searching through the house and finding nothing amiss, plus the cat happily purring, she chose to accept that she had apparently gone out without locking the door. There was, it would seem, always a first time, she thought.

She removed her coat and hat, placing them carefully onto a peg inside a cupboard. Then she unloaded the colourful knitted shopping bag onto the kitchen table, pouring scorn onto the head of the idiot she had bumped into. She smiled to herself as she remembered his fearful surprise as he reeled backwards. He had looked like a frightened rabbit, she thought. A scruffy tyke if ever she had seen one.

All seemed well until she crossed to the kitchen range to make a pot of tea. The kettle, which she always left simmering, was now off to one side of the hot plate. It was only a matter of an inch or so, but its position on the range was a matter of domestic servant discipline. Regulating the position of the kettle was not one of Mrs Sparrow's duties. That was cook's domain and she was absolute master in her own kitchen.

Mrs Sparrow was certain the kettle had been singing when she had left the house, and she had been the last one to leave. Feeling a little un-nerved she crossed to the kitchen window and looked out into the basement area.

"Now," she told the cat, "I either made a mistake or you have been making yourself tea," she stroked and looked fondly at the cat, "or I'm starting to lose my grip," she said, smiling.

After thinking things over, Mrs Sparrow decided it best not to say anything. Clearly, she had forgotten to secure the kitchen door when she popped to the Camden shops. With the house-staff, having their afternoon off, no one was ever likely to know. She put the kettle in its place, where it immediately began to simmer. She made herself a cup of tea and relaxed with her knitting. Mrs Sparrow certainly thought the kettle business was strange, but she put her slight disquiet down to imagination.

Grech crossed the road and hired a taxi from the rank. The driver was somewhat surprised by Grech's enquiry to take him to Highgate Cemetery, "Do you mean off Swains Lane, Highgate?"

Grech nodded, "If that is the Highgate cemetery!"

The driver looked at Grech critically, "Have you got the fare? It's a long journey by cab. You'll be better off getting a bus."

Grech showed him a white five-pound note.

The driver shrugged and said, "It's your money guv, but I think you'd be better off buying a wash and brush-up. That'll only set you back tuppence."

Grech ignored the remark and got in. He sat back and took the cream envelope from his pocket. He weighed it in his hand and judged it was quality paper, not cheap. He smelt it. The distinct aroma of cigar tobacco met his nose. He took from his pocket a small penknife and slit the flap. Withdrawing the single page, he eyes swam over the words. Then quietly, so the cab driver couldn't hear, Grech whispered, "So, my revered Lord Stickland, you have ears in both houses," he folded the paper and placed it back into the envelope, "It seems I am not the only traveller that has traitorous allies."

With the envelope, now safely back in his pocket and having arrived in Swains Lane, Grech paid off the driver. "Where is the entrance?" he enquired of the driver.

The driver grinned, "Depends whether you're alive or dead when you arrive mate. Someone as grand as you, it's questionable. What are you, a share holder?" With a laugh, the cabbie reset his meter and was gone.

Grech stared after the taxi, remembering the fate of a taxi driver who became too clever. He looked up at the sullen grey sky and turned his collar up against the rain.

Making his way along the road, he followed the high wall that separated the dead from the living. A sign told him this section was Jewish and according to records he'd studied, it hadn't been used for some time.

Grech thought the practice of burying the dead was offensive, unhygienic, a waste of good land. A practice not permitted after the middle of the twenty first century. Now here he was, soaking wet, trying to hunt down archaic ancestors.

He had to find a way in without drawing attention to himself. Coming to heavy wooden gates, he found them locked. He pushed hard at the small wicket door set in the right hand section. It was rotten and gave a little. Making sure no one was interested in what he was doing, he put his puny weight against the door again.

Three times he did this before it swung open. Quickly he passed through the door and slammed it shut. He turned and leant his back on the gate. What a nightmare, he thought. Everywhere was overgrown. Pathways had disappeared. Roots of vines and ivy straddled what evidence of paving there might have been. Everything smelt of decay. Grech pushed at some foliage and immediately drenched in rainwater. He was not very happy.

He tried pulling some of the tall weeds aside, only to cry out as thorns pierced his skin. He turned and decided to make his way toward a stone roof he could see, some thirty yards away. After much struggling, he managed the short distance. He found the building to be some sort of mausoleum. He kicked hard on the stout wooden door. His anger grew as he realised that finding graves relating to the Galen family was probably as unlikely as his chances were of ever getting back to the year 2102. He fought down the sudden rise in frustration and told himself that he had come back with one aim, and the plan to achieve that was working better than he could have expected.

He saw a narrow pathway, leading off between the tombs. Soon he came into an area where the undergrowth had been hacked back. He could clearly see rows of markers. It suddenly became clear that had he chosen the right gate, he would have had a slightly easier journey.

Grech searched amongst the soaking knee high grass for over two hours, without finding so much as a clue as to whether or not there were Galens interred within these walls. However, historical records that he had trawled through as a young man, clearly showed there were.

He had always held the view that he would simply walk in, consult a list and confirm at least, some of his family history. It had been a dream, a driving ambition based upon childhood conversations.

Grech felt too tired to be dispirited or angry. Finding a door that looked inviting, he pulled hard and very gradually, the protesting door opened. All there was inside were four, moss covered walls, the roof having fallen in. Grech was about to leave when he saw some faint but regular lines of script on a wall. By pure accident, he had stumbled upon the room of names. He had read of the existence of this room. A sacred room filled with script from floor to ceiling, all in the special Yiddish form of Hebrew.

Now, all he had to do was look for the names, familiar family names. He excitedly clawed at the moss with his nails. Stopping to examine script then quickly moving on. After what seemed an age he stood back staring. There, carved in the stone were lists of names beginning with the letter G.

Grech ignored the fact that every step he took was over rotten timber boards and joists, which collapsed as he gradually made his way along the wall. After a dozen or so slips and falls, he found what he was looking for. His finger traced each letter. 'GALEN'. At last, here was his family. He had no idea who they were, but they were Galen, and so the fable he had been carrying in his mind since a child, was true.

He slumped against the wall, slid down and buried his head in his arms. He did not cry. He wanted to, but couldn't. He had never cried. Not even as a child. He only felt the white anger he felt for the name Stickland. Grech got to his feet. Then, spreading his hands over the Galen names, he reaffirmed his oath for vengeance.

As best he could, he cleaned himself up and made his way back the way he had come. He turned south and walked on through the steady slate-grey rain. Turning into Highgate Hill, he walked until he was lucky enough to find a taxi. He offered the driver five pounds to take him to Whitechapel. The driver looked him up and down and refused. Grech pushed ten pounds through the cabbies door. The driver took the notes. Grech had his ride.

Once again, Grech sat back in the taxi and rested. He would have to find new lodgings. That was not going to be easy for a man who looked as though he hadn't two pennies to rub together. He'd moved many times in the short time he had been through the Gate. He had travelled many miles in many guises and now, here he was on the hunt again. He'd clean himself up, collect his bag from Whitechapel and move down to Limehouse.

Grech was almost asleep when the taxi began meeting heavy traffic. Eventually a harassed police constable informed the driver there was a serious incident in Kings Cross, making the journey into or through the city impossible. Like other drivers, the cabbie turned around and headed for Regents Park. Once again, he found nothing but parked vehicles. Finally, as the taxi nosed its way across to the north side of Baker Street, his passenger decided he would walk.

Grech turned east into Marylebone Road. He knew if he walked to Great Portland Street station, he might be able to get a train direct to Whitechapel. The rain peppered the pavements, causing pedestrians to look for somewhere to wait out the storm.

Joining others, Grech edged under cover on the front steps of the Royal Academy of Music. His eyes wandered over the posters displayed on boards marked 'forthcoming attractions'. Staring back at him was the picture of a woman. The poster proclaimed a grand charity concert in aid of European war orphans. Grech looked at the photograph again. He was sure he had seen her before. The face was too striking to be mistaken. Working his way through the people to the poster gave him no problem. No one was too enthusiastic about standing against a rather grubby individual.

He read the script beneath the photograph. Her name was Grace Woodhall, famous pianist. He searched the face again. There was nothing wrong with Grech's memory. He was certain he had seen a photograph of the woman, in a copy of a Cromer Newspaper. He checked back on the poster. The concert was to take place the day after tomorrow at the Royal Albert Hall. All the details were there.

Glancing up the steps, he looked through the glass doors into the entrance hall. What appeared to be a programme board displayed times and names. Grech wandered up the steps and stared through the glass. He was right. Chalked clearly on the board was the name, Miss G Woodhall – Rehearsal Room G2.

The hall was empty. Grech pushed the door. It swung inwards. His ears immediately caught the sound of a piano beautifully played. A crowd of young people came busting out of a room to his left and piled through the main entrance. Grech saw a broom leant against the corridor wall. He edged casually forward and took possession of it without a challenge from its owner. He then used this to slowly, brush his way toward the sound of the piano.

Within seconds, he was looking through a window set in a door, above which hung a small sign requesting complete silence. The number of the room was G2. Through the glass, he could see a woman playing the piano. She wasn't so much playing the instrument, she was casting a spell that, for a moment, held him captivated. At her side stood a young woman who, as he watched, turned a page of music.

Although the pianist was sideways on to his position, Grech recognised her as the woman whose picture was on the poster and he had seen in the newspaper. He was about to move when a voice over his right shoulder said, "Isn't she wonderful?"

Grech jumped. He looked round at a tall, elderly man with a shock of grey hair and goatee beard. The face was smiling at him, "Oh please, I am sorry I crept up on you. Do not continue your work on my account. I too am a great admirer of Mrs Brandon's playing. I wish I played my violin with half the feeling she achieves."

Grech knew the broom he was holding, was as good as a staff badge. Thankfully, he had been mistaken for a cleaner.

"Surely sir," Grech affected a bemused voice, "you mean Miss Grace Woodhall?"

"Oh I see. You still prefer her maiden name. Those of us that have been fortunate enough to follow her career from the orchestra, were pleased she continued to occasionally play, even though she has a full family life outside music."

Grech scratched his head, "You will have to excuse my ignorance sir, but you say her married name is Brandon?"

"Yes, surely you remember, married a police officer, years ago. Absolutely no musical talent I'm afraid, but I'm told an excellent detective. They say he's a very senior officer in Norfolk. Not the kind of work for people with real talent of course, but there you are, it takes all sorts to make this world go round," the man sighed heavily, "so, I suppose we ought to thank our lucky stars she appears at charity concerts. Oh yes, what a wonderful talent." With that, the man slowly walked away and began climbing the broad staircase to the floor above.

Grech took another, longer look at the woman. His eyes were not relaxed now. They were sharp and glistened like pieces of coal. He was not listening to the piano any more. His mind was on information he had acquired in Cromer, about a certain Detective Superintendent Brandon leading the hunt for him, and a large close-up photograph in a newspaper of the Brandons', opening a local Charity Fete. Grech laid the broom aside and left the building. As he passed through the doors, the piano became silent. The rain, if anything, had worsened. He spent a few moments reading the details of the concert, particularly noting where and when it was to take place. His thin face now a deathly white.

Walking quickly, he descended the steps and turned left towards Great Portland Street. High metal railings separated him from the glowing windows of the Academy. He quickly glanced to his left, and there, framed in one of the windows was a woman's face. The face was Grace Brandon. She hadn't just casually looked through the window at the falling rain. Her eyes were staring, fixed to his, just as a trapped rabbit would watch the approach of a ferret. Her eyes followed him as he turned quickly away. They bore through his back as he hurried into the blanket of rain.

In the London Borough of Stepney, Lockhart Street would not have won prizes for the design of its houses or for the tune, the rain played, as it gurgled its way through fractured guttering and spilled to the paving below. Typical of the housing stock of east London, the dwellings thrown up in the 1850's at £80 apiece, were squat, flat-fronted, narrow terraced properties, constructed of mean yellow-grey brick with front doors, opening directly off even narrower pavements.

Charlie felt depressed by these streets. He knew them so well. During his childhood, his father had often brought him here to pay duty visits to relations. These trips were, for the most part, short on conversation and long on warm silences. His grandfather's particular slice of Lockhart Street backed onto the Tower Hamlets cemetery. To a small child, the close presence of this borough facility was very unsettling. He was not used to the open stillness of graveyards and the morbid fear and excitement they triggered.

Although a high wall stood between the back of his Grandfather's house and the tombstones, Charlie's imagination often worked overtime. He would stare at the dark wall from his Grandfather's scullery window, but could never work out whether the wall was there to keep the local children out, or more frighteningly, to keep dead relations firmly in.

In accordance with their plan, Bob had started cold knocking at one end of the street, while Charlie began at the other. Frank was left in the car, just to make sure the children's games didn't include stone-fights, snooping to see if the tyres could be let down or a game of kick-the-coppers car. All accepted children's past-times, in London's docklands.

It had crossed Charlie's mind that Grech could suddenly appear out of one of the houses, challenge them and start a second blitz. After all, it was local knowledge that all coppers went around unarmed, except for their wooden truncheons. One crumb of comfort each of them had, as the enquiry in Lockhard Street commenced, was that shootings were extremely rare and killing a copper was almost unheard of. It was the 'almost', that placed caution in Charlie's plan.

After about ten minutes of futile enquiry, Charlie saw Bob step back into the road and wave to him. He made his way through a group of small children that were playing their version of tin-can-tommy, in spite of the constant drizzle and joined Bob.

He was standing at the edge of the pavement, looking up at the cracked first floor windows of number two-hundred and twenty. The dull panes of glass had net curtain, probably butcher's mutton cloth, draped across the lower section of each window. None of them showed a sign of life.

Bob pointed, "The people next door say this place is split into two tenancies. An old couple live downstairs, the rooms above are rented to a man. They say they haven't seen any of them for a while. The man is possibly fifty-ish, long grey hair, always scruffy. Short and thin. Eyes are deep set like coals. Speaks softly, and only when he's forced to. Bit of a queer fish. They say he scares the hell out of the kids. The owner of this palace and a few others in the road, owns the newsagents at the corner of Ropery Street. Frank's dived round to get the story and hopefully a key."

They stood for a while, leaning against the decaying brickwork, watching the children. Boys were busy inflicting pain, while girls demonstrated the first pangs of motherhood, nursing young ones. These children were out in the street come rain or shine. Two youngsters broke away from the others and raced over.

"Are you coppers then?" Yelled one of them.

"Nah," said the other, "can't be. Their feet ain't got boots on."

With that, they fled along the soaking wet pavement, back to their bedraggled gang.

Bob smiled at Charlie, "Funny thing about kids. They see everything, and yet when you ask them whether they have seen or done something. They shove a thumb in their mouth and innocently shake their heads."

Charlie lit another cigarette, "It's the code of the East-end. They're born to it. Deny everything, until they know they're not in trouble, or they think they're safe. It's as natural to them as yelling their lungs out. It's called the playground mentality. Before they go to school, they can speak without shouting. One day at school, that's all it takes and whammo! They come home, shouting their bloody heads off."

"Have you any children?" Bob asked.

Charlie flicked his cigarette away, "No," there was a long pause, "I could give lots of reasons. War wound, chicken pox, measles, rickets, lack of funds, but the truth is we just never clicked, if you know what I mean. Anyway, it's a bit late now. June and I, well, we're happy enough." Charlie lit another cigarette.

Bob looked away to where the kids screeched with laughter, chasing each other in circles, without pausing for breath. For some reason, he was sorry he'd asked Charlie the question. He felt embarrassed. He knew there was more to Charlie's answer than he was prepared to say.

Frank arrived with a large key. The owner had told him he hadn't seen the elderly couple or the other tenant for a while. There was no formal letting agreement, or rent book. They would just call in at the shop on an agreed day and pay whatever was due. The rent always had to be up front, just in case the tenant felt like doing a moonlight flit. The place was a furnished let, but the owner never bothered to call.

Charlie sucked hard on his teeth. He didn't like any of that. In the East end, one name for a property like this was 'dosser's drum'. In other words, a slum with a few sticks of furniture, in return for an exorbitant rent. If you didn't pay, you'd get visited quick enough. Then, if you were extremely lucky, you'd be out on the street with a full set of teeth and what you stood up in.

When they got through the door, they were hit by the stench of what they assumed was rotting waste or a failed sewage system. Bob turned and gently closed the door. Curiously, very little noise from the street penetrated into the house. In fact, they could feel the silence. It seemed to wrap round them like a cloak.

Bob whispered, "Funny, that sewage smell. I thought every house in the east-end had a lavatory in the yard?"

Charlie's eyes were looking up the staircase. He nodded, "No need to whisper Bob. The noise we made coming in, if anyone's about they'll know we're here."

The air seemed thick with disturbed particles of dust that floated in the dim shafts of daylight, filtering through the cracked fanlight above the front door. Charlie put a handkerchief over his mouth and nose. The place was filthy. Mice leapt from stairs or poked their heads from wide cracks in the skirting board to see who or what was passing. The stench of decay was so heavy it clung to their noses and coated their teeth like varnish.

Charlie ignored the downstairs and led Bob straight up the creaking staircase. At its head was a small landing off which was an equally small scullery. The only fitting here, apart from hanging traces of mould, was a heavily stained butler sink. A single cold tap continuously hissed a fine jet of water at them, like a venomous snake. Bob leant over and applied the necessary pressure. The hissing gradually subsided. Two doors led from the landing. The first room contained a chair of sorts and rough wooden table. The remainder of the contents couldn't be described as furniture. Charred papers and several burnt pieces of wood in the fire-grate provided the answer. Whoever spent time here had been in the process of burning the furniture.

There was just sufficient daylight to see what a filthy dump it was. Charlie had been tempted to try the light switch, but on looking up, he saw the light socket was as empty. Bulbs obviously cost money and were not the tenant's first consideration.

The room to the front of the house turned out to be the bedroom. A small canvas camp bed and some filthy blankets provided the only reason for calling it a bedroom. Charlie looked around. There was very little to get excited about. He and Bob opened the two fitted cupboards, one either side of the fireplace. Like Mother Hubbard's, he found them bare.

Disappointed, Charlie reached down and tipped the bed over. He smiled at Bob, "At last, treasure!"

In turning the bed over, they saw a large canvas holdall. The bag gave every impression of being empty. Charlie leapt on it, opened it and turning it upside down, shook it furiously.

Gradually, items fluttered like confetti to the bare floorboards. Charlie and Bob carefully sifted through the scraps of paper and card. By the look of the teeth marks, the local rodent population had thoroughly inspected each piece.

Their trawl finally found what appeared to be the lid from a small cardboard box, with a label that identified the missing contents as 50 rounds of point three-two rimless ammunition, also, a small scrap of paper, on which was just one identifiable word. They both looked at this for some time before they agreed the word was 'primers.' There were other screwed-up scraps of paper. These appeared to list dog and horse racing results, plus coastal tide tables. Charlie returned every one of the scraps to the holdall.

"Well Bob, we seem to have found the jottings of a loose mind alright, a suggestion of ammo, dogs and tides? Take these," he said, handing the bag to Bob.

Charlie then crossed to the fireplace. Embers from what had been a small fire felt cold to his fingers. He combed through the ashes and finally pulled out a small fragment of pale green card. Carefully he wiped its surfaces. It was clearly the remains of a railway ticket. The letters 'To Ingat...' were readable but the rest had died a slow death in the fire. On the reverse was part of a number and the word 'conditions'. That and the rest of the confetti went into the holdall.

Bob followed Charlie to the door. He had almost passed through onto the landing when he said, "Ingatestone! That's it Charlie. Ingatestone Railway station is just a walk from Mountnessing and that is a spit from ex-Mucky Mary's."

Charlie turned and smiled, "Young man, you've just earned yourself a large pint. Let's get out of this stinking place."

As they descended the stairs, the cloying sickly smell became heavier. Charlie's memory switched onto the probable cause. He looked at Bob and frowned, "I hate to pour cold water on this party, but are you thinking what I'm thinking?"

Bob took his handkerchief from his mouth. He too had cause to remember incidents where this sickly smell was present, "You mean the old couple never did a flit?"

The first two ground floor doors they tried were unlocked. There was nothing in them but old furniture that had seen better days. They walked quietly to the far end of the passageway then tried the third door. Charlie rattled the handle but the door wouldn't open.

"Must be the scullery," Charlie whispered.

Both men listened. They could hear a heavy buzzing sound. Something like electric clippers or a thousand flies around a cowpat. Whatever it was, the sound came from the other side of the door.

Charlie looked questioningly at Bob, "I take it you are no stranger to post-mortem incidents?"

Bob's eyes never wavered from the door. His voice was unnaturally forced, "I've been to one or two, yes." His face lost some of its colour.

Charlie gently pushed Bob to one side, "Better let me."

Charlie raised his right foot and sent it crashing against the door lock. The door flew back.

The air was immediately thick with massive blowflies. They rose, like a black cloak from the bodies and covered Charlie and Bob, causing them to reel back and grope for handkerchiefs.

Every germ-infested fly in the world seemed to be in that room. The two men needed only a second to look at the two still forms. They were seated on chairs, one either side of the sink, where they had been propped. Each had an entry wound in the back of the head. Both had large exit wounds in the forehead. Large white maggots had already started their ghastly work.

Charlie quickly closed the scullery door, thankfully trapping most of the flies inside. The defenceless old couple were no longer missing, and the cause of the stomach-wrenching stench was no longer in doubt.

Seconds later, outside in cool rain, they both leant heavily on the brickwork, pale and badly shaken. Although they had both seen death before, neither had quite expected the massacre they had found. After a few minutes of heavy breathing, Charlie turned and locked the front door. He then patted Bob's shoulder.

"You okay, old son?"

Bob smiled weakly and nodded just as Frank drove up.

"Get us out of here Frank and to a secure phone. We seem to have found two of Grech's calling cards."

With the car windows wound fully down, they didn't stop until they pulled up outside the Police Station in the East India Dock road.

"You two wait here. I'm going to get the local peelers to visit Lockhart Street. They'll need more than the usual gloves and masks. I shouldn't be more than five minutes or so." With that, Charlie disappeared up the steps and into the building.

Frank turned and looked at Bob, "Your face looks as grim as your suit smells, don't throw up in the car. Get some fresh air, but don't walk out of sight."

Bob sank down into his seat and loosened his tie. He wasn't into walking or conversation right now.

"I suppose Charlie was referring to the old couple?"

Bob didn't answer. He sat still and just nodded. He'd seen the bodies at Mucky Mary's, but these were something else. Two old people trussed up like chickens, nightmare stuff. He wondered what the old couple had gone through before they met their deaths. How they must have pleaded before those filthy cloths were stuffed into their mouths.

Charlie was a little longer than he said, but seemed satisfied when he climbed back into the car, "Surprisingly, they all seemed to know what Operation Phoenix meant, which I must admit was a relief. They raised no questions, just listened and acted. So, this is how it goes. Frank, you take Bob and I to Russell Road where you'll drop us. Then you head for Norfolk. It's essential Stolland and the boss see the contents of that holdall as soon as possible.

Meanwhile I'll have briefed the boss about Lockhart Street over the phone, any problems?"

Frank grinned, "No problem. I'll do anything to get that smell out of the car."

Charlie turned to Bob, "I take it you have some spare kit at your parents place?"

Bob raised his head. He was gradually regaining some of his colour, "I think my people will hand me the tin bath in the yard."

Without turning round, Frank said, "Don't forget to scrub well under your arms!"

Bob managed a very weak grin.

Chapter Sixteen

On reaching Russell Road, things didn't go quite the way Charlie planned. Before Frank could pull away and start his journey to Norfolk, Charlie signalled him to reapply the handbrake.

Charlie's father appeared at the window making frantic signals. He was pointing at Charlie, making it obvious there was a phone call for him. Bob and Frank waited in the car while Charlie disappeared into the house.

"Charlie," Alan's voice sounded agitated, "I have to be very quick, so listen. It seems Victor Grech has paid a call on Grace while she was rehearsing at the Royal Academy of Music. God alone knows how he knew she was there, but somehow it seems he did. Anyway, briefly Grace is okay but a bit shaken-up. The Met have a personal protection team with her. They are taking her to the flat in Eaton Walk and staying with her until I arrive. I am leaving now and should be there in a couple of hours."

"Do you want us to go there from here?" asked Charlie.

"No. She's safe enough. You stay put."

Charlie sketched out what had taken place at Lockhart Street. There was a long pause while Alan thought his way through the information.

"Right, send young Woodhouse, with the holdall to Norfolk. Stolland must see that lot. Tell Woodhouse to stick like a clam to him, and get him down to you in London as soon as possible. He had better come to Eaton Walk. I'll phone you later, when I've spoken with Grace. Don't waste time Charlie. Get that car on the way to

Stolland, and pull in all the favours you can in the east end, to find out where Grech is."

Charlie replaced the receiver and walked out to the car.

Alan was tired when he eventually drove into the Mews at Eaton Walk. He was questioned by two police officers as he got out of the car and again as he walked into the entrance to the flats. This time, the officer was dressed in the uniform of a hall porter.

On reaching the second floor flat, he was not surprised to find two more CID officers inside, with Grace. The moment he came through the door Grace was in his arms. As soon as Grace calmed down, Alan took her through into the lounge where a woman constable handed her some tea.

"Now my dearest girl," Alan said kindly, "In your own time, tell me exactly what happened."

The two male CID officers went back into the hall and quietly closed the door. The WPC remained seated close to Grace.

"Well, as I told you over the phone, I was working through the music I am to perform at the concert. Everything was going beautifully when suddenly..." Grace stopped speaking her lips trembling. Alan took the cup and handed it to the WPC. Grace searched for and found her handkerchief.

"I know the music so well, I was ahead of myself. Suddenly I was no longer playing the piece. Well, I thought I wasn't. The room seemed to have darkened and I saw a man's face where the keys should have been. It was a face so cruel, so full of evil, I felt faint. I couldn't breathe.

The man seemed to be holding a bouquet of lilies to my face. There was a sickly smell all around me like a thick fog. It was suffocating." Grace looked pleadingly into Alan's eyes, "Alan, it was the day you came home wearing that old jacket, you remember? The one you took from the boot of the car. At first, I thought it was an odour from the jacket, but it wasn't. Then you told me where you

292

had been and I realised you had been close to that solution for preserving bodies?"

"Formalin," Alan said softly.

"Yes, that's it, formalin. The flowers, they seemed to reek of it. The little man, the one I felt I had seen leaving the marsh. I knew it was his face. He was grinning, urging me to reach out for the lilies. I was so scared Alan."

Alan took both her hands in his and kissed them gently, "You possibly had one of your premonitions," in a quieter voice he added, "you are safe darling. Nothing can harm you."

"But I saw his eyes, Alan, I saw flashes of so many things, dreadful things. He is death walking."

Alan placed a hand under her chin and softly raised her head so he was looking deep into her eyes, "Grace, listen to me, it's over. We can withdraw you from the concert and get you safely home."

"No. Please, I must tell you. I promise it wasn't imagination, I saw his face as clearly as I am seeing you." Grace tried to compose herself, "It was as though, just as suddenly I came through a mist and incredibly, I was still playing. It seems I hadn't missed a note. But, I stopped at that moment. I could feel him. I got up from the piano and ran to the window and there he was, walking quickly along Marylebone Road. I saw his evil little figure just as I had seen him leave the marsh. He suddenly stopped, turned and looked directly up at me, and Alan, he knew me. I know he somehow knew who I was," Grace shook as the tears flowed down her cheeks, "he's not alone Alan." sobbed Grace.

"Darling, please rest," Alan took her into his arms and held her tight, "Grace, you simply must rest, now."

"You must believe me Alan. I know he is not alone. He has help and you must not go to the 'barge house'." Her face cleared and Grace appeared to slip into unconsciousness.

The WPC went to the telephone. Within five minutes, a local doctor arrived. She examined Grace, gave her a sedative and Grace was put to bed. According to the doctor, she would probably be fine after a good sleep. The WPC made some more tea and after ensuring Grace was sleeping peacefully, she settled down with a book, in a chair by the bed.

Alan struggled to understand what Grace had told him. Her dreaded visions had proved themselves accurate in the past. Foreboding edged into his mind. In an effort to bury the unease, he reviewed what Grace had said. There was nothing new in the thought that Grech had purchased help. He knew that was the only way Grech could have appeared in two places at once, but what had Grace meant by the barge house? Was it the name of a pub or club? This puzzle was still in Alan's head when Stolland arrived. He had arrived at Eaton Walk white faced looking as though he had been drawn through a bramble hedge backwards.

"That chap of yours, the driver. He's as mad as a march hare. Where on earth did he learn to drive like a lunatic?"

Alan smiled, "Yes. He's a product of the driving school at Hendon. I think he took me at my word when I said you should be brought here to Eaton Walk without delay."

"Well, I can assure you that I, plus a thousand other motorists, would have taken bets on our not surviving that journey. I tell you, he's an absolute speed freak! He would have made a first class fighter pilot. Their life expectancy wasn't long in your last war!"

Alan couldn't tell whether Stolland was praising or damning Woodhouse, "Do you want me have a word, get him replaced?"

"Certainly not, it was quite exhilarating actually."

Stolland was soon staring through a lens at the scrap of label from the bag, lifted from Lockhart Street.

"Well, what do you think?" Said Alan.

Stolland put down the magnifying glass and shook his head, "I can't be sure. If it's what I think it is we may have a far worse situation than I first thought. I would like to keep this particular little item quiet, if you don't mind. Okay?"

Alan frowned, "If you must, then you must, but, sometimes I wonder if we have the same objective! Or should I say planned outcome?" Stolland looked hard at Alan, "We both know you've no idea how far weapon technology has moved in the years that separate us. This scrap of information could be vital to your damned outcome! Just leave the clues and soul searching to me. I need you Alan, as a guide through your time, not as a badgering superior officer. I prefer to work with you, but not under your damned direction!"

Alan lowered his voice, "Right now I don't need you coming at me like some preening prima donna. Cut it out. Remember I am not the bloody enemy here. He's from your time, but he's committed murder in my time. That makes him material for our hangman's rope, have you got that!"

Stolland turned square to Alan, "Look, this rotten business is every bit as bad for me as it is for you. It's no good our getting up tight with each other," he paused, "Alan, believe me if we slip up, it'll be more than embarrassment that spoils our day."

He fought shy of telling Alan that he had strict orders to ensure that Grech's interrogation takes place nowhere other than the other side of the Gate. An examination under a strict medical regime by the tribunal, would take place immediately before Grech's termination.

A door quietly opened, "Gentlemen, can I suggest you discuss your business disagreement quieter and preferably in the kitchen, with the door firmly shut?"

Alan and Stolland stared at the WPC. She gave them both the look of a very upset nursing sister who will not have noise on her ward.

"Sorry," they said in unison.

The silence between Alan and Stolland deepened. Neither wanted suspicions between them, but these were inevitable. Alan walked over to the window and stood looking out into the street. Should he tell Stolland that in the event of Grech being taken alive, he would receive a military court martial, no hint of press or public.

Sentencing, execution and burial would probably take place in the Tower of London. These actions would be necessary to ensure the public knew nothing of time shift or the Gate. The Home Secretary himself had laid down these ground rules to Alan at a private meeting, before they left London for Norfolk. His final comment had been, "As a politician Brandon, you learn to try and keep things undeniably simple." Alan decided he should keep his thoughts to himself.

Alan shared a room with Stolland so Grace remained undisturbed.

Next morning she was as bright as a button. Grace was up first, arranged breakfast for everyone, including the personal protection team. She was halfway through the front door when Alan appeared in pyjamas and dressing gown, bleary eyed, enquiring what was happening.

"I'm on my way, with my CID friends, to the Royal Albert Hall, for my rehearsal with the full orchestra, dear."

Alan opened his mouth to object.

"Now please Alan, don't be annoying. I'm fighting fit and have a date with the orchestra that I will not be late for. Now, look after Mr Stolland for me and I'll be back before you know it."

With that, she placed the morning paper in his hands, kissed him on the cheek and they were gone. Without troubling to get properly dressed, Alan wandered through into the kitchen to be surprised by there being a different WPC laying the table for his breakfast. Alan quickly excused himself and dashed back to the bedroom.

Thirty minutes later, Alan and Stolland presented themselves at the kitchen, bathed dressed and ready for whatever the day might bring. After breakfast, Stolland started examining the contents of the bag again while Alan phoned Custom House. He asked for Charlie and was told he had mentioned something about having a trawl through a road, next to the river, in North Woolwich. Charlie had left to walk round to Bob Fuller's house.

Alan rifled his pockets and found his notebook. He quickly thumbed through the pages. A minute later, Bob's phone was ringing. Relief flooded through Alan as Bob's voice answered, "Fuller, has Sergeant Friar reached you yet?" Alan tried to sound relaxed but it didn't quite work.

"Hang on sir, he's just arriving. Is there a problem?"

Before Alan could say another word, Charlie took the phone, "Sir, What's happening at your end?"

Alan explained what had occurred and that Grace had gone off for a rehearsal, with an escort, "Is there any point in Stolland and I going to Lockhart Street, just to have a look round. See what's going on?" Asked Alan.

"Probably still smell a bit of the old couple but it might be worth having a word with neighbours. It's possible they may have an idea where Grech has holed up. Mr Stolland may even spot him. We have heard that one of the local tearaway's, Barry Scrivner was seen, mouthing off in the Bridgehouse pub last night, not unusual for him but he was full of bounce. As far as we can gather, he's suddenly interested in North Woolwich. If it's okay with you sir, we'll go and have a quiet sniff around?"

"Okay, but anything definite, get back to us," said Alan, "either here at the flat or through the Met Information Room."

As soon as he put the phone down, he recalled what Grace had said about a barge house? Alan picked up the phone and dialled a number. It rang for some time without an answer. Alan settled for having a word with the Met. See if they could trace a pub or some such, with barge in the name.

Charlie's mood brightened. He was happy not to have Mr Stolland tramping round North Woolwich with him. He grabbed his coat and joined the others. As he did this he heard the phone ringing, by the time he got to it, the ringing had stopped. Just to make sure all was well, Charlie dialled the information room at Norwich.

"What contact have you got with Mr Brandon?"

"We have him as booking mobile in London. We have his number at Eaton Walk or you can get him via the Met. Anything we can do?"

Charlie thought for a minute, "No, it's just a thought. If he rings in, tell Mr Brandon I'll ring him as soon as Bob and I get back from Barge House Road. Oh, and add, we've spoken to Jack Cousens of the Dock Police at Pier Road nick. He's meeting us. It's part of his ground, so he could open a few doors. He's picking us up. Shouldn't take more than an hour or so to run our eye over the area. Evidently, most of it's still flattened, so God knows why a villain like young Barry Scrivner should be interested in a bomb site. Did you get the drift of that?"

Charlie heard the chuckle, "Enough to let your boss know." Charlie replaced the receiver and went out the front door.

Charlie and Bob walked out of the North Woolwich railway station onto Pier Road. Turning left, they crossed over the cobbled surface, dodging between the crawling traffic, bound for or leaving the Woolwich Ferry. A London Transport bus, its destination board showing '101 East Ham', came almost to a halt, as the driver wrestled with a bad tempered gearbox. Charlie nodded towards the bus, "Wouldn't catch me trying to drive one of those things. Haven't the temperament for stop-start driving."

Bob smiled up at the driver, who chose not to return the greeting. "Guy," he said.

Charlie frowned, "You know him?"

Bob looked puzzled, "No, not the bloody driver. Guy's the type of bus. They're all fitted with crash-gearboxes. Evidently, they're a nightmare to drive. Talk about aggravation."

Charlie watched as the driver won the fight to select a gear to take the bus towards Albert Road. The whole world seemed soaked from the fine rain that had set in.

"I hate fine rain." chirped Bob, "I don't know why but it seems to drill right through your clothes in seconds."

Charlie smiled, "Cheer up, smiler, perhaps it'll blow over before long."

They reached Albert Road the same time as the shuffling bus. They were in plenty of time to listen to the driver playing another tune on his gearbox. Their pace deliberately slowed as they turned right and passed the entrance to Albert Road police station.

They had walked on some thirty yards, when they heard a heavy door slam, immediately followed by the clatter of steel shod boots on granite steps, accompanied by a string of foul language. Obscenities obviously aimed at someone in the police station, undoubtedly referring to someone's questionable parentage.

Seconds later, a ragged figure pushed roughly passed them. By his dress, or the condition of it, he looked a real tramp, a gentleman of the road. He was Charlie's height, looked in need of two or three shaves and wore the filthiest fawn mackintosh that ever graced the human frame. On his tousled head was a battered cap that was more grease than cloth, and on his feet were old army ammunition boots, laced with GPO string. The vagrant spun about and raised his hat, "Spare tuppence for a cuppa guv?"

Charlie laughed as the aroma of best bitter assaulted his nose. The tattered bundle shoved his way roughly between Charlie and Bob, then seemed to lose his balance, flailing fingers clasping hold of Charlie's coat lapels, "Nice to see you Charlie, I see you're still fraudulently drawing plain clothes allowance."

Charlie's mouth split into a wide grin. He straightened the crumpled figure and quietly introduced Bob, whose face gradually unfroze, "Meet Detective Inspector Jack Cousens of the Port of London Authority police. He's been playing this tatty role for years. Even the locals believe he's a booze-ridden itinerant of the first order. When he needs a break or just wants to wash and change to go home, he contacts them and they nip out in the van and arrest him. His collar is always felt in a very public place."

Jack staggered back and then made a fake grab for Bob's shoulder, "And, if I might say so young sir, my arrests always contain an element of drama - always highly dramatic!"

To anyone watching, it seemed the drunk had failed in his attempt to tap the price of a pint from two pedestrians.

But to those grinning faces peering from the police station windows, Jack was providing another flourishing performance worthy of the Queens Music Hall. With a melodramatic stagger, Jack weaved off, ahead of his sauntering colleagues. Charlie and Bob shortened their step to match Jack's erratic progress. They followed him along Albert Road to the point where it bends round to the left, following the line of the high wall that separates Albert Road from the King George V Dock. All this time Jack's singing tried to compete with the noise coming from the busy, slow moving traffic. Once or twice, he doffed his soiled cap, saluting and serenading bus passengers, only to draw mild abuse from some and smiles from the majority. Occasionally, coins rattled the pavement and Jack was not slow in retrieving them, with an alcoholic, "I thank you kindly, sirs."

Barge House Road, or what was left of it, lay to their right. It was exactly as the German bombers had left it. The narrow, heavily cambered cobbled road surface now cleared of debris as far as the slipway, into the river. A string of blitzed warehouses decorated the excuse for a footpath.

To their right, sagging roofs and shattered window frames clung to cracked and blackened brickwork scorched by fires long quenched. To their left, most of the buildings were floorless to the sky or reduced to mounds of brick rubble amongst which weeds battled for space, providing explosions of yellow, red and pink flowers. Hidden beneath their nodding heads lay deep, water filled basements, the half-concealed entrances of which occasionally soak the inquisitive explorer.

Half way down, on the left side, one building still stood proud amongst the ruins and caught their attention. Its pockmarked but imposing front, set some yards back from the road, had been the headquarters of the British Steam Navigation & Transportation Company. Their fleet of blue funnelled ships had once graced many of the London Royal group of docks. Structural damage to this hall of business was extremely severe, with large cracks

300

springing through brickwork; buckled metal joists, defeated key stones no longer capable of bearing spanned arches and cast-iron columns that increasingly vibrated, as if signalling the loss of compression strength. Above all this hung several tons of grey/blue welsh slate, which still clung tenaciously to spars and roof trusses, apparently defying gravity. The fractured rear of this building, not visible from the road, remained in place simply because it formed part of the massively strong steel-reinforced dock wall.

Charlie and Bob had both seen Jack turn into and stagger across Barge House road, a few yards ahead of them. Carefully picking his way over the piles of debris, he seemed to be making for the front entrance of the BSN &TC building. Surprisingly, the imposing front door still hung in position.

Charlie and Bob viewed this move with mounting concern. To them the sagging gaps in the outer fabric raised serious doubts about Jack's plan. That's if he had one!

They took in what they could of the ruins around them. The street seemed deserted enough. The only sign of movement came from the nodding grey heads of dockside cranes, working the other side of the dock wall. These swung and swivelled, beating time to the fine rain that was now becoming more insistent.

Charlie had another pull at the wet cigarette end in his mouth, "Let's try and get into that building where Jack's making for. Get out of this bloody rain."

The word rain brought with it a sharp crack. They both looked up, startled by the thought that nearby brickwork was collapsing. In the same instant, they both saw Jack throw up his arms and disappear amongst the rubble and weeds.

At first, they thought he'd simply stumbled, but he didn't reappear. Concern for Jack's safety increased as the seconds began to mount. They had just increased their pace when there was a twinned noise of thud and crack. These came from further along the street. Whatever it was seemed to come from opposite the old Navigation offices.

"They're shots Bob! Make for that porch!"

Charlie took off a split second after Bob, running hard across the uneven brickwork, trying to keep low and weaving where the ground made it possible. A whole fusillade of shots peppered the brickwork around them. They both dived into the dip where they had seen Jack disappear. He lay sprawled across a granite kerb stone. His left arm bleeding heavily, but he still managed a cheeky grin and a thumbs-up.

Three further sharp cracks followed by fading whines underlined the welcome, as rounds ricocheted from the rubble above them. It seemed they had walked straight into what must be a private war. Crazy heaps of blitzed rubble, absorbed most of the sound of gunfire. Anyone close enough to hear it would probably associate the bangs with dock working. The only people likely to be visiting Barge House Road were those having business on the bombsite, or those idiots suckered into paying the place a visit.

Charlie groped in a pocket and handed Jack a large handkerchief, "Sorry Jack, it seems I've invited you to the wrong party. I thought we might run into a villain or two but I didn't count on being shot at. Whoever it is, they obviously knew we were coming."

Jack was doing his best to stem the flow of blood, "Can't be young Scrivner, he's more of a quick stab in the back merchant."

Charlie leant over Jack and tried to help tighten the makeshift bandage, "There's more than one gun here, and they know coppers don't come out tooled up for this kind of party."

Charlie had finished doing what he could for Jacks arm, "Okay to move Jack?"

Jack gave a grin, "No good staying here, the roofs leaking. Anyway, I think they're moving to get a better view of us. Best make for that wonky front door. Make our way through the old Navigation building and up into the dock. The wall's breached at lower basement level. You ought to be ashamed Charlie, coming home and upsetting the locals like this," Jack's face creased into another painful smile.

Charlie changed his position so he could clearly see the twenty or so yards of open ground that separated them from the front door of the building.

"I just hope that bloody door's not jammed or locked,"

"It wasn't when I came through it a few hours ago," said Jack.

The sound of a bullet striking nearby brickwork made him duck down quickly. The force of its arrival spewed mortar over the three of them.

"Well," Charlie said, "our neighbours are either bad shots or they haven't a clear shot. As soon as we break cover, it'll be different."

Bob pushed over alongside Charlie, "If we are going for that door, I suggest we do it now. I'd rather go while they're unsure where we're lying. They think they've got Jack so three will be a surprise."

The words spurred Charlie into action. He hurled himself up and forward across the rubble toward the porch. His one thought was to throw open the door. The others could then dive straight through. Looking neither right nor left, he thundered up the three steps onto the porch and folded himself into the protection afforded by the bricked recess.

A second later, the arrival of the two others slammed the breath out of him as they joined him in the bricked recess as several bullets struck the brickwork above their heads.

"Now chaps, let's have an orderly queue and I think we can dispense with knocking," panted Jack, "with any luck no-one will be at home."

Using his foot, he reached out as far as he could and pushed at the door. With relief they watched it swing slowly inwards, giving a loud jarring screech. The timber framework on the far side of the door disintegrated as several rounds smashed into it.

"Impatient buggers aren't they!" Bob shouted as he threw himself to one side, diving through the gap left by the half open door. More rounds smashed through timber and brick.

"Time to go?" Said Charlie and grabbing Jack, flew through the doorway, landing neatly on the unfortunate Bob.

Jack groaned as they all crawled along the entrance hall floor, "This really is no joke. It's raining outside and I'm bleeding inside. It's just not my day."

Charlie and Bob looked at Jack. He looked deathly pale but still insisted on grinning back at them.

"Jack, can you keep going?" Charlie spluttered through the dust.

Jack eased himself onto his side, "Yes, take no notice of my makeup, I put too much talcum on this morning."

Charlie grinned and looked round quickly, "You can bet those shooters are not going to be content staying their side of the street. They're going to come looking for us, so we've got to move."

Their temporary shelter turned out to be a beautifully tiled entrance hall. Litter, glass and masonry lay everywhere. Daylight filtered in through massive gaps where windows or brickwork had blown away. Ahead of them, in the gloom, a grand staircase stretched up, out of sight. It was not hard to see that not so long ago the building must have been impressive.

Hugging the floor tiles, they crawled forward. Jack led them to the very back of the hall, where they saw a narrow recessed door. Jack got to his knees and put his weight against it. The door gave grudgingly. Set into what was no more than a cupboard space was a narrow iron spiral staircase.

A fresh hail of bullets found their way through gaps in the outer walls, each round shattering floor tiles. A single bullet rebounded and ploughed across Bob's thigh. "Persistent bastards aren't they," he said, gritting his teeth.

"It was your fault," said Charlie, "The least you could have done was close the front door properly on the way in."

Incredibly, they all burst into fits of suppressed laughter.

Jack slid onto the spiral staircase, "Down we go. I suggest best done on your backsides, rather than feet. And watch it, the anchorage has sheared part way through," he demonstrated this by pushing on the iron framework. The whole staircase swayed sickeningly, "worry not lads," he said, "escape lies at the bottom, its only two floors down and a crawl over some brickwork then we're out."

"It strikes me," Charlie said quietly, "if this has been set up, wouldn't you think they'd have closed that way out. If you know about it Jack, you can bet your boots they do."

Jack shook his head, plaster dust cascading to the floor, "I doubt it. It's my bet they want us in here. They could have nailed us easily before we got through that bloody door. It's unlikely they'd know about the breach in the dock wall. Even I didn't know about it until I explored these cellars. No, they'd have to be really local to know about the breach."

"Well, we'll soon know. Off you go, Jack boy. Bob, can you manage?"

Bob nodded, "It's only a scratch."

Charlie patted Bob's shoulder, "Good lad, I'll hang on a minute to see if they're coming in. Good luck each."

The staircase swung like a slow pendulum, as Jack and Bob fumbled their way down into the darkness. Charlie backed onto the head of the stairway and squatted down. He then dropped down further so that just his head was level with the hall floor. There was not a hint of movement. Encouraged by the silence and comforted by the security within the gloom at the back of the hall, Charlie relaxed a little. Small comforts eagerly clung to by the hunted, and Charlie certainly felt on the side of the hunted.

Time passed and the icy coldness of the metal stair treads struck up through the seat of his trousers. He could hear the muffled movements of Jack and Bob as they descended into the blackness. He shifted his position slightly to avoid the cramp that was already invading his legs. The staircase groaned and swung alarmingly, reminding him of Jack's warning. Charlie didn't want to think too much about the sheared anchorage. From the swaying he guessed the bottom fixture had gone completely, leaving perhaps one stressed bolt through the spindle at the top.

He preferred not to look up, although the chance of seeing the anchor point, in the gloom, was remote. He concentrated his gaze on the front door. Time seemed to be standing still. The urge to light up a cigarette was strong but fortunately for Charlie, the urge to preserve his life was stronger.

He pulled up the left sleeve of his jacket, noticing how filthy it was. He strained to see the dial of his watch. He drew his right hand across its face and, for the first time, noticed his hands were shaking. Charlie's mouth creased into a grin as he told himself it wasn't a lack of nerve. It was pure bloody excitement. He was the fox, and those outside were the hounds. His mind held this thought. On reflection, he didn't much like the idea of being the fox, trapped as he was. He'd never really been one for blood sports.

Cleaning the dial of his watch, he had a second look. The others had been gone about five minutes or more. Assuming Jack and Bob must have got where they were going and having heard nothing from outside, he slowly uncoiled, so that he was now standing. Pins and needles rocketed through his legs. He knew it was time to move.

Charlie carefully twisted round to start down the stairs, allowing his left hand to slide down the steel rail. The whole structure slowly spun. He halted, waiting for the staircase to steady. Then he heard a different sound. It was a very distinct crunch.

As a small boy, playing Cowboys and Indians, he recognised the noise you tried to avoid, as you silently approached your enemy's camp. The sort of noise you might make if you were trying to cross a rubble-strewn porch for instance, placing a size nine on brittle mortar. Silence again descended.

Charlie held his position and opened his mouth wide. This let breath pass slowly in and out of his mouth, with little sound. A gamekeeper had taught him this trick for reducing his own body noises, while hearing everything going on around him. More hungry seconds ticked by, crammed with silence. Charlie still had a view of the door. He tried to will the staircase to remain steady. Then, just when Charlie thought he had imagined the noise, the half-open front door began to inch backwards into the hall. At first, the movement was so painfully slow. Charlie was convinced he was seeing things. Then, there was the movement again, so very slow. The same protesting screech they had caused when opening the door began to repeat itself.

Finally, the figure of a man appeared in the shattered door frame. He was tallish and in one of his hands, he held a gun, while in the other, was what appeared to be a small canvas bag. Charlie silently lowered his head. In the deep shadow, he was sure he couldn't be seen.

Just then, a very faint voice called from below, "Charlie, we're down. Come on."

As Charlie heard this, he also heard a scratching sound and a plop. The man with the satchel swung his arm in a shallow arc, as if to skim a stone across water. The satchel, now giving off a thin trail of smoke, spiralled across the tiled floor towards Charlie. It spluttered and fizzed as it came, sliding round and round, pushing its way through the litter, towards him.

Charlie tore his eyes away. He dropped down the swinging staircase, his feet stuttering over the treads, in what he knew was the flight of his life. Darkness held no fears but what was above him drove him downwards at break neck speed.

He managed to call, "A bomb, it's a…"

The detonation, when it came totally destroyed what remained of fragile stability. In what seemed to be a grand theatrical gesture, the ornate roof buckled and caved in. This shuddering avalanche displaced walls, causing them to fall domino fashion. Like playing cards, they folded and fell. The thunder of this explosion gradually gave way to a huge rising cloud of grey dust.

To the beat officer, who was patrolling Albert Road, the rumbling crash signalling the demolition of yet another blitzed building, was not a special or an unusual occurrence.

A little later, a gang of four men appeared, walking away from Barge House Road. They were all dressed in builders-type overalls, covered in the usual dust and carrying weighty plumber's canvas bags. They laughed and talked as they made their way casually along Albert Road. The constable recalled the nearby racket of jackhammers just before the collapse. He'd clearly heard these as he was leaving the station. Add to that, the continuous thunder of rivet hammers coming from the other side of the dock wall, constant traffic noise and countless other assaults on his ears, it sounded just like any other normal docklands day.

He nodded to the approaching group. He envied the freedom they had in their work. He pulled his cape closer around his shoulders, thinking it must be nice not to have to wear a uniform that makes you stand out like a sore thumb. In passing, one of the men smiled and remarked that it was as well the old Navigation offices were down at last. The constable agreed. It was one less death trap for the local kids. He made a mental note to put an entry in the Daily Occurrence book, on his return to the station.

He watched the men as they made their way along the road. He didn't really envy them. Their job was dirty and dangerous and it was unusual for anyone to give them credit for a job well done. Bit like being a copper, he thought. He looked at his watch, noted the time and hoped the rain would last just long enough to help lay the thick dust.

Charlie's ears were ringing painfully and he had the air sucked out of his lungs. The fall was a heavy one but miraculously the staircase stayed upright. It swung and creaked alarmingly, threatening to collapse, taking Charlie with it. Brick debris and dust continued to fall for what seemed an age, drifting down where Charlie clung like a limpet to the handrail.

Choking dust blotted out what little light there had been. Bob's voice came from below, "Charlie, Charlie, you okay? The stair bolts have gone at the bottom. Just follow the stairs down. I'll do my best to hold it steady."

Charlie held a hand over his mouth and moved slowly downwards. It seemed to take forever but soon he felt hands guiding him away from the stairs and over a brick strewn floor. Jack's voice came to him out of the blackness, "Charlie, hang onto Bob. I'll guide us. We've got to get out of here before the whole place caves in."

Fearful groans came from above, as joists and arches began their journey to collapse. To Charlie the distance they travelled through the basement could have been no more than thirty to forty yards but it seemed to take an age. Suddenly all three were scrambling and clawing upwards, over bricks and shattered timber.

Gradually the blackness gave way to a half-light. Dust was still so thick it was all but impossible to see. Bob suddenly called for him to climb into a narrow gap in the brickwork. As soon as he had done this, Charlie realised he was out. The dust dispersed and he was sitting on a heap of wet wreckage, in the open air. They were in the open expanse of the Royal Albert dock. All three looked like cement dust clowns, covered from head to toe, but grinning like apes.

Charlie slapped Jack on the back, "Thank God for your escapades Jack. Your wanderings, certainly through that building saved our bacon."

Jack, who was holding his arm across his chest, shook his head, "We've still to get away from here without attracting too much attention. I reckon whoever set us up for that lot will think they've done a good job. You two stay where you are. I'll nip across to our dock phone and arrange some transport." With that, he hobbled away.

Charlie and Bob crawled into a dip so that they were out of sight. Whatever Jack was up to, they were happy to leave him to it. The two lay back and soaked up the fine rain that now turned the dust into neat plaster casts.

It was a forty minutes later that a dark green van pulled up beside their particular heap of bricks. The back door opened and Jack stepped out.

"Listen my lucky lads, all hell's breaking loose just round the corner from the dock gates. Our lads are everywhere. Charlie, your boss Mr Brandon used some heavyweight with the Met. They're busy raiding anything and everything that contains the name barge house. My lot put two-and-two together and stormed the pile of bricks the other side of this wall. Pity the tip came a bit late for our party, but that's life." Charlie tried to interrupt but Jack was in the chair, "Charlie, to answer your question, the team that tried to do us had it away before our cavalry arrived. I phoned your folks and evidently your lad Frank has turned up. He's on his way over to pick you up. My lads at the gate will direct him in. Look for a green Riley. And if I were you two, I'd lay very low for a while, give that trigger happy crew the impression they've won."

He smiled, "Don't fret Charlie, I'll be in contact and claim the pint you owe me for giving you the conducted tour."

Jack looked at Bob, "You have to admit it, being with Charlie is better than dishing out parking tickets." With that, Jack waved and was back in the van.

Bob grinned through the cement dust, "Well, he's right enough. We could both do with a scrub. He pulled at his clothes. Do you realise Charlie, every time you and I get together, we end up looking and smelling like something the cat dragged in."

Charlie smiled and lit up a cigarette.

Chapter Seventeen

The Grab and Bucket Pub, next door to the Seamen's Hostel in the Victoria Dock Road, was busy. It was just after seven when Barry Scrivner pushed his way in. The four men with him went straight to the bar. Barry said something to them, then made for a table tucked away in a recess by the fireplace.

"Hello Mr Grech," he slid too easily into a chair opposite the small figure, "you'll be pleased to know that things went well. In fact, it went so very well my lads are thinking they ought to take up demolition full time."

Grech noted the blatant cockiness.

"Well, Mr Grech?"

Grech lowered his newspaper, but didn't reply.

"Mr Grech, you owe me a lot of money, and my crew need their pay. Money well earned, wouldn't you say, Mr Grech?" Barry stabbed a finger at the lowered newspaper, "Your special edition told you that. What goes into print can't lie eh?" Barry referred to the headline in the London Star.

Grech ran his eyes across the article again.

'Collapse of Woolwich Building

Three Missing. Police sources confirmed today, the probable deaths of three men, last seen entering a derelict building in Barge House Road. North Woolwich. Demolition was taking place in the area at the time. Who the men were or why they had gone into the building, despite the presence of warning notices, remains unknown. Dangerous conditions prevented an immediate search by the emergency services.'

A stop-press article on the back page reported that efforts were being made to trace contractors responsible for work in Barge House Road.

"See that, neat job eh?" Barry's finger repeatedly stabbed again at the headline, "National press headlines, what speaks can't lie, eh Mr Grech? Now, I think a job like that is worth its settlement, don't you?"

Barry looked over his shoulder to make sure he had an audience. His four companions laughed and raised their glasses to him. Others in the bar either buried their faces in pint glasses or looked away. Whatever was going down was none of their business.

Barry made a great show of turning back to Grech. His face was now deadly serious, "Getting your three into that bloody building wasn't easy, took a lot of ammo. My lads took risks for you and now they need to put miles between the bizzies and where they're going. Even you should know how that feels Mr Grech!" Barry's voice was strong, laced with spite and threat. He relished the opportunity to demonstrate the local clout he carried. He'd have even more weight when it got round who'd organised the Woolwich job. He'd learned his trade early, using the school playground to hone his reputation with a razor.

Grech looked up slowly from the paper. His black eyes bored into Barry's and he whispered, "The job called for three men to be found, apparently killed by the sudden and unexpected collapse of a building. Your job was to plan that incident. To recruit what labour you needed, and achieve *exactly* what I required," Grech placed great stress on the word 'exactly', There was no mistaking the implied violence, "nothing too onerous I would have thought. Especially for someone of your capabilities, a professional like you. Simply trap them, render them unconscious, using materials immediately available. Then place the unconscious bodies in the right spot, and topple a wall or two."

Grech let that sink in.

"My task was equally simple. Supply the target, and find the money. Before I hand over the money, I want your assurance that examination of the bodies will confirm no other injury, other than that probably caused by collapsing brickwork?"

Barry looked round again at his supporters. This time when he turned back, he was sweating, just a little. His collar felt tight and he didn't quite know where to place his eyes. His posture had changed. There was now a visible fraction of uncertainty. He tried to cover this with an ounce of bravado.

"What are you worried about? I did the business on em! Don't play hard man with me. It won't wash."

Barry snapped his eyes away from the cold stare. He didn't like Grech, one bit. But, he did appreciate the cash he'd produced since their first meeting. He'd tagged along because his old man said he must. It was handy for their business. Apart from that, he didn't need this skinny little git!

With the speed of a snake, Grech's thin hand shot out. He grabbed Barry's right wrist, turned it outwards with a grip so tight that Barry yelped in agony. At the same time, he was jolted up out of his chair and halfway over the table to save his arm being broken. This happened in full view of his team and by a man at least twice his age, one-third his weight and almost a dwarf!

"You will remember, you staked your life on this business going perfectly," there was a pause, "didn't you Barry?"

All Barry could do was to control the urge to scream and try to ease the pain that was now shooting through his arm. Grech smiled. It was not the smile of a caring person. It didn't reach the hard black eyes that bored into Barry's. Grech was enjoying this moment. He cared deeply about getting the right message across.

"You see Barry, it's very, very important that these policemen or bizzies, as you call them, get their exit from this world, without a suspicion of murder?"

"Yes, of course, yes," Barry yelped.

His wrist released, he slumped onto the table then slowly slid back into his chair. He didn't like being made to look a fool. Threatening Barry in a bar full of locals was not good for Barry's image or his business. It certainly did nothing for Grech's health. Barry was already working on what he would do to this little gnome, probably in his uncle's butcher shop.

Grech read what was in Barry's mind, "You are a good lad Barry. Just don't take it into your head to follow your friends to the seaside. You are too special, too busy to wander," with that, Grech slid a thick package across the table, "now, your next little task is a simple one. Find me a Steward who works on the MV Galen Empress, she's a sea going motor vessel, berthed in the Albert dock."

Barry interrupted, "I know, I know. She's been tied up there a while. Talk about the filthy rich...."

Grech's rage showed in his brittle eyes, "Shut up and listen Barry. All you need to know is that it's important this steward keeps his mouth shut tight, and I mean shut! Find him, and don't be too long about it. When you have the man, contact me at Pennyfields. I'm lodging under the name Gentry, I'd rather you didn't forget that, Barry. One last point, can I remind you that it wouldn't pay you to harbour thoughts of forming your own company, if you understand me?"

Though nothing of what had passed between Grech and Barry was overheard, the discomfort suffered by Barry was visible. This was the East end, where painful disagreements were part of everyday life. However, there was little chance of a fracas raising too much interest inside or outside the pub.

Grech folded his paper and left without another word. Barry swaggered across to his pals, "I'm going to slit that git's throat from ear to ear."

He needed to look top man in front of his mates, but he still looked over his shoulder as he made the threat. Stories about Victor Grech, were beginning to circulate. That Lockhart Street business made Barry sick to his stomach. It wasn't good business to knock off a couple of local pensioners. It's the sort of job that gets the local crushers angrier than a swarm of wasps.

It was just after ten when Barry and the four men left the Grab and Bucket. The pavements were still busy but as they made their way along the Victoria Dock Road, pedestrians thinned out. Barry took his leave by the railway station and made his way home. He'd had a profitable but tiring day, not to mention an unforgivable knock to his pride.

His mind sped back to Grech. He loathed him. How anyone could tie up and gag an old couple, then put their lights out, was truly out of order. It was time someone did for that heartless bastard and Barry felt he was the one to do it. The snuffing would earn him some local credit. A smile spread across Barry's face, he'd enjoy doing for Grech.

The four men, lately employed in Barge House Road, were all lodging south of the river. They filed off the train at North Woolwich, with the intention of using the foot-tunnel to cross to the South side. Being total strangers to the area, they hadn't counted on the tunnel closing at ten. They dived across to the ferry terminal but found that too, had closed down for the night. They stood and chatted about getting a train back and taking a tram through Blackwall tunnel.

The terminal was completely deserted. All lights apart from those required by the river navigation rulebook, had been extinguished. Still chatting and laughing, the men walked casually to the edge of the landing stage, put their bags down, stood in a row and began relieving themselves of some of the ale they'd drunk. They giggled like children as the four streams of steaming urine, curved to join the river water, some ten feet below. A slack tide sluggishly pushed against the black timbers of the landing stage. It wouldn't be long before the water left the high water mark, starting its regular journey down to the sea.

A succession of soft thuds joined the noises coming from local factories. The four, half-turned in silent surprise, then like marionette's whose strings had been cut, they folded one by one, and splashed into the dark water. A small man in dark clothing emerged from the shadows. He walked slowly to where the men had stood, looked down for no more than a second, kicked their bags into the water and walked away.

Grech gave little thought to the money that filled the drowned pockets of the men. After all, they had obliged him by falling into deep water. His gloved hands worked as he unscrewed the silencer from the pistol. He placed both items in his pockets and, being in no hurry, walked at an easy pace to the railway station, where he boarded the last train to Canning Town.

Lo Wey's café was one of the many Chinese eating houses in the heart of London's China town. This small but thriving section of Limehouse, just off the West India dock road, grew as hardworking Chinese catered to satisfy the needs of merchant seamen, shipping into or out of the London docks. The blind alley, leading from Ming Street, to Lo Wey's café, was far from pleasant. It was a typical narrow unlit passage, which ended at Lo's dimly lit door. The worn sign above the entrance confirmed that food and accommodation was available, all at reasonable prices. Services also promoted by distinctive smells that continuously lingered in the alley.

The thin little man in the dark scruffy clothes that made his way confidently through this passage had no illusions about this place. Its appearance or aroma meant nothing to him. He was a tenant of Lo's, quite happy to accept what that meant. Most people, including the local police, managed to find reasons for avoiding this area, whenever choice was available.

Grech opened the front door into the small lobby, which immediately set a bell jangling. He reached up automatically and strangled the noise.

Ignoring the half-glazed door leading into the café accommodation he walked to a second door. He unlocked this and before starting the climb the stairs immediately ahead of him, he tried the light switch. The stairs remained steeped in shadow. The one fly speckled bulb, swinging from the twisted flex above his head, had blown. This one bulb had been defunct since before Lo had given him the conducted tour. Grech slowly climbed the three flights to the attic. The condition of the steep stairs advised against swift movement. Passage up or down was clearly announced into the café by the movement of ill-fitting joints.

The room Grech had rented was small, more like a cupboard, but came complete with window. This window, Lo had stated, was a very special feature, and was the reason why he was asking double rent. The window, once unlocked and swung fully open, could, if the tenant so wished, form an emergency escape route. Not a journey for the faint hearted, but by carefully negotiating adjacent roofs and a series of ladders, the tenant could depart unseen, exiting into Pennyfields. This, Lo had explained, was the road behind Ming Street. Grech was not slow in appreciating this unique feature. The alternative exit, plus the stout lockable door to his room, was well worth the additional rent. Equally clear was the fact that, Lo was not slow in welcoming a tenant who clearly placed his skin before money.

As for the remainder of the Chinese community, it seemed they were happy not asking or answering questions. They preferred the use of their own native language, insisting they didn't understand or 'spek engrish'. This statement always accompanied with an inscrutable smile. This made life difficult when trying to obtain information.

The private world of little China was exactly what Grech looked for when adding to his accommodation register. He chose not to use this room every day. He felt safer switching from one lodging to another. He did this for many reasons but mainly to avoid becoming a familiar face.

All these thoughts sifted through Grech's mind as he laboured up the ancient stairs, making as little noise as possible. As he reached the head of the stairs, he paused before crossing the small landing to the door of his room.

The landing area had a tiny skylight in the ceiling, but this was a moonless night, so the space at the top of the stairs remained as black as the inside of his hat, with darker shadows thrown in.

He stepped quietly forward and ran his fingers lightly down the door. He barely touched the surface, feeling every outline of the flaking varnish. Some three inches above the floor, he found what he was searching for. A split match, jammed tightly between the door and its frame. It was where he expected it to be.

Grech felt pleased that he had dodged into the Troxy cinema, off the Mile End road, to escape the rain. The only part of the programme he found entertaining was a scene where a match was slid between the door and the jam, to detect movement of a door. It was certainly a very useful tip.

He unlocked the door and went in. As he stepped across the threshold, the toe of his shoe kicked something that slithered forward across the bare boards. Closing the door before putting the light on, he stepped forward. In the dim light given off by the lamp, he saw a slim book, the edge of which poked out from under the bed.

Lo, being an attentive proprietor, had pushed his rent book under the door. Grech reached down and picked it up. Lo's handwriting was impeccable. Room number nine. Tenant Mr W.S.Gentry. Grech felt gratified. He had taken the name from a red lorry he'd seen being driven towards the dock. Placing the book on the washstand, he returned to the door and locked it. Then he wedged the back of a chair under the door handle, as insurance. Another tip he had picked up from the film.

Grech crossed the room and groped under the bed, dragging out a battered looking leather case. Although it was far from new, the locks were solid. Taking a key from his pocket, he unlocked it and searched through the few contents. He opened a large brown paper bag and tipped out the contents.

A small calendar marked 'Favourite Views of Cromer', fluttered out. He put this aside, after thumbing

318

through the promised views. He couldn't remember what had prompted him to buy it, unless it was simply to get change for some reason. Along with the calendar, there were several large bundles of five-pound notes, which had fallen onto the bed. He placed these back into the bag. Then, taking out what seemed to be a large black cigarette case, he operated a catch. A slide opened and he was staring intently at a small illuminated screen. He used a control on one side of the case to scroll through displayed information. It took several minutes before he arrived at some text that held his attention.

Grech then carefully made detailed pencilled notes, often referring back to the screen. Following this, he again concentrated on the screen. After a few minutes, he whispered to the room, "It seems I have to push things along."

He closed a slide over the screen and placed the case carefully into his inside jacket pocket. This he buttoned down carefully. Seeming satisfied, he carefully removed two other objects. Treating them with great respect, he very slowly removed their covers and examined each in turn. They were about the size of half a cigar box. Ranged along one side, were a number of recessed buttons and a minute screen. Satisfied all was well, he replaced each into its cover and put them both on the bed. He then withdrew a canvas holdall from the suitcase. Into this, he placed one of the boxes, all the money and several other items that could have passed for small hand-tools. Grech patted the holdall, as though it was now special to his needs.

The second box still lay on the bed. He looked at it in deep thought. His eyes then swept the room, as though searching for something. He went over to the door, stood with his back to it, and again surveyed the room. His thin lips parted.

He crossed to the washstand, opened a drawer and slid the second box inside. Taking the calendar, he turned to the current month, counted the weeks forward, into the following month, and selected the third Sunday. He pencilled a ring around the day.

In the margin, he wrote the words 'S returns to Albany Street to celebrate his birthday!' This he underlined heavily, twice. Grech's eyes glistened as he did this. He then did a most curious thing. Folding the calendar very carefully, he placed it at the very back of the same drawer, as though intentionally hidden. Having done this, he placed the holdall and suitcase back under the bed, out of sight. He turned off the light, dropped onto the bed, closed his eyes and slept soundly.

Someone pounding on the door woke him from a deep sleep. He lay for a second, trying to pull his tumbling thoughts together. He checked his watch. It was just after 3pm. Looking around the room, he made certain his luggage was out of sight. The pounding came again.

"Alright, alright, I'm coming!" he called.

Grech unfastened the window latch and allowed the window to swing fully open. He swiftly crossed back to the bed and removed his gun from under the pillow. He was ready now.

Walking across to the door, he whispered, "Who's there?"

Lo Wey answered in his quiet, polite manner, "You come now Mr Gentry and talk to man in Café. He is very anxious to speak, please."

Grech visibly relaxed. He thanked Lo and heard him pad back down the staircase. It took Grech a few minutes to secure the window, put the gun in the waistband of his trousers and throw on his long coat. He quickly locked his room, split a match and place it in the door jam. He couldn't afford simple mistakes.

He didn't enter the café part of the building straight away, but looked for Barry through the cracked glass of the door. One glance found him standing by the counter, trying desperately to look inconspicuous. The pose adopted by Barry wasn't very well managed, mainly because of his expensive looking suit, light tan suede shoes, western shirt and gaudy tie.

Barry didn't look pleased when he spotted Grech.

"At last," he said, "I've been round every bloody chink café in the district looking for you. Why didn't you say this drum was off Ming Street?"

Grech sat at one of the tables and ordered tea, "Can I assume you've found my steward?"

Barry took out a handkerchief and wiped the lino used by Lo to cover tabletops, "You really do pick crappy places to stay."

A grinning Lo appeared with the tea. One pot, two dishes and a small bowl containing what looked like cane sugar.

Grech poured hot liquid from the pot onto leaves at the bottom of each dish. He offered the green tea to Barry.

"Not on your bloody life. I don't drink chinky tea."

Grech chose to ignore this. Instead, he sipped his tea, "I take it that you have achieved a quick result?"

Barry continued polishing the lino tabletop, "To answer your question, yes I've found your pigeon. A real prize too, he's ripe because he's pissed off. The owners are as rich as pigs, but they pay next to nothing. Still live in the world where servants get zilch."

Grech waited for Barry to finish his burbling.

"She's loading in the Albert dock, something to do with a trip, but at the moment she only needs one of the crew sleeping aboard. He's staying at the Seamen's hostel, except for the odd night that he has to spend on board."

Accepting the information and weighing every word, Grech said, "Is that it?"

Barry looked hurt. "What more did you expect?"

Grech sipped more green tea, "Did this person say how long before they leave?"

Barry was looking very uncomfortable, "No, but it won't be too long now."

Grech changed tack, "How much exactly did you say he'd get for his trouble?"

Grech watched Barry's eyes. He had now transferred his cleaning from the tabletop to the sleeves of his jacket, "I just said you'd see him right."

Grech knew he was lying, "How much?"

Barry looked even more uncomfortable, he looked around nervously, "I have to make my bit so I reckon a tenner for him and say, twenty for me."

Grech smiled his thin smile, "Barry, you've done well. If this works out I'll give you enough money to buy another suit. Now, I want you to get him to the Eastern, you know the public house at the corner of Burdett Road, at eight sharp, tonight!"

Barry stopped grooming his sleeves, "That's a bit tight. Suppose he can't make it?"

Grech's eyes hardened, "There are some things, Barry, that are as urgent to you as breathing. Don't let me down!"

Barry went to say something, but just as quickly closed his mouth.

Grech nodded, "Just make sure he sees this little job as a golden opportunity. I'm sure you can persuade him."

Barry looked down at his hands and started to wipe them.

"There is one more really small job I want you to do. I wouldn't trust this to just anyone Barry, so you should see how important the task is," Grech waited for the reaction from Barry. He didn't react.

"It is so simple, but it has to be exactly as I say. A man of your standing knows that presentation is everything. For a lady, flowers mean so much, wouldn't you say?"

Barry didn't answer, he knew it was best to listen and let Grech explain his small job.

"I want these particular flowers arranged and boxed exactly as I say. I will see to the delivery," Grech then explained the special surprise. It was involved and Barry didn't like one or two aspects of the task, but didn't dare refuse.

"I'll do what I can."

Grech watched him carefully, "Of course you will Barry. After all, it's business isn't it? If you feel you are not up to this particular task, I may have to take my business elsewhere. And that would make me very unhappy."

Barry hated Grech's soft voice. In fact, he hated everything about the poxy dwarf. He knew Grech would top him as soon as look at him. Barry had always hated guns. They could be traced, plus they were bulky to carry around. A blade was quieter and didn't need reloading. In the hands of an expert, and Barry felt he was an expert, a knife was so much more professional, even artistic in the right hands.

Grech's voice broke in on Barry's thoughts, "You will need extra funds for this small matter and to ensure they are packaged *exactly,* as I have said," the word, 'exactly,' was once again heavily weighted. Grech pushed a packet at Barry, "Don't forget now, Barry, I want this task done perfectly. Oh, by the way before I forget, did you pay off your friends yesterday?"

Barry's face turned very pale. It was unlike Grech to make small talk. He immediately thought Grech knew he had taken half of everyone's cut from yesterday's job. His anxiety rose as he thought Grech had seen them after Barry had spilt from them at the railway station. Barry decided to bluff his way out.

"Yes, of course I did. We split the money five ways before they got onto the train. They were well pleased. Probably down at the coast right now, having the odd drink or two."

Grech's lingering look worried Barry. It worried him on the bus. It dogged his footsteps walking along his road, it nagged at him over his tea and it was still his companion when he collected Nicky Richards, the steward. He'd served two years borstal with Nick and felt he could trust him.

"Just watch this geezer, Nicky boy. Do the job whatever it is, snatch the cash and do a runner. He's not one of us, he's a shooter, and I don't mean peas."

The Eastern was well packed by eight. A woman of uncertain age and liberally supplied with port and lemon, was doing her best to coax something from an out of tune piano.

Grech worked his way through the crowd to the end of the bar. He settled for a spot where he could see both bar entrances. He had only been there two minutes when he saw Barry and another man appear through the Burdett Road entrance. They made their way over to Grech. Introductions over, Grech called for drinks.

"How long you been with the Empress then?"

Nick looked at Barry then at Grech, "What's that to do with you? Barry just said you wanted some information. That doesn't include my sheet."

"Fair enough," Grech said, "I just want to know that my money's well spent. That you're more than a one-trip wonder. You're no good to me unless you know the boat backwards."

Nicky was on edge. He'd been put on his guard by Barry's warning, "Look mister, I know the boat backwards, and I know the tight git that owns her. I'm a steward to the officers see, not the bloody captain, first mate or greaser. Ask me what you want to know and then, I'm off."

Grech placed a white fiver on the bar immediately in front of Nick. Then he slowly placed another, over the first, "If you tell me what I need to know, plus let me have a look round the boat, there's plenty more of those in it for you," he watched Nick's eyes flick to Barry, "Don't you worry about Barry's take, I'm going to settle up with Barry after the job." Grech's assurance didn't go down well with either of them.

Nick's eyes again wandered over the money, "That's not enough cash to risk my job mister."

For the second time that day Barry looked worried.

"Okay," said Grech, "it's only fair you're happy. You guarantee me a couple of hours undisturbed aboard the Empress, and I'll give you another ten now, plus twenty more when I get my result. Are we in business?"

Barry was smiling broadly, "Bloody hell Nicky, you can see he's good for it. It must be worth him getting a quick glim. You can have a few beers on that lot."

Nick still looked puzzled, "What's this all about? What exactly do you want to look at?"

Grech straightened up from the bar, shrugged and opened his hands, as though coming clean, "Okay Nick. You're no fool, I saw that as soon as I looked at you. Now, believe this or not, my family was seen off by the Sticklands. Your bosses, right?"

Nick nodded, as though at last he'd been seen as someone who gets respect.

Grech needed the right words, "Look, I'm a time-served engineer. Some time ago I worked for the Sticklands, on development. I came up with an idea and like a fool gave them a drawing. Doesn't matter what it was, but it was a positioning device I'd dreamed up."

Grech drained his glass and ordered more drinks. He did this purposely, letting his story sink in.

"You said they were tight. Well, I'd say they were worse than that. They took the idea, developed it and didn't pay me a brass farthing, not a thing. Well, I couldn't prove a damned thing. You know the old story," Grech winked one of his beady eyes, "after a while, they planted stuff at my home, had me turned over and framed me. It's the Stickland family tradition, their empire against the little people. You know the way it works. Well, long story short. I went down," Grech played the part he'd seen in the film, perfectly.

For once, Barry was silent. Pictures flashed through his mind. He'd never heard Grech say so much about himself. It might just come in handy to know the poisoned runt had form. Grech going down for theft could come in very handy. It might give him an edge. Barry could hear the chink of gold. He may even be able to cut a thicker slice of cake from the Sticklands, if it came to shopping Grech. Perhaps Lord Stickland might hand over a tidy packet to avoid the slippery slope to disgrace. He'd have to wait until Grech had done all the work and got the evidence in his hands. That would be the time to play grass. He told himself Nick mustn't know either. After all, friendship is one thing, but this, as Grech would say, was business.

Barry's attention returned to the waiting Grech. There was a quick exchange of looks between Nick and Barry.

Nick slapped the bar, "I knew it. It's the sweet taste of good old revenge."

Grech continued to play victim. He ordered more drinks, "I know he's using my idea. He's produced it from my drawings. He'll trial it secretly, using the Empress. If it works at sea, he'll turn these out by the thousand, and make another fortune. You're in his crew you must know how two-faced he is?"

Barry reacted, as he knew Grech would expect him to, "Come on Nicky my old mucker. You must ride this one. That Stickland needs a right shafting," he turned to Grech, "look, we want in on this. If we help you prove what this git's done, it must make us all seriously rich, right?"

Grech looked at Barry as though he was his long lost son. He reached over and shook his arm, "Don't you worry Barry, the second we pull this off, I'll make sure you both get every penny you're owed, and a lot more. I'm just after getting my own back!"

Grech knew how much contempt he had for Barry but he was at a loss to know why he felt sorry for Nick. To Grech, pity was unknown and had no value. It was a new feeling, which made him very uncomfortable.

Nick still wanted chapter and verse, "Are you saying, all you need is time to look at control equipment on the Empress, a rapid in and out? No damage done?"

Grech hid his thoughts and smiled, "Two questions and the answer to each is yes. No one gets hurt, nothing's taken, a dead clean job which can never be traced to you or Barry," Grech paused and raised a finger, "but, until it's all tied up and the results are in, not so much as a whisper to anyone," turning to Barry, he said, "no one's saying you've a loose tongue but, when I say no one knows that especially includes your family. When it's all over and I've paid you both off, then everyone and I mean everyone will know!"

"I'm in," said Nick.

Barry grinned like a Cheshire cat, "So when do we do the job?"

Grech looked at Barry, "You've done your bit well. Now, in order to stay clean, you have to keep your head down. As soon as Nick gets me on the Empress and the jobs done, we'll be in touch. Then we wait for the result."

Barry faltered, "What's this? Why do we have to wait for the results? What results?"

Grech kept the conspiracy theory ticking over, "It won't be enough to claim he's bent. Got to have hard evidence, proven evidence to screw him. Enough so that Stickland, can't and won't want to go to law. Then, my dear Barry, he'll pay us a cool million." Grech let the sun, sandy beaches and fun, sink in.

"Then," he leant back, allowing greed to take its natural course, "then my dear conspirators, we will tap him for some more. Preferably from a spot where the police aren't so busy." Grech enjoyed seeing the light in the eyes of the two opposite him.

Barry pulled on Nicky's arm saying, "Now I bet you're happy working for us?"

Grech heard the words and almost reached for Barry's throat, but checked the temptation. Barry's demise certainly would be a pleasure to look forward to.

The smile on Nick's face said everything, "If you say this jobs kosher, it's okay with me. I'll set it up. It'll have to be on my shift. So I'm the only one around. We take turns to sleep on board. The owners completely rely on the PLA bizzies for security. I'll figure a way round them. I'm due to be aboard the day after tomorrow, so I'll be here tomorrow night, same time to brief you."

More drinks and after handshakes, they parted. Grech left first, managing the walk to the bar door with just about the right amount of sway. Barry and Nick stood at the bar and watched him go.

Barry said, "You know Nick I think this is where both our ships come in. We'll time this dead right. If it's the last thing I do, I'm going to use my blade on that git!"

Nick shook his head, "Not until we've our hands on the money!"

Barry put his arm around Nick's shoulders, "Fear not old pal."

The following night, as arranged, Grech met Nick in the Eastern. He appeared quieter without Barry but seemed sure of himself.

"You meet me outside the Seamen's mission in Victoria Dock Road, tomorrow evening at seven. I'll kit you out with duds that'll carry you through the dock gate. One more thing, no tooling up. You know what that means?"

Grech smiled, "It's okay Nick, regardless of what Barry may have said, I don't believe in violence. You and I don't need it. A clean job is what we need, don't we?"

Nick looked at Grech, "Now, when we get near the gate, we'll split. You follow a few yards behind. No point the bizzies seeing us walk in together. Oh, you'd better be carrying some kit, a bag or something. As soon as you're through, make for Shed 47. The shed numbering is plain enough. Tied up there will be a skiff belonging to PLA Lighterage. Take no notice of the clutter. It's fitted out for dock maintenance. I take it you can row a boat?"

Grech looked thoughtful, "I've never done any rowing but it can't be that difficult."

Nick shook his head, "Well for Christ's sake make it look as though you're a natural. Take her down towards the lock. That's at the far end of the wharf, after the last donkey."

"Donkey?" Queried Grech.

"Christ, where do you come from. A donkey's a crane, right?"

Grech tried to cover himself, "Of course."

"Well, you can't mistake the boat. The Empress is all white. She's tied up at the end of the sheds, just before the lock. Come up on the starboard side. You'll be sheltered from the dock bizzies that way. I'll make sure there's a jacob over the side, so you can shin up. Don't forget to tie the skiff off to the ladder. Got all that?"

Grech slowly nodded his head. He guessed a jacob must be a ladder, "Sounds quite a lot, but I think I've got it all. Are the dock police likely to search my bag on the way through the gate?"

Nick grinned broadly, "If they do, it'll be the first time they've moved their feet since the gates first opened. But, if anything goes wrong, it's down to you to talk your way out. I've never seen you before, right?"

Grech nodded again.

Nick wished he felt just a touch more confident, "The Empress will be yours for as long as you need, but I'm not talking hours and no bloody lights above the main deck, and no flashing torches, plus no noise. Remember, those bizzies are responsible for security and they're quick to react. With Stickland's back-handers, there's a lot to lose if they foul up. Once I go aboard, they'll expect me to check the auxiliary motors every couple of hours to keep lights and power ticking over. Apart from that, I usually get my head down. They won't expect to see movement on the open decks," Nick then passed a sheaf of papers to Grech, "I've made some rough drawings of deck spaces. If there's a glitch, I'll wait by the head of the ladder, but I'm gone the second you're over the rail, okay?"

Grech took a quick look at the papers, "These are fine Nick, thanks. I won't need you, I'm just going to check some of the controls and make some measurements. I'll push off in the skiff as soon as I've finished. It's easier if you stick to your normal routine. Don't forget the ladder before your relief arrives. Can't have them spotting something like that hanging over the side. I'll be in touch through Barry. If anything goes wrong, as you said, you've never seen me and I'll deny you ever existed, okay."

"Too bloody right," said Nick. The two had a drink then parted for the second time.

Chapter Eighteen

Both Charlie and Bob slept well after the trauma of the previous day. They had spent the evening having the physical problems patched by a local doctor and a certain loss of pride, for walking slap bang into big trouble, restored by Alan Brandon and Stolland. The long sleep in their respective parent's houses did much to revive aching muscles but the dented pride still rankled. Both men again scrubbed like mad, to dislodge the last particles of Barge House Road from their bodies. Following a late breakfast, they settled down to write up their own accounts of what had occurred.

A little after ten, with the morning sun streaming through Bob's parents front room window, Charlie made the promised call to Alan.

"Anything turn up from the trawl in Barge House Road?" He asked.

"Well, considering the state of that collapse, I still can't work out how you three managed to get out alive. The way it went down proves whoever did it, knew exactly what to do. It had ex-military stamped all over it. There's little doubt Grech has had considerable help, in spotting the right boltholes, putting his finger on the right contacts, recruiting crews, etc., it's incredible."

"That's the whole point, Alan. Whatever he does, he seems to know how, where and when. He's certainly jerked us around."

Alan was doubly pleased that Charlie had been able to rely on Jack Cousens. He also realised this had only been possible because of friendship outside the job.

"You were damn lucky you had Jack Cousens. If it hadn't been for Jack, you and young Fuller would have ended up as foundations for a new housing scheme. You take it easy. I have a few things to tie up, then Stolland and I will be over."

Charlie replaced the handset and felt for his cigarettes. He didn't fancy the idea of forming part of anyone's foundations.

Bob Fuller had taken a quick walk round to Clever Road to pay a call on the Tate family. He wasn't best pleased with yesterday's result and felt they might have heard a whisper. The door was answered by May Tate. She was still red-eyed and looked as though her world had crumbled.

"If you're after Ben, he's shot over to the Ville, to meet our Billy. They've let him out a week early because of Jimmy's death. Come in if you like. I don't suppose they'll be that long," her quiet voice showed how tired she was.

Bob trailed along after her as she shuffled back to her kitchen. Jimmy's death had certainly rubbed the edges off May's legendary temper. They sat drinking tea beside the black kitchen range, while a small alarm clock pecked away on the mantel. Bob was finding it hard to make general conversation.

Suddenly May said, "I suppose you've heard Barry Scrivner's been recruiting from the other side of the river. A Charlton firm, I heard. That cocky sod was bragging about it in the Peacock. Not local amateurs either. The talk is they were all tooled-up. He's crapping bricks because he knows what'll happen when Billy catches up with him," May's eyes never left the small fire that was burning in the grate, "If Billy does for Barry, that'll mean I'll have lost both my boys. He'll be strung up for sure and I'll never have another night's sleep." May wiped her eyes, "Bob, I'm glad Billy's coming home, but I dread what might happen. Can't you do something to keep them apart?"

Bob laid a hand on May's arm, "Don't go fretting yourself May, I owe Billy a lot and we always got on.

When I was growing up and in a spot of trouble, we never took that trouble home. Your Billy saw to that. He was the one that sorted things out. You tell him from me, that it's my turn to help him. Let us turn over the likes of Barry. You know it's for the best May. Try your best to persuade him to pop round, I'm staying at Mum's. It's not the copper talking May. You tell him, as far as I'm concerned, it's our local business."

May smiled at him, "You're a good boy Bobby, even though you are a copper."

He left May, dabbing her eyes and staring into the embers of her fire. For the very first time, he understood just how much she'd lost by Jimmy's death. He'd been her favourite and she'd doted on him. Little wonder that she dreaded what Billy might do.

Bob closed the front door quietly, recalling how easy it would have been for him to end up on the wrong side of the law. As a youngster, he was always in and out of scrapes. You couldn't grow up in these streets without shaving strips off the margin between legal and illegal.

By the time he'd walked to Charlie's house, he was convinced they could benefit from Billy's help. News of the heavy type had a habit of penetrating prison walls. Especially rumbles on who was working for who, or with who? Whatever happened, he had to persuade Billy, the simplest route to Barry was a straight line, using the force of law as a steel ruler.

Charlie looked less whacked when he opened the door to Bob, "I've just spent an hour on the blower talking to the boss. We, and I do mean, you and I, are going on a day's leave. Frank's taking us up to Cromer. The boss and Stolland are on their way here now. They're going to take over this end. Stolland needs his crack at Grech."

Bob eyes showed he was stunned.

"Sorry Bob, we haven't a choice. It's an overnight breath of fresh salty air, then it's back here tomorrow. Then being five handed may make it easier."

Bob let go his frustration, "That's bloody charming that is. Come on Charlie that's just not possible. I've spent the last hour with May Tate. With any luck, Billy Tate will be round to see us this evening. Charlie, there's no chance he'll play ball with your boss. It needs us here, not swanning off just when we get this break."

Charlie just stood looking at Bob, an unlit cigarette dangling loosely from his lips.

Bob wouldn't give up, "I'm damned sure he'll put his weight behind finding our shooters. This really is the worst of all moves we can make."

Charlie recovered his cigarette, "Are you telling me our Billy Tate is chalked up to pay us a visit tonight? How can that be, he's still a slated guest at the Ville."

"You're wrong, Charlie. They're giving him the key to the door today because of Jimmy's death. He's probably loose right now."

Charlie lit up, scattering fresh tobacco smoke.

Bob had the floor, "And there's more. Barry's been recruiting. Word has it it's a foreign firm. South of the river stuff, according to May Tate. With Billy loose we might even have a lever to screw Barry into telling us who was behind Barge House road?"

"Just a minute," said Charlie, "you're saying Barry went south for a crew."

Bob smiled, "What I'm saying is, that Barry is in the frame for recruiting a professional team. Now, he couldn't afford a crew like that in a month of Sunday's, out of his own pocket. Not even if he had the key to his old man's piggy bank. He had to have the readies for a heavy crew, with guns, willing to top coppers! And they don't come cheap," Bob drew breath. Charlie continued to puff on his cigarette, "now, with our combined local knowledge, and forgetting the Police Gazette, who do we know south of the river that fits that bill?"

Charlie smiled, "Well, let's see. We know that Barry can't cross the road alone, let alone a river without his old man's say so. He hasn't got enough pennies to ride the free-ferry, or the personal bottle for shooters. Add to that he hasn't brain enough to blow his hat off, so my old son, I reckon you're broadly hinting at Master Liam

Rooney & Co. Renowned in old fleet circles as the Looney Rooney's."

Bob smiled, "You've got it in one!"

Charlie almost danced a jig, "Last time I heard about that team, they had a cover firm operating out of Charlton, demolishing blitzed buildings."

"Exactly, Charlie, and you can't get more blitzed than the old Navigation building. It all fits Charlie, so for Pete's sake let's talk to Billy, before packing our buckets and spades."

"Sounds kosher enough," said Charlie, "Bob, my friend, your few words with the redoubtable May Tate, could have saved us a mile of shoe leather, but I'm afraid the boss still has us chalked up for a trip to Cromer, and that's etched in stone. But, we'll go after we speak to brother Billy Tate. We can still be up in Cromer late this evening, or the early hours."

A smile a mile wide spread across Bob's face.

Alan, Stolland and Frank arrived at Russell Road. They all sat in Mrs Friar's best room, drank tea and made plans. The overnight trip to Cromer was still on with Frank driving Charlie and Bob in the Riley.

It was with some concern that Mrs Friar made her fourth trip into the kitchen to brew another pot. She was fast running out of tea and felt her house had become an annex to a police convention.

The group were still discussing the best approach to Billy when he arrived. May Tate had obviously talked him round, relying on Bob to do his best. Bob went to the front door and took Billy for a stroll up the road, before bringing him to meet the others. By the time he walked into the meeting, Billy was unexpectedly relaxed. He shook hands with everyone and took the cigarette offered him by Charlie.

Billy surprised Alan, "Well Mr Brandon, there's nothing like getting down to why I'm here. It's no secret that I hate that toad Barry Scrivner. He set our Jimmy up for his skills and when it suited him, he had him killed. We still don't know why. Jimmy never had a bad bone in his body, but he was still done in. Mum's told me what you said Bob and I'm happy to co-operate with you and Charlie, for old time's sake. But, and I mean this, it's got to be done right. Barry must get the rope for Jimmy's death."

This opener from Billy seemed to take everyone, apart from Bob, by surprise.

Alan understood Billy's feelings, "You have to be realistic, Billy. Securing that type of sentence depends on many things, including removing all doubt that Barry killed Jimmy, or was party to the actual killing. No one can give you a written guarantee on a death sentence verdict. The jury will decide whether Barry is guilty and the judge will pass sentence. We are not in the business of pursuing personal or family feuds."

Before Alan could go on, Billy jumped to his feet, "Listen, you came to me, remember! I've just done hard time for a crime I didn't commit. Again, set up by that scum Scrivner. Now if you really want my help, then let's get one thing clear. My price is, I want Scrivner tapping the boards, and I want my sheet torn up. Not even a bloody search file number, lingering around CRO files. Like I said before the trial, at the trial and ever since the bloody trial, I didn't have that stuff in my yard, knowing it had been lifted and it's my brief's opinion, that's enough to make my conviction unsafe. It's the only charge I've ever faced. It's the one blot on my character, and I want it off!"

There was no doubt in anybody's mind that Billy was steaming. He meant what he said and wanted no other settlement. Whoever shot Jimmy was to hang and Billy wanted his character back, unstained.

Bob stood up, "Billy, let's just cool down a bit. We all want justice for Jimmy. So sit yourself down and think. We are all on your side in this."

Billy slowly sat. His voice was now more controlled, "An appeal's in my brief's hands. He has written evidence that blows holes through Scrivner's evidence, so do you blame me for getting up tight. I've just done time for that scumbag. I want it over, finished! Besides, I want to be able to go back to work without you bizzies knocking on my folks door."

"Billy, I apologise," Alan desperately wanted to bring the temperature down, "I wasn't trying to hand you a line or talk down to you. You and I got off on the wrong foot. If what you are saying is true, then, I promise, you'll have that clean sheet. However, you must see, we can't wait around for an Appeal Court ruling. We have to act right now, against a firm that probably wouldn't give Barry Scrivner the time of day. Except, it seems he may have been the fixer with access to the man with the money. Now, our target is a serial killer. His name is Victor Grech and he is the key to this wretched business, including your brother's death. But, if you've any doubts, if you feel we are setting you up, if you....."

Billy slapped the table, "Don't give me any more if, but or maybe. Either you need me this side of the table, or I work on my own to get that bastard! Waiting for the bizzies to do what was right when I was banged up, didn't do me a lot of good!"

Bob was afraid of this. He knew that if Billy thought he was being fed tripe, he'd back off and be gone for good. Bob chanced his arm, "Excuse me cutting in, sir. Look Billy, I told you before, our boss can't make promises he's in no position to keep. Regardless what you may think, we have to stay within certain rules, or scum like Barry will pay a slick brief and walk away," the room was quiet again, Bob went on, "we're here, off our ground, or as Mr Brandon might say, acting outside our normal police areas, but I can assure you, we're not a vigilante gang Billy. Just for now, put aside your personal grief.

The person or firm we're after executed four people in my police area, four totally innocent people. I saw them Billy. I was there, looking down at them. One was a woman, about your mum's age. She had taken two in the head Billy. As if one wasn't enough, that bastard walked round a counter and gave her another one! Perfect strangers to me, but I'm telling you Billy, it was a bloody massacre, in both senses of the word. Listen to yourself and what you're claiming Billy. They were innocent too. It's possible that, whoever worked that trigger nailed your

Jimmy. Think Billy think! Barry's no bloody gunman! You know that. He's only a mouth, with a yellow streak as wide as the Mile End road."

By now Bob was pacing the floor around Billy, "Don't hand us all your grief Billy. I still wake up at night sweating because of that woman's face staring up at me or I dream about two old pensioners in Lockhart Street gagged, bound and shot through the head, just like Jimmy. Face the truth Billy. Barry is a cringing blade man, part of the cancer that's ruining life for people like your mum and dad, but I promise you, he's not the man that pulled the trigger on your brother!"

The air in the room felt electric. For the first time in his life, Bob was centre stage. A part he'd never played before. No one else wanted to speak, let alone stem the flow.

Bob, slightly embarrassed, opened his hands and shook his head, "Billy, if you help us nail this whole crew, I'm sure we'll have your brother's killer and, you'll be able to live with the way it turns out. You'll be helping to pay back the anger people feel. They're every bit as bitter as you. There's one more item to put on the scales. You're going to need character witnesses at your appeal. If you help with this business, our business, I'm damned sure Mr Brandon will make the best character witness you'll ever get."

Bob still felt Billy was in two minds. He gave it another shot, "You remember when you first taught me to box Billy, before we went to Dockland Settlement. You clouted me so bloody hard I went down and didn't want to get up. You knelt over me. You said you have to control your anger, your temper, think your way out. Then make every move count. Boxing, you said, is an art and you were painfully teaching me the rules. If I wanted to box in the ring, I had to fight by the rules of the ring. Well, police work is a bit like boxing. The same rules apply. You have to control your anger. You can't afford serious mistakes and you have to think and plan every move you make. Otherwise, those that assault, rob, murder and threaten win

337

every time. Learning ring craft from you was a painful business. I know, because you taught me the hard way." A wide smile accompanied this last sentence.

Billy looked across at Bob and smiled, "Hey, and I thought I had all the mouth. You'd make a bloody good brief or better still, a politician. I didn't teach you so bad did I? You're okay Bob."

Billy turned to Alan, "Okay Mr Brandon, let's make a new start." They all smiled and relaxed.

Alan quietly drew a deep sigh and took his pipe out of his pocket, which was a sure sign he needed to think. He looked across at Bob, smiled and nodded. It was the only way to thank him without actually applauding.

He turned to Billy, "Well Billy, if you ever need my help, and providing it's mine to give, then you won't have to ask twice. Now, we have to know everything you know about this Barry, and what's more important, who he's teamed with," he paused, looking across at Bob, "Then, we can push on."

Billy raised a finger, "Okay, I'm in, but this business stays between us. It wouldn't do anyone any good if it got out that I was playing your side of the street. Let those out there continue to think I've a private score to settle."

Bob showed his pleasure. He liked Billy and had a lot of respect for him. He had always been a bit of a character, but there was no real villain in him. Kids in the East End looked up to him, especially those still trading leather at the Settlement.

Billy took the lead, "When I was first in the Ville, I was banged up in fours. You never open your mouth. It's very unhealthy. After a while, keeping tight-lipped paid off and I found myself in two's. After about three months, the lad sharing my cell got parole. My next cell-mate was a chink. He was up for helping himself to sizeable chunks of Millwall dock. We spent a lot of time talking about his family. Life can be tough if you've slit eyes, so you tend to stay in your family group. Bit like the poor old Jews, clinging to Whitechapel, I suppose. Anyway, back to the chinks. Being tolerated in a confined group with low intelligence, suddenly becomes more doubtful if some wise arse puts it about you're from North Korea.

Some lags on the landing claimed they had family away fighting in the Korean War. Anyway, one day in the sluice, they nailed him, just because some of them thought he was a red. I pulled them off him and slapped one or two. I dragged him out. We were both in front of the governor, ended up in solitary. When we got out and put back on the wing, he thanked me and asked me to go round to see his folks when I got out.

He lives off Pennyfields. His uncle, named Lo Wey has a café off Ming Street. I'm going down there tonight, about eight, to deliver a letter. If I hear anything, or get a smell of Barry, I'll be in touch."

Alan stood up and shook hands with Billy, "Thanks Billy. I know how difficult it must be, and we won't come tapping on your door to see if there's news. You can contact us via this number," he handed Billy a slip of paper, "just say you're with Operation Phoenix. That will open all the doors. Set up a meet somewhere, one or all of us will be there."

Bob walked Billy to the door, "You're doing the right thing Billy. We'll do this together. Oh, and watch your back. If the other side get a whisper, well you know what Chinese whispers are."

They shook hands warmly and Billy left. Bob went back to the room. As he walked in, Alan was explaining the action.

"You can get off up to Cromer, stay overnight, and come back tomorrow afternoon. It will be good for June to know Charlie's still in one piece and for the girls to have some male company for a few hours. As for Mr Stolland and I, we're off to have a word with Jack Cousens and walk that bombsite in Barge House Road. According to you Charlie, the building you were in had all but collapsed. Doesn't it strike you as strange that a charge in a haversack could bring down a building that withstood the blitz?"

"Not if it was almost ready to come down," said Charlie. "When we went in through that door, we didn't inspect the place, but it did seem more than a bit knocked about."

Alan nodded, "I take your point. But it would be nice if we could find evidence that explosive thrown through the door, had been helped along by other prepared charges. I'm not saying I'm right, but if there were set charges, then it underlines the planned ambush theory. How many detonations did you hear?"

Bob looked at Charlie, "When Sergeant Friar was playing Tarzan on the spiral staircase the explosion seemed to rumble on, like an echo. I suppose it could have been more than one detonation."

Charlie agreed, "To tell you the truth, I was busy praying the bolt at the top of the stairs would hold long enough for me to get to the bottom. I just remember seeing the trail of smoke from the bag and diving down. I suppose we were all lucky the bag didn't spin through the doorway, before it blew up. If it had come through, June would be drawing the old widow's shilling."

Bob added, "You know, the more I think about this, the more I'm convinced you could be right Mr Brandon. Whoever set this up had every chance of putting a bullet in any one of us before we made the door. The more you think about it, the more it seems they were set on driving us through that door, like cattle into a holding pen."

Charlie lit up a cigarette, "It does seem that the object was to get us into that building."

"See it from their point of view," Alan added, "if the building collapses on you, the probable conclusion would be that falling masonry killed you. After all, these bombsites throw up several deaths every year. However, say you were hit by a bullet, well that's murder."

Charlie took a long drag of smoke, "You know, if it hadn't been for Jack Cousens knowing that dock wall had been breached, we'd still be trying to claw our way out. I'll give him a buzz to make sure he knows you're going to Barge House road."

Charlie got up and left the room. He was back in a second, "He's next door, so you can go round."

Alan seemed surprised, "Jack lives next door?"

Charlie grinned, "Who do you think talked me into becoming a copper? He fed me the Police Gazette all through my school years. They've never had kids of their own so it was natural for me to grow up with two homes."

"Well," Alan said, "we had better get going. Mr Stolland and I have a date at the Royal Albert Hall tonight. Grace is playing my favourite Rachmaninov's piano concerto and that's seventeen and a half minutes of music we are not going to miss."

Charlie smiled, "Give Mrs Brandon our very best wishes. What time does this happen?"

"As near as you can time these orchestral charity events, it should begin about seven thirty. We'll be there to make certain all goes well. She has her own protection bunch and a certain WPC who acts like a second skin, but I'll feel better being there. Grace is scared stiff but she's just as adamant the performance will go ahead. She's amazing, rarely does public concerts now but never turns down a request for charity performances... still has the skill to provide spell-binding performances."

With thanks to Charlie's long suffering parents, Alan and Stolland joined a bandaged Jack Cousens, while Charlie and Bob climbed stiffly into Frank's car.

Frank was beginning to know the way to Cromer. He was happy snapping off the miles while Charlie and Bob slept. He looked in his rear view mirror and smiled. He was hoping the return journey to the East End would hold more for him than chauffeuring.

Grace had to be at the Hall early in the afternoon for final orchestral rehearsal. She seemed to take everything in her stride. Other performers came and spoke with her, treating her as the star she was. The conductor, Sir Clive Reason took the orchestra through each of the pieces faultlessly and the mood just couldn't have been better.

At four thirty, all the musicians and soloists sat down to a beautiful meal, courtesy of the organisers. Following this, each of the special guests retired to their particular dressing room for a rest, before dressing. On opening the door of her dressing room, Grace found the whole room covered in bouquets of flowers. She and the WPC were still opening cards from well-wishers when Alan and Stolland arrived. She seemed so very excited.

A large side table overflowed with yet more cards and boxes of flowers. Grace insisted on seeing each one. Alan watched her undoing ribbons, opening boxes and giving cries of delight as she read encouraging notes from so many kind friends. Alan watched this excitingly beautiful woman, who he had fallen madly in love with so long ago. She was still the sparkling slip of a girl he had first seen on a chilly November evening in 1922, outside the Albert Hall. He loved her then, as he adored her now.

She turned from the flowers and looked up at him, "Oh darling," she said, "isn't it all too wonderful," she looked at Stolland, "do you know Peter, it was outside this building that Alan and I first met almost thirty years ago. He was a quiet, shy young constable and I had just finished playing. He tried to report me for some silly motoring offence, but ended up being the love of my life."

She turned back to Alan and kissed him warmly, "Thank you for those wonderful years, darling."

The room filled with her warmth and laughter. Far off, thunderous applause welcomed the beginning of the concert.

Stolland heard a soft tap on the dressing room door. The WPC immediately rose from her chair, but Stolland indicated that he would answer the knock. He opened the door. Standing in front of him was a young boy, dressed in the uniform of a Page. On his pillbox hat was a ribbon bearing the name Simmonds Hotel. The boy thrust out the large oblong box he was holding.

"Special delivery," the boy stuttered, "for Miss Woodhall, sir."

Stolland smiled at the boy, gave him a half-crown and took the package. The boy saluted smartly and ran off towards the stage entrance, obviously in a rush to get back to his post at the hotel.

Stolland turned toward Grace. She was still struggling with her flowers, laughing at something Alan had just said. Stolland felt the box in his hands. It felt unusually heavy for flowers. The wrapping seemed to be a very fine silk. Its colour, in the soft light of the room seemed to be pale green and gold. A wide blood-red ribbon secured the wrapping to the box, tied off in a large bow. There was a small envelope under the ribbon. Stolland slipped the envelope out, preparing to hand it to Grace.

He suddenly became aware of utter silence in the room. Only the distant opening notes of the orchestra cut through the absolute quiet. His eyes lifted from the box to Grace. She was standing, facing him. All the gaiety gone, washed away by a look of absolute, stunned horror.

Alan was standing by her side staring at her. The WPC had left her chair and seemed to be moving in slow motion towards Grace.

"Please Peter," Grace's voice faltered, "please don't open that box, please God, don't open that box!"

Both Alan and the WPC reached Grace at the same moment. She collapsed in their arms.

Stolland ran from the room, taking the box with him. He ran through the long corridor, bursting through swinging fire doors, down the steep staircase and out into the street. There was no sign of the Page that had delivered the package.

Under the light from a street lamp, Stolland removed the wrapping and slowly slid aside the lid of the box. Inside, wrapped in a waterproof bag, lay white lilies. Their beautiful petals sullied with droplets of what appeared to be dark red blood. He moved the stems and leaves aside and saw the stiff pitiable body of a young black kitten. Its tiny throat sliced from ear to ear.

Stolland caught his breath and turned aside gagging as the overpowering smell of formalin surrounded him. He staggered back from the box into the arms of two uniformed constables that had joined him. Stolland knew instantly that this was Grech's doing, although the choice of blood donor was probably the work of another sick mind. One of the constables replaced the lid on the box. Stolland carried it back into the Hall where, after wrapping the offering in a sheet, he secured it in a cupboard in the doorkeeper's office. He would decide later where the package would end up. Stolland pocketed the key and made his way unsteadily back to Grace's dressing room. He had to control the rage he felt.

Grace was on a couch, attended by a doctor. She was still very pale but was conscious and whispering something to Alan. He crossed to a phone and turned his back on the room.

"Nothing to worry about Grace," Stolland offered, "just another box containing flowers, please don't worry. Everything is fine."

Grace looked at him and gave him a weak smile. Stolland knew it was no good. She had seen what was in the box before he had opened it. She must have already told Alan, only the WPC and doctor had questioning looks on their faces.

After ten minutes and some hot sweet tea, Grace was fine. She insisted that her performance would go on, although the doctor felt doubtful as to her ability.

Grace looked at him, "Young man, during the recent war, my home was turned into a hospital for wounded. Someone in our beloved government failed to tell the Nazis it was a hospital. The Luftwaffe took every opportunity to break our windows. I never once cancelled playing for those patients, in spite of the breaking glass and I am not about to fade away now."

During the interval, Grace remained adamant that she was not about to disappoint the audience. On cue, she walked out onto the platform, to overwhelming applause. With Grace now safely seated at the piano and a beautifully gowned WPC at her side, Stolland stood at the entrance to the platform and watched Alan. It was so obvious how deeply Alan loved his wife. Again, just for a single moment, deep sorrow reflected in Stolland's eyes. He had known that feeling. In that same millisecond, sensing someone was watching him, Alan turned to say something. What he saw was something so deep, so acutely painful, that he immediately gripped Stollands arm. "Are you okay," he said, in a concerned whisper.

Stolland's eyes immediately cleared, "Yes, sorry," he stammered, "I'm fine. Alan, do you want to know what was in that box?"

"No," Alan whispered, "I'll tell you."

Stolland shook his head, "Well, I'll be damned."

Alan held up a hand to listen to Grace's first few notes, "She told me," Alan murmured, "the box has white lilies, blood and the smell of death. Grace also said, the man that sent the message was the same man she saw outside the Royal Academy. Actually, she is more concerned for the safety of the young Page. Grace told me to ring Simmonds to make sure he was safe."

Stolland felt sickened. A tug at his arm brought his thoughts back. A police constable handed him a note. It said, *'Page found. Being brought back to the Hall from hotel. Please wait.'*

Stolland remembered the envelope. He reached into his pocket and slid the card from the envelope. It was blood stained. The words were clear enough, **'*Do not look for death – he will find you soon enough!*'**

Grace continued to play, defying the horrible events to cloud the beauty, of the concerto. Its soft repeated phrases filling every corner of the hushed auditorium.

"Are you married?" Alan's whispered question came as a shock. At first Stolland was not certain he had heard the question correctly. Dragging his eyes from Grace, Alan repeated the question.

Stolland's thoughts again flooded into a dark place. A sad place buried too deep, too far away to talk about. Stolland shook his head and turned away. He walked through the corridor, every intervening door reducing the sound of the music, until with relief Stolland was standing, shaking in the cool evening air. How could he answer that question? The rapid approach of a car pulled him back from whatever misery it was that haunted him. The pain in his misted eyes gradually faded.

"Mr Stolland, sir?" The question came again. The driver of the patrol car was talking to him, "I believe you or Mr Brandon want words with this young man."

A pale faced Page slid from the rear door of the car. He was not the sure and steady young man who had handed Stolland the box. This was an uncertain young man, full of curiosity and doubt.

"Did I do something wrong, sir," he said, touching his Page's hat, in an uncertain salute.

Stolland gave him a broad grin and placed an arm close around his shoulders. Hugging the boy to him, he looked like a father greeting his son.

"Not at all young man, quite the reverse actually, we are hoping you can help us with our problem."

He took the boy inside, into Grace's dressing room and watched the boy's face. The Page was all eyes, "Cor, this is smashing. The other lads won't believe this," he sat swinging his legs on the couch.

"You are doing a real man's job. Would you like a beer?"

The Page's face lit up, "Blow me. My mum would kill me if I said yes."

Stolland smiled, "Will ginger-beer do the trick?"

Receiving a grin and a nod, Stolland handed the boy a foaming glass of ginger beer and a slab of chocolate cake.

"Now, can you tell me," asked Stolland, "what the person was like who gave you the box for Miss Woodhall?"

"Course I can, I'm a trained observer I am, and I'm going to be a detective when I'm old enough and grown a bit. I'm in the trade now, so to speak. Has to keep my eyes peeled in my job."

"Well," asked Stolland, "what did your powers of observation tell you about this particular person."

"He was no regular gent. Scruffy, stunk of the stuff mum puts down the sink. Grey hair too long. Little geezer," the boy chewed on the cake, "very old I'd say."

"Just how old would you say?"

The Page scratched his chin, "Well, must be forty, thin as a twig, scrawny as a chicken with pip. Queer eyes, not one home and one away. More hard like, shifty. Bit like a bookies runner. Good with the gelt though."

"Gelt?" Quizzed Stolland.

"Gelt, money, gave me a fiver to do that job. Blimey, I thought to myself, he's one of them with the brass alright."

"Is he staying at your hotel?"

"You are joking governor. Mr Defarge wouldn't have him in our place. Give it a bad name he would."

"Is Mr Defarge the hotel manager?"

"Lord no," laughed the Page, "he's much higher than that. You just ask him. He's the head doorman, medals and everything he's got. Paid to keep the riff on the move he is."

"If that's so, how did you manage such a neat little trip then?"

"Well, I was on my break see, when this cove spots me at the back door in Park Street. So I thought, as I was on my own time it had nothing to do with his nibs, Mr Defarge. Anyway, this sort gets me a cab, pays off the driver for a two way, and that was it."

"Have you seen this man before?"

"No. He's not the sort you see and forget, creepy he was."

"Did you happen to notice which way he went when you left him?"

"Sorry sir, I was too busy checking out the fiver."

Stolland took a white five-pound note out of his pocket, "I want you to do me a special favour. How old are you?"

"Fourteen and a bit, this is my first job."

"Right, you are a grown man now, so we can talk man-to-man, right?"

The Page's head nodded but the eyes stayed locked on the fiver.

"That man you saw is wanted by New Scotland Yard. If you ever see him again, don't let on you have spotted him. Just go straight to the nearest constable or dial Whitehall 1212, got that."

"Sure. That's easy they're always giving out that number on the wireless."

"Just tell them who you've seen. Now young Sherlock, tell me if this is the man you saw." Stolland showed the Page a copy of the hologram taken of Grech.

The Page studied it for a second, "That's him alright."

Stolland took the Page's name and home address, gave him the fiver and put him back in the Police car.

"Take my detective friend to the Simmonds Hotel, rear entrance and make sure he gets inside without a problem," he exchanged smiles and thumbs up with the boy, "well done, Sherlock!"

Stolland waited for Grace and Alan to return from the platform. Grace looked much better. She and the WPC went into the dressing room to change. As soon as Stolland had Alan alone, Stolland told him exactly what had taken place.

"Do you think the boy's safe?" Alan asked.

"I doubt if Grech will consider him a threat, but you never know."

Alan thought about this for a moment, "Look, get onto NSY and have that boy taken home. He can go back to his job when we have Grech locked away. Make sure the hotel management understand the lad's a witness, helping with enquiries, also have a word with his parents, otherwise they'll be worried stiff. If necessary, get them off on a short break somewhere. We don't want another body courtesy of your Mr bloody Grech."

"It wouldn't be a bad idea," offered Stolland, "to have the hotel quietly notify us of anyone showing interest in that boy's home address, and that includes other staff. Its something Grech might try."

Stolland went off to telephone while Alan rang Cromer. Half an hour later, they were in the car, covered in flowers, heading for Eaton Walk.

Chapter Nineteen

Grech remained in his room. He didn't wish to attract attention, so apart from a quick visit downstairs to the café, he waited for time to pass. He packed and repacked his canvas holdall, making sure it held just essentials and the money. If checked, he could always claim he was a sparks. If they found the money, he'd say he'd just sold his van.

He crossed to the washstand and checked the second box and calendar was still snug in the washstand drawer. He passed some of the time staring out of the window, listening to the chaotic noise from the streets below. It was while deep in thought that he missed the sound of someone climbing the stairs to his room. The first he knew about it, was when a heavy tapping rattled the door.

Grech's mind flew from what was going on in the street. In a single, silent movement, he was across to the bed. As he straightened, his gun appeared in his hand. As always, he placed it behind his back, tucked into the waistband of his trousers. He then put his coat on. He failed to notice that he had left the canvas holdall on the bed.

"Who is it?" He asked softly, but with an edge in his voice.

"You had a visitor Mr Gentry. It was that man who came before. Name Scrivner I think. He urgently wanted to see you. Was holding a newspaper and seemed very angry. Perhaps that has something to do with big headline?" With that, Lo pushed a copy of the paper under the door.

Grech bent down and picked it up. He unfolded it and read the headline. 'Four found shot dead in Thames at Woolwich Reach.' The sub-heading read, 'Gangland killings may spark more violence.'

Grech read it again. How could that be, he asked himself? Why hadn't the bodies floated further down with the tide?

"Where is Mr Scrivner now?" asked Grech.

Lo's answer didn't please Grech. "I told him you were in but sleeping. He is coming back in one hour. He kindly left paper for you to read. He say, you may want to talk about loss of friends? Perhaps some people get very upset with him. He is very angry. Paper shaking when handed it to me. I do not like this man. He is bad to have in my café. Not good for Lo's business, Mr Gentry!"

Grech was furious. He managed to contain his anger. He hadn't wanted to leave the room until just before the meeting with Nick, but this changed matters. Barry Scrivner had become a liability. It was time to terminate their association.

Grech steadied his thinking. Through the door, he told Lo to say he wasn't in his room, he had slipped out, saying he would phone the Scrivner house and arrange a meet. While he was doing this, he was hoping that Nick hadn't told Barry the arrangements for visiting the Empress. He had to avoid seeing Barry today, at all costs. If he did bump into him or if Barry turned up with Nick, he'd have to face it out, do the Empress job, then silence Barry for good.

What Grech knew was that Stickland would take the Empress out just before tomorrow's high tide. It was a secret from everyone, except the police, port-handling authorities and certain crew. Like everything else Stickland did, his movements were never for public consumption or advertised in advance. Stickland had the clout to do this. She would slip through the lock gates, out into the river and be away. If necessary, she'd call in at Tilbury to replace any crew, reporting late. Next day, for those interested in such things, newspapers would print a few lines, stating that the Stickland family had left the country on business.

Grech, of course, had access to history. He knew when the boat would leave because, like all football, horse and dog results, such facts were newsworthy, faithfully recorded in the papers of the day. It followed that these items were available to him, by scrolling down the text displayed on his personal information system. His eyes glowed with satisfaction he would always be one jump ahead of the idiots around him.

Grech hurriedly put on his coat, and gripping the holdall as though it was a precious child, left the room. He locked the door and placed a split match in position. On the way down the stairs, he checked that the landing light was still faulty. This time, the darkness on the stairs would work for him.

At the door leading into the café, he called to Lo Wey that he was leaving to see friends in Stepney. Lo shuffled from behind his counter and watched him start down the alley. His hooded eyes following the black clad back. He silently wished not to see his tenant again. Lo had an uneasy feeling about the story in the paper, and the last thing he needed was a lodger who may attract the attention of the police, or who had violent friends. Lo had enough suspicion to contend with, without having another dragon living in his home.

Grech quickly turned left out of the alley, away from the announced route to Stepney. He kept to the inside of the pavement until it met Poplar High Street. Turning east, he slowed his pace to that of other pedestrians, keeping as close to buildings as he could, thus giving him the option to dive into a shop if he spotted Barry. The footpath was crowded, most people making their way to or from shops. He turned left into Woodstock Terrace and followed it along to the East India Dock road. Here, he turned right, then left into Crisp Street market. As usual, the street market was comfortably busy.

Making his way along the centre of the road, he came to Moody's Pie Shop. He was just about to go in when he saw Barry standing in the queue at the counter. Luckily for Grech, the flash suit made Barry stand out like a traffic light. Barry was in the act of turning towards the door. Grech thought he'd been seen. He let the door go, turned back into the market and pushed his way, as quickly as he could, through the crowds. He dare not look back. His mind was now in a complete panic.

Grech knew if Barry had seen him, he wouldn't be able to deny the shooting at Woolwich. He'd have to think up a reason that Barry would swallow. He turned right into Willis Street and ran into the council flats. He ran as fast as he could up the stairs leading to the first floor. He stood leaning against a wall for a second to get his breath, taking the opportunity to look over the balcony.

Barry was standing with his hands on his hips looking first one way, then the other. His face was red from running and with obvious anger. Grech knew he would have to think quick. Behind him, a door clicked open. An elderly woman was coming out of her flat. She looked at him.

"Hello dear, you waiting for me?"

Grech put a strained expression on his face, "Sorry lady but I've just fallen on the stairs and knocked the wind out of myself. Is there any chance of something to sit on?"

The woman smiled, "Come on. You come in and sit down."

In a second Grech was inside the tiny kitchen. The woman turned and closed the front door. "No rush, I was just on my way round to Mrs Duncan's, but half hour won't make any difference."

Grech made full use of that half an hour. He chatted away to the woman as though they had been friends for years. When the woman looked up at her clock, it was Grech who said, "Is that the time? I'd better go. I'm feeling so much better. He felt in his pocket, brought out a half crown and passed it to the woman.

"Please don't be offended. Have a drop of something good, for being kind to a stranger."

The woman took the coin and waved as he started back down the stairs. What a very nice man she thought. Obviously, a tallyman, but well brought up.

Taking a chance, Grech walked straight out of the stairwell, as though he had finished a planned visit. If Barry was still waiting, Grech would face it out. There was no sign of Barry. He turned right, doubling back to the main road. In no time at all, he was seated in the Rex cinema. For nearly two hours, Grech watched a gangster film and a newsreel. When he emerged from the Rex, it was raining. Grech turned up his collar and decided to catch a bus to meet Nick.

Nick was waiting when Grech arrived. By the sodden state of his coat, he'd been waiting for some time.

"At last," he said as Grech smiled, "I got here a bit sharp, had to collect some gear for you," with that, he handed Grech a sack, "you can't be too long on board. I've just been told we're sailing tomorrow so the crew will be arriving anytime after midnight. They'll start running everything up, usual bloody panic."

Grech nodded and dived into a public toilet. He came out wearing overalls, a dark blue reefer with PLA plastered over the back and a somewhat large black woollen cap.

"At least you look the part."

Grech handed Nick a roll of notes, "Have you spoken or seen anything of Barry since we last spoke?"

Nick was in a state of shock, he was staring at the number of white five-pound notes in his hand, "No, not seen anything of him. Do you know how much you've just handed me?"

Grech looked at him and shrugged his shoulders, "What's right is right, Nick. I didn't want Barry to know what your first cut would be," He winked, "doesn't do to let Barry know too much. Let's get going, we don't want to get you any more soaked than you are. Just stick to your side of the bargain and you'll have a good time with that, when you next meet your girl."

They parted company out of sight of the police at the gate. Nick had been right. The dock police didn't give him a second glance. They were keeping tucked up in their hut, out of the rain, which was now falling as if it had a date with Noah's flood.

Grech walked quickly as though he knew exactly where he was going. He turned down the quayside, avoiding the twinned railway tracks, watching for Cargo Shed 47. He came to it. Ignoring the continuous unloading that was going on, he walked over to the quayside.

Tied up alongside a PLA waste barge was Nick's skiff. Grech climbed down and jumped in. Nick had been right. It looked as if everything but the kitchen sink was aboard. He didn't make a bad job of the oars and quickly pulled free from the side. He rowed out between the towering sides of the cargo-passenger vessels and headed down towards the lock. He passed the MV Rangitiki. She was ablaze with light and people were swarming all over her decks, regardless of the rain and lateness of the hour. He relaxed. Everything was going well. He was even rowing the boat in the direction he wanted to go.

Soon he saw the white hull of the Galen Empress. She was bigger, more luxurious than he'd expected. By the look of her, there was not a speck of dirt on her. It was almost immoral that one individual should have enough money and power to own a vessel of that size, when everywhere else post-war poverty reigned supreme.

Anger mounted in Grech. With so much food and fuel rationing still in place, plus acute shortages of materials vital to a country's recovery after such a war, how did a man like Stickland manage to run a life so totally remote from what was going on in the rest of the country? Then he remembered the letter he had found in Stickland's house in Albany Street. The more he thought of this, the more Grech hated Stickland. He could now see, first hand, what he had only read about, in his own time.

Grech heaved on the oars and was soon alongside the ladder that Nick had managed to rig. He tied off the skiff and rapidly scaled the Empress's side. Nick was crouched below the rail, "Don't hang around. Time is very short. Try making all your movements away from the dockside. Remember what I said, the engineers and rest of the crew will be coming on anytime now. Good luck and thanks for the cash." With that, Grech was alone.

At about the same time, Billy Tate walked down the alleyway and entered the world of Lo Wey. As he entered the café, conversation subsided. Every head, apart from Lo Wey's, was bent over bowls filled with strange but succulent steaming morsels. Lo came from behind his counter.

"May I offer you some tea, or some food? We have excellent choices."

Billy held up his hand, "No thanks, I've already eaten. Are you Lo Wey?"

For the second time that day, Lo Wey was on his guard, "I am. How can I help?"

Billy smiled kindly, "It's more what I can do for you. I have a letter from I think it's your nephew. I've just come out of the Ville and he asked me to bring this." Billy handed Lo the letter.

"You please sit while I see what my nephew has to say."

For the next five minutes, Lo scanned the short letter. He ran his eyes over the words again, then slowly he read it again.

"Your name is Billy?"

Billy nodded. Lo apologised and left the table. He was back in a second carrying two small glasses and a half bottle of whisky.

"Not our usual drink, but I think you might drink to my nephew's good fortune in a spirit not unfamiliar to you?" Lo smiled. They drank.

Billy said, "Now I've delivered the letter, I'll go. I want to have a wander round the area. Hope to bump into someone I know."

Placing a friendly hand on Billy's shoulder, Lo looked quickly around, "Please, stay for a moment. A man in a hurry cannot think clearly and you have need of a clear head?"

Billy smiled.

"My nephew writes that you saved his life. I am like a father to that boy. He has no parents now, so I suppose you have saved my son. Is there anything you need, anyway I can help you. Perhaps you need money?"

Billy shook his head and smiled, "No way, all I did was slap a couple of cons who had him trapped in the sluice. It's nothing."

Pouring a little more whisky into Billy's glass, Lo whispered, "Nothing you say? My friend, to save a life is special, to save my son's life is everything. We Chinese accept such a deed as a most honourable debt. Is there nothing I can do to repay your kindness?"

Billy looked around the café, "Perhaps there is. Do you ever get locals in here. I mean English locals?"

Lo nodded vigorously, "Yes, I have two. One is my tenant and the other visits him. He has the mouth of a fool and can bring much trouble."

Billy listened, but Lo had stopped speaking.

"You mean this man makes trouble for you?"

"No not for me. This man comes to see my tenant, but I think he means much trouble. To speak honestly, I wish they would both go away from here. My tenant is older, small and never speaks much, but I think he is the tiger, the most dangerous of the two."

Billy took a chance, "Lo, is this younger man from a family called Scrivner? Is he Barry Scrivner?"

Lo's eyes dropped to his hands, "You know him?"

It was Billy's turn to nod, "Lo, can you describe the older man to me?"

Lo moved his head closer to Billy's, "I am sure we should not talk too loudly about this. He is older. Thin, has a long, pale face. Has thin lips, a face unused to smiling, and when he does, the smile never reaches his eyes. I have never seen such dark eyes. The man you call Scrivner called here today, very angry. He was very upset with my tenant because something bad had happened.

Scrivner left without seeing him. Some time later my tenant, Mr Gentry, left to go to Stepney."

"Is your tenant coming back?" Billy said.

"Yes. He has my attic room."

Billy patted Lo's shoulder, "Listen Lo, I need to make a phone call urgently. Have you a telephone?"

Lo rose from the chair and waved so that Billy followed him round, behind the counter, and through a bead curtain, where he left Billy to make the call.

Billy grabbed his arm, "Lo, this is very important. If you owe me a favour, what I ask you to do will pay that debt, okay?"

Lo nodded.

"If your tenant or young Scrivner comes back while I am on the phone, let me know. It would not do if either of them saw me here. Is that okay?"

Lo smiled, "I like this. I do not like them, you stay here, I will let you know."

Lo spoke to one of his customers. This elderly Chinese man rose from his table and left the café. If Barry or Grech showed up, Lo would know about it before either of them entered the alley.

Billy made the call and put the receiver down. He waited just five minutes and the phone rang.

"Billy, it's Alan Brandon. I understand you may be on to something."

Billy told him exactly what Lo had said.

"Do you think we could get into this attic room and take a quick look before the tenant comes back?"

Billy paused, "I don't know what time he's due back, but it's got to be worth trying. I'm sure Lo will go with it."

Lo nodded and smiled as he ushered his remaining customers out of the café. He had felt it best to close. His customers would not ask why. It was not their business. His elderly lookout would not budge from his post until Lo gave him the signal.

When Alan and Stolland arrived, they left their car in Garford Street and walked casually along Ming Street, to the alley. Billy led them to the café. Once inside, Lo extinguished all the lights, locked the café front door and they made their way up the stairs to the attic.

Lo produced a key and they were in. Lo waited outside on the landing, what was happening was none of his business.

Alan and Billy just watched, while Stolland moved around the room slowly, examining everything. He eventually came to the washstand. Opening the drawer, he knelt down and with the aid of a torch, took his time trying to see what was inside. After a few minutes, he slowly withdrew the box. He was handling it as though it would explode any moment.

Alan whispered, "You look as though you've got a bomb."

Stolland held up a hand for silence, "You are as close to the truth as you ever want to get, my friend."

With that, he placed the box carefully on the bed. He then returned to the drawer, easing it further open. It seemed to stick. Something was jammed at the back. He carefully manoeuvred the drawer until he freed the item. He opened what seemed to be a folded card.

"It's just a calendar." Alan said.

Stolland smoothed out the card, "Not just any old calendar, Alan. This is rather special, I think."

Stolland pointed to the heading over a view of a pier, "Views of Cromer," Stolland flicked through the attached pages.

"Only one date is marked," whispered Stolland, "Sunday twenty-fifth of next month, it seems we may have time on our side!"

"So," said Alan, "As you say, it seems our friend doesn't intend to do anything until next month, and if I'm not mistaken, Albany Street is where Stickland has his main home."

Stolland didn't reply. Instead, he returned to the bed and took up the box. He opened a panel and spent some moments peering inside.

"Well," he said, "it seems Grech doesn't intend to make any drastic moves for a short time. At least, that's how it seems."

Stolland went out onto the landing to where Lo Wey was waiting. "We would very much appreciate being told if your guest intends to vacate this room? It would be very wise not to say anything about our visit. He could be most upset."

Alan quickly scribbled Charlie's telephone number on a piece of paper and handed it to Lo.

The smiling Chinese shuffled his feet, as though he was rather nervous. Imagination was taking over. He had not planned to go to his ancestors so soon. He thanked Alan and said he would wait below.

Stolland went round the room again, placing everything back exactly as it had been, especially the contents of the drawer. Re-locking the door, they trooped downstairs and handed the key back. Thanking Lo, they left the café. For his part, Lo was quite pleased they were gone from his little corner of Limehouse.

Billy joined Alan and Stolland in the car as they headed off to Eaton Walk. By the time they arrived at the flat, Alan was smiling as though his face would split, "Billy my son, you have earned the biggest meal I can rustle up. We'll fix you up with a room for the night, then tomorrow we'll wait for the crew to arrive at Charlie's from Cromer and make our big move on Grech."

Stolland was quiet, he finally said, "Yes, thanks Billy, well done, without you we'd probably still be scratching."

Billy smiled and felt relieved he hadn't bumped into Barry otherwise he just might have spoiled Alan's day.

Alan told Stolland to brighten up, "At least we now know where he's living. Plus it seems he doesn't intend to make his move just yet."

Stolland shook his head doubtfully, "Okay Alan, but were we supposed to think that? What we saw as a clue to his intentions could so easily have been a plant."

Alan held up a hand, "Fine, I admit it all seemed rather too pat, too simple. But we have to hope Grech has made one simple slip? He may have all the cards in his hand, but perhaps he may have given us a glimpse of his hand? Remember Stolland, it was your lot dealt us this hand. We didn't ask for the visitation of a serial killer. So, let's relax and pray we have Grech under lock and key tomorrow. Besides, we have a fail-safe key. Lo is on the spot. He'll tip us the second Grech makes a move. Lo's snoops will know where Grech goes."

Stolland glanced round. It was fine. Grace and the WPC were hopefully well asleep and Billy was in the bathroom.

Stolland lowered his voice, "Alan, when Grech passed through the Gate, we know he took certain things with him. One of these was a type of bomb. Up until this moment, I thought we were dealing with Grech and one device," he paused, "now, I'm not so damned sure."

Alan also looked around anxiously. There was still no sign of Billy, "I think I already know the answer, but I'll ask the question anyway. What does, now I'm not so sure, mean?"

Stolland lowered his voice to a whisper, "The bomb is not a bomb as you understand it. This is an extremely dangerous device, far worse than you could visualise. In my time, we call it a sanitizer. Environmental scientists developed it to rid large areas of resident infestations."

"What sort of residential infestations?"

"All life forms. In other words, if you had a plague of rats in an area, you cleared the people out and set one of these off. When you returned, there would be no forms of life from worms, to bugs to rats to cats, alive."

Alan's shoulders dropped, "Your lot don't do things by half, do they? Is that what you meant when we were at the War Office, and you said a weapon worse than we could imagine?"

Stolland nodded, "This device was first developed some time after the trouble in twenty-sixteen, purely to fight alien disease and other infestations harmful to man.

That is why we refer to it as a sanitizer. As usual, when the dust cleared, out came the damn politicians! Armed with their old ambitions and rescheduled it as an offensive weapon. The military were delighted, used it straight away. It took out people, etc., leaving anything that was not a life form, free for them to take over. To the military, it was and is a perfect weapon. No residues, no side affects. Wham then its all clear to casually walk in and take over. It's a childishly simple device. You simply adjust it to take out from one square yard to several hundred square miles."

Alan felt sick, "Look, don't say any more about this now. We must change tack. I'll phone Charlie and get the three of them back a.s.a.p. Grech must be taken alive but we can't nudge him into activating this box of tricks."

Stolland heard Billy returning, "Go and make that call."

Alan nodded and left.

While all this had been going on, Grech was aboard the Empress. He found the family accommodation without difficulty. Four cabins, each one having its own services, a large dining area and all interconnected by a series of heavily carpeted walkways. This accommodation took up most of the upper sundeck, to the rear of the bridge.

By its position and isolation, it was plainly exclusive to family. Discreet but obvious signs, displayed on all approaches warned that the area was strictly out of bounds. The design made Grech's task, a simple one. By measuring the exterior of the area, he had all the information he needed.

With a pencil, he did a few quick calculations and within seconds had the exact centre of the area. He made a few adjustments to the device and slid the box silently, deep into the darkness of the overhead ducting. Grech's lips creased into a smile. His work on board the Empress was over.

He collected the small tools he'd used, placed them into the holdall and, making certain he left no sign of disturbance, he left the deck.

Climbing down the ladder into the skiff was a simple matter, as was the row back to the barge. He tied the skiff off exactly as he had found it and climbed onto the quayside, where unloading and loading remained in full swing.

Grech looked along the dock and noticed several buses drawn up. He sauntered along to where they were, destination boards simply displaying the words, 'Not in Service'. After a few minutes, he realised these were transporting seamen from one of the many passenger boats. Grech crossed over to a group and took a chance, "Are the buses taking you out of the dock?"

A swarthy faced man, about the same age as Grech, turned and looked down at him, "Yes mate, we're all travelling back to Tilbury, for paying off."

Grech put on the tired old man look, "Do you think I could get a lift up the road. Save getting more wet. It's been raining all night. I'm soaked from working on the lights over there." Grech pointed over his shoulder.

"Sure," the swarthy man clapped Grech on the back, "I don't suppose this lot will mind sharing a seat with a little sparks. Jump on."

The bus pulled away and left the dock without so much as a wave from the dock police. Grech watched the road and soon he noticed a spot he recognised. He jumped onto the open platform and as the bus slowed, he gave a wave to the seamen and left the bus.

Grech did not arrive back at Lo's until just after three in the morning. He let himself in and walked slowly up the stairs. At the landing, he felt for the matchstick. It was missing. His stomach lurched.

He unlocked the door and eased it open, without a sound. As soon as there was enough of an opening to go through, he passed in and re-locked the door. Putting the light on, he crossed to the washstand. The drawer slid easily out. Grech knelt and looked at the box for some time, he was certain it had been touched. He slid the box to one side and felt for the calendar. His groping fingers found and withdrew it. He saw straight away that there were a few new creases in the cardboard.

Surprisingly Grech eyes shone with satisfaction. He almost laughed but it wasn't in his nature to laugh, even when he was on his own and pleased with a positive result. Instead, he whispered to the room, "You see how easy it is to fool these people. They only see what they wish to see." The spark in the eyes faded. "Now," the same whisper continued, "it is a good time to settle accounts with Lo Wey."

Grech had just started down the stairs when he heard Lo Wey call him, "Ah, Mr Gentry, you are here at last. I waited to tell you that the business with Mr Scrivner is all too much. Many men came to see you. They threaten me. I had to let them into your room. They pushed me out. I am a weak, humble man. I go away, but wait to hear you return. Perhaps it is best if you leave now. I will say you are coming back?"

Grech listened to Lo, whispering his story on the darkened staircase. He felt no hatred toward Lo. There was little a poor weak chinese could have done to stop these men.

"Who were the men, Lo? Were they Barry Scrivner's friends?"

Lo adopted a very mild manner, becoming the humble man he was hoping Grech thought him, "I think they know him. They do not like me for sheltering you. They are very angry you not here. They curse me too."

This worried Grech. If Barry had recruited more men, to pay back for the death of his team from Charlton, things were dangerous for Grech. And he knew there was still work to do.

"Look, Lo," he drew the wilting chinaman, into the room, "you have been very helpful and I am going to need friends like you."

Grech went over to his holdall. He drew out a bundle of five-pound notes, "If I give you this money, you keep this room for me?"

Lo nodded then allowed his eyes to grow as large as they possibly could. He tried to push the money back into Grech's hands.

"You are most welcome friend and already generous and can have the room for as long as you need. Perhaps it is best to leave a few things so visitors can see your presence?"

It seemed to Grech that every sentence Lo pronounced ended as though it was a question. But he seemed to show genuine concern.

"Fine Lo, and your idea may work well. Look, you take this money and I'll keep the key to the room. I will stay away for a while. If Barry Scrivner or his associates come looking, just say I am away a day or two on business. It is important Lo, that I can trust you?"

Lo smiled the inscrutable smile of one used to implying complete trust. To him, the business of the English was not his concern, especially if it involved his skin.

Grech waited for Lo to descend the stairs. He quickly checked the contents of the holdall, particularly the fine jewellers tools, he had used on the Empress. He then added the box and calendar from the washstand drawer. Carefully he closed the holdall, went out of the room, locking the door. He made his way down the stairs and out of the café.

Lo watched Grech's back as he once again disappeared into the shadows of the dimly lit alley. Lo had known many of the worst experiences life had to offer, but in his mind, this Mr Gentry was the worst of all fiends. Making certain his tenant had in fact departed Lo bolted the front door, his thoughts far from generous. He was too old to have these foreign devils bringing such trouble to his house.

The small cobbled alley settled into its shadowy indifference, while Lo's worried eyes lingered for several minutes behind the glass, then they were gone.

Chapter Twenty

By nine the next morning, Mrs Friar's front room was again full to bursting. Charlie, Bob and Frank had left Cromer a little after five. Alan, Stolland and Billy had a good breakfast and left Eaton Walk sharp at eight. Jack Cousens managed to stagger round on time from next door. As usual, the over worked Mrs Friar was doing her best to fill them up with tea.

As the last drop was squeezed from the pot, Charlie ushered his mother into the warm kitchen and quietly but firmly closed the door. Obviously, there was police business to discuss.

Alan called the meeting to order, "As you know, yesterday was a particularly heavy day. I have no intention of going over every detail. Grace is brilliant. She and her escort left at dawn for my daughter's home in Cambridge, where they will stay for the time being. While I'm on the subject of Cambridge, George Wright continues to make progress."

"Do they know yet whether his eyesight is affected, sir?" Charlie's hushed question brought a steadying influence into the room.

"To be truthful, I never raised that point, because it's still too early to know just how affected George will be. The main thing is, he's making progress, good progress according to my daughter, who it seems lives at his bedside."

The uncertainty of George's condition continued to leave empty spaces in their conversations.

Alan coughed, "You will be relieved to know that the young Page-boy from Simmonds and his parents are on their way to an address on the Isle of Wight, until Grech is stopped. I'm sure the boy will enjoy the holiday," Everyone around the table grinned.

Alan cut short the amusement, "Mr Stolland, Jack and I spent some time trawling over that brickwork in Barge House Road. Long story short, we found around thirty spent cartridge cases, behind the walls of shattered buildings opposite. We had to draw the conclusion that as only one aimed round hit a target, unfortunately that was you Jack, it seems the aim of the shooters, was to drive you three into a trap."

Jack, Charlie and Bob muttered in agreement.

"This opinion was confirmed later by Jack. Being an ex-munitions navy-type, he ran his eye over what was left of the brick supports. On three, he found residues and marking which, in his humble opinion, could have been plastic explosives, probably something like military eight-o-eight, probably in support of the satchel charge, delivered through the door.

The additional static charges, timed with a fraction of a second gap between each, would have a textbook effect. Load bearing walls would drop out allowing floors, etc., to fall like a collapsing house of cards.

Also, amongst the rubble, we found traces of cable rigs, leading to each detonation point. Whoever did this job were experts in their trade. That probably makes them a professional demolition crew using a cross between industrial and military kit. We can therefore say, without much doubt, what you three survived was a planned attempt to make your deaths look like misadventure."

Charlie lit a cigarette, "Well, at least it's nice to know someone cared enough to put some thought into it."

Alan frowned, "Yes, Charlie. Three coppers nosing into a blitzed building, dying under collapsing brickwork is tragic. Even to Joe Public. But it doesn't raise sweat amongst the criminal fraternity. However, three coppers shot to death in the execution of their duty, now that would send alarm bells ringing. Am I right, Billy?"

Billy suddenly took an interest. Here he was to give a professional opinion. "Sounds right, Mr Brandon, the other side gets up tight over cops and guns. The chill probably comes from their knowing the bizzies are going to be crawling all over them. Topping a copper is seen as bad for business." Everyone smiled at Billy.

Alan continued, "Yes, thanks Billy. You should all know that if it weren't for Billy, we would still be running around trying to spot our master villain. Well, yesterday, Billy went to Limehouse, to deliver a letter, just doing a friendly post run. Up until Billy walked into that café in Limehouse, we had been on the back foot.

Even with the help of Mr Stolland, we have always been three streets behind and that is putting it mildly. Now, thanks to Billy's foray, not only do we know where Grech is, we also know what he may do and when he may do it. Oh, and in case you think Billy, as a civilian, shouldn't be in on this meeting, I think he's earned his spot. He's acted extremely responsibly and is due our special thanks." There was unanimous agreement.

Alan went on, "You should also know that I've given Billy the opportunity to duck out at this point and maintain his local credibility. None of this is easy for him. In fact it could be positively unhealthy. However, he has asked if he can see it through. I welcome him and fully appreciate his remaining a full operational member of this team."

Billy looked at those around him and was pleased to see smiles and even a friendly slap on the back. It was the first time in his life that he felt people, outside the boxing ring, were respecting what he had done. Up to now, the law had always seemed remote, unfeeling, unless they wanted to know something. It was good to feel of value and on the right side for a change.

Jack leaned across, "Well done Billy, I'm dead pleased."

Billy's hands were sweating. He had rarely known praise and was embarrassed. It felt good to be amongst these people.

"Right," said Alan, "you've heard enough from me. It's time to hand over."

Stolland coughed, "Well, as Alan said, as a direct result of Billy's work, we were able to drop in at Lo Wey's café, in Ming Street, yesterday evening. We immediately got a result. We have evidence that shows Grech is indeed living above the café. We also know what he may use as a weapon, and when he may use it. I have some personal reservations on these last two points. You know what they say about chickens and eggs. However, Alan, Billy and Jack are aware of these concerns.

Grech also has the advantage in this game. He leads, like any scum terrorist, choosing the time and place. We naturally follow. He is super-intelligent. He is extremely cunning and we all know how ruthless he is. Death, yours mine, anyone's, counts for nothing. It's all small change to him. He doesn't leave stones unturned. He thinks every move through and then thinks it through again. When we jump on him, we are only going to get one chance! We must secure him totally, before he is surprised or panicked into what he will see as his final response.

I must impress on you, he has absolutely nothing to lose, and that makes him as dangerous an enemy as you will ever have to face. He's an extremely cunning opponent. Certainly smart enough to outguess most of us. And, most certainly, smart enough to have realised we may drop into his latest bolt-hole."

Stolland pushed his own suspicions to the back of his mind. He felt what they found was a deliberately laid trail. He concentrated on the faces looking at him and tailored his words to fit the mood.

"But," cautioned Stolland, "we know who his main target is. We're not sure if he'll go for just this man or try to wipe out what's left of the line. You may recall that most of his family was lost in a cruising accident, a while ago. Since that time, the target has chosen to keep those few that survived, together under one roof. I'm told, he feels that way, he can more or less guarantee their safety.

However, the incident has not dulled his Lordship's love of cruising. He follows his own path in everything he does. He runs his family, the same way he runs his many business interests. Somewhat callously and allowing no opposition. We have received information that he and his family leave, on a business trip, aboard his own boat, the Galen Empress today. In fact, she's already making her way out of the Royal Albert dock. I understand that the risk to Stickland, once aboard his boat, is extremely low. This assessment of risk having been undertaken by the Chief Constable of the Port of London Police, and passed on through the Home Secretary.

The Empress, has evidently been under twenty four-hour police guard and surveillance, since the risk became apparent. We have no rational argument, which would convince a character like Lord Stickland to put off this trip. He evidently replied, 'Oh no, not another one', when told of Grech's aim to kill him. He evidently has a long list of people who've threatened to murder him. So, not only is Grech intent on his purpose, it seems our victim is equally intent on assisting him.

I am assured it would be impossible to persuade him to toe the line, any line. That comment is straight from the Home Secretary. We must accept the opinion of others and hope that the items seen yesterday, is indicative of Grech's true intentions. If correct, then time seems to be on our side. We must take this opportunity to finish this business."

Charlie smiled, "Carpe Diem?"

"Exactly," said Stolland, "grasp the day. Now, it's likely that Grech will be at Lo Wey's café today. Our plan is to go there and hopefully arrest him. We know Grech is armed, he's already demonstrated he will use a gun. We also know that Lo Wey has co-operated and seems more victim than collaborator. So, in order to try and make this arrest with as little fuss as possible, Billy has suggested that he goes into the café first.

We will not attempt to follow until Billy comes out, into Ming Street, and gives the signal that Grech is present.

If he's not on the premises, Billy will return to us and we'll leave the area and think again."

Alan said, "It is possible we may have to keep the alley and café under observation for some time in order to snatch Grech. If we have a no show today, Billy has already come up with an idea we will use.

You also know this is strictly a 'Phoenix' operation, in other words our affair. However, we have no doubt, limited information has been passed to the Met. They probably know we are operating here. But, if things go wrong and one or more of us are in trouble, don't expect the cavalry. It won't happen. I repeat, we must not go into that café, until we are certain Grech is alone. If he is in the café itself and there are other customers, we wait for Billy to say the snatch is on. If Grech appears out of the alley, we'll close on him and make the arrest. Charlie, you and Bob are to cover that rat-run out into Pennyfields. Now no heroics from anyone, let's do this by the book."

The room was suddenly very quiet.

Stolland looked at his watch. "It's just after eleven. I suggest we leave this operation until three. That way we can be certain, business in the café will have dropped, hopefully to nil. Grech may have returned to his room, and any kids normally sculling around, will or should still be in school."

Everyone nodded.

Charlie got up and stretched his legs, "You don't have to be in on this unless you want to Billy. It could get nasty and we don't want anything happening to you."

Billy smiled, "It's okay, Charlie. I reckon I owe this one to our kid. Besides, it'll be nice riding with the cowboys. Blimey, my folks wouldn't believe it would they?"

They all knew what he meant. Charlie then left to ask for more tea. He'd remembered to rescue some Brook Bond from Cromer, to relieve his mum's straining tea caddy. It was going to be a long wait until three.

Charlie took Frank on a drive around the streets of China town. They didn't slow up as they passed the alley leading to Lo's café. It was enough that Frank had a good idea of the road lay-out, just in case they had a chase.

Charlie suddenly said, "What do you think of Billy Tate?"

The question caught Frank out, "Well, I thought he had your vote?"

"He has," answered Charlie, "but what would you say if, after his appeal, we were to do what we could to make his life easier?"

Frank thought for a minute, "You mean bring him into the job?"

"Well, he's shown enthusiasm for this type of work."

Frank shook his head, "Don't you get the feeling it might be something to do with his wanting to see the killer of his brother topped?"

Charlie smiled at Frank, "You know your trouble Frank Woodhouse, you've no faith in human nature."

They both grinned.

"Well, just let's see what happens today and at his appeal. Now, we'd better get back and take the gang out for a bite, before they eat my folks out of house and home."

The Empress had slipped her tugs and, with a pilot in command on the bridge, and a fast police launch escort, was making her way down river. Every member of the crew had reported as instructed, so a delay at Tilbury was unnecessary.

The passengers were settling down and, as was always the case, Lord Stickland had gone straight to his cabin and shut himself away. He was never interested in the drab passage down river. The boring Essex and Kent shorelines held no interest for him.

He crossed to his desk and took up the telex he had received prior to leaving dock. His eyes scanned the text. He screwed the paper up into a tight ball and threw it forcibly through the open window. It fell into the grey looking water where it joined other unwanted rubbish, caught on an ebbing tide. Stickland watched it for a second, as he mouthed the words, "Jealous ignorant fools, worried by idle threats."

At ten minutes after three, Billy appeared at the entrance to the alley. He put his thumb down, then tucked both hands into his pockets and strolled across the road into Garford Street. He paused alongside a green Riley, parked by the Church, said something to the driver, threw away a match he had been chewing, and walked on. In Ferry Road, he unlocked a car, got in and drove it slowly along Pennyfields, stopping to pick up two men. Some time later, both cars parked in the car park of the Bull Inn at Barking. The raid on Lo's café was off.

Not long after this, at a point just off Sheerness, the police launch, which had escorted the Empress down river, pulled away from her side. A river pilot looked up to the Empress's bridge, from the deck of the launch and saluted. The Captain of the Empress smiled, waved his thanks and gave orders to increase speed. She was on her own now, heading out to the North Foreland. After which, she would turn, beginning her run to the Atlantic.

The few passengers that now stood at the rail of the sun deck, occasionally stared at people crewing small scrappy looking boats, that fought to avoid the elegant bows of the fast moving Empress. Lord Stickland saw little point in joining his family. He was engrossed in papers that lay on his desk. They outlined proposals to buy out a mining company in Cornwall. A short stopover in Falmouth would be necessary. He reached for the telephone.

Stickland smiled, it was nice to have an ex-Royal navy sea captain jumping to attention. He personally didn't have much use for these navy types. The war had finished, so they were of little consequence now.

Over dinner at the Bull, Alan outlined his intentions for the next day. Part of this was that Billy was to return with Bob and Charlie to the East End. Hopefully they could pick up Barry Scrivner's trail and, with luck and Lo's help, get a handle on Grech's trail.

If Alan had been in Goulston Street, Whitechapel, he would have seen a small black coated figure edging through the throng of pedestrians in the area known as the Jewish quarter. Grech smiled to himself, as he brushed shoulders with the serious grey bearded, black coated men. He was back amongst the Jews. Nothing wrong with that, he thought. After all why not, he was Jewish by descent. It was here that he should feel most at home.

He turned left into a passage that led into the centre of a tenement building. By the look of the brickwork, he guessed it to be over one hundred years old. Everywhere there were children and lots of noise. He came to a set of worn steps leading up into the gloom.

A single knock on the door of number twelve brought a man, obviously Jewish, dressed as always in black, all except the obligatory off-white prayer shawl.

"I am told at the salt beef shop in Middlesex Street, you might have a room for rent?"

The man looked down on Grech, through steel-rimmed spectacles, "Are you able to pay? Too many times I have people who end up at my door as charity cases."

Grech drew a few silver coins from his trouser pocket, "How much? I am not rich but I could afford eight shillings a week?"

The prospective Landlord smiled and stepped aside, "Just the sum I was going to ask, for room only of course. It is a small room with just a bed and a chair, but it does not ask questions and eight shillings is no fortune."

Grech found himself depressed by the cupboard that miraculously found itself promoted to a room, by a simple knock on the door. Washing and other facilities were on the landing and consisted of a communal sink with a single cold tap and one water closet. Introduction to this made Grech revise the previous estimate of the building's age.

Such a fine example of Dickensian decay could not be less than one hundred and fifty years old and still with all original features intact. Grech had no idea how many people occupied the building, or the flat for that matter, but as he wasn't forced to share his cupboard with anyone, he gave up trying to count voices or footsteps. He tried to open the high small window that graced one wall of his room. This turned out to be impossible. He lay down on the bed and using his canvas holdall as a pillow, he slept.

The next morning, it was raining. It wasn't torrential, but blundered toward the fine penetrating variety that quickly soaks the unwary and keeps the wise nodding behind windows.

Smoke from hundreds of chimneys fought hard to get away from the street. Grech tried to find a convenient moment to wash, but was embarrassed by so many children's curiosity. He did his best, then returned to his room and completed dressing.

He removed his coat from the bed, which had doubled as a blanket, and with his bag firmly grasped in his hand, made his way out into the milling hubbub that was Middlesex Street.

Shabby tenements surrounded and depressed him. He looked at each pile, wondering how much the owner had paid Hitler, not to bomb his building. Then Grech recalled the terrible holocausts and wished the thoughts had not entered his head.

In spite of the grimness of Whitechapel, Grech began to feel excited at remembering what today should bring. His enemy would die today. He turned about and walked east to Brick Lane. Here Grech made several bulky purchases, and was delighted to see a Public Baths sign. Within twenty minutes, he was lying back in a bath filled with warm water. His few pence entry fee had provided a towel of sorts and a worn square of dark green soap. All he had to do now was to enjoy his bath, dry himself, put on the clean clothes he had just bought. He could then walk out of the baths a new man. For the first time, since making the time shift, he felt as if he belonged. In his cubicle, he could lay back and enjoy his twenty minutes of complete privacy.

The time sped by and it was with some shock that a hammering on the door indicated the impatience of the next bather. He towelled himself dry, still feeling quite relaxed.

Putting on the newly bought clothes was a treat because although they were second hand, they were clean and of fairish quality. After clearing the pockets of his old garb, he tied his filthy clothes into a bundle, placed the used towel on top and left the lot beside the bath. He pocketed the remains of the soap and made a clean exit from the cubicle. His next task was to find somewhere to eat.

Grech left the baths and walked in the general direction of the Commercial Road. Reaching the Mitre pub at Aldgate, he went in and was soon enjoying a spam sandwich. He had taken two bites when he felt a sharp point, pricking the back of his neck.

"Now, here's a surprise lads. A fully togged Jewish Rabbi, complete with the hat and long black coat of the faith, stuffing his gut with gentile fodder."

The food dropped out of Grech's mouth. He could see the two young thugs in front of his table, but the owner of the knife pricking his neck stood behind him. The voice was unmistakable.

"Barry, my friend. What's all this about?"

Barry hid the knife and slid round to sit alongside Grech, "My pals told me you were up here. Hiding your scrawny little form were you?"

As he said this, Barry ran his free hand round Grech's waist searching for the gun. "Not tooled up Grech? What an error, my friend. Bad luck for you, eh?"

Grech's mind was reeling. Barry was no hero. Well, certainly not on his own anyway. Now he had enough support to play hard man. One of his companions was Chinese and Grech knew where he had seen him before. Grech's mind flew to the holdall. It was at his feet and in it was his loaded gun.

"Look Barry, I had urgent business up here. I was having a bite to eat, before going back to Lo's place, hoping you'd drop in."

Barry sneered in Grech's face, "Of course you were, you little prick! You were going to tell me all about my mates getting paid off after the Barge House job." Barry's anger brought flecks of saliva to his lips, "You topped them, you snivelling little toad! Now, I'm copping the grief due to you. So, my little disguised Jewish Rabbi, you're going to perform a sacred ritual, for my two mates. Patrick has come all the way over from Charlton to see you dance. His brothers were the ones you dipped in the Thames, remember? Patrick wants your eyes out first. So you can scream and grope about a bit. Now, he's our guest so I suppose we'll have to grant him first jab, eh?"

Barry pushed Grech's head down hard into the food on his plate, "Now, I don't care what my old man says, you're for it. I'm going to watch you twitch as you bleed to death."

It seemed to everyone watching, that Grech was struggling to get his face from the food. Actually, he prolonged the struggle because it gave him the opportunity to grope into the holdall, for the gun. Barry gripped Grech's hair and dragged his head up.

"Upsadaisy old-un! Don't want you suffocating in your food now, do we?" The three laughed, but the comedy never reached their eyes.

Customers in the bar melted away. This fracas was one that didn't concern them. Gangland quarrels were frequent enough in the Mitre, so non-interference was a rule of the house. The burly landlord had quickly recognised Barry. He put towels over the pumps and backed off. It wasn't Barry that worried him, it was the weight behind the name he carried.

Barry grinned at his two friends across the table. He was like a child having fun.

"Right then, let's take this toe rag down to St Katherine's, take his eyeballs out and pin them to his liver. Then he can go in the dock. He can explain on the way down what happened at Woolwich!"

With that, Grech pulled himself upright and pushed the pistol hard into Barry's stomach, "Have you any idea what that is Barry? You're only allowed one guess, so you can't afford a mistake, can you?"

The two thugs, the other side of the table, couldn't see what Grech had done.

"Now just tell your friends that you and I need to talk. They should walk out and go home." To emphasise the point Grech again rammed the gun into Barry.

Grech saw Barry's eyes flicker down to his left hand. He read the fear in Barry's thoughts.

"Don't do it Barry. You're not in the same league. The knife is not that quick," he paused, "or is it?" The menace in the last three words fell on Barry's ears, like cold winter snow.

Grech whispered, "It's alright Barry, you won't even hear the gun go off, the silencer is very efficient, shame to spoil the suit!"

Barry couldn't believe it. He stared down at the folds of the black coat and saw the gun. He imagined the damage a bullet through his guts would do. He had a split-second nightmare. Barry began shaking violently. A small pool of urine started to form under his shoes. He had always suffered from a weak bladder.

"Okay Grech. Okay. But if you try shooting me, my mates will start at your ankles and work their way up!" He was shaking so much his words came out in a high-pitched warble.

Grech whispered in Barry's ear, "Try, Barry? What's this try to shoot you? It's a surety Barry. From this distance, your spine will explode and become part of the wall. Now, like a very good boy, tell your school friends to lay whatever toys they have on the table, get up and leave, quietly and now! One wrong move, just the hint of one, and you are very, very dead, and so are they!"

The ice in Grech's voice petrified Barry.

"They either do it right now, or we end everything right here, including you, them and whoever else wants to join in! I've got sixteen flat-nosed bullets to share out!"

Barry's eyes were wet with tears. He looked across the table, "I can handle this. Back off. I'll see you in Lo's."

They didn't move. They were staring at Barry.

378

Patrick said, "If you think I'm about to turn my back on my brother's killer to save your arse Barry, you're crazy!"

The Chinese youth reached across to control the anger of his partner. He smiled at Grech, his thin voice betraying the acid of his words.

"Listen old man. We do not want poor Barry hurt. You can be most certain that we will wait. We will see you another time to play this game. We know your face, and Patrick will have his blood revenge for his brothers."

With that, he increased his hold on Patrick's arm and dragged him stumbling and cursing through the door. Two knives were on the table. Grech used his free hand to sweep them onto the floor but didn't take his eyes from Barry's.

He smiled into Barry's face, "You are such a child Barry, trying to play a grown man's game. You are a tragic waste Barry. Trying to act strong is going to get you killed for sure. Now, you are all alone. I have a silenced gun. You have a knife. Who do you think will win? Drop the knife!"

Barry stared down at the gun. He hated guns. The knife clattered to the floor, Grech kicked it spinning away.

Grech whispered, "The right decision, for once you thought like a man, a foolish one maybe, but a man. Now, how did you and your little gang get here?"

Barry couldn't believe the question, "What's it to do with you?"

Grech pressed the gun further into Barry's stomach, "My patience is not endless, boy," he quietly repeated the question.

"By bloody bus," Barry spat the words, "how'd you think, we grew wings and flew!"

"Always the clown, Barry, now, you and I will get up and walk out of that door. Not the one your friends have taken. Once in the street, we will get into a taxi and go for a ride. If you make one move, say just one wrong word, even look the wrong way, I will kill you! Very painfully you will die. I have nothing to lose since you decided to end our business relationship."

With his right hand, Grech took hold of a gaudy silk handkerchief, which was sticking from Barry's top pocket. He wiped the crumbs from his face, picked up the holdall and stood away from the table. The folds of the long black Rabbi's coat now covering the gun.

"Barry, you don't know it, but you're actually helping to make history. You ought to feel proud of that. Unless we can come to some understanding, you'll never live long enough to appreciate it. Now walk!"

The door chosen by Grech as an exit led, via a small lobby, into a cobbled delivery yard. This brought them into Braham Street. There was no obvious sign of the two young villains. Barry walked slightly in front of Grech.

On reaching Leman Street, Grech hailed a taxi, "You're such an expense Barry. But, with luck, you'll learn, if you live long enough."

"If you top me, my family will roast you over a slow fire."

"Barry, if they are anything like you, I have little to fear."

Grech pushed Barry into the cab and told the driver to head for Limehouse. As the cab did a U-turn toward the river, Barry was still threatening.

"It's all gone wrong for you, Grech. My people have got you marked. There's no where for you to run. My family and the Rooney's will nail you. You're just a weird old man with no where to go."

Grech was sick of Barry's bleating threats. He hated the fact that Barry was nothing without the protection of his father and his organisation.

The cab turned into the Highway. An area still filled with its share of blitzed buildings.

"Stop here please driver," called Grech.

He bundled Barry out of the cab. The driver watched this performance. Grech thought he was becoming curious enough to start asking questions.

"Take no notice of him," offered Grech in a tired voice, "bit weak in the head. An idiot, gets it from his mother's side. I have to do everything for him. You know how it is, who'd have kids eh?"

Grech paid the driver, who nodded sympathetically at Grech. Barry started pissing himself again. The urine ran across the cracked pavement into a filthy gutter. The driver watched, then shook his head. Barry was too busy watching his last chance of help put his cab into gear and drive away.

Grech pushed Barry violently forward, signalling he wanted him to walk ahead. The damp patches on the seat and legs of his trousers plainly showing the route Barry's courage had taken. They came to a low wall. Behind it the ground dipped down into a typical bombsite, covered in tall weeds.

"Go on ahead of me, across that," Grech pointed across the open space, "run, Barry, run, and if you slow down or stop, I'll kill you!"

Barry's face betrayed his fear. He set off across the uneven ground. He stumbled, cried out and slipped again, but as he gained ground and the distance between him and Grech widened he felt an ounce of hope. Every juddering step over the uneven bricks increased the chances of Grech missing his aim. As he ran he cried, his tears torn between anger and fear. Seconds were passing and still no shots. He started to gain a little bravado.

He was tempted to look back but as he tried, he lost his footing and stumbled. He lost precious seconds in gaining his momentum again. Grech followed Barry round a corner, out of sight of the road. Barry didn't look back and was now running hard.

Grech leant against the remains of a wall, steadied the gun and fired two shots. Barry staggered on a few yards then collapsed like a rag doll.

Grech slowly walked to where Barry's body lay. He kicked Barry viciously in the stomach. There was no response. Grech actually smiled, then paused for a second as though a stunning idea had struck him. Slowly, he removed a cream envelope from his inside pocket and bending down, he tucked it neatly into the inside pocket of Barry's jacket. Having done this he rose to his feet. His black eyes glistening hatred for the worm that now lay dead at his feet. He then tucked the pistol into the waistband at the back of his trousers, arranged his long coat, adjusted his wide-brimmed black hat and casually walked back to the road, swinging his bag. It was not a bad day.

Having reached the Highway, Grech clambered over the low wall, taking some care to brush the dust from his shoes with Barry's handkerchief. He straightened his coat and gripping the holdall, he hailed a passing cab. Not once had he looked back to where Barry lay like a discarded tailor's dummy.

Sitting comfortably back in the taxi, Grech asked the driver the time.

"It's about half past two sir," said the driver.

Grech smiled. He felt comfortable dressed in his recent purchases, even if they did make him look like a Rabbi. There was nothing wrong with being a Rabbi. They were renowned for respectability, understanding and kindness. Grech felt at home in this religious garb. They were nearly new and, apart from a little mortar dust here a scrape there, perhaps a speck of food, a little crease, they were as clean as new.

The cab drew up at Liverpool Street station. Grech thanked the driver for his courtesy. He gave an excellent tip and entered the main concourse. He looked up at the station clock. It showed it was exactly a quarter to three. He casually strolled to the booking hall, enquired for a train to Cromer and purchased a first-class single ticket on the six-ten express service. It would be a long wait, but he preferred the express to the very slow, earlier service where he would have to make two changes.

Having time to spare, Grech left the station and mingled with the crowds until he came to a second hand bookshop. Becoming curious, he wandered in. Browsing the shelves, he searched for some time before he seemed to land on what he was looking for. Grech removed a leather bound pocket sized book, studied its cover carefully and took it across to an assistant.

"You want I should wrap the book?" Asked the elderly man.

"No, why buy such a book and hide its messages behind a paper bag?" Whispered Grech, adopting the guise and gait of the Rabbi.

The assistant smiled, nodded in agreement, passed back the book and accepted the money. As Grech left the shop, he felt complete, with a holy book of his supposed faith carried openly in his left hand. Grech was simply copying what he had seen at least one other Rabbi do, since arriving in the East End.

He wandered into Middlesex Street and found a small Jewish café. He relaxed in a corner, immediately feeling safe. He was just one among so many men wearing the black. He ate a plain meal of chicken soup and bread.

One or two customers smiled and nodded to him, possibly accepting his clothes for the badge of a Rabbi. Although he didn't support a full beard, he hadn't shaved for some time and his grey whiskered chin help in his disguise. Life amongst such people felt strangely comfortable.

Having left the café, he continued his walk through the tattered streets, making his way west. Finally, he came out into Houndsditch. Here he consulted his watch and found it was exactly four. He would continue his slow amble around the dusty streets, sticking to the roads thronged with pedestrians, coming and going about their business.

To the passer-by, he acted and looked the harmless and confused elderly man, carrying a holy book in one hand and the remainder of his world in a worn holdall. He would eventually return to the station, in comfortable time to catch his train. Grech stared in a jeweller's window and saw that the time was now four-fifteen. He stood reflecting on the change he had made in the Stickland family history. The beautiful Empress would require a new owner. Grech's task was over, all he had to do was clear up a little personal matter in Norfolk.

Before Grech's taxi had reached Liverpool Street, a patrolling beat-officer, had heard weak cries for help, from a bombsite, off the Highway. As a result, within half an hour, the wounded Barry was in Poplar Hospital. Though his condition was poor, he was desperate to tell the police or anyone willing to lend a sympathetic ear, everything about the scum that done for his friends, and tried to kill him.

An alert police Inspector put two and four together and connected the business to Operation Phoenix. Frustrated surgeons trying to get to work on their patient, insisting Barry should have a chance of life, while an equally insistent Alan dragged words from him as he sped vigorously towards the operating theatre. Barry's weak hands fought with nursing staff as they tried to sedate him.

His mouth worked ceaselessly, telling everything he knew. In just a few minutes, he had spilled the beans, including the business about the Empress and Nick Richards.

On hearing this, Alan flew out of the room and contacted the Coastguard Service. The hunt was on for the Empress. Returning quickly to the theatre where Barry was losing the battle for consciousness, a constable on the door handed Alan an envelope. He quickly explained that while going through Barry's clothes, he had found a letter that could have come from the Home Office.

Alan pulled out the single sheet and read the contents. His face tightened. It was obvious to him that a certain senior member of the government had written to Lord Stickland, advising him of questions before parliament, regarding the acquisition of certain Galen holdings. Alan's eyes flashed to the date at the head of the note. The note had been written on the same day as Alan's meeting with the Home Secretary.

Alan was stunned. What was this private and confidential letter doing in Scrivner's pocket? How did he get it? Further questioning would have to wait until Barry came round following the operation. Alan tried to control his flaring anger as he telephoned his Chief. David Long's opening words were cut short.

"David, I have in front of me written evidence to show that one of your colleagues, sitting on your side of the table at the War Office, revealed the subject of that meeting. It is also likely that the content of the letter, written to Lord Stickland, by your eminent colleague, may have been available to half the bloody villains and briefs in London!"

All David could manage was a descending, "Oh my God!"

Alan rasped out, "We're going to have to wait four bloody hours, at least, before we can question Scrivner to find out what he was doing with it. He, by the way, has been shot by our Victor Grech!"

David Long was silent for some minutes.

"Alan, I expect total silence on this until you have questioned Scrivner further. We will speak again when the air is a little clearer and you have cooled off! I don't want you saying something we would both be sorry for." David rang off.

Alan kicked himself for the way he had handled David. It wasn't his fault that the political club had closed ranks.

Alan rang the coast guard. They knew the location of the Empress but were having difficulty in raising her. Arrangements were in hand to intercept her at sea.

Not two miles West of where Alan was using the telephone, Lo Wey was leaving an Oriental Food Importers office, when he plainly saw Grech step from the kerb, and begin to cross Bishopsgate.

At first, he almost called out, but stopped himself. He knew Barry was angry and searching for Grech. His first reaction had been to warn Grech, but their business was not Lo's. Neither did Lo want to invite trouble. The Scrivner family business involved criminal violence, whereas Lo preferred the less demanding employment of wok, rice and noodles, plus a little laundry business on the side.

He watched Grech walk slowly, certainly casually between the crowds, towards Liverpool Street station. Lo followed, drawn by natural curiosity. Grech entered the station and threaded his way to the train indicator board. He studied this for some time, then his attention seemed to focus on one particular chalked notice. It announced that the six-ten for Cromer would now leave at six-forty, making an additional stop at Chelmsford. The staccato voice of the station announcer broke in, repeating an announcement about the delay and additional stop.

Lo saw Grech shake his head in frustration clearly showing disappointment. It was clear to Lo that Grech was about to make that journey. Lo walked away, ensuring to keep well clear of Grech. He entered a public phone-box and made a call. After this Lo left the station and made his way home. This was no longer his business.

Billy arrived at Charlie's parents to learn that Alan was at Poplar Hospital. He gave the message to Frank, telling him everything Lo had said. He then told Frank he would leg it to Liverpool Street and keep an eye on Grech. Billy would look out for the others, hopefully boarding at Chelmsford.

Frank looked hard at Billy, "As you've been told before, you don't have to do this. Grech's a shooter, he's our problem."

Billy shook his head, "Wrong Frank. He's every buggers problem. You just make sure you're at Chelmsford. Be there Frank, or I'll deal with him. We can't afford a gunny like him running lose."

Frank shook hands with Billy and told him to take care. He dropped him off on the way to see Alan at Poplar Hospital. Once there, Frank relayed Billy's message.

Stolland gave a broad grin, "We've got him. If only Billy doesn't lose him or over-play his hand, we'll have him."

Alan gave a half-smile, "Yes, it's all coming together. But we can't touch him on that train. We have to stop him before he can use that gun."

"I think we all agree on that," said Stolland.

Alan turned to Frank. "Get the others over here. As soon as Mr Stolland and I are free here, we'll all get up to Chelmsford to board the train as Billy expects.

As Frank was leaving, Alan called, "On second thoughts, you grab Charlie and Bob and take them to Chelmsford. I'll drive Mr Stolland direct from here. That way, some of us should make it. Get tickets for all of us through to Cromer. Don't let's get thrown off by a ticket inspector for evading the bloody fare."

A little earlier that afternoon, walkers on the cliff at Berry Head, just outside the fishing village of Brixham, Devon, had their first glimpse of Stickland's boat. She was cruising about three miles east of the Head. The duty coastguard watched her progress through his binoculars. She was certainly a grand sight, with her raked bows slicing through a calm blue sea. Though painted white overall, she looked more like a naval sloop than a private boat. The coastguard, Harry Pinner, consulted his movement sheet. He looked through his glasses again. Yes, there was little doubt she was the Galen Empress, making for Falmouth. Harry could clearly hear the unusually heavy static from the radio, which was in a small room to the rear of the lookout tower.

"Tea up," a voice called from the door.

Harry lowered his binoculars and turned, grateful for the steaming mug that reached his outstretched hand. He turned back to gaze at the white hull, just in time to see what seemed to be a sudden mist appear all around the vessel. The sea appeared to flatten and shimmer violently for just a few seconds, then whatever had caused the disturbance, was gone.

In forty-two years keeping watch, he'd never seen anything like it. Harry looked down onto the cliff edge and saw a dozen, or so walkers, all talking excitedly and pointing toward the Empress. She was rapidly losing speed and as he watched, she began a wide turn. At first, Harry thought there had been some sort of explosion under water. Perhaps a boiler had exploded or something?

As he watched, she continued her turn until she had completed a full three hundred and sixty-degree circle. The bow wave had disappeared and she now seemed to be dead in the water, just drifting.

Harry pressed the alarm button on a handset linked to the RNLI station at Brixham. At the same time, he read the position of the Empress off from a scale set in front of him. She was in trouble. Within ten minutes, the lifeboat and a pilot launch was speeding towards the Empress.

Two trawlers on their way into Brixham diverted to close with her. The radio behind Harry burst into fresh life. It was the naval sea rescue tug, Arthur. Ordered to sea to rendezvous with the Empress, she was proceeding at maximum speed. The coxswain of the lifeboat acknowledged the call.

The clock on the coastguard tower registered five-forty two, when the coxswain of the Brixham lifeboat called stating that some type of serious incident had occurred on board the vessel. There had been several deaths. All the dead appeared to have been located in the passenger accommodation. All other persons and deck spaces appeared unaffected, except for what seemed to be minor pressure injuries. Because of the nature of the incident, the naval tug Arthur was taking the Galen Empress in tow. The message ended with a request for Police to meet the vessel on arrival at RN Devonport.

Chapter Twenty One

Billy arrived at Liverpool Street station, just in time to join the rush hour. Crowds of people, scurrying like ants, all trying to board trains with just one thought in mind, getting home!

Certainly, the pandemonium prevented any hope of spotting Grech from ground level. He had to get above the crowds. Billy looked around. All he had to go on was a quick glance at a fuzzy photograph and a description of clothing more suited to the garb of a Jewish Rabbi, than a hunted killer.

The only additional clue was the canvas holdall he was last seen carrying, but trying to spot one man humping a bag in a crowd who all seemed to be carrying bags of one sort or another, seemed a bit hit and miss. Billy looked up. Above him, running the length of the station was a pedestrian walkway. A bird's eye view seemed the best option. At least he would stand more chance up there than rubber necking at ground level.

In two minutes, he was there, with an excellent view of the main concourse and, more importantly, the entrance to platform four, the platform from which the Cromer train would leave. He stared down, trying to separate the face he'd seen in the photograph, from the sea of faces beneath him. Then a possible solution struck him like a house brick. Railway staff may think he was seriously cracked, but it was better than what he was doing.

He threaded his way through to the comparative sanity of the main booking hall. He'd expected it to be packed, but surprisingly, most of the clerks were free. Billy took a quick look at them. Only one looked slightly

Jewish. Billy adopted the most anguished Jewish look he could muster and approached that window.

"Sir, I am terribly sorry to bother you when you are so busy, but my father is getting the train to Cromer this evening. He's left our home without the pills he needs for his bad heart."

The booking clerk turned his dead eyes on Billy. His face remained unmoved, as though carved from chopped liver.

Billy tried his appeal again, "Please, you must help me sir. He is an old man, a Rabbi, who will surely die without his pills," Billy wrung his hands for effect, "I don't know what to do. Help me please. He's carrying a holdall, an old one."

Billy remembered to allow his hands to describe a small holdall. At the same time, he left agony on his face, the way he had seen the traders in the Jewish market do, the day they settled their bills.

The Clerk's eyes flickered. It was like watching a winter's dawn over Hackney marshes. Light gradually crept in.

"Wait, wait. You say a Rabbi? Has a bad heart? He's your father?" As he said these short sentences, the clerk's voice pitched higher, "Hold on and don't worry so much. Calm yourself."

With that, the Clerk turned on his stool, looked along the line of booking clerks and called, "Has anyone sold a ticket to an old Rabbi, travelling to Cromer. You know, long black coat, black hat, maybe looks sick?"

"Carrying a holdall?" Added Billy.

"Yes, yes. He has a holdall."

The heads of the other clerks began to shake and lips set themselves like closed purses.

"An old black coated Rabbi, carrying a holdall?" At the far end of the line, a voice piped up, "Little old boy with peculiar staring eyes?"

"Yes, that's my father, the Rabbi," shouted Billy.

He raced to the window, spraying sorry, to the three people he almost knocked over. The end clerk looked pleased, "I served a man. Could well have been a Rabbi, wore a long black coat and hat. I think he carried a holdall, yes I'm sure he did. Black eyes, let me see, he's booked on the..."

His speech dwindled as he slid off his stool and went over to a table. He took his time thumbing through slips. "Yes, name of Grech. Seat sixteen, facing the engine. Coach A. It'll be the one nearest the engine, at the far end of platform four. Any trouble finding him, get the station announcer to broadcast over the loud-speaker."

The clerk turned and grinned at his colleagues. He liked to appear helpful sometimes, although it wasn't strictly part of railway policy.

After thanking everyone in the booking hall, Billy went out and began making his way back to his perch. The crowds seemed to have increased. Billy changed his mind and made his way to a phone kiosk. He knew exactly where Grech planned to be so there seemed little point in staring down faces.

Billy rang Charlie's house. Mr Friar senior answered and told him to hang on. While waiting, Billy realised his part in the job was almost over. Charlie might even tell him to go home. It was the last news he wanted to hear.

A long minute passed before Charlie came to the phone. Billy gave him the full story. To Billy's relief, Charlie laughed as he listened to what had taken place in the booking hall.

"Listen Billy, we're just about to leave for Chelmsford. You nip back to your favourite booking clerk and get a ticket close to Grech. Watch every move he makes but don't tip him off. Look out for us boarding at Chelmsford. If things go pear-shaped, get word to us somehow, good luck Billy boy. Oh, and remember to get a receipt for that railway ticket and anything else you buy."

This last comment made Billy grin. He was obviously part of the team, and on expenses! Billy returned to the booking hall, to the same clerk.

"You were very kind. I have spoken with my father and feel he couldn't possibly travel all the way to Cromer on his own. So, may I also have a first class ticket to Cromer, with a receipt of some type?"

The clerk smiled politely at the caring son, thumbed through the reservations again, and issued a docket for a seat just two rows away from the Rabbi.

Coming from the booking hall, Billy bought a paper and then went to the buffet where he ordered a beer and ham sandwich. The girl behind the counter gave him a cheeky grin, and handed him a beer and a plate, on which crouched a curly spam sandwich.

"Spam is all I can offer you, at the moment," she whispered in a seductive voice, "do you want mustard with that?" Her eyes flying to see if her supervisor was watching the brush with flirtation.

"No thanks my love, I'm on duty see," smiled Billy, "but can you see if I can have a receipt for this lot?"

"Till receipt do you?" The girl asked, smiling for all she was worth.

Billy returned the smile and accepted the proffered receipt. He couldn't really believe what he was doing. Just a few days back, he'd been banged up for something he hadn't done. Now, here he was, playing detective, and getting a first class ride to the seaside for his trouble. The only down side to this was, he was playing detective, just as he'd done when he was a kid, playing cops and robbers in the street. This sudden dip in his mood passed in a flash and he almost laughed outright when he wondered what some of his old school mates would think if they knew.

Billy checked his watch. There was still some time before the barrier on platform four would close. Billy waited it out in the buffet, getting an occasional smile from the spam girl at the counter. She was very attractive in a peroxide sort of way. He watched her as she moved around collecting used glasses and dishes. He judged she was around twenty. Billy tore his mind away from what was on offer and looked around at his fellow drinkers. He was safe. No one resembled Grech. He kept an eye on the platform entrance through the window. Twice he saw a person go through the barrier who could easily have been Grech. One even had a holdall, long black coat and hat. Unfortunately, most men catching that train seemed to be sporting dark coats and bowlers, typical city types.

The flow of passengers dwindled to a trickle, as the time for departure drew near. Billy looked at his watch, six-thirty-three. Billy drained his glass, gave the cheeky lass a special grin and left. By the time he reached the entrance to the platform, departure whistles were sounding. Along with two other people, he ran to the nearest carriage door, opened it and piled in.

As he walked slowly through the carriages toward the front of the train, he told himself to concentrate. Not be distracted by the novelty of the game he was playing. If Grech suspected for one moment he had been tumbled, he would disappear in a breath.

Despite the rush hour crowds, this train seemed to have plenty of seats available. The reason was probably that the first scheduled stop for this particular train would have been Colchester, then Norwich and Cromer. This evening, for some reason best known to the railway, they were also making the additional stop at Chelmsford for extra passengers.

Billy gradually worked his way forward, taking his time, passing from one coach to another until he eventually came to the first class accommodation. Billy rather liked the groups of two or four well-padded seats. Each group separated by a small table, where place settings implied the availability of tea brought to the table.

As Billy entered the two first class coaches, a train conductor, complete in white monkey jacket and matching gloves, raised his eyes in an authoritarian way, requesting sight of Billy's ticket and seat reservation. Billy returned the look and produced the documents.

After the monkey jacket had read every word on the seat docket, he handed them back, and regally waved Billy forward without comment. Billy knew that his clothes weren't up to first class standard, but was determined to leave his mark. With a vice like grip, he pressed a penny into the conductor's white-gloved hand, squeezed and smiled broadly.

"Thanks my good man." He didn't turn to see the impression or tortured expression his generosity had left.

The seat reserved for him was to the left of the centre aisle, in a group of four. Luck was with Billy, it was an aisle seat. There was only one other passenger in this group. A woman who looked up from the book she was reading, smiled briefly and returned to her book. Billy noted the title. It was a favourite of his, John Buchan's, The Thirty Nine Steps. He glanced forward and sure enough, he saw the crown of a black hat just visible above the back of a window seat, two rows ahead.

Billy settled down, listening to the rapid click-clack, as protesting steel wheels nudged heavily against bossy points. Room lights, in drab terraced houses backing onto the line, were coming on, providing fleeting points of interest for passengers. People moving about in these rooms, seemed oblivious to the fact they were actors performing one act playlets, ranging from relaxing gymnastics, exiting with braces down from outside loos, yawning, eating, stretching, scratching and pulling at their clothes, not once realising their immense entertainment value to the travelling public.

Billy decided to read his paper. The foot of the woman opposite him caught his shin. Billy swallowed the pain and apologised for not arranging his long legs out of her way. She smiled and said she was sorry. He was embarrassed, turned crimson and assured her it hadn't hurt. He felt he ought to say more but didn't know what to say. He tried, "I see you're reading the Thirty Nine Steps."

She smiled again and said, "Yes, have you read it?"

He wished he hadn't spoken. "Yes," he said, "It's a great story."

She nodded, "Thank goodness true life's not quite so dangerous."

He smiled back, showing his agreement.

Around him, the ritual shaking out of The Times or Telegraph papers, occupied a few of his travelling companions. The woman returned to her book. Billy unfolded his Daily Mirror, leafing through to see what the cartoon, Jane was doing. Then he noted the Korean War was not going well. The thought struck him that he was still young enough to join up, go and do another bit. The idea was immediately discarded, his eighteen months National Service as a guardsman at Windsor, had been enough soldiering for him.

Soon the rain came. Billowing sheets of drizzle, painting a gloss on dark slated London suburb roofs, spattered against misting carriage windows and distorting the glistening scenes that lay beyond. Billy resisted a childlike urge to wipe the gathering mist away. He was here to watch Grech, not stare out at the downpour.

The Cromer Express engine settled to its task, reaching and maintaining a comfortable speed. After a while, Billy folded his paper and placed it on the table. Not wishing to join some of the passengers around him, induced into a commuter slumber, he got up and walked forward, opening the half-glazed sliding door that gave access to toilets and carriage exits.

Opening the right hand toilet door, he slid in and bolted the door behind him. He tried to shut out the thought that he was travelling with a man who may well have shot his brother, Jimmy. He told himself that so far, he had made a good job of tagging Grech. Now, all he had to do was to get a look at his face, without raising suspicion. He waited two or three minutes, then unbolted the door and left.

Taking his handkerchief from his pocket, he began wiping his eye as though an eyelash or piece of grit was giving him trouble. At the same time, he slid back the aisle door and slowly passed through. Gaining his own seat, he completed wiping his face and smiled to himself. Grech was certainly the man under the hat. Although he seemed to be dozing, head-down, there could be no mistaking that ferret-like face.

The monkey jacket arrived. His gloved hand placed a miniature cup and saucer in front of Billy and the woman. He asked in a high nasal voice if she would, "take coffee?" The woman declined. He then turned to Billy.

"And, you...sir?"

Billy looked up, "I'd rather a large cup of tea."

The monkey jacket sniffed and straightened his back, "There ain't tea this evening, sir. It's only served till four." With that, he minced to the next group.

Billy checked his watch. It was seven-fifteen. The chap at the booking office told him they would arrive at Chelmsford around half past seven. He uncurled his long legs, rose from his seat and slowly wandered back down the train. He had noted that Grech still appeared to be dozing. On reaching the last carriage, Billy took up a position by a door.

Soon they drew into a very wet and windy Chelmsford. Billy dropped the window and looked out. The rain was cool after the stuffiness of the carriage. As the train came to a squealing halt, he searched for familiar faces. Five figures suddenly ran quickly across the platform and tumbled through the open door. The cavalry had arrived.

They all waited in the corridor for the train to start, with Bob leaning out of the window, making sure Grech didn't attempt to leave the train at Chelmsford. As soon as they were comfortably under way, they found a group of unoccupied seats.

Alan shook Billy's hand, "Nice to see you again Billy, you've done really well. Have you seen him?"

"Yes, he's two rows from me. When I last checked him out, he seemed to be dozing, probably had a rough day."

They all grinned. "Okay," Alan said quietly, "It seems Grech's settled so here's the way we play it. We are going to wait until he's clear of all other passengers. That may mean waiting until Grech gets off, clears the platform and is heading for the exit. Now, with luck we'll crowd him at that point. Hopefully we'll be on him before he knows what's hit him. Billy, you must be right up behind him. As soon as you get the chance, grab him from behind so his arms are pinned. Got that?"

Billy gave a broad smile, "Don't worry. I'll enjoy that."

"We can't afford him to get at his gun. The last thing we need is a shooting incident."

"What about units waiting at the station," asked Charlie, "what if Grech spots one and explodes?"

"There will be no marked vehicles or uniforms," assured Alan, "I have arranged that the only police on the station will be CID, and they'll be kitted out as railway staff. The only vehicle that Grech might see, apart from civilian cars, will be the odd railway lorry and perhaps a scheduled bus."

Alan again turned to Billy, "We will remain towards the rear of the train until we are just outside Cromer. Then, we will move through the train to coach B of first class. This will put us close behind Grech when he dismounts. Billy, as I said, you must exit immediately behind Grech. We will take our cue from you. Once you grab him, we will be there like a bad rash. Whatever we do, we must remove his gun and I want him totally disabled. Just remember he'll have nothing to lose!"

Alan was sucking on his empty pipe. It was obvious he was feeling tense. Grech was armed and Billy wasn't. But Billy was probably the only one who wasn't known to Grech. He would have no reason to suspect him. It was too risky putting anyone else so close.

"Are you sure you're up for this Billy?"

"I'm looking forward to getting my hands on him. Just let me judge when to whack him."

"Fine," said Alan, "if anything goes wrong and Grech tries to leave the train early or something else happens, Billy, you are not to risk your life under any circumstances. Just get back and tell us. Now, let's settle down. Good luck to everyone."

The train made its way smoothly through Essex, crossing into Suffolk and on into Norfolk. Billy noticed

Grech get up twice and go to the toilet. On each of these occasions, he left his holdall perched on the rack above the carriage window. He never once glanced along the carriage when returning to his seat, or seem vaguely interested in those around him. All seemed well until they were about ten minutes from Cromer.

Grech suddenly rose from his seat and walked to the toilets. Billy watched him try each of the two toilet doors. He must have found them occupied because he immediately made his way back, shuffling passed Billy's seat, to the toilets between coaches A and B. It was pure bad luck that Alan chose that very moment to advance his group forward, ready for their arrival at Cromer.

Stolland was leading the group, but was looking down at his feet as he negotiated some heavy luggage stacked in the aisle. Grech's whole attitude changed. He took one glance at Stolland, turned about and quickened his pace back through the swaying coach.

He passed Billy in a hurry. On reaching his own seat he grabbed the holdall from the rack and pushed forward, through the sliding door into the exit lobby. Billy instantly knew something bad was about to happen. He rose from his seat, pulling his coat on. The speed of Grech's move had surprised Billy. He kicked himself for not being ready to react.

At the same moment, Billy realised the train was slowing down. He glanced out of the window. Faces stared up at him. Repairs to the track or line maintenance accounted for the men at the side of the track. The trains speed continued to slow. Billy moved towards the sliding door.

Grech's back was towards him, just the other side of the glass. Billy felt a tingling in his body. The adrenaline rush he always had just before going into the ring surged through him.

A woman and small girl, about four years old with blond curly hair, stepped from one of the lobby toilets. Billy saw Grech reach forward, grab the child and scream something to the woman. In the same second, Billy saw a gun appear in Grech's hand. He was through the sliding door in a second. There was no time to warn Alan and the others. Grech was on his way off the train or he was going to shoot a number of people, including an innocent child.

The woman was now screaming. Billy grabbed her and pushed her back through the sliding door space, into the safety of the carriage. He spun round to confront Grech, whose face was filled with hatred. His small black eyes seemed to deepen until all Billy could see was the brim of the black hat over two white sockets each holding a piece of coal.

"Get back or I'll kill this child," screamed Grech.

Spittle flecked Grech's mouth. He looked insane. He dropped the holdall to the floor and reached behind him. Billy saw the window drop, then Grech reached out for the external door handle.

The train was now beginning to increase its speed. The thundering noise of the engine, only separated from the first carriage by the coal tender, seemed to drown the warnings and pleadings from other passengers. Billy held both hands up. There was just four feet between him and Grech. The trouble was the short space also contained a small child and a loaded gun.

Billy called above the noise, "That's a tiny child. She can't do you any harm. If you want to jump, do it. But, you're not going anywhere with that child!"

Grech seemed to hesitate.

Billy pleaded, "Let the child come to me. No one's going to interfere with what you want to do."

The tiny girl was screaming and struggling, but Grech held her fast, her kicking feet clear of the floor. Billy could clearly hear the cries of the mother for her child. He turned cold inside. Suddenly, it was all too clear what he had to do. Grech thrust the gun forward, and at the same time, kicked back against the door. There was a tremendous crash as it flew outwards, whipped wide open by the force of the slipstream. Rain and steam came pouring in.

Grech and Billy stood, glaring at each other. The train was now travelling quite fast. Billy took a step forward, at the same time he grabbed the little girl's arm. In the very same instant, he saw yellow flame erupt from the gun and searing pain enveloped his head and chest.

Grech seemed to half turn and lose his balance, tottering backwards. His fluttering hands fought the air as he attempted to regain his balance. He lost his footing and dropped the gun, releasing hold of the girl in the same instant. Billy fought the pain and dragged the child into his arms.

In a second, all the air that had filled the lobby disappeared as a London bound train exploded across the space where the door had been. As if plucked by invisible fingers, Grech disappeared into the thundering darkness.

No one heard Grech's tortured voice as he screamed for help. No one saw him torn apart. In that split second, no one cared. Tomorrow's assassin had stepped into history.

To those pushing forward into the lobby, it was all over in a second.

Billy, still grasping the little girl, lay sprawled on the floor with blood staining his head and chest. The mother of the child, fought her way passed two elderly men, to kneel and very gently release Billy's fingers. She lifted and hugged her child to her, allowing her tears to join the little girls. They were both staring at Billy's face.

"That was for Jimmy," he said. Then he lost consciousness.

The train driver responded to the emergency signal and brought the train to a grinding halt. Kind hands reached down and drew the woman and her child back into the coach, away from the blood stained floor of the lobby.

In the extraordinary silence, punctuated only by the steady puff and pant of the stationary engine, the passengers slowly parted to allow a shocked Alan and his team through.

Bob quickly knelt by Billy. He felt for a pulse, then shouted, "Get this bloody train moving into the station."

Stolland stepped round Billy and stared down into the darkness of the track. Alan pulled at his arm.

"Leave it for God's sake man. What lies out there isn't worth one of the people he's slaughtered. It's Billy you should be concerned about."

Stolland slowly nodded in agreement and bent down. He picked up Grech's gun and the holdall. The gun would provide ballistic evidence for Alan. The holdall, and what it held, would be taken back through the Gate.

With Billy made as comfortable as possible, the train moved smoothly forward towards the station.

Alan knelt down. He clasped Billy's shaking hands together in his, "You hold on Billy, you're one of our team and we'll get you through this, I promise."

No one else said anything. Even the small girl had stopped sobbing.

The train hadn't completely stopped when Charlie had dashed off to use a phone. By a miracle, the maintenance crew had already used their track telephone, to summon help. As a result, an ambulance with a doctor had arrived at the station. Charlie spotted them and brought them running to the platform. Billy was quickly stabilised and removed to hospital, along with the woman and her little girl.

Alan perched on the exit step of coach A, looking at what little remained of the door, its torn hinges and smears of blood. His mind, trying to take in the misery Grech had caused, in such a short time. He looked up at Stolland and offered him a tired smile.

"Well Mr Stolland, it seems, as a species, we haven't progressed very far, have we?"

A uniformed officer stood in front of Alan, "Sir, we've received a message from Mrs Brandon. She has been trying to get in touch with you, says it's extremely urgent."

Alan nodded his acknowledgement, rose up and walked slowly to the station office. Alan dialled Clare's home.

"Hello Grace, sorry I haven't been in touch. We've been rather busy." He changed the receiver into his other hand, fishing his pipe from his jacket pocket.

Grace sounded worried, "You sound very tired Alan, but thank God you've phoned. I'm not sure where you are or what's happening."

Alan tried to soothe Grace.

"Please, please Alan. Just listen. I was sitting in Clare's lounge when suddenly I felt dreadful. I was in a dim lobby, full of noise. In front of me was a small man, I recognised him as the man you called Victor Grech. He was standing with his back to an opening. He was holding something out to me. It was like a black box. The whole business was over in seconds, but his face Alan, he was laughing like a maniac. Then he was drawn backwards into the blackness."

"Darling," whispered Alan, "be my best girl and relax. You probably dropped off to sleep and had a bad dream brought on by the incident at the Albert Hall. Is Clare with you?"

"Yes, she's sitting right here with me. I'm alright Alan. It was just that I was suddenly so frightened for you. Has anything happened, are you coming here soon?"

"Grace, I promise, I'm fine. We are all fine. Look, why don't you have Clare drive you over to Patchets in the morning. I'll be free by then and I'll join you both for a good lunch. That is a promise."

"But," Grace said, "What about…"

"Grace, there is no need to worry any more. It's all over, that evil creature will never harm anyone ever again. Please darling, stop worrying and rest. I'll see you and Clare tomorrow."

Alan stuffed his pipe back in his pocket and slowly put the receiver on its cradle. He was hoping what had flashed into his mind, was wrong. Was this a warning, had he spoken too soon? He hurried from the office. Stolland was walking towards him.

"Stolland, where's that holdall?"

Stolland turned and pointed back towards the train, "It's on the floor in the lobby."

Without asking why, Stolland followed Alan at a run. Alan leapt up the carriage steps into the lobby, followed by Stolland.

"What's in that bloody holdall?"

Stolland shrugged. "I have no real idea. I shoved the gun into it, placed it down and then we concentrated on Billy." With that, Stolland undid the fastening. "Do you want me to tip it out here?"

Alan stopped him, "Do you recall when we were at Lo Wey's. You drew a box of some type out of a drawer in a washstand?"

Stolland smiled, "Yes, of course, and a calendar."

Alan nodded, "The box is a weapon, right?"

Stolland nodded again, "Yes, it was what I feared Grech had with him, a really nasty piece of kit. It's a sterilizer. It clinically removes the enemy, but leaves everything else intact. Not even a broken pane of glass."

Alan remembered what Stolland had said at the London briefing about Grech, possessing a weapon more fearful than they could imagine.

"Yes, Stolland please spare me the history. How does the blasted thing work?"

Stolland shook his head, "Sorry, I can't tell you that. It's enough for you to know that it's a simple mechanism for triggering a type of power, to ensure every single life form within a pre-determined area, will die instantaneously. As I said, it's attraction to the military is there are no harmful residual problems. You can just move in."

Alan sat down hard, "I don't believe this... for Christ's sake Stolland. Forget the bloody lecture, don't you see!" Alan's mind was in turmoil. He knew what would be in the holdall.

Stolland took hold of the bag, and lifted it onto the table between the two seats.

"One calendar, several rolls of what appear to be five pound notes, the gun and silencer, plus..." Stolland slowly, very very slowly lifted out the device, "plus the box, or as we know it, the Sanitizer."

Alan breathed out slowly between his teeth. "Well, at least Grech didn't have the chance to use that bloody nightmare!"

"Sorry sir, but I think he did," said Charlie, appearing in the lobby.

Stolland spun round. Charlie had a telex in his hand.

"HMG thoughtfully didn't include us in their first circulation, need to know and all that. It seems the Galen Empress is in Plymouth. The crew, apart from a couple of stewards survived, but all the Stickland family are dead. And that's official."

Charlie read part of the telex, "'cause of death unknown. Post mortem being carried out.' Some sort of incident aboard the boat, seemingly restricted to the family accommodation."

Alan slapped the table. His conversation with Grace racked into his brain. Damn. Grech must have got to the Empress while they were in Limehouse and there he was thinking they had Grech's main weapon safely in the holdall. He held his head in his hands.

"Just when I thought we were getting a handle on Grech's thinking. Even daring to assume we were, at last, dealing a few of the cards."

Stolland's face was white. He turned the box onto its side. "I'm afraid Grech may be still dealing one last hand from the grave."

He slowly turned the box towards Alan, "Don't touch it. Just look at the small window. There's an indicator showing the device's condition."

Charlie leaned over Alan and they both looked.

"What are we supposed to see?" Said Alan.

Stolland's voice was controlled but unnaturally quiet, "You must appreciate I'm a policeman, not an arms specialist or a military type. In the short time I had for briefing on this weapon, I was told that the indicator must read 'black' to show the device is in a safe condition."

Alan and Charlie guessed what was coming at the same moment.

"And," there was a crushing pause, "bright yellow when activated. To me, this device clearly indicates it is running. This is the blind hand that Grech's dealt us, and it's all spades."

Alan, Charlie and Stolland's eyes couldn't snap away from the brilliant yellow indicator, regardless of the stinging beads of perspiration, now running into their eyes. Alan wiped away the sweat and cleared his throat, "What else does it tell you?"

Stolland coughed and loosened his collar, "Nothing. All other information is displayed on a screen, hidden beneath the top panel and that is unfortunately locked down."

Alan paused, and then very slowly whispered, "Then open it."

Before Stolland could reply, Alan said, "No, don't tell me. The powers that be, the other side of that damned gate, thought you would never have need of a key, right?"

Stolland nodded.

Charlie chipped in, "What exact type of key do we need?"

Stolland's head slowly moved from side to side. "Something like, a miniature driver. The type a scientist would use."

It was Charlie's turn to wipe the perspiration from the tip of his nose. "Well, that really helps a lot. Do you mean a fine type of socket, or perhaps a screwdriver?"

Stolland nervously coughed again, "Yes, perhaps. But it would have to be very, very fine."

Alan wiped perspiration from his eyes, "Ideas please, Charlie?"

Charlie stared at the floor, "Ruben Weiss, jeweller in Church Street. He'd have fine tools. I know where he lives."

Alan was up and running. "Put that lot back in the holdall," he called over his shoulder, "and let's get going. Charlie you commandeer whatever you find on the forecourt and drive us to your jeweller friend. If he can't help, I suggest we drive as far away from civilisation as we can get, dump this gadget and run!"

As they ran for the forecourt, Alan called to Frank and Bob to hold the fort. Charlie pounced on a parked police area car. The traffic officer was known to Charlie and handed him the keys, without a murmur. Alan and Stolland piled into the back, Charlie said, "Not that it's important Mr Stolland, but if we do have to run from this bloody thing, what's its killing range?"

Stolland looked into the distance, "Not to labour the point Charlie, but if it's the type I think it is, we'd be fairly safe three miles from its point of detonation."

Alan turned to Charlie, "This is not the time to ask Mr Stolland the legal definition of 'if' and 'fairly', just bloody drive!"

Chapter Twenty Two

The bell rang through the house. Charlie's impatient finger tried again. "Don't tell me he's chosen this time for a bloody holiday!"

He rang again, this time hanging on the button. The sound of footsteps came towards the door.

Charlie called, "Ruben, it's Charlie Friar on police business. We must speak quickly."

Bolts were drawn and the noise of a heavy chain pulled through a hasp greeted their ears, before the door inched open.

"It really is you, Charlie boy. Something happened down at the shop?"

"Listen Ruben, and please don't ask why. Every second counts. We need your finest jeweller's tools. We have to open a nasty object and we need to see if any tool you have will do the job. Now Ruben, time will cost lives. Can you help?"

Ruben didn't wait but shot back into his house. Less than a minute later, he was back on the doorstep.

"Charlie. It would be better if I did the job myself. I know the tools and what they can do." He held on to a bundle, wrapped in fine chamois leather.

Charlie called to Alan, "Mr Weiss says he should do the job. The tools may not help, but he will know if they can be of use."

"Thank Mr Weiss," Alan shouted from the car, "but he needs to be around in the morning to open his shop. We'd rather keep this in the family."

Ruben smiled, "You take great care now Charlie. Don't worry about the tools, they can be replaced."

With a wave, they drove on.

"Where to?" Said Charlie.

"It's your bloody ground," yelled Alan as Charlie threw the car round a bend.

"Then I'm off to the Overstrand golf course. We can throw it off the cliffs, as a last resort." Charlie steamed for the B1159.

Chances were they would meet little traffic and be able to cut off over the golf course towards the cliffs. The only people likely to be about on a golf course, in the dark, were either courting couples or those like himself, trying to defuse bombs.

In the rear of the car, Alan tried to hold Stolland steady as he opened the roll of tools. He swore a few times as he tried to compete with Charlie's piloting.

Eventually, Charlie came to a small track running over the course between the eighth and ninth holes, A section full of bunkers. But, this way also led to the notoriously steep sandy cliffs. He drove like a bat out of hell, straight across the smooth velvet of the eighth green and into the deepest bunker he knew and applied the brakes. Unfortunately, the front of the car met the turf wall of the bunker, before the brakes halted the car.

"Sorry folks, but the tour ends here. I should add," said Charlie, pointing over the front of the car, "the cliff begins twenty yards over there, just in case you feel we are going to need it!"

Alan and Stolland readjusted their positions and began work. With the aid of the car's interior light, plus the traffic officer's torch, Stolland studied the recessed locking pin.

Alan looked at the clock in the car, checking it against his watch.

"Sirs," Charlie felt awkward, but had to ask, "as my stint at the wheel is complete, and I now feel like a spare brush in a glue factory, can I step out and have a cigarette?"

Alan and Stolland both said, "Yes," at the same time. They looked at each other and grinned.

"No good getting uptight about smoking killing him, I suppose," said Alan, "we should be far enough from houses and people, if it goes up."

Charlie smiled and said, "Always supposing they're not in a nearby bunker, playing happy families."

"You are joking," whispered Stolland, not taking his eyes from the box, "our arrival here must have put the fear of God into anyone fool enough to be within ten miles."

Twenty long anxious minutes ticked by and Stolland was down to the end of the tool roll. Charlie smoked his way through three cigarettes while Alan bit hard on the stem of his cold pipe.

"Got it," said Stolland. He looked at the other two with triumph in his eyes and perspiration glistening on his forehead, "Gentlemen, I think we're in."

Slowly he withdrew the minuscule socket attachment, turning it anti-clockwise. A second ticked by, then another, then another.

Click! A metal panel rose as if controlled by a hidden springs. They all peered at the small green screen that was now exposed. The first thing they saw displayed, was a row of seven boxes.

"What are they?" Asked Alan.

Stolland ignored the question for a second, then whispered, "Authorisation boxes, at least I think that's what they are. We need to enter a code into each one. If we are lucky, it will then refresh to a screen indicating the settings applied by Grech."

"How on earth do we know what Grech used, would it be numbers or letters, or what?"

Stolland thought for a while.

"It will more than likely be numeric. All the boxes must carry a number and we must not include a zero. Now think hard, what seven numbers would he know off by heart? Numbers that Grech could not forget?"

Alan broke in, "Not his name. That contains only five letters."

Charlie climbed back into the car, "What about a work security number he had the other side of the Gate?"

Stolland thought, then shook his head, "Unnecessary, he had scan identification. I think we ought to try a straight run of seven numbers. That would be simple to enter. Say one through to seven?"

Alan interrupted, "Just how many tries to do we get?"

Stolland replied, "Just the one."

Alan was working hard with a pencil on the car clipboard.

"We just can't wait for the bloody thing to go active. Look, you two leave. I'll give you thirty minutes. Then I'll try something I've just thought of."

Stolland looked at Alan, "You may outrank me in your time, but I have more understanding of this device. You two go. I'll use your figures."

Charlie smiled at them both, "Hold on! I saw that film too. The Corporal always has the sticky end so as you both outrank me I'll do it. I don't intend walking away. Let's get these numbers in and take our chances. We've been here long enough and I think there's a storm coming, plus I'm parked in a bunker!"

Alan looked at Stolland then at Charlie, "So be it."

Far out, over the sea, lightening stretched its fingers across the dark night sky.

Stolland said to Alan, "Read your figures off slowly. If my nervous fingers catch the wrong digit, we'll all melt into the ether."

Alan held his piece of paper up to the roof light, "Seven, one, one, two, five, one and four." Alan drew a deep breath.

Stolland repeated, "Seven!" There was a soft click, as the depressed key went home. The same soft click followed the remaining six numbers.

Stolland finished keying. Looking up from the panel, he smiled and firmly pressed the execute button. The screen blinked, refreshed and changed its display. It had accepted the code.

Charlie felt a little sick, so he lit another cigarette.

Stolland smiled, "Where did those figures come from, Alan?"

Alan shrugged, "Truthfully, it was a wild guess. I just felt that with a man like Grech, centred on family revenge, the name Galen is the spark that initiates his actions, drives his hatred. 'G' is the seventh letter of the alphabet. 'A' is the first and so on. It was cute of Grech to use his old family name. He couldn't use his own name."

"Why?" Questioned Charlie.

"Because my dear Corporal, the letters making up the name Grech carry one digit less than Galen. Work it out. Although each name has five letters, Galen carries one more digit, see?"

Charlie scratched his head, "I'm sorry but all this has me rattled."

Alan held up the paper, "Remember, one digit in each of seven boxes. Count the digits."

Charlie read,

$$'G = 7, R = 18, E = 5, C = 3, H = 8 \ (6)$$
$$G = 7, A = 1, L = 12, E = 5, N = 14 \ \ (7)'$$

Charlie nodded, "Oh, yes. It's so simple when you see it written down."

Both Alan and Stolland laughed with Charlie.

"I owe you a pint," said Charlie.

"Make that a dozen," said Stolland, "now let's find out what Grech intended for us."

Alan and Charlie settled back in their seats as Stolland trawled through the screen information. After ten minutes, he smiled.

"Well, it seems we were destined to leave this earth," he paused, making a great show of checking the car clock, "in just a little under seven minutes. It's set to cover the maximum area for this pretty toy, so that equates to," there was a pause, "anyone within three miles from here would have been on the coroner's list. It's safe now, so that's the last you'll see of it." Stolland closed the panel and put the box back into Grech's holdall.

The atmosphere in the car had brightened considerably.

Alan turned to Charlie, "Are you a member of this club?"

"I am, and fully paid up."

Alan smiled, "I fervently hope, when you play your next round, the Green Keeper doesn't realise you were the vandal that ruined his eighth green and this bunker."

Half an hour later, the area car arrived back at Cromer railway station. To Alan, the hours that followed were crammed with rushed meetings and telephone calls. The worst of the telephone conversations had been the one to Billy's parents. He assured them Billy was in excellent hands at the Norfolk and Norwich Hospital and that surgeons didn't see any reason why Billy should not make a full and quick recovery. Alan gave them the name of the surgeon and the contact number.

Then, right in the middle of dealing with a dozen things at once, Alan received long-winded call from the Home Secretary, who felt that the whole matter had been rather conveniently resolved.

Alan, with steam coming from his ears, could not voice his true feelings. After ensuring all the necessary actions had been wound up, he left the team making their own arrangements for the remainder of the night, and drove home.

On arriving at his home, Alan was so very pleased to find Grace and Clare there. They had evidently chosen to travel back instead of waiting until the morning. Grace had lots of news, but felt her prime concerns for Alan were, bath, supper and bed, in that order. Alan cancelled supper and fell into bed following a quick bath. He was asleep before his head touched the pillow.

At ten the following morning, a clean-shaven, freshly suited Alan arrived back at Cromer railway station. He walked through the booking hall and barrier, onto platform two. He immediately noticed a large canvas sheet, which covered one end of a single carriage. This, it turned out, was coach A from the previous night's train. It had been detached and shunted into its current position, for close examination. The tent-like structure, erected over the business end of the carriage, contained several white-coated figures, all busy examining, noting and photographing.

These technicians were not conversing, just emitting the odd, mmmm! Each discovery of a minute particle of skin or hair resulted in the greatest care to ensure safe transfer of the item into a specimen vial. Not wishing to interrupt their labours, Alan moved over to his team, who were further along the platform. Anxious to know what results had been gained from the over-night trawl of the track he wished everyone a good morning.

Before he could ask the question, Stolland smiled broadly, "You'll be pleased to know that most of Grech, including some traces which had applied themselves to the front of the London bound locomotive, have been recovered. Should you want to look at the collection, it's over there, in that tin bath."

Stolland pointed to a large galvanised tub, which was on the platform, some twenty feet from them. Out of common decency, an old canvas had been used hide the contents. A small card, hanging from one end, displayed the words, *'All donations gratefully accepted!'*

Alan's smile faded as he realised the public could also view the card. "Get that bloody card off, and let's get to work."

He turned to Charlie, "Exactly how much of Grech did we get?"

Charlie stubbed out his cigarette, "Well, we have enough to do a positive ID. His head was intact, although completely severed from the body. The legs were split, but we do have a left and right…"

Alan drew him aside, "Charlie, until everything is tied up and we know there are no more bloody surprises, you and the others will refrain from treating this as a Fair-Play outing. We all feel happier now that Grech has gone but, we still have to dot the 'i's and cross the 't's."

Charlie shrugged, "Sorry Alan. I suppose it's just letting off a little steam."

"I know Charlie, I know, but until Stolland has gone and that Gate no longer exists, let's all continue doing our jobs. Now, what else is happening?"

Charlie lit another cigarette, "The Coroner and Pathologist have both been. They had a good look then walked the track. The body and tissue traces are being forwarded to Norwich for the formal PM."

Alan frowned, "What time did they dig you out?"

Charlie pointed to Frank, "We got yanked out of bed at six. Messrs Lawrence and Balls said they had a full day, so we couldn't complain. They were here when we arrived. We went over everything."

Alan patted Charlie's shoulder, "Sorry I went off half-cock. I had no idea they'd want to get down here at dawn."

"That's not the half of it," said Charlie, "Friend Stolland, dragged Frank and Bob along the line by torchlight, we had most of Grech found by the time the BR people arrived. Then Stolland insisted he and Frank supervise the railway people shunting the carriages around. I don't imagine Frank will want to play with his train set for a while. It's been quite a night for him."

Alan couldn't help smiling. He'd had the gall to turn up bright and shiny, while everyone else had been hard at it.

Stolland joined them. "Do you want to see what we've salvaged?"

"Fortunately for us all Mr Stolland, I am quite happy for you and Sergeant Friar to oversee the anatomical collection. I'm sure you'll have identified the deceased and made a formal statement to that effect for Mr Balls."

"Who?" Said Stolland.

Charlie grinned, "Now, don't tell me you don't know Clifford Balls. He's our very own County Coroner. You ought to be acquainted. After all, your lot have certainly been keeping our Coroners busy lately."

The team followed Alan into the station waiting room.

"Now," said Alan, addressing his team plus other police officers, "a formal statement will be made by the Chief Constable to the press later today. It will be announced that the person responsible for a number of recent deaths, died yesterday evening, while trying to evade arrest. The Home Secretary has agreed that the press can have a field day. They will be free to use whatever language they think fit to describe Grech, serial killer or whatever they can dream up. No one, and I underline those words, will provide them with information over and above the official handout issued and approved by me.

However, as there will be no trial for Grech, certain details of the victims and the circumstances of their deaths will be included in the press release. There will naturally be a submission of evidence for the Coroner's Court. These papers, your statements, where relevant, will stay on file. My team will all be required to provide statements and submit corroborative evidence where applicable."

Alan held up a piece of paper, "I have been informed that ballistic and other scientific evidence will be used to link the gun dropped by Grech, to rounds taken from each of his victims. Also, I'm sure you join me in thanking all the coroner's officers, from each force, and the medical and scientific teams that work round the clock to support our efforts. You must admit, it's comforting to know you weren't the only ones hard at work last night.

Given that Mr Stolland must present himself elsewhere, in the very near future, the remainder of you will continue to work here in Norfolk, following up this matter, until the whole affair is closed. In short, that means you Mr Fuller will remain here, in Norfolk, until further notice. Detective Sergeant Friar will lead the team to tie up lose ends with Essex, Met and PLA police. There will be a full meeting of everyone involved, and by that I mean people like Jack Cousens, etc, in one week's time, at Police HQ, Norwich, to be addressed by the Home Secretary."

Alan looked at everyone smiling, "Any questions?"

Bob sprang to his feet, "There is one small point sir, what about lodgings. Do I commute or move over? It's a bit too far to claim cycle allowance."

Alan held up his hand to silence the laughing that broke out. He looked at Charlie, "Have you any ideas?"

Charlie shrugged and said he would have a word outside the meeting. Alan ended the meeting and made it almost to his car when he summoned back for a telephone call. The caller was Vincent Lawrence.

"Alan, greetings from the sterile land of the mortuary, I have just been speaking to a colleague in Plymouth. It seems that the first indication as to the cause of the Stickland deaths appears to be cardiac arrest. However, there is some evidence of blood in the mouth and ears. I was interested because of our Cley bodies. There seems to be certain similarities and I thought you might have a slight interest in these facts."

Alan thanked Vincent, who chuckled.

"Tell me, Vincent," Alan asked carefully, "do you intend to slip down to Devon and have a peek yourself, just to satisfy your quaint curiosity?"

Vincent chuckled again, "Good heavens, no man. I'm up to my armpits in carbolic, old boy. Can't simply swan off, just thought it might interest you. Let me know if you want me in on anything." Lawrence rang off.

Alan placed the receiver lightly back on the cradle and sat thinking. The phone rang. It was the Dockyard police at Plymouth. Chief Inspector Roy Southgate explained that he had received instructions to contact Alan with regard to the Galen Empress.

"We have received orders to allow you access to the vessel, sir, also an Inspector Stolland? The instructions are headed Operation Phoenix?"

Alan was getting used to being thunderstruck.

"It was considered you might want to take a good look at the accommodation side."

Of course! If there was a second device, and there must have been. Whatever remains of it, if anything did, Stolland must have back. He cursed his own stupidity.

416

With all that had happened, he'd completely overlooked the Empress.

"Yes, I am much obliged to you Inspector."

He went to continue, but Southgate beat him to it.

"I've been informed that the Navy are arranging your transport. We'll be ready for you when you get here. Goodbye for now, sir."

Alan thanked him, put down the phone and walked quickly from the office. He told Charlie to get onto Police HQ and find out exactly what the Navy were proposing.

He turned to Stolland, "Surely this box thing would disintegrate once it's triggered?"

"No," said Stolland, "the device will still be intact. We'll have to turn that boat over until we find it. What a fool I am. I'm sorry, my mind was still on Grech's gift to us."

"Don't flog yourself to death, I'm just as guilty."

Charlie appeared, "You'll never believe this. There's a Navy plane at Norwich, waiting to go to Plymouth. I've just spoken with the Navy dispatcher. They're expecting to fly you to Plymouth, where a car will take you to the Empress. When you finish, they'll fly you back," he smiled broadly, "fly Navy eh sir, talk about company transport."

Alan returned the smile, "Yes Charlie, that's right. Mr Stolland, myself and you! Now, tell the others what's happening and organise transport to Norwich."

The smile on Charlie's face dissolved, "But I'm terribly airsick, ask June."

Alan looked hard at Charlie, "Alright Sergeant, delegate that duty to Woodhouse and you stay in charge here, does that suit you?"

Charlie looked deeply moved.

The aircraft flying Alan, Stolland and Frank to Plymouth was a twin-engined DC3. The pilot, a very young looking Lieutenant, picked out every bump in their path, causing the aircraft to rise and fall as it nosed around a storm, before finally dropping in at Plymouth.

Alan felt quite envious of Charlie, and wished he too had been able to remain in Cromer. The young Lieutenant smiled down at them from the cockpit, as they walked rather unsteadily to the car. Judging by the width of the smile on Stolland's face, he'd obviously thoroughly enjoyed the ride in the ancient flying machine.

Inspector Southgate took them aboard and straight to the passenger accommodation, where he left them to their business. They were astonished at the sheer size of the Empress. The lavish family accommodation was like walking into London's Savoy Hotel. Everything was immaculate.

Moving slowly through the inter-connected cabins, to the main dining saloon, they saw chalk marks outlining where bodies had fallen. Two bathrooms still had water in the sinks and towels lying on floors. Some spilled talcum powder clearly showed an outline of a hand upon a cabinet top.

Stolland went into Lord Stickland's cabin. This was the largest of all, with both lavish sleeping and business rooms. He said nothing but walked slowly around it. Then, with the other two in tow, he walked the family accommodation, as though working something out. He then returned to Stickland's quarters.

"This is where the device will be," muttered Stolland, as though speaking to himself.

He went over to the desk, which was set against a wall. On the desk was a neat pile of unopened mail and a steel letter opener, in the shape of a sword.

Stolland took up the letter opener and looked at it most carefully. Having apparently found what he was looking for, his eyes moved upwards. There was a small grill in an air-vent channel. This wasn't the only vent in the cabin. There were many others. Stolland placed the letter opener back on the desk and knelt down so that his eyes were level with the desktop. Again, he found something. He rose and pressed the tip of his forefinger onto the polished desktop. He then looked at the tip and smiled.

"Rust, just a minute speck, but none the less, it's rust."

"Rust?" Asked Alan.

"Unless I miss my guess," said Stolland, "The child may have a clean face, but behind his ears, dirt exists."

Alan was still puzzled.

Stolland returned to the air vent above the desk. He climbed onto the desk and carefully examined the screws holding the grill in place. He pointed at the screws.

"These have been removed and put back. It's my guess either Grech failed to clean every speck of rust from the desk surface, or he used a cover to stand on, and one or two specks made it onto the desk. I bet you, we find similar specks inside the channelling."

The other two continued to watch as Stolland took from his pocket a small penknife. He quickly removed each of the four screws. He then carefully removed the grill. In doing this, very small particles caught the light as they drifted down. It seemed Stolland had made his point.

"I need a torch."

The words hadn't finished being formed before Frank was handing him what looked like a cigarette lighter.

"It's a torch sir. Not a bad beam for such a small battery."

Alan smiled, "It's nice to know, Mr Woodhouse, that we have been able to assist Mr Stolland in one or two small ways." Frank grinned up at Stolland.

The beam of the torch penetrated the darkness inside the channel. Stolland looked down at the pair.

"We've found it," he whispered. In seconds and with the aid of a mop handle, supplied by a steward, who had been waiting in the corridor, Stolland had the box in his hands. It was almost identical to the one from the holdall, though somewhat smaller.

He quickly checked the small aperture, and looked at Alan, "It's been triggered, and we know it obviously functioned."

Stolland replaced the grill.

Alan looked puzzled, "I thought you said one of these would clear an area of one square mile plus, yet we have just a small accommodation space affected."

Stolland nodded, "What we have here is the previous one's little brother, extremely effective in very small areas."

Placing the box in the canvas bag, Alan indicated it was time to leave. The trip back to Norwich was a far smoother affair. The aircraft seemed to find continuous ribs of silver clouds, off which to bounce. so minds were kept permanently entertained. Both Alan and Stolland sat deep in their own thoughts. Amidst the drone of engines, they each silently mulled over recent events. Their sadistic killer was history and both devices were in their possession. Stolland could return to his own time and, with luck, Operation Phoenix could be put to bed.

Suddenly Stolland leant across to Alan, "Wasn't it the writer Michael Hadley who coined the phrase, 'Count not the dead'?"

Alan who was half-asleep looked across, "Who coined what?"

Stolland repeated, "Michael L Hadley, wrote a book on German submarines.

Alan squinted at Stolland, "Who wrote what, on what?"

Stolland smiled and waved a hand at Alan, indicating he should return to his dozing, "It's okay Alan, you can relax. I was forgetting. He hasn't got round to writing it yet."

Alan half opened his eyes, looked to his right, through the round disc of plexi-glass. Far below, slowly appearing from beneath the exhaust scorched grey wings, he could see tiny points of light, changing and winking at him. They reminded him of a diamond necklace, stretched across a bed of dark velvet.

He heard a bracketing sound as flaps extended and the engine note change, as throttle settings adjusted. He felt the plane bank to the left, then level out. He listened to the rumbling whistle as the extending undercarriage pushed down and out, into the wind. Further rumbling came as flaps were finely tuned. Soon they would be on the ground again. He felt a judder and screech, as both wheels met the tarmac. The tail-plane sank as the speed decreased. Brakes squealed in protested, bringing them to a slow, loose roll.

Within minutes, all engine noise was gone. The only noise was the occasional ping of cooling metal. They remained in their seats, waiting for something to happen. The door to the cockpit dropped back into the cabin. The smiling face of the pilot appeared.

"Sorry you chaps, this is as far as Doris can take you. Evidently road traffic laws in Norfolk prohibit us from taking you to your door." With a salute, the cockpit door slammed shut.

As soon as they stepped from the aircraft, the engines were turning over, throttled up and she was negotiating her way back to the runway. It was clear the crew had no wish to spend the night in Norfolk.

Immediately they were in the car, Alan looked across at Stolland, still clutching the small canvas bag.

"It's time you went home. It's time you left us to count our dead."

Chapter Twenty Three

Although it was still late summer, the weather on the marsh seemed undecided. A few low-angled shafts of pale sunlight pierced the ominous clouds, caressing and encouraging the few birds that splashed and dipped in the marsh water, to feed quickly and be gone.

The rising, pulsating North Sea wind tugged hard at the green and gold grasses, in a hurry to change the straw-coloured hues of summer into the mellow shades of autumn. In the middle distance, fine dark heads of long stemmed reeds bounced and reached high, as if to snatch at the feet of rising birds, who recognising the change as a warning of things to come, were desperate for protection.

Beyond the high shingle bank, the soft overnight caress of a slumbering North Sea became increasingly restless under pressure from the prodding wind as clouds, saturated with moisture rode over the horizon like a division of cavalry, casting hungry eyes on the richness of the dry land. Soon, the whole of the marshland resounded to the thud of foaming waves jumping onto and then clawing at glistening shingle.

When the wind driven rain came, it beat onto the glass and steel of the car parked close under the shingle bank, each raindrop falling like the slap of a blacksmiths hammer.

The wild-wind rain, throwing aside any pretence to be summers gentle companion stormed ashore, leaping unbidden up the beach, bounding across the head of the bank and then, like a marauding giant, used the top of the car to launch itself out into and across the darkening marsh.

Alan consulted his watch and drew his mackintosh around him. Looking across at Stolland he said, "Can't wait for this lot to blow over. It may last another hour. Come on, I'll walk the last few yards with you."

The main problem between them, had been obtaining some sort of guarantee that once Stolland had returned through the gate, the breach to their world, would close forever. The last thing either side needed was another maniac with a grudge, tumbling through the hole, armed with a space age weapon of mass destruction.

At the very last minute, Stolland produced his box of tricks. He displayed the text of a document, addressed to Sir Nicholas Folland. The closure of the Cley facility upon Stolland's safe return, was guaranteed. Sir Nicholas felt they had no option. Control was not in their hands. It was, at least, something tangible to demonstrate intent. Sir Nicholas added a time limitation, which suited all sides.

There were those present who remembered the results of the Munich Agreement, and Chamberlain's triumphal return to Croydon, waving a piece of paper. Alan hoped that Stolland's document held more veracity, than Hitler's written assurance.

"Are you sure you have everything?"

Alan sounded like a father, packing his son off to do his National Service. Stolland smiled, nodded and looked down at the late Victor Grech's bulging holdall.

"I think I have everything, even Grech's ashes."

He twisted round to face the rear seat where Charlie and Grace sat, "There must be so many ways of saying thank you. But whatever I said, it would not be enough," the two looked back at him awkwardly, "so, I wish you happiness. Enjoy the peace you have in this time and place." He didn't wait or expect a reply.

Charlie shot out a hand, which Stolland took, "You just take great care getting through that gate." They shook hands.

Grace leant forward and gently kissed his cheek. He left the car.

The few yards of path seemed too short for things between Stolland and Alan. They had passed the whole of the previous evening going through all the loose ends. Alan had supplied Stolland, with copies of every report arising from operation Phoenix, including his own hand written letter, explaining the unplanned death of Grech. Alan had a feeling that Stolland was going to need it. He hoped he was wrong.

Stolland stopped, "Alan, you shouldn't come any further."

There was a long pause. The wind whipped between and around them, causing both to hold onto their hats.

Stolland continued, "I wish I'd planned what I was going to say, but I haven't. I hoped for something rather eloquent. But again, I'm just a plain speaking copper, as Charlie would say."

Stolland stopped talking and looked out across the marsh. His eyes following a flight of birds, blown on the wind, like washing on a line.

"This is a good time, Alan. You have a wonderful family, the loyalty of friends and a beautiful place to live. I'm sorry my task spilled into your life," he shrugged his shoulders, "but, as policemen, we can't always choose when and where we serve, can we?"

They stood for a few seconds, shaking hands warmly. Alan looked along to where he knew the gate waited, "You never told me if you have a wife or children."

Stolland looked into the marsh, his face clouding over.

"We have no time and I come from a time where life is very different."

Alan wanted to say more, to push Stolland, to find the out more about the real Peter Stolland, "It's such a pity you never felt able to tell us. Be very careful my friend."

Grace sat, watching this parting, "You know something, Charlie? Look at them. They're like two peas from the same pod, even down to the clothes they chose to wear."

Charlie nodded, "If it wasn't for the 150 years between them, they could be brothers or father and son."

Alan returned to the car. He climbed behind the wheel and watched as Stolland walked very slowly forward. He looked round once. For a split second, he looked lost and uncertain. He half raised a hand in a salute, then stepped forward, and was gone.

A gust of wind roared over the shingle barrier, in what seemed to echo the closing of a door.

"He didn't want to go," Grace said.

She had moved into the front passenger seat beside Alan, and was dabbing at her eyes with a handkerchief.

"He's worried about something Alan, something on the other side. I saw it clearly in his eyes."

Alan started the car, "Well my darling, whatever it was that's worrying him, we'll never know."

Alan reversed the car round and slowly drove back towards the main road. Grace and Charlie turned and stared at the shingle bank, while Alan looked in the rear view mirror. Through the gusting rain, the ruin of the old coastguard station looked misty and remote. The shingle margin was now empty. Peter Stolland had gone from their lives.

The meeting at police headquarters, addressed by the Home Secretary, was a resounding success. That is, if you are the type that wallows in political syrup. All politicians have a way of turning everything to their advantage, no matter what the subject or result.

There was little doubt that by the time the Chief Constable, David Long, wound up proceedings, there was a feeling that Sir Nicholas Folland had led Operation Phoenix, every inch of the way. No mention of their visitor from 2102 was made, or of the existence of the Gate. Alan looked around the hall, noting that every police officer involved in or connected with the operation was there. Also many others, who had assisted, been affected by or brought their expertise to the Grech affair, these included doctors, local authority officers and officials, representatives from the Navy, including their pilot and his crew.

Towards the end of the meeting, Alan was speaking with Charlie when Sir Nicholas Folland called him to one side.

"Just as well that only a very few of us here know where Mr Stolland came from, eh?" He nudged Alan's arm and winked, "Look Brandon, I think you ought to know that the appeal hearing for your man Tate has been brought forward. It's the least we can do in view of his current circumstances, going to be damned embarrassing though. I have taken advice. Seems his conviction was quite appalling, in view of evidence the Crown now has. There was a conspiracy to accuse Tate, something to do with local criminals. Anyway, those responsible are charged, the result is a foregone conclusion. It will mean Tate has his clean record. As I say, this matter has caused some embarrassment in the House, lot of red faces and all that. Pity it couldn't have all been handled quietly. Cost the state a pretty penny I can tell you. PM's not too pleased. Neither is his uncle. He tried the case you know, sent young Tate down. Thank God, I wasn't personally involved. Awful lot of money in straightening out the matter too, I wouldn't wonder.

Still, the voters must have their pound of flesh, justice must be served, eh? No doubt, you'd like to give him the good news yourself. How is he by the way?"

Sir Nicholas, ever the politician, didn't pause for an answer, "Shot to pieces I understand. Hope the fellow gets on his feet soon. As I say, Brandon, a jolly good show all round. I was saying earlier to the PM, we British come together when the bugle sounds eh? I think I can be justly proud of the way I drove the whole thing forward, eh?"

Alan didn't try to answer or offer an opinion. Sir Nicholas was a politician after all.

"I suppose you feel rather relieved this whole business is over, eh? So you should, so you should."

Alan nodded. He wanted to say there was an awful long way to go before George Wright, Billy Tate, or others would feel this business was over. Grech had savaged his way into and out of so many people's lives.

Sir Nicholas went on.

"Yes sir, I think I can truly say this business will have done none of us any harm in the long run."

Alan was furious, "There is one point which I feel I must mention, Sir Nicholas."

"Go ahead old boy, go ahead."

"During the latter stages of my investigation, a letter came into my possession, delivered by hand to Lord Stickland's Albany Street home. The date on the letter was the very same day as our meeting at the War Office. You do recall that meeting?"

Sir Nicholas's face turned sheet white.

Alan went on without waiting for the answer, "The letter had been stolen and was kept by the thief until he was searched. Now, it is highly likely that copies may have found there way around the criminal fraternity. However, I have retained what I take to be the original."

Sir Nicholas looked as though he was going to pass out, "I must say Brandon, if this is some kind of joke it is in extremely poor taste!"

Alan smiled, "Oh no sir, I could never say I was joking. I believe it is far from a joke. In fact Sir Nicholas I would say I never laugh at deliberate criminal acts, especially when the perpetrator is a highly placed and supposedly trusted member of the Government."

Sir Nicholas's voice shook, "Brandon, I must ask you what your intentions are. If that letter was ever released to the press, it would be a disaster."

Alan slowly nodded, "The trouble is, one should never play both sides of the street. The letter is safe in the Operation Phoenix file, and will remain secret until after the year twenty-one o-two. I hope you are more prudent in your future choice of friends?"

Sir Nicholas Folland's jaw dropped.

"Now, you must excuse me Sir Nicholas, my Chief is coming over."

David Long came across and told Sir Nicholas his car was waiting. As soon as he had turned his back, David was at Alan, "What on earth was that all about?"

Alan assumed a look of absolute innocence, "Oh, the Home Secretary was just easing his springs a little. I think it's called preening in political circles."

"I hope you didn't say anything that reflects on me?"

"Relax David, I just told him a few truths in a diplomatic way, anyway, while I'm being diplomatic. I have an announcement to make. I'm considering retirement."

David Long stared at Alan, "You must be joking!"

"No. I want Grace to have less sleepless nights. I'll speak to her and then, when she and I have talked it over, I'll let you have our decision."

David Long looked around the room, "So, you rocket the Home Secretary, and slide off the stage. I rather hoped we could finish with the service on the same day."

"Well, it's early days. I'll let you know."

The next day, Alan went to see Billy. He was pleased to find him looking more comfortable. In fact, he looked considerably happier than usual. The young woman and her little girl from the train were at his bedside along with his mother and father. It seemed he was having enough excitement, so Alan relayed the message from the Home Secretary and withdrew. He did promise to call again with the whole team. His impression was that the little girl had already made up her mind that Billy was her hero who needed kissing every two seconds.

The long autumn, winter, spring and early summer months that followed saw many changes in the lives of those touched by Operation Pheonix. The crimes committed by Grech began to fade, as reporters found other tragedies to fill their columns. Occasionally Grech's brief rampage found its way back into newsprint, with the stories of his victims and how their families were coping. One daily newspaper went so far as to print photographs of the street in which the murderer had lived during his childhood and the school he had attended, until being expelled for violent conduct. Who was going to contradict such reporting? Certainly not the officers involved in the case. Sadly, George Wright had to take a medical discharge from the police. He, Clare and Grace had a very proud day at Buckingham Palace, where he received the Kings Police Medal for Gallantry. Although most of the time bound to a wheelchair, he is totally committed to walking again. Unfortunately, his eyesight is limited to one eye but in spite of this, he is studying hard for his new future, as a seascape artist. Many knowledgeable people, including connoisseurs, agree he has natural talent, and insist on buying his paintings before they are dry.

He was able to purchase the rebuilt Linnet from the owner. It is his wish to sail her in the summer months. The marsh gang, to a man, naturally volunteered to crew. Clare insists she must be his first and only mate! I think she and George see the Linnet as their future home.

Charlie was promoted to Detective Inspector, making him head of Cromer Division CID. In the opinion of David Long, he will make Detective Chief Inspector before retiring.

Fred Fisher retired. He and Spike moved into a bungalow in Bucklers Lane. Fred insists the arrangement was purely so that the Marsh Gang had an HQ near the marsh. In response, Charlie pointed out it also gave them immediate access to the Duck Pub.

Bob Fuller married Sylvia Cash and set up home in Cromer. He has a new future in Norfolk CID working directly for Charlie. Sylvia's friend, Ellen Thurston, often arrives for weekends and holidays.

Frank Woodhouse chose to revert to uniform and took over Fred Fisher's beat. He's the new occupant of the Police House at Salthouse and seems to be making a first class village policeman. It seems he spends a lot of time in Fred's company, and is an apprentice member of the marsh gang. He also has regular visits from Bob and Sylvia, plus Ellen, who it seems shows a keen interest in walking the marshes.

Barry Scrivner and a number of other east-end villains received sentences for being concerned in certain crimes committed by Grech.

One of the best surprises for Alan and Charlie was when David Long telephoned them to say Billy Tate had applied to join the Norfolk Constabulary. Given that he now had an unblemished record, had walked through the physical and educational entrance examinations, and had at least two distinguished sponsors, there was no valid reason to refuse his entry. When asked who, other than themselves, had supplied Billy with references they were told Jack Cousens and Sir Nicholas Folland.

"Well, Jack's word is good enough for me," roared a delighted Charlie, "but I don't know about the other one!"

Chapter Twenty Four

August brought Clare to Patchets on a surprise visit. It wasn't often she found time to visit her parents home, what with being a busy junior doctor and helping to rebuild George's life.

Clare had just driven George to the quayside at Blakeney from the convalescent home where he had been living since leaving hospital. The final work on the adaptation of The Linnet was now complete. Clare explained these alterations would enable George to live aboard. He could now embark, disembark, move around the boat and operate her, all without assistance. The only thing George couldn't do was take the boat to sea on his own.

In the opinion of George's doctors, there was no reason why George shouldn't live on The Linnet if he chose to. The more Clare talked, the more Grace noticed she was unhappy about something.

"Clare," Grace said softly, "how will George manage his treatment if he does choose to live on the boat?"

"It shouldn't be a problem," there was a delicate pause, "If he behaves himself and doesn't have falls or other accidents, he will go into hospital every six months or so, for a short stay."

Grace crossed the room. Her eyes signalling to Alan that it was time he made himself scarce. When the door had closed on Alan, Grace sat next to Clare.

"Darling, you should be bubbling over but you are not. Something is wrong."

Clare rose and poured herself more coffee, "Is this the bit where you say physician heal thyself?"

"No darling, I'm just worried."

"George and I spoke for a long time yesterday. I thought we would discuss the wedding. Tie loose ends, talk about the arrangements, but he never mentioned it. In fact, he changed the subject more than once. Just now, at the boat, I got the impression he really wanted to shut himself away. Deep down I feel he considers himself pitiful, even finished as a capable human being.

I know I have very little real experience as a medical doctor but I think I can recognise depression when I see it. The condition usually follows when a patient realises, no matter how hard they try or whatever equipment is available, he will never be fully independent again. I watched him moving around the boat. He smiled in all the right places, as he found his way around the new gadgetry, but I know him and something is wrong."

"You mean about your being married?"

"I don't know, I just wish I did."

"Surely this can't be George. He's so very positive and he loves you. That's obvious. Maybe, he was just having a bad moment."

"When I said I would pop over to see you while he was with the fitters, he barely heard me."

The telephone rang. Both women sat listening to its metallic jangle until Alan picked up the receiver in the hall.

"Phone Clare," Alan's voice called.

Grace used her handkerchief to wipe away the tears that were forming. She recalled, how many times a simple word or look or the lack of either, from Alan had broken her heart. Alan came in bearing the tray of coffee.

"That was George," Alan chirped, "he's so thrilled about The Linnet. Wants us all to go down to the quay and have tea on the boat. Do you think he'll be fit enough to get married at the end of the month? Oh Grace, before I forget, he asked if we could supply the tea things. I said you would arrange something."

Grace smiled as Clare came back into the room.

"Would you mind terribly if we drink the coffee quickly and get to the boat. George says I've been gone too long."

Grace left them to arrange a few things for tea. It was so handy being a director of a hotel.

Alan looked at Clare, "Wedding nerves are terrible things."

"Have you been listening?"

"No, my sweet child, but I do know something about being a thoughtless man. Try putting yourself in George's place. He's just scared stiff you're building yourself into an arrangement that you will, one day soon, regret, maybe even want to get out of."

"So, what do I do?"

"Just show him you are one of the pair. Love each other with every breath and stop believing something is going to come along to spoil everything. What you both have is wedding nerves. We all had them dear girl. My God, I should know. Remember, I was a poor copper when I asked a rich man's daughter to wed me."

Clare walked across to her father and kissed him on the forehead, "You really do know me don't you?"

The afternoon and evening spent with Clare and George removed all doubts as to whether problems existed. They didn't. Alan and Grace took there leave meaning to drive straight home, but without meaning to, they found themselves driving out onto the Cley marsh.

Since the end of Operation Pheonix, the cordon was no longer necessary, so the army recovered all their tents and lighting. The marsh was once more a tranquil place.

Alan parked the car near the bank, close to where they had said goodbye to Stolland.

"Do you think he is alright?"

Alan turned to look at Grace, "How do you mean?"

"There was something very sad about the way he walked those last few steps. It was as though he was walking to the scaffold."

"That's imagination, Grace. He was naturally a bit sad to leave. After all, he was fond of you and he got on well with Charlie and others. I must admit I found him rather difficult at times."

"I think sadness didn't come into it. I think he knew what he was going to face."

Alan got out of the car and walked along the shingle path a few paces. Grace joined him, "I know this sounds silly Alan, but I have had the feeling all day that the Gate is still here, still sitting there like some demon, waiting, threatening."

Alan was suddenly serious, "Oh come on now, Grace. The Gate no longer exists. You know that. Stolland promised..."

"Peter Stolland was doing what he was instructed to do. He may have promised too much."

Grace walked forward. She looked around and shuddered, "No Alan. I am right. My feelings told me it was here. Can't you feel it?"

Grace took off her coat, leaving her arms bare. She handed the coat to Alan, "Alan please do this for me. Stay where you are. I am going to try something." Alan took a step forward, "Please Alan. Trust me."

Grace again stepped forward carefully. She held her bare arms out in front of her as if she were sleep walking. She moved forward, perhaps ten paces and stopped, as though meeting a wall.

"Alan," she called softly, "fetch your torch from the car and look at this."

Alan collected the torch and joined her.

"Shine the torch on my arms, darling."

Alan caught his breath. In the light of the torch, the small pale hairs on Grace's arms were standing upright. Alan took off his own jacket. He rolled up the sleeve of his shirt and thrust his arm forward. The same thing happened.

"There, what did I tell you Alan, the Gate has not been disconnected."

Alan was totally mystified. He repeated the exercise while trying to steady his thoughts. The next thing he said to Grace had to be plausible, for Grace to swallow.

434

"That is not the affect of the Gate, Grace. It's straight forward static electricity."

Grace looked at him as he led her back to the car.

"Watch," he said as he withdrew his comb from his jacket. He passed the teeth through his hair a couple of times then ran the comb over his arm. Once again, the hairs stood up on end, "There you are. Any boy with a chemistry set knows how to manufacture static. Ask any girl with a nylon petticoat."

Grace turned and looked at the shingle bank. She didn't answer but slowly walked up the bank. Alan shook his head and followed. Grace stood on the top and looked down along the margin between the marsh and the bank. She said nothing to Alan as he laboured up and stood beside her.

Grace closed her eyes for what seemed an age. The moonlight came from behind a cloud, painted the scene in silver light then rushed to hide again.

"You are so wrong Alan. The Gate is right there, where we were standing. I'm not asking you to believe me because that is the last thing you want to believe."

"Grace, my darling girl, the army had powerful generators standing right there, where we were. These transformers are extremely powerful. They floodlit this place until Grech died. Then they were withdrawn. They have caused the static. It's known in scientific circles as residual static. That is what you found, not an entrance to some throbbing science fiction tunnel."

"When did the Gate become science fiction, Alan? Aren't you confusing proven fact with your science fiction? Anyway, I think you are wrong. We shall see."

First thing the next morning, as soon as Alan had the telephone to himself, he rang Mullards laboratory at Hackney, he gave his name and asked to speak to Professor Bob Willis.

"Hello Alan. You had me worried, I thought you might want to arrest me."

In seconds, without mentioning anything about the Gate, Alan described what Grace and he had seen at the shingle bank. He asked what would be the likely cause.

"There might be a simple explanation for it, but without examining the circumstances, the scene, etc., I couldn't say. Is it important?"

"Well, not vital, it was just something weird that Grace came across. I think it would be nice to settle her curiosity."

"We have an 'A rated team at Norwich, I'll get them to pop over and check it out. Do you want them to contact you?"

"'A' rated?" Queried Alan.

"I mean they are all checked out security-wise. No one will ever know they've been. I don't see how it can be anything special anyway."

Alan requested that Bob inform Charlie of any result. He gave the number and thanked Bob for his help. He then rang and briefed Charlie.

"For God's sake Charlie, keep what they tell you to yourself, whatever the outcome. The last thing I need right now is Grace to discover she's right." Charlie seemed to understand what he had to do.

Duty and honour having been satisfied, Alan sat down to a healthy breakfast of the Clare variety.

The days leading up to the wedding, came equipped with stress. Alan lost count the number of times he asked for a clean shirt, etc., only to end up being led to the linen cupboard or the wardrobe, or a drawer. Full English fried breakfasts were not available and a quiet evening reading the paper was not permissible. Nothing, as far as the women of the house were concerned, was going to plan!

His trip with Charlie to Brody's, for their rental outfits became a complete fiasco. The trousers were too long, jackets two sizes too large, and Charlie's waistcoat was ridiculously tight, etc. To all adverse comments, impeccably dressed young male assistants repeated the same phrase, "But this, sir, is how they are being worn this year."

The final straw came when Charlie tried on his grey top hat. It fell straight over his ears. He took it off and dared the young man to tell him, that's how they were being worn this year!

Instead, the young man simply smiled, like a patient uncle, "Sir, we do not wear our hats, we simply carry them to complete the ensemble." Alan and Charlie just sighed.

When Alan dropped Charlie at Cromer, his wife June came to the front gate, "Alan, I have had a message from Bob Willis. He was trying to reach you or Charlie. He said he was phoning from the lab at Hackney."

Alan and Charlie's ears began to pick up the distant jangling of alarm bells.

"What did he have to say?" Asked Charlie, trying desperately to ignore the bells.

"Well, strange really. He said you'd understand. Evidently, a number of tests have been made, right across the spectrum?" June shrugged indicating it was all double-dutch to her.

"There doesn't appear to be an explanation for the presence of the detected phenomena? Oh, and to say you should ring him if you weren't sure what he meant. Sound's just like he was talking about ghosts or something, doesn't it?"

Alan smiled, "Yes, thanks June, we do understand."

Sadly, both of them realised, their particular ghost had left his front door wide open. The only question was, did he do this on purpose or was it just bad housekeeping?

On the big day, everything went brilliantly. Alan and Grace were so proud of Clare. She looked positively radiant. The short drive to Cley church went without a hitch.

On Grace's arrival, all their guests had arrived and were standing in bright sunshine. The marsh gang conducted everyone to their allotted places to await the arrival of Alan and the bride. The car bringing the bridesmaids drew up. This seemed to put Grace into a tizz, because she hadn't seen hide nor hair of George.

Five minutes later, Clare and Alan appeared which added to Grace's discomfort. The Groom was still absent. Alan brought Clare to the door where she organised her dress and formed up with the bridesmaids, while Alan gave a thumbs-up signal to Harold, who smiling broadly nodded to the organist. The result was a thundering fanfare from the organ, which sounded like a hundred state trumpeters.

To everyone's utter amazement, George Wright stepped into the main body of the church from the Vestry where he had remained hidden. He walked very slowly, with the aid of sticks, forward to where Grace sat thunderstruck.

"Well, dear Grace, beautiful mother-in-law to be, I was determined this was one wedding I wasn't going to miss."

Everyone in the church heard George's soft words. They all stood and applauded, including Alan. Handkerchiefs were out, even though the bride was still waiting for Alan to lead her to the altar.

The only people who knew about George and Clare's plans, had been Charlie and June. It was to be their wedding surprise and thank you to Grace.

Charlie rose from his place as Best Man and guided George to the front pew. George's face was an absolute picture of determination and pride. As everyone settled down, a strong chord on the organ announced the bride was about to join them.

The weather just couldn't have been better. Even Alan began to relax, determined to enjoy the whole day.

Far out over the Cley marsh, the first signs of a summer storm crept in. It's arrival unnoticed in the hotel ballroom, where guests were dancing the evening away.

Grace took a break, from circulating amongst the many people who wanted a quick word. The service and reception had all gone so beautifully. Grace felt so very proud of her daughter and new son-in-law. She lingered by one of the large windows overlooking the marsh. The dark sky lit up as lightening fingered its way through heavy clouds. The only outside light was a decorative street lamp, faintly illuminating the car park entrance.

Grace watched as puddles began to form in the small circle of light given off by the lamp. She looked away, smiling broadly at guests enjoying themselves. She relaxed and returned to look through the window. A dark figure of a tall man had appeared and was now standing under the lamp. The shadow thrown by the brim of his hat hid his face, but Grace knew he was watching the window where she was standing.

Grace looked around at her guests. The atmosphere reminded her so much of her own marriage. She saw Alan chatting to the Tate family. Here, she thought, was a picture of the contented father. Grace smiled at everyone she passed as she walked slowly over to Alan. Slipping her hand into his, Grace whispered to him, "My darling, I think our missing guest has arrived."

Printed in the United Kingdom
by Lightning Source UK Ltd.
129163UK00001B/53/A